To
Diane
Honorary

SPARTAN
HONOR

Savage
PRESS
14172 E Carlson Road • Brule, WI 54820
(218) 391-3070 • www.savpress.com

SPARTAN
HONOR

JOHN F. SAUNDERS

First Edition

Cover Design: Jillene Johnson

ISBN: 978-1-937706-24-1

Library of Congress Control Number: 2020902158

Published by:
Savage Press
14172 E Carlson Rd., Brule, WI 54820

Email: mail@savpress.com
Website: www.savpress.com

To all those who have gone on before us.
We raise our glasses high in your honor.
We will see you on the other side.

Honor your gods. Honor your country.
Shields high. Spears straight.
Forward. Forward. Ever forward.
Honor to Sparta.

Alcman
Spartan poet, member of the Kryptea

Chapter 1

Keith Masnick woke up in a dark cell. His clothes were gone. It was cold. Goose bumps pebbled his pale skin. He didn't know how long he had been out. His mouth felt like it was full of cotton balls. He tried to swallow and couldn't. His back ached and his elbows and knees were rubbed raw. They must have thrown him around when he was unconscious. No major damage that he could detect. And what true Spartan couldn't take a little punishment?

The black cloth bag was still tied loosely around his head. He could see nothing. He shook his head, trying to shake it free, but it held fast. He took deep breaths in through his nose to steady his racing heart. He strained his ears for sounds. There was only silence. Masnick knew that sensory deprivation was one of the primary tools in interrogation. That was alright too. There was nothing he could do but wait anyway. They would come when they were ready. They might even be watching him now.

Some type of thick, wide leather collar had been fastened around his neck like a dog's collar. He could smell the sour scent of fear and sweat on the collar. He wondered if the collar had been used before or if it was his own fear he smelled.

He was seated upright in a metal chair that prevented him from lying down or moving. That was alright too. He wasn't tired. He could tell that his hands were fastened in front of him with handcuffs secured to a length of chain bolted into the floor. He wiggled his bare legs. His feet were not shackled. He wondered why not. It might mean they were careless. It could mean they felt that it was unnecessary. It might be nothing. He stretched his legs, feeling around him. The only thing he felt was the bare concrete floor and the base of the chain that held his wrists to it. He swept them again. Nothing except empty, bitter cold air.

He calmed himself. He sat quietly. He needed to be ready. It would only get worse from here on. He knew he needed to save his strength. The years seemed to tick by.

In reality, he didn't have to wait very long. He heard footsteps and the release of an electronic lock. The metallic creak of a steel door. The casual flipping of a light switch. The strong earthy smell of men who worked with their hands. There was no speech, but by hand signal or prearrangement, men began to move around him. Someone began loosening his hood. The hood was removed. Masnick blinked hard at the purposely bright lights of the cell.

He found he was indeed sitting upright in a metal chair. The chair's framework was solid, but the seat and back were made of wide mesh. He understood why. It was not meant for comfort. The chair legs were screwed and bolted into small metal plates in the floor. He glanced around. There was nothing else in the cell. There was a drain in the center of the floor. The walls

1

were mortar and brick. There were no windows. A large overhead light secured behind a metal lattice was the only light source in the room.

There were two men. The smaller of the two was thin with a shaved head. He wore a jacket that zipped all the way up to his neck. He was nervous, with black weasel eyes. The other man was a giant with long black hair. The giant wore heavy tan canvas work pants, but only a black vest on his upper body. His gargantuan arms were covered in full sleeves of tattoos. The tattoos seemed Nordic in design. Vikings. Wolves. Long boats. Ravens. Thor's hammer broken. The giant man seemed immune to the biting cold. The man was smiling. He had a bright smile like a wolf.

"Welcome, to Valhalla. I am Finris Wolf," he began.

"The Norse Man," Masnick continued for him. "Loki's enforcer."

Finris smiled. He made a mock bow toward Masnick.

"Yes, thank you for knowing my name. I am flattered that the great Prometheus of the Spartans is aware of me. It is an honor."

Masnick tried to sneer but couldn't manage to hold it.

"What do you want with me? I never had a beef with the Norse Men."

Finris leaned back against the open cell door. He had a relaxing smile.

"True. But we have business with you, Prometheus. You have information we have been asked to retrieve."

"What information? I'm no snitch."

Finris leaned in closer, but well out of striking distance of Masnick's legs.

"But you are. You are a snitch. Cyrus told us so."

"What do you want?"

"Are the Spartans rebuilding?"

"The Spartans are done as far as I know."

"Where is Frank Kane?"

"How should I know? Dead, I hear tell."

"You were friends. Brothers almost. If he were alive you would know how to contact him."

"That was a long time ago. I haven't seen Frank since the Spartans fell. That was years ago."

Finris nodded his great head as if he knew that was what Masnick would say. He stroked his square chin. The broad smile returned. Finris neither believed nor did not believe Masnick. He was a pragmatic man.

"You will tell me what I want to know. We both know that. Sooner or later you will answer all my questions. . . truthfully. Happily."

Before Masnick could respond he heard the click-clack of high heels approaching down the hallway outside his cell. They drew closer like an indomitable tide until they were followed by a tall attractive blonde woman. Her

Germanic heritage shone through her sharp features and soft mouth. Her eyes were large with tweezed brows that arched upward into a delicate intelligent curve. She was wearing a navy-blue wool business suit. Her feet were clad in small black boots with flirty fringe at the top. She had two small diamond earrings in each ear. It was a statement of some kind. With women, everything was a statement of some kind.

"Finris, are you starting without me?" the woman asked.

"No, Heather, I'm just spending a few minutes in conversation while waiting for your arrival."

"And threatening our guest, I imagine."

Finris stepped out of the doorway. Heather entered. She looked tiny, almost doll-like next to the giant.

"If I had my say, we would use the old ways. Iron and fire. I could pry the information from him."

"At what cost, my wolf? If he were to die, then where would we be? What benefits would await us then? No, your ways are too harsh. They are unpredictable." Heather turned back to Masnick. She scanned him from head to toe. She shook her head like a teacher finding crayon marks on a school wall. She made a clucking sound with her tongue. "Has he been given water?"

Finris shrugged.

Heather turned to the thin man. "Earl, go bring me a bottle of water."

Earl hesitated until he got a nod of approval from Finris. They remained silent while Earl hurried away. Masnick was tempted to say something to fill the void, but he knew there was nothing he could say that would make any difference. They all waited, unmoving like someone had hit the pause button on a DVD. Eventually they heard Earl returning. He jogged into the room with an unopened bottle of water. Heather took the bottle and twisted the cap loose. She stepped toward Masnick. She looked disapprovingly at his shackles.

"Is all of this necessary?"

Finris shrugged. "Spanish Johnny says he is a dangerous man and we would be wise to fear him no matter how he presents himself."

Heather flashed a knowing look and removed the bottle cap.

"Here," she said offering the open bottle to his lips. "Drink."

Masnick would have liked to have refused the water as a sign of strength, but he was very thirsty and there seemed no point in showmanship. He opened his mouth and she poured a little inside. She waited for him to swallow and then repeated the action until the bottle was empty. She gave the empty plastic bottle back to Earl. She placed a cool hand on Masnick's right cheek as if testing for a fever. She stroked his black hair back from his forehead. It was as gentle as a lover's touch and nearly as erotic.

3

"Is that better?" she asked. Masnick nodded.

"Thank you."

Masnick held her gaze measuring her. She smiled a motherly smile. She leaned in close and gave him a chaste peck on the same cheek she had touched. Her soft lips seemed to burn the flesh.

"We are going to have so much fun," she whispered into his ear.

Heather straightened upward and turned to Earl.

"Put his hood back on," she said, which Earl hurried to do.

"I hear he likes to dress like a woman," Finris said. "Let me give him to some of my men who are not repulsed by such things. A rough night or three with them will break his soul."

Heather laughed a soft girlish laugh that sounded like tiny cymbals. "You men and your brutality. So homophobic. I will start to break him tomorrow or the next day."

Masnick heard the light click off and the door clang shut. He heard the sliding of the electronic lock into place, the sound of three sets of footsteps as they disappeared. The cell fell back into silence. He thought he heard the throaty bark of a large dog off in the distance. It was followed by more barks. A shiver shook him. It wasn't the cold.

Despite Heather's charm, Masnick had seen the dark hollow that should have held her heart. He had heard the quiver of excitement in her voice. Unreasoning fear reached for him and his bladder emptied onto the screen mesh of the chair seat. She would take her time. She would savor his questioning. She would not stop until she had broken him. For the first time in his hard life he was terrified.

2

Frank Kane sat in the dark watching the stillness of his house from a chair in the backyard. He cinched his fleece lined Carhartt jacket around him and snugged his watch cap down a little more over his shaved head. He had thought this was his refuge, his hidden fortress. In his hubris, he had convinced himself that they would not be looking for him. He would be forgotten. He would be left alone. Five minutes had changed that. Five minutes that promised more blood on his already bloodstained hands. He looked at the back of his huge scarred hands. The thick veins looked like worms under the brown skin. He flexed one massive hand and then the other. People would die if he did what they asked. People would die if he didn't.

Frank took a cigar case out of the breast pocket of the jacket. The worn black leather case held three Churchill-size cigars. He smiled. He wouldn't need that many tonight. He took the cutter from his pocket and snipped off the end of the cigar. He moistened it with his mouth. The saliva wetted the Connecticut wrapper. The ritual complete, he sighed. His warm breath came out as steam in the late February air. It looked like a dragon's breath from the mouth of a dark foreboding cavern.

The gentle night breeze was helpless to prevent the torch lighter from lighting the tip of the cigar. He drew in the smoke and savored the familiar taste. He blew it out and watched the white smoke hang in the air above him like a summer cloud. He glanced at the band. Casa de Garcia it read. Frank had always smoked Montecristos. Apollo, his best friend from his days in the Spartans motorcycle club, had turned him on to their distinctive taste and slow burn. They were reportedly the most popular cigars in the world. He had smoked the ones from Cuba and their self-named cousins from the Dominican Republic and could tell no difference. Apollo had told him that after Cuba fell, the tobacco growers had fled with the seeds for all of Cuba's popular brands. Frank wondered what would happen with the United States starting to trade with Cuba again. Would they both keep the same name?

He took another deep draw on the cigar. He had stopped smoking Montecristos in favor of the Casa de Garcias. They were both hand-rolled in the same factory in DR. The Casas used less ideal leaves but still burned smooth and slow. A Montecristo cost fifteen bucks a stick while the Casa was only a buck fifty. Frank was wealthy, but he abhorred spending money on himself.

He took another draw. Five minutes, that was all it had taken to change his world. Five minutes. It had begun innocently enough. Jenny, the young girl he acted as ad hoc guardian for, had been leaving for a date with her new boyfriend. It was the first real date she had been on since he rescued her from some bad business in Atlanta. He had been both happy and a little concerned to meet her new boyfriend, Jacob.

Jacob had turned out to be someone Frank had known when he was the chief enforcer for the Spartans motorcycle club. Frank had called him The Jake back then and had mentored him until the Spartans had fallen years later. His surprise had turned to concern. It wasn't that he didn't trust The Jake. The Jake was like a younger brother. Frank trusted him with his life. It was when The Jake had handed him a special cell phone. It was not coincidence. Things rarely were.

Frank took a pull on the cigar and tried to blow a smoke ring. He failed. He never had been able to blow one and a part of him liked that he failed the challenge but kept at it. He replayed the call in his head. It had been from David Carpenter, also known as Helios to the Spartans. He had been a Spartan God along with Frank and Masnick and Spanish Johnny and a dozen or so others.

"They have Masnick," Carpenter had said.

Frank had not responded. There were too many "theys" out there. Too many enemies. Too many touched by the Spartans' rise and brutality.

"I gave him up to Cyrus." Carpenter continued.

Frank could picture Carpenter on the other end. He looked like Kevin Costner with more hair. He was handsome and he knew it. Carpenter gathered information and traded it. He was a wizard with a computer. He believed he could discover any secret in the world with enough clicks of a computer button. He could have been right. He was a spider with a huge web. His work with the Spartans was a large part of why they had become so successful.

"Why?" Frank had asked.

"I had to. Cyrus asked me to find him."

"So, Cyrus made it out?"

"You didn't know? Interesting. Do you want me to tell you who else is still alive from the old gang?"

"No. That's all past history."

"Then you aren't reforming the Spartans? You aren't settling old scores?"

"No. Why would I want to do that?"

Carpenter laughed. "Because you are Frank Kane."

"And?"

"They are afraid of you, Frank. All of them. You were their enforcer."

"No reason to be. I'm out of that business. It ended after the compound in Asheville fell."

"I understand. Do you want me to tell you how I found you?"

"No. It doesn't matter."

"Not even a little curious?"

"No."

"Just a hint. I traced the car. The one you used in Texas."

"Good for you. Let's talk about Masnick."

"Right, sorry. Cyrus asked me to locate him. In the spirit of full disclosure, Masnick was a CI for the feds."

Frank had laughed. "I know. He came to me for advice. I gave it to him. The feds had him cold. The question was what to do about it. We used his info to focus the feds on our enemies. Win-win. No harm to the Spartans."

"You amaze me. I had no idea. You are very good with keeping secrets. I know you guys were close friends. . ."

"Masnick is insane and a genius. But yeah, on some level we were friends."

"Cyrus wanted me to find him and you. I had to give him something."

"Why not give him me?"

"We are friends. . ."

Frank had laughed again without restraint. It was deep and full and spontaneous. The sound had shocked them both. Carpenter had recovered quickly.

"The truth is, I think it would be more valuable to me to know where you are than to sell that information. I never really liked Masnick. He was too mercurial for my tastes."

"The truth. Damn. That must be a first for you, Carp."

"It is a rarity, I confess. Cyrus gave Masnick to the Norse Men. I don't know where they have him . . . yet. They mentioned something about taking him to Valhalla. Wherever that is. Obviously not the real one. What would be the point? The Norse Men are so weird. I should know soon."

"And you want me to go save him? Why?"

"Honor. Spartan honor. That is also who you are."

"Why did Cyrus give him to the Norse Men?"

"To draw you out. They hope they can catch the big man himself. They don't want Masnick. They don't give a damn about past transgressions. They want you."

That had been the gist of it. It hadn't been much. Just enough. Frank would go. Carpenter knew that when he had called. Honor was Frank's Achilles' heel. Masnick had been a good friend, if you can be friends with a nut job like him. Masnick had saved Frank's life a few times. Carpenter's knowledge of where Frank lived was the unspoken threat if it was needed. It wasn't.

Frank would have to put together a go bag. He would have to go to his storage locker and get gunned up. The Norse Men were white supremacist assholes. But they were tough. They wouldn't just give Masnick back. He would have to take him.

Keep it simple with the fire power, he thought, a couple of handguns and the Benelli twelve-gauge shotgun. No way to accurately trace a shotgun blast back to a particular shotgun. For some reason, despite all of his legendary prowess with a handgun, Frank was only average with automatic weapons. Spray and pray. And he wasn't much better with long guns. Scott Rehm, who the Spartans called Pan, had once said that an angry man with a shotgun could rule the world. Frank liked shotguns.

He would need some ammo, but no need to hoard. He wasn't planning on shooting his way to Masnick. Frank recognized the irony. That was exactly his plan when he went to Fort Worth to rescue Elliott's brother. Kill them all and let the gods sort it out. That hadn't worked out so well. Fuck it. Better take an extra couple of boxes just in case, he thought.

Carpenter had said they had taken Masnick to Valhalla. Frank knew where that was. He had an idea what to expect when he got there. Some things you couldn't learn on a damn computer. Some things couldn't be ferreted out with clicks on a keyboard. Some things you learned on the ground by listening. Some things you learned when you did time in prison with assholes like the Norse Men.

Frank sat in the cold dark and worked on the cigar. He would need a plan. He would need to already be in place when Carpenter called. But before they broke Masnick. How long could Masnick last, he wondered? He pondered his options as the cigar burned down.

3

The Jake pulled his black Honda Accord into the empty parking space near the front of Ruth's Chris Steak House. Jenny smiled appreciatively.

"Wow, you really are trying to impress me. Do you think an expensive dinner will win me over?"

"If it would, we would eat out every night."

"You say the sweetest things in the weirdest ways, Jacob."

"Call me Jake."

Jenny looked slightly puzzled. "You told me everyone called you Jacob."

The Jake smiled and brushed a loose strand of brown hair back from her face.

"They do. But my close friends call me Jake. I like it better."

He was staring at her with his huge dark eyes. He seemed so earnest and vulnerable. She thought she might melt into the seat. She was falling hard and fast. She recovered enough to whisper out an answer.

"Jake, it is."

Jake leaned over and lightly kissed her. The movement was so quick and so light she didn't respond. It was almost like a butterfly had actually kissed her. She did manage a quick smile.

Ruth's Chris was the best steak house in Greensboro. It was expensive without being ridiculous. The food was predictable and good. Jake opened the door for her and then led her into the restaurant. The hostess seated them in a secluded booth with a wink at Jake.

The waitress arrived within minutes and asked if they would like something to drink. They both ordered sweet iced tea. When she had gone with their drink orders, Jenny leaned across the table.

"It is alright if you get a real drink. I don't mind. I would get one, but they will card me."

"I like iced tea. And I rarely drink alcohol."

"Like a good boy scout," Jenny teased.

"No. I am far from that. Drinking just isn't my thing."

Jenny felt a twinge of embarrassment. She was kidding, but sometimes he seemed to take everything so seriously. She really liked him. Jenny and Caron had been visiting the University of North Carolina at Greensboro. They had stopped in at a new little coffee shop, The Black Broth. It was Jake's place. It was small and hip and crowded. They were thinking about leaving because it was packed when she saw him for the first time. He was behind the counter in a blue tee shirt with the company logo over the left breast. He looked like an athlete, lean and strong. His thick dark hair was tousled and a touch long, like he needed a haircut and knew it. When he had looked up to see her there was an instant connection. Something like electricity struck her from across the room. It was primal.

He stopped what he was doing and let a waifish tattooed, pierced, sullen, slump-shouldered Goth girl behind the counter take over. He walked with long strides across the room to where Jenny stood rooted. He had introduced himself and led her by the arm to a small, unoccupied table. His touch had felt like electricity on her arm. He had swept up the clutter of empty coffee cups and debris himself. She had started going to The Black Broth everyday. Usually she wouldn't have gone back without Caron backing her up. But the fact was she never went back with Caron. Caron had her own boyfriend, DC. Jake was her secret.

"This place is awesome. I've never been here," she said.

"Really? Frank never brought you?"

"Frank doesn't like to go out to eat. Why did you bring me here, Jake? Are we celebrating? Is today your birthday?"

"No. It is not my birthday. I just wanted our first date to be special."

"Is this our first date?"

"Official first date."

"What about all those times we walked around Tate Street? Or when you took me shopping at the Shoppes on Friendly? Or the late nights talking at your store? What were those?"

"Those were hanging out. Getting to know each other. Deciding if we were worth each other's time. This is a date, a real date."

"And that little kiss in the car, is that part of the first date too? I thought that came at the end of the date."

"Sorry. I couldn't resist. You looked so pretty it just happened."

"It was nice. I liked it."

Jake smiled nervously.

"There are some things we need to talk about."

"Wait. You can't break up with me on the first date."

"Don't be a goof. I'm serious. There are some things I need to tell you before this goes any farther. To see if you want it to go any farther."

"This is a pretty heavy talk for a first date, Jake. And where do you see this going? Should I pick out a wedding dress? Where do you see us in five years?"

Jake reached across the table and took her hands in his. He looked at her like a man going to confession.

"I like you, Jenny. I like everything about you. I liked you the first time I saw you. I want to continue seeing you, but I don't want there to be any lies between us. I don't want to not tell you things now that could ruin us later. If when I am done, you don't want to see me again, I will understand. I will be hurt, but I will understand."

"What did you need to tell me so badly?" Jenny asked, smiling. He was such an idiot sometimes.

"I'm not who you think I am. I mean I am, but I am more than what you see. I'm not just a guy who own his own business."

Jenny smiled indulgently like a mother might smile at a child who has stolen a cookie from the cookie jar. Men were such children.

"And who are you, Jake? Besides being awesome."

"I am a Spartan. I was a Spartan. I knew Frank from back in the day. We rode together."

Jenny lurched back. She pulled her hands free.

"Is this some kind of a setup? Are you after Frank?"

"No. I mean partly. I was told where Frank was. I came here to see him. I found out I liked Greensboro. The weather is nice. The people are friendly. It's big enough but not too big. I decided I wanted to put down roots here. Go straight like Frank has. We were very close in the Spartans. He was my mentor."

"And what did he teach you? How to be a biker?"

"He taught me how to kill men. He taught me how not to get caught. He taught me loyalty and courage and honor."

She gasped. She had told Frank tonight that her new boyfriend reminded her of a younger Frank. It was true. Jake was a younger version of Frank. She looked into his face. He was so handsome. He didn't look like a killer. He looked like a kid. Like a million other kids. Like her.

She knew the siren call to violence. She had felt it once herself when a football player named Zach had tried to rape her. She had held a knife to his throat daring him. Part of her had wanted to cut his throat. To take his life. To actually see him die by her own hands. But she hadn't.

"You need to know the truth, Jenny. You deserve the truth. I am trying to go straight."

Jenny didn't know what to say. It was a shock. She took in a deep breath through her nose and held it as she gathered her thoughts. She tried to calm her pulse. What did she want to do? Storm out? Make a scene? Never see Jake again? No, she realized that in her world it didn't matter. In some twisted way it made perfect sense. Since the bad business in Atlanta she hadn't even dated anyone. She had been drawn to a boy she met on vacation, but he had been another outlaw friend of Frank's. Nothing had happened and she had come home. Alone again. Caron, her best friend, had found DC. She was happy. What did Jenny want?

Jenny relaxed. She placed her small hands over his.

"I know that was hard to say. It was hard to hear. I don't know what is ahead for us. Nobody does, but starting out with lies is never good. I want to keep seeing you as long as you want to keep seeing me when you learn all my secrets."

"Do tell."

"Not tonight. Those are enough revelations for one night. You will just have to keep dating me if you want to discover them."

"I think I can do that. Nothing that has happened in your life would affect how I feel about you."

This time she reached up and traced her fingertips along his face like a blind woman seeing for the first time. She smiled, and with perfect timing the waitress returned with their drinks.

"Are you ready to order?" she asked.

"Give us a couple more minutes," Jake said, and picked up the menu for the first time. "We are going to be here a while."

"Are you celebrating something special?"

Jake smiled. "Our first date."

The waitress beamed. "I will give you a few minutes." She looked at Jenny. "You are a lucky girl."

Jenny returned the smile and then turned it toward Jake.

"I know."

The date lingered on. They ate salads, and thick steaks served on five-hundred-degree iron plates with sides of asparagus and mashed potatoes. They talked and joked and each made secret plans about their futures. The time raced until it was nearly nine thirty.

"We better go," Jake said. "She might get one more paying guest if we finally leave."

Jenny looked embarrassed. "I know. I worked as a waitress. We live for tips."

"Don't worry. I will take good care of her."

Jenny liked that he was so deferential to the waitress. She considered it a good sign.

Jake paid the bill in cash and they left. He held the car door for her, and Jenny got inside. He got in the other side.

"Thank you for tonight. I know it really was hard for you."

"The truth always comes out. I'm glad you listened. Glad you are willing to give me a chance."

Jake leaned over to kiss her and hesitated. Jenny wasn't one to miss a second chance. She reached up and grasped the front of his shirt and pulled him toward her.

"This time, a little slower."

Jake was a good kisser and so was Jenny. They sat locked in an awkward embrace kissing until another car pulled into the parking lot. The loud slams of car doors and men's voices broke their building passion. Jake turned to see who the newcomers were.

The men were both from eastern Europe by their heavy accents. They wore expensive dark suits with starch-stiff white cotton shirts. Bold-colored power ties were the only splash of color on their attire. He stared at the military style haircuts. He stared at the stiff swaggering strides. He knew these men. They were Russian gangsters. He had worked with one of them using the alias Stephan. One of the Russians was named Yuri. He was in the heroin business. He and his consorts had hired Jake through Carpenter to remove a competitor in the same business. Jake didn't like seeing them in Greensboro. This was his home now. It presented complications. It posed questions.

Jenny turned his face back toward hers. "It's still early. I know a nice place we can go for some after-dinner coffee and dessert."

Jake smiled. "I think it is closed by now."

"I know the owner. I think he would open up for us."

"Let's go find out."

Jake snapped his seat belt on and started the car. He backed out slowly. He would have to think about the Russians some more. Not tonight. Tonight he was on a date. He could find them later. Russians thugs were always easy to find. They were thugs. That made them predictable.

4

Deputy Sheriff Jeff Maurer drove toward his home in Zaneville. It was late and he was tired. But he kept it at the posted speed limit. His shift was over with the completion of the local high school basketball game. The basketball game was long over. A team won. A team lost. The bleachers were deserted. The school parking lot was empty. Everyone was home to wherever they were sleeping. His wife, Cathy, would be asleep by now. She was a history teacher in Zaneville and always got up early in the morning. Even on Saturday. She was pregnant with their first child. If it was a boy they had decided on Will, if it was a girl, Natalie.

Maurer had always wanted to be a cop. Ever since he was a small boy it had been his dream. His goal. He had avoided the usual teenage infractions that might mar his record and keep him out of the police academy. He had played sports in high school, football and basketball. He worked hard shaping his body for law enforcement. After high school, a couple of years of community college improved his resume, then off to the Marines where he did a tour in Afghanistan. It was mostly behind the lines, supply depot stuff, but it looked good on his resume.

After his time was up, he applied to the academy and was accepted. Reality set in on graduation. There were no jobs. Anywhere. He wanted to stay in his home state of Ohio, but couldn't find a post. He had signed on as a night watchman for a while. Biding his time. Searching the internet. Calling old friends. Asking favors.

The sheriff's office in Blackwater was small. There were three ladies that handled dispatch, nine officers, and the sheriff. Jim Long liked to be called the High Sheriff. He had been the high sheriff for as long as anyone could remember. The sheriff was described by everyone as tough but fair. One of the deputies had died of a sudden heart attack and Jeff had applied to fill the post. Still he was shocked when he got the job. Sheriff Jim Long became his mentor.

He smiled. Maurer was exactly where he thought he should be. At the bottom rung working his way up. Maybe eventually end up in Dayton or Cinci. That would be sweet. A lot of big-time crime up there. Lots of badasses needing to meet a no-nonsense cop like him. Baby steps, he told himself. One step at a time.

The radio squawk broke his daydream.

"This is dispatch. We have a reported 10-16 at the Manor trailer park."

Maurer clicked his radio on.

"Roger that. I am in the vicinity."

"Sorry, honey, I tried to raise the high sheriff, but couldn't get him. Sure you don't mind?"

"Not a problem."

She gave him the address.

His heart raced a little as he turned around on the road. A 10 –16 was domestic disturbance. It wasn't much, but it was a lot more action than directing traffic at a basketball game.

The drive to The Manor took less than six minutes. It was a worn-down trailer park for people barely scraping by. These were hard times. Most people were only a couple of paychecks away from The Manor themselves.

Maurer threaded his way down the gravel road inside the entrance, past the weedy overgrown tracts. The trailers were old and well used. Children's toys and broken bicycles littered the hard-packed bare dirt yards around each trailer. Old chairs and sofas rested on empty porches. A mongrel dog with its ribs sticking out darted past in the dim light between two trailers. He turned on the light bar on top of his cruiser. He wanted to let the people who were still awake know he was a cop. He let the siren stay quiet. Most people would be sleeping. No reason to wake the whole place. Sheriff Long was big on public relations.

He used the searchlight mounted outside his window to scan for the trailer's number. He might as well have left it off. The shouts and screams were loud enough to steer by. Maurer goosed the accelerator a little and hurried to the commotion. There was a weak streetlight ahead and the trailer he sought was set up ten yards away. A man in jeans and a green camouflage jacket and an orange camouflage hat stalked outside.

The man was a little under average height. Maurer couldn't tell his weight under the coat for certain, but he figured the man was bone thin. The man turned as Maurer eased his car to a stop. He let the light bar announce his presence. That was usually all it took. The thin man turned back to the house and threw a can of beer at the side.

"The cops? Damn you, Darlene. You called Five-O on me."

"I didn't call nobody. One of the neighbors must have called because you are making an ass out of yourself."

"You are a lying bitch. You called them. I know you did."

"Go to hell, Dwayne."

"If I go, you're going with me, whore."

"Whore? You're the one shacked up with Connie from the diner. She's the whore. She knew you were my man."

Dwayne seized on the opening. "That's right, baby. It ain't my fault. She seduced me."

"Liar. You been drooling over her big tits since high school."

"That ain't my fault neither. That's hormones. Men are made to lust after women. That's the way God made us. Nothing would have happened if she hadn't let me."

15

"Go back to your Nazi buddies at your lodge. I'm taking the kids to momma's."

"You ain't taking my boys. You hear me. You ain't taking 'em. Next time I come back I won't come alone. Let's see you keep me out then, you fat cow."

Maurer smiled. He appreciated the calmness of his marriage more every day. He got out of the car and approached Dwayne with a slow, nonthreatening stride.

"Sir. I am going to have to ask you to step away from the trailer."

Dwayne turned toward Maurer. He scanned the deputy from head to toe. Dwayne took his hat off and threw it down on the ground. He stomped on the hat.

"This don't concern you. It's between me and my woman."

"Sir. You are creating a disturbance. I am going to have to ask you to vacate the trailer park."

"Or what?"

"Or I will arrest you."

"You and what army? You get all badged up, turn into some Rambo wannabe?"

"I don't need an army to handle trash like you."

"Trash? I'm from the Lodge, you dumbass pig piece of shit. I'm a Norse Man. You know what that means around here?"

"No. What does it mean?'

"It means you can't do shit to me."

"Is that right? Well, I don't know anything about the Norse Men or the Lodge or what or who you think you know, but I do know you can't break the law."

Dwayne stared at Maurer as if he were from another planet.

"You're a fuckin' idiot," Dwayne said. "I ought to beat your ass just to teach you a lesson."

Maurer smiled. "I would not recommend that course of action, Dwayne. Just go home and let's call it a night."

"This is my home."

"Not tonight it isn't. You need to go somewhere else. Go to your Lodge or whatever you called it."

Dwayne shook his head and kicked a clod of dirt. He picked up his hat and beat it clean against his jeans leg. The hat left a smudge of dust on the old pants.

"Alright. I guess you're right. She don't want me no more anyway."

"Good choice, Dwayne. Tomorrow you guys can try to work it out."

Dwayne nodded and extended his hand toward Maurer. Maurer reached to shake it. Dwayne's punch came without warning. It was a big looping left. Most men would have been caught off guard. Maurer was not. It took him a millisecond to process the threat. He ducked below it and struck Dwayne with a hard uppercut to the stomach. Dwayne stumbled backward a step, tripped over a broken rake and then set down on the ground gasping for air.

Maurer reached back for his zip tie hand cuffs.

"That was foolish. Now you are under arrest for assault on a police officer."

Dwayne drew a knife from somewhere and lurched to his feet.

"You ain't arresting shit. I'm going to cut your pretty face right off you."

Maurer took a step back. He drew his collapsible baton and snapped it open. He could have drawn his sidearm and shot Dwayne. But that would lead to a mountain of paperwork and recriminations. Non-lethal force was always the best option.

Dwayne crabbed from side to side with the hunting knife extended before him. He waved the blade back and forth, looking for an opening. Occasionally, he would dart forward and slash at Maurer, who moved easily out of his reach. Dwayne was wearing a maniacal grin.

"Now, law dog, let's see how tough you are."

Maurer didn't answer the taunt.

When Dwayne lunged the next time, he struck him across the top of his knife arm. The bone snapped. Dwayne screamed. The knife fell to the dirt. Maurer used the baton to punch Dwayne in the stomach again. As Dwayne clutched at his broken wrist Maurer tackled him to the ground. Dwayne was screaming and thrashing. Maurer flipped him onto his stomach and pulled his arms behind his back. He hooked the nylon cuffs to his left wrist and right forearm above the break. He got to his feet and picked up Dwayne's knife. He put it on the hood of his car.

He returned to Dwayne and started patting him down.

"Anything in your pockets? Anything that might cut me?"

Dwayne was crying.

"I'm sorry. I'm sorry. She just makes me crazy."

Maurer found a zip lock bag with three nondescript capsules inside. He put that on the hood beside the knife. There was a ring with a set of keys, a wallet, a lighter, some change, and an unopened condom. Dwayne must be an optimist, Maurer thought.

He helped Dwayne to his feet. Darlene came outside. She ran over to Dwayne.

"Oh, baby. What has this son of a bitch done to you?"

"He broke my damn arm. For nothing."

"He attacked me, ma'am."

"He's lying. I didn't do nothin'. He just hit me for no reason."

"Don't worry, baby. I get you out."

Dwayne stared at Darlene like she was his guardian angel, which she might have been.

"I love you."

"I love you too, baby."

Dwayne started crying again.

"Can't you just let him go? He didn't mean nothin',"

"No, ma'am. He assaulted a police officer. I have to take him in."

The night lit up with approaching headlights. Three trucks came flying in, kicking up rooster combs of gravel and dirt. The trucks slammed to a stop on the other side of the deputy's car. The doors popped open and a half dozen men climbed out of the different cabs. They spread out in a loose semicircle facing Maurer and Dwayne.

5

When Jenny came home she saw that Frank's light was still on in his room. She knocked on his door. He was reading Plutarch. For some reason, it did not surprise her. Frank was a complicated man.

"Can I come in?" she asked.

"Of course. I was waiting up for you."

"I'm sorry I'm late. I know my curfew is . . ."

"Never mind that."

"Nothing happened. We just talked."

"Jenny, you are a grown woman and I trust you. I waited up because we need to talk."

"About Jake?"

Frank smiled. "We can talk about that if you want to."

"He told me he used to be in the Spartans with you."

"He was."

"He said you were his mentor."

"That was nice of him to say. I taught him what I could. I felt responsible for him so I tried to look after him."

"He said you taught him how to kill people."

The statement hung in the air between them. Frank sighed.

"I did. It was what I knew how to do."

"And Jake?"

"Listen, I knew a lot of men when I was a Spartan. Some of them were good men within the context of being outlaws. Apollo, Blanco, Reaper, Hendo, Pan, they were all guys I trusted with my life. But they were not good men. They were criminals. They aren't the kind of men I would trust with you. Jake is different. He is special. He is one of the only men I knew who was a good man. And I mean that."

Jenny nodded. "We had a long talk about a lot of things."

"I figured you would. Are you going to keep seeing him?"

"Yeah. Maybe there is something wrong with me. I mean I am only attracted to outlaws."

"Maybe there is something wrong with you."

"Gee, thanks."

"There is something wrong with all of us, Jenny. But you maybe less than anyone else."

"Good recovery. I really like Jake. For all he told me, I still think he is a good guy too."

"He is. He'll look after you while I'm gone."

"Gone? Where are you going?"

"To help an old friend."

"Do you have to?"

"I wouldn't go if I didn't think I needed too. You know that."

"I know. You do the things you need to do. How long will you be gone?"

"A few weeks? It is complicated." Frank picked up a note card and handed it to her. "Here is the number of the cell phone I will be using."

"Is it another prepaid?"

"Of course. Is Caron staying over at DC's tonight?"

"Yeah. It's the weekend and all."

"Give them the number too. If something comes up and you need me, call."

"Where will you be? I mean if you can tell me."

"Ohio."

"Must be a good friend."

"Like I said, it's complicated."

"Does Jake know what you are up to?"

"I don't know. He might. I doubt it. I will stop in to see him before I go tomorrow. Have a little chat."

"You aren't going to talk about me, are you? About Jake and me dating? I mean, that is so weird."

"No. We have other things to discuss. I'll leave you and Jake up to you and Jake."

"I just don't want you scaring him away. At least not yet."

Frank got up from his chair. He laid the book on his seat. He motioned Jenny to come to him. He gave her a warm hug. Frank Kane did not hug. Frank Kane was not a toucher. Frank Kane was learning to be a regular person.

"Jake may be one of the only people on this earth that isn't afraid of me."

Jenny looked up into Frank's rough face. "Damn. You didn't tell me Jake was an idiot."

Frank laughed and Jenny laughed with him. Her crazy world seemed to make sense again.

"I will check in when I can. Don't worry about me. Just look after yourself."

"I know, schoolwork, eat right, no parties, blah blah blah."

"I am starting to sound like an old woman."

"No. I just know the drill. Go help your friend. Do what you do. I got this. Really, I do."

"I knew I could count on you, Jenny."

"I'm glad you waited up, Frank."

"Me too."

6

The leader of the group was a giant with long black hair pulled back into a ponytail. He was wearing heavy canvas pants but only a vest over his upper body. His massive arms were covered in tattoos. He didn't seem bothered by the cold. He was the first to speak.

"What's going on here, officer?"

"Nothing to concern you, sir. This is official police business. Move along."

"And what are you going to do with Dwayne?"

"He's under arrest. I have to take him down to the station."

"He didn't do nothin'," Darlene yelled. "This cop just jumped him for no good reason."

"Is that right, officer?"

"That is not correct. I must ask you again to return to your vehicles. I am taking this man in."

"Help me," Dwayne hollered. "He broke my damn wrist. Don't let him lock me up. I didn't do one damn thing."

The giant shook his head.

"Dwayne is a fool, but he is our fool. Let us handle this, officer. Just release him and everyone goes home in one piece."

"I am sorry, I cannot do that. This man is in my custody. Now stand aside, sir. I am taking him in."

"Not going to happen." The giant smiled a warm smile, but the words were cold.

"I am a police officer in performance of my duty. If you hinder me then you will face arrest as well."

Some of the men laughed. One slowly drew a pistol and let it dangle obviously beside his leg. A second and third went back to their trucks and returned carrying shotguns or hunting rifles. Maurer drew his side arm. He held onto the back of Dwayne's shirt and pointed his weapon at the men.

"Put the weapons down, now," he shouted.

Two more men drew pistols from behind their backs.

The strangers made no overtly aggressive moves. He noticed that everyone except the giant now had a weapon drawn. Maurer had his gun up and was sweeping it from person to person. He was outnumbered and outgunned. If the shooting started, he was dead.

The giant brushed some unseen dirt from one of his massive arms.

"It's your call, officer. This doesn't have to be bloody. It's entirely your call."

"I told you to stand back, sir. This is official police business."

"Don't let him take Dwayne," Darlene screamed.

"Help me," Dwayne screamed. "Don't let him take me in."

"Let him go. Just walk away. Go home to Cathy and your unborn child in Zaneville."

The casual mention of Cathy shook Maurer. How did this man know his wife's name? How did he know she was pregnant? How did he know he lived in Zaneville? Who were these guys?

"I will not ask you again to back away," Maurer shouted. "I will fire."

Some of the men surrounding him began to laugh. The air seemed to crackle with the tension. Maurer pointed the Beretta at the giant. The giant smiled. Maurer increased pressure on the trigger. They had him, but this jerk wasn't walking away from here either.

The sound of an approaching siren seemed to take the air from the situation. Backup, Maurer thought. Just in time. Thank God, someone had called the sheriff's office and they had sent backup. The sheriff's car skidded to a halt. High Sheriff Jim Long bolted from behind the wheel.

"Break it up. Break it up." He shoved a couple of roughnecks out of his way. "What's going on here?" He pointed a long finger at Maurer. "Stand down, officer. I said stand down. Holster that weapon. Do you hear me?"

Maurer lowered his weapon. He reluctantly holstered it.

"Sheriff, I got a 10–16 call," Maurer began. "This man was asked to leave the premises and attacked me with that knife." Maurer pointed toward the hood of his car. "When I arrested him, these people showed up and threatened to take him from me. They are all armed. Thank God you got here when you did."

"Goddamn it. Finris, what do you have to say for yourself?"

"The kid is telling it pretty straight."

"All this shit for a 10–16? A fucking pissass 10-16?"

"Dwayne is one of us. I couldn't stand the thought of him locked up."

"I won't press charges, Sheriff," Darlene said. "We were just fighting is all. Everything's fine now. Isn't that right, baby? We gonna work it out like we always do."

"That's right. 'Cept he broke my damn wrist."

Sheriff Long nodded as if he was sorting the facts. He approached Dwayne and spun him around. He took out his own knife and cut the cuffs.

"Collect your stuff, Dwayne, and get along to the hospital to have that wrist seen to."

"But Sheriff. . ." Maurer started.

The sheriff held up a finger to silence him. He turned to Finris.

"See to your boy, Finris. We are done here."

Finris smiled.

22

"Thank you, Jim. I appreciate your expert handling of the situation."

The Norse Men loaded Dwayne into one of the trucks and they all left. Maurer stood fuming.

"Now settle down, son. You only been on the job here a month. It's bad business to be locking up ever redneck and shit kicker in town just because they have a fight with their old lady."

"He tried to cut me."

"But he didn't. You could handle his kind with one hand behind your back. You were never in any danger and you know it. Come by my office tomorrow noon. I want to talk to you."

"But Sheriff. . ."

"Not another word. This is my town. I know how to run it. Get on home. That's an order, Maurer."

High Sheriff Long got in his own car and disappeared into the night. Maurer was momentarily lost. He was trying to sort it all through when Darlene walked up and placed a crone's wizened hand on his arm.

"Don't worry yourself, son. You tried to help. But this is Blackwater. That's how things are done here."

With her words still heavy in his ears, Maurer climbed back into his car and drove to Zaneville. All the way he thought about Finris' words. How had Finris known his wife's name? And all that other stuff? And what did it mean?

7

Frank slept late. There was no need to get started early. Most of the places he needed to go didn't open until nine. He packed carefully. He had to have the right look. He dressed in old blue jeans and his beat-up Timberland work boots. He put on a white tee shirt and his Carhartt jacket. He took a pair of shooting gloves, glove liners, his fleece lined Carhartt Sandstone bib overalls, and a second pair of jeans and put them in a large garbage bag. He tossed in his electric screwdriver, a lockpick set, his fake I.D. in the name of Frank Carsons and three flannel shirts. He left the bag on his bed. He locked the house and started his errands.

His first stop was the Army Navy Store. It was the perfect place to resupply. The building in Greensboro was old and worn. Paint peeled from the old wood and hung like burnt skin from the building. Inside was a dusty and cluttered array of surplus military and camping gear. Frank went to the back to the section marked "gently used", which actually meant old and half worn-out. He started with a dark green Mossy Oak tree-patterned camo hunting parka. It was lined with Thinsulate for warmth. It came with a hood and a vast array of pockets for storage and hand warming. It was supposed to be Gore-Tex coated and waterproof. He took a size larger than he normally wore to layer and disguise his body shape. In the coat he looked like a big fat guy. He liked it. Hide the lion, show the clown, he thought.

He got a pair of ragg wool gloves, three pairs of wool socks, two sets of thermal long underwear, a bright yellow sweatshirt that said Marines in bright red on the front, a couple of watch caps, one in black and one in bright orange, and four plain gray tee shirts. Finally, he bought a large olive-green canvas duffel bag to put his stuff in. He paid cash and was offered no receipt. Frank smiled. Trying to make a little extra profit, he figured.

His next stop was Walmart. He found a shopping cart with a wobbling front wheel and started searching the aisles. He bought a five-gallon Coleman water cooler and a twenty-five-quart Igloo marine cooler. He found a small Coleman 10,000 BTU one-burner propane stove, three canisters of propane, a Wenzel camp coffeepot that held nine cups, a zero-degree sleeping bag, a white twin sheet to use as a sleeping bag liner, a blow-up mattress, a regular-size pillow, a towel and a nondescript black backpack.

He searched the outdoor section until he found the night vision gear. A salesman unlocked the cabinet and let him look through the choices. He bought a Yukon NVMT night vision goggle. The monocular covered the right eye only. It had 1X 24 mm and used no magnification so that users could see a clear image, with no distortion in depth perception. It was small, lightweight and secured to the head with headgear. It could also be flipped up when not in use.

Frank again paid in cash and locked his new gear, except for the coolers, in the lockbox in the back of his pickup truck. He could sort through it before he left. He stopped at the nearest Harris Teeter grocery store and bought a case of bottled water, two bags of ice, two giant packs of beef jerky, some plastic kitchen utensils, a box of mosquito coils, a gallon jug of Clorox bleach, a bottle of Windex, some large black garbage bags, a case of paper towels, a hard pack of cigarettes, a bag of red Solo cups, a case of Budweiser, a loaf of bread, coffee, Splenda, and a big jar of crunchy peanut butter.

He stopped at local pawn shops looking for a specialty item. He found it at the second one. It was a tool belt with a full set of tools. The leather of the belt was old and heavily stained. The tools were chipped and worn. They had seen a lot of rough use over the years before the owner had decided to part with it. Perfect. There was a good assortment of other used tools, so he chose a sturdy bolt cutter, a crowbar, and a shovel to add to his collection.

With his preparations nearing completion he turned toward The Black Broth. He needed to talk to The Jake before he left.

The Black Broth was busy. College students and hipsters with skinny jeans stood outside smoking exotic cigarettes and drinking huge to-go cups of coffee. The inside was busy too. A line of customers stood patiently, waiting to be served. Most of the tables were occupied. Frank went inside and stood at the doorway. A young male barista stared at him like he was the coffee police come to bust them. This was not a working man's coffee shop, his look said. Go to the service station and get a cup of your coffee or if you were feeling rich, get one at Krispy Kreme or even that sludge they served at McDonald's. You do not belong here.

Frank stood quietly until Jake caught his eye. Jake motioned Frank to come around to the back of the counter. There were murmured words and sighs at the unfairness of it all. Frank followed him out of the coffee shop to the private parking area behind the building. It was deserted. Cigarette butts littered the ground around the garbage dumpster. Discarded paper napkins danced in the breeze.

"Frank, it is good to see you. What do you need?"

"It is good to see you too, Jake."

"I know you got questions. About me, about Jenny, about Carpenter."

"Yeah. But that must wait for now. I got to leave town for a little while."

"Carp?"

Frank nodded. "He wants me to find Masnick. The Norse Men have him. He's trying to run down the location for me."

"But you already think you know where he is."

Frank nodded again and smiled. "I got some idea. Do you know anything about it?"

"No. Carp didn't say anything to me. He only asked me to give you the cell."

Frank walked around in a circle; his hands stuffed into the jacket's pockets. "I need you to look after Jenny while I am gone. And her friends, DC and Caron."

"Consider it done. You expecting trouble?"

"No. Just like to know that is handled. It will help me focus."

"I got your back. You know that."

Frank extended his hand with a piece of paper. There was a number written on it. "Here is the number to my cell if you need me."

Jake looked at the paper and memorized the number. He tore it up in front of Frank. "I got it. You can count on me, Frank."

Frank reached out and pulled Jake into a bear hug. He held it for a second before releasing Jake. "When I get back, we will have that talk. A long talk."

"I hear you."

"Don't break her heart. You hear me. She matters."

"It's not like that. It just sort of happened. It was an omen."

Frank smiled. "Everything happens for a reason."

"I believe that."

"Me too. Listen, I got to go. You call me. If there is any problem, I can come back."

Jake spread his arms with his palms face up. "What could possibly happen?"

Frank laughed. "You always were the funny one."

8

Jeff Maurer parked in front of the police station. He hadn't been able to sleep and he was on edge. He hadn't told his wife about it. He lied to himself that he didn't want to worry her. But the truth was that it scared him. Every time he closed his eyes he replayed what had happened at the trailer park. He had so many questions.

Jeff got out of his car and went inside. He said hello to Helen, who was working the desk and the phones. He walked back toward the high sheriff's office. Jim Long was seated at his desk. He was talking excitedly on the phone. He held up one finger as a signal for Jeff to wait. Long completed his conversation and put down the phone. He motioned toward one of the two chairs across from his desk.

"Have a seat."

Jeff sat down.

"Listen. You did good last night, son. It was a tough spot, but you handled it well, like a professional."

"Handled it? You released my prisoner."

Long leaned his chair back. A broad smile split his face. "Exactly. No one got hurt. Everyone went home. Except that peckerwood whose arm you broke."

"That's what I'm talking about. You just let him go. I defended myself within the parameters set by this department."

"I never said otherwise."

Jeff jumped to his feet. "It makes no sense. I thought about it all night. I thought you were afraid of a civil suit for excessive use of force or something and that was why you released him."

"Simmer down. There are some things you need to understand if you are going to work in Blackwater."

"Like about the Norse Men?"

"Yes, like about the Norse Men."

Long rubbed his crew cut with his big right hand. "The Norse Men are a powerful group in Blackwater. They do a lot of business here and bring in a lot of money this town needs."

"They threatened me. They had guns."

"I know. I know. And I hate that for you, son. They can be a bit rough. They help look after this town. They keep some of the predators away."

"I thought that was our job?"

"It is, but we don't work alone. We need their help. You see how safe Blackwater is? We don't have drugs ruining our kids' lives. We don't have gangs roaming our streets. We got to have one of the lowest violent crime rates in the country."

"But at what cost? They aren't above the law."

"I never said they were. Only we tend to cut them some slack. This is a small town; we all have to live in it."

Jeff stared down at the floor. He finally said what had him scared.

"The big one. . ."

"Finris."

"Yeah, Finris, he said something about my wife and our baby. Something about keeping them safe in Zaneville."

Long didn't answer.

"How did he know all that?"

"Like I said. This is a small town. Everybody knows everything about everybody else. He probably heard it somewhere."

"It sounded like a threat."

"Now, I am sure you are mistaken about that. What kind of an idiot threatens a man's family?"

"But I don't live here. I live in Zaneville. I just work here."

The sheriff's voice took on a twinge of steel. "That's right. You just work here because there are no other jobs out there. You work here because I want you to work here. I went to bat for you and got you this job over a lot of other applicants. And it is a job. It pays your bills. You will do what I ask you to do as long as you work for me."

Jeff was startled. "Yes, sir. I never meant to demean this job."

"It just sounded like you weren't all that happy with your situation here. Implied I might need to be looking for a replacement. One that can roll with small town police work better."

"No, sir. I never meant that. I like my job. I want to keep my job."

High Sheriff Long smiled. "Good. I would hate to lose you. You are a valuable asset to our police force."

"No chance of that, sir. You would have to kill me to get me off this job."

Jeff extended his hand and the high sheriff took it.

"Get back to work."

Jeff smiled and started to back out of the door.

"One more thing," the high sheriff said. He bent at his desk and opened the top drawer. He took out a plain white envelope. It was thick.

"Here, this is for you. We don't have the budget for raises, but here is a little bonus. Something for your kid's college fund."

Jeff took it without speaking. He was stunned. He knew what it was without opening it. He zombie walked out of the office, past the front desk, out of the building and got into his car. He knew he was in trouble. Deep, deep trouble.

Finris sat behind his huge teakwood desk. The top of the desk was bare, except for a laptop computer and a scale map of the compound. He stretched his giant arms behind his head. He smiled at the memory of last night. He cherished the look on the young cop's face. That smug look of authority transforming into a look of fear. And then, when Finris had mentioned his wife and unborn child, sheer terror. He replayed it over and over in his head. It was good to be Finris Wolf.

His phone buzzed and he answered it.

"What's up?"

"The truck is on the way," the voice said. "It cleared customs and should be here in a couple of days."

"Excellent. Any problems?"

"No. The big cats make the customs turds nervous as hell. Everything went smooth. Just wanted to give you the heads up so you could be ready."

"Thanks. I'll pass the word."

Finris hung the phone up with a press of a button. Things were going very well. Loki would be proud. He would have to go see him soon. The old bastard liked his updates on business. The phone calls at the prison were recorded, so everything had to be handled old school, face-to-face.

There was a delicate tap on the door.

"Enter."

A young girl appeared. She was about nineteen years old and very thin with barely any breasts. She was wearing light blue lingerie and knee-high black boots. She lowered her head so that her bright red hair fell like a curtain over her expressionless face. She was carrying a tray with food on it.

"I brought your lunch."

"Bring it over here."

The girl raised her head slightly and walked to the desk. She placed the tray in front of Finris. The lunch was simple. There was a large crystal glass of water. Steam rose from the slab of meatloaf and vegetables. She unrolled the napkin and placed the silverware on either side of the plate. She took the napkin and walked behind the desk to where Finris was seated. She placed it across his lap. Her hand lingered there. A salacious smile crinkled her mouth.

"Is there anything else I can do for you, my lord?"

Finris grasped her hand and pressed it harder between his legs. The girl smiled and began to rub him.

Heather strode into the room.

"Am I interrupting something, Finris?"

Finris smiled at her and released the girl's hand. He looked up into her tiny face. "Have them send you to me tonight."

The girl's smile held its wantonness. "And will you have something for me after we play, my lord?"

"That will depend on how well you play,"

"Leave us," Heather snapped.

The girl's face slipped into banality and she walked from the room.

"Really, is this even necessary?"

"The girls must be seasoned while they are here. I have explained that to you. In her own way she must fight to stay here."

"I understand that part of it. But why do it at all? Those are the old ways. We are going in new directions now. There is plenty of money without all the risks."

Finris cut a portion of the meatloaf and ate it.

"You do not understand, even though you say you do. I like risk. I like the old ways. And there is never enough money."

"Men are pigs."

Finris smacked his lips. Whether over the food or in mockery, it was hard to tell.

"Yes, men are. And I am only a man."

Heather walked over and sat on the edge of the desk. Her short gray skirt and high heels made her long legs look much longer than they were. She crossed them and swung one in a rocking motion.

"Nils will be flying in next week. Will we be ready? He will be angry if we are behind schedule."

"Of course. Don't worry about your brother. I can handle him."

"You don't know him like I do."

"Perhaps I know him better than you do. Leave him to me."

Heather sighed and got off the desk. "We shall see."

Finris ignored her remark. "Are you starting on Masnick today?"

"No. I think I will give him another day to fear the questioning."

Finris shrugged. "Whatever you say. I just want to be there when you interrogate him."

"You will be. I promise. When it is appropriate."

Heather walked toward the door. "Enjoy your lunch."

"I will. Oh, I just heard the truck is on the way. It should get here in a couple of days."

Heather spun around. Excitement lit her eyes. She clapped her tiny hands before her chest.

"That is wonderful. I will check on the lab and see how the process is proceeding."

"You do that. I will check on you later. I don't want this fine lunch to get cold."

Heather's step was as light as a wisp of smoke as she floated from the room.

9

Frank removed all the tags and stickers and store labels from his new gear. He tossed it all in the dryer on the heavy-duty setting to break it in. He filled the five-gallon cooler with tap water and secured it to the back of his truck. He took the case of bottled water and dumped half of it into the ice chest. He poured out the water from the remaining bottles and crushed each one with his hands. He put the empties in a garbage bag. He put most of the Budweiser in the ice chest and emptied and crushed a few, which went into the garbage bag. He dumped one of the bags of beef jerky and put them both into the garbage bag. Frank opened the plastic bag of Solo cups, crushed a few and tossed them in the same garbage bag.

He put the bleach, Windex, and a couple of rolls of paper towels and the large garbage bags into a white kitchen garbage bag. He dumped a third of the loaf of bread and resealed the bag. He used a large spoon to scrape out some of the peanut butter from its plastic jar.

Frank carried both garbage bags out to his truck. He placed the white bag behind the passenger's seat. He shook out the black bag in the back seat and floorboard. He went back inside the house and got the bread, peanut butter and plastic utensils. He put them in a plastic grocery bag and took them out to the truck as well. He put them on the seat. Anyone who looked inside the truck would assume he was living out of it.

He stuffed a handful of Splenda packets into the empty coffee pot and placed the rest of the box in the kitchen cabinet for the girls to use. They loved Splenda. Although lately there had been some discussion about using something called Stevia, whatever that was.

The dryer dinged the completion of its cycle. Frank took all the new clothes and crudely folded them up. He stuffed all the old and new clothes into the duffel. He put the mosquito coils, the lock pick set, the electric screwdriver, cigarettes and a box of Casa de Garcia cigars in the small backpack.

He loaded the clothes and camping gear into the lockbox in his truck. The small backpack went behind the driver's seat. He went to his cash stash and took out five hundred dollars for travel money. He also got two packs of money out of his secret stash. Each envelope held five thousand dollars. Best not to leave a paper trail. He hid the money under the back seat of the truck in the folder that held the owner's manual. No one ever looked there.

Just one more stop before he hit the road. He went to the storage unit he rented. He got the guns and ammo he wanted. He hid one pistol, the Kimber Solo with the 2.7-inch barrel, in the left outside pocket of his coat where he could reach it with his left hand. The gun was all sleek rounded edges and high-grade steel on an aluminum frame. It carried six rounds of 147 grain hollow-point death in the magazine. If he was stopped by police, he could easily slip the all-black gun from his pocket and into the door well of the truck. The twelve-gauge Benelli pump shotgun went in the lockbox in the back of the truck, under the camping gear along with all the ammo. He started to take the Glock, but decided on the H&K MK23. It was the .45 caliber Navy SEAL handgun he had gotten when he did the job in Fort Worth. It was incredibly accurate and had the knock down power he liked. With a twelve-round magazine and its KAC Sound Suppressor, it may have been the most lethal handgun Frank had ever used. He placed it in the very bottom of the lockbox. He wrapped it in the Dragon Skin bulletproof vest.

He cranked the engine up on the old truck. It was one o'clock. He should get to Blackwater by ten. He shook his head at the thought. The damn Norse Men in prison couldn't keep their yaps shut. They loved to drop hints. But after a while the hints painted a clear picture. You just had to connect the dots. They were building a compound in Ohio in a place called Blackwater. It was going to be their Valhalla. It was going to be a place where only the best of them could ever hope to go. Valhalla, a place of unlimited food and drink and women for true Viking warriors. Idiots.

Frank decided he would stop in Tennessee and pick up a new license plate. Should be easy enough to get one along the way. It shouldn't take more than a few minutes.

10

Frank stopped at a Wendy's on the way out of Greensboro. He didn't usually eat fast food. He ordered a Bacon Double Cheeseburger, large fries and a Dr. Pepper. He ate his meal in the parking lot and tossed the trash into the back of the cab. The thick, greasy smell of fast food seemed to fill the cab like a cloud. The rush of carbs made him feel a little sleepy, but he ignored the feeling until the caffeine from the soft drink kicked in. It was a final layer of camouflage for the truck.

He took I-40 West and linked up with I-74. Then he just headed north for I-77. It was just shy of four hundred highway miles to Blackwater. That translated to about six and a half hours for the truck. Adding in the detour to Bristol, Tennessee, it made the entire drive about seven to eight hours tops. Easily doable for Frank and would put him into Blackwater at the right time. Carpenter had given him a Medusa quest. One that would turn a normal man into stone waiting for a destination. Frank was not that man. He was a man of action.

The highway was busy. There seemed to be long haul trucks everywhere. Maybe the economy was finally turning around. The drive gave him time to think about The Jake. There was no one exactly like The Jake. It was on a deserted stretch of highway north of New Orleans that he had first met him.

The Brutes, a small one-percenter bike club in New Orleans, had contacted the Spartans about patching over. Cyrus had been dubious. New Orleans was five hours away from the nearest Spartan club. It was like being in some old-time fort out in Apache territory. Help from your brother Spartans was too far away to do you any good. But Carpenter had been intrigued about the criminal possibilities in New Orleans.

Frank had been bored and offered to go have a look. Hendo and Reaper had come with him more to party than to offer any opinions. The Brutes MC was small, only six guys. Not enough to stand alone with any power against the other criminal enterprises already well established in NOLA. In the end, after a long week of partying, the Spartans had agreed to patch them over but declined to let them stay in New Orleans. However, they did offer to relocate them to Tallahassee to bolster their small club there.

Instead of heading back to the East Coast, Frank had taken Highway 61 north through Mississippi toward Memphis, where he had some club business. The lonely route wound through the Homochitto National Forest. He had spotted The Jake outside a gas station in St. Francisville.

Jake looked to be about fourteen or fifteen. Maybe even younger. A worn overstuffed backpack hung from one shoulder. The kid was thin, with thick black hair and dark nervous eyes. He radiated helplessness and vulnerability.

Not a good thing in Frank's world. Frank thought he was probably a runaway. He was easy prey for the hunters and there were always hunters.

He was dressed in baggy blue jeans, old high-top tennis shoes and a red hoodie sweatshirt. It was a good color. Ancient Spartans always wore red. Frank had thought it might be an omen, so he had given him a second glance as he filled the tank on his bike. He watched the kid sipping on a Diet Pepsi and eating a pack of Skittles. As Frank watched he noticed new features. The eyes weren't nervous, they were searching, watching everything around him. His build was also misleading. What Frank had first taken as a sign of malnourishment was something else, something more akin to leanness like a marathon runner. His movements were too balanced, to precise for someone who was apparently lost on the road. Even the clothes seemed to be more a disguise than the product of days or weeks spent sleeping outdoors. It intrigued Frank.

"Hey, kid. You looking for a ride?"

Jake had lowered his head as he spoke. The voice was timid and nervous.

"Yeah. Are you heading north?"

"Tennessee."

The dark eyes had scanned Frank. They had seen the six foot four, two-hundred-and-thirty-pound outlaw biker. They had swept over the strong features and thick beard. They had noted the Spartan rockers. The eyes processed and made a decision. Jake's reply was in a different voice. It was stronger, more confident. All the traces of prey were gone.

"Sorry. I think I will wait for someone else."

Frank shrugged. "Suit yourself, kid. This is a bad stretch of road. Not much traffic. Lot of chicken hawks use it."

"I can take care of myself."

Something had changed in the kid. For some reason, Frank believed him. Before he could say anything else an old white Ram pickup truck slowed as it passed him. The truck stopped and a thin redneck hopped out.

"You looking for a ride, kid?"

Jake had smiled at Frank and in a quiet voice said to Frank, "This looks like my ride." Then to the truck in the weak voice he called, "Yes, thank you. I need a ride."

"Well come on, boy. We ain't got all day."

Jake hurried forward and the redneck let him slip inside before following him and closing the door. The truck spit gravel as it hurried away. Frank finished filling the gas tank, rehooked the nozzle and tightened off the gas cap. Something seemed odd about the situation. It seemed staged somehow. Why would the kid get in that truck? It screamed a warning on the most elemental level. Frank decided to follow them. He didn't want anything to happen to the kid.

Jake sat pinned between the two men. The driver was fat and smelled of kerosene and bacon. The thin man on his right just stunk of days old sweat and beer. The thin man reached in the back and got a beer out of the cooler.

"You want a drink, kid?"

"No, thank you. I am too young to drink."

"Wonder what else he thinks he's too young to do," the fat man said.

The thin one drank the beer in one long gulp and tossed the can into the back. He stared at Jake like a man with a new present waiting to be unwrapped. He put a hand on Jake's leg and squeezed it. Jake squirmed and pulled his leg away. The thin man laughed and put his hand farther up on his leg rubbing his thigh.

Jake pushed the hand away. "Stop. Get your hands off me."

"That's what your wife says, ain't it, Joe?" the fat man said and laughed.

"Shut the fuck up," Joe said.

He grabbed Jake's hair and jerked his head to the side.

"You don't never tell me no. You hear that, bitch."

Jake's struggles only made Joe get a firmer grip on his hair. He wrenched the head back and stared into his frightened eyes. "Don't fight me. You going to do whatever I say."

Joe started rubbing Jake's crotch.

"I bet he's got some girly panties on under them jeans," Fat man said. "That would be something wouldn't it, Joe. If he was wearing girl's drawers under his pants."

"You a sissy, boy? You a little girly boy?"

"Please," Jake whimpered. "Just let me out. I won't tell anyone. I swear."

"You listen up. Only way you get let go is you do what we say. You be real good to us and we'll let you go. Might even give you a couple of bucks for the road."

"If you don't," Fat man said, "we'll feed you to the gators like we did the last one. Ain't that right, Joe?"

"Shut up. You act real nice now, you hear me?"

"Yes, sir. Just please don't hurt me."

"Whooee, Joe, fresh meat. It's been awhile since we had us any fresh meat."

"Turn off's coming up soon. Don't miss it."

"I won't. We got us a special place for you, girly."

Both men laughed and Joe released his grip on Jake. Jake slumped into the seat.

The truck drove on for another five minutes before turning off onto a side road into the thick trees. The dirt track banged along, twisting and turning until it stopped in a small clearing near a sluggish green river. The truck stopped. Fat man put the truck in park but left the headlights on in the twilight.

Joe threw his door open and dragged Jake out of the truck. He pushed him to the ground in front of the light. Jake backed up slowly.

"Get them clothes off, girly."

"Best listen to Joe, girly, there's gators in that river that will swallow you whole."

"Hurry up now."

Jake removed his sweatshirt and stood holding it in his hands.

"Now those pants," Joe ordered.

"Hips or lips?" Fat man asked.

"Both. We going to have us a time with this one."

A smile crept over Jake's face. "Do you want me to take your pants down for you?" he asked.

"Yeah. Get over here and undo my belt. I got something for you."

"He likes it. I told you when I saw him he was going to like it."

Jake walked to Joe and stood quietly. He undid his belt and then knelt before him as he pulled his pants down. Joe's erection strained against his dirty white underwear.

"Now the underpants."

Jake reached upward to pull the underwear down. Neither man had seen him take the small pistol from the top of his left shoe. Jake placed the gun beneath the man's scrotum and pulled the trigger twice. The blast was muffled by the proximity to the target. Joe screamed and fell to the ground holding his crotch. Everything in a straight line upward was vital. Joe was dead already, but the pain kept him thrashing on the ground. Jake shot him above the heart. Joe's screams echoed in the stillness.

"Oh, my God. You shot Joe. You shot Joe."

"On your knees, you fat fuck."

The fat man was crying. He crawled over to Joe's body. He shook it as if he could wake the dead man.

"You killed Joe. You just killed him."

Jake stepped up to the fat man. He pointed the gun at the fat man's head. The fat man was blubbering.

"Please. Please don't kill me. I didn't do anything. It was all Joe's idea. Please just let me go."

Jake hesitated. The fat man saw his chance and swatted upward at the gun hand. The gun flew from Jake's hand onto the ground. The fat man sprang to his feet and shoved Jake off his feet. All pretense of sorrow was gone. The fat man glared at him.

"I'm going to bust you up. When I get done there won't even be enough to feed the gators with."

There was a whistle from behind the fat man. He turned toward the sound and his head exploded. Frank Kane walked up to the circle of light. He stepped over the fat man and offered a hand to Jake.

"You alright?"

Jake took the hand and stood up.

Frank walked over to the tiny revolver and picked it up. Frank had never seen the North American Arms .22 magnum revolver. He had read about it. He turned the gun over in his hands. It was tiny. The gun was thinner than a twelve gauge shotgun shell and light at just over six ounces. The barrel was only an inch long and it fit in the palm of his big hand. It carried five rounds of Hornady's 45 grain magnum rounds. He handed the gun to Jake. Jake took the gun and stared at Frank.

"You've done this before," Frank said. "How many times?"

"The thin dude was my fourth with the gun. I burned two others."

"All pedophiles?'

Jake nodded.

"The bait trick seems to be working, but you can't use it too often or the cops will get wise. What were you going to do next?"

Jake put the gun in his pocket. "Take their money. Steal the truck. Dump it up north."

Frank nodded. "Not bad. You got gloves?"

Jake shook his head. He seemed embarrassed.

Frank slipped his own gun into the holster at his back. He was wearing latex gloves.

"That's okay."

Frank went to the bodies and took out their wallets. He removed the cash and handed it to Jake.

"Spoils of war."

Jake put the money in his pocket.

"You got a story behind you or do you just like killing pervs?"

Jake started to lie, hesitated and told the truth.

"When my sister turned nine my dad started raping her. I tried to stop him, but I wasn't strong enough. My mom knew but she didn't give a shit."

"You go to the cops?'

"They wouldn't have believed me. My dad was the town doctor. He was a big deal. One night he got too rough, and she died. He told everyone she fell down the stairs. It didn't matter."

"But it mattered to you."

"I was weak. I couldn't protect her, so I got strong. I did push-ups and sit-ups and ran, and then I waited. I waited two years until everyone had forgotten.

I slipped some of his sleeping pills into their nightcap and waited for them to go to bed. I replaced the battery in the smoke detector with a dead one we had removed. Then I used one of his cigarettes to set their bed on fire. I watched until the flames got too big, then I went back to my room crawled into my own bed and waited for the firemen to come."

"What about the gun?"

"It was my mom's. She got it for protection. Before the fire, I stashed it and a box of ammo in the shed behind the house. I went back later and got it."

"What happened to you?"

"The inheritance went to me, so my aunt took me in so she could get at it. She was a cokehead and her and her boyfriend worked hard to snort up as much of it as they could. I stayed there for four months, took some cash and then hit the road."

"From where?"

"Florida, where I killed the first one. I shot two more in Alabama. And you know about the last one."

Frank nodded. "Did you touch anything in the truck?"

"No. I was careful not to."

Frank went back to the truck and got Jake's pack out of the back. He turned the truck off and doused the headlights. He left all the doors open.

"You want to come along or have you got something better to do?" Frank asked.

"Can you teach me?"

"What?"

"How to kill men. Can you teach me?"

"Maybe. In my world there are a lot of bad men that need killing. If you are up to it."

Jake took the backpack out of Frank's hand.

"Let's go."

11

Mary walked along the highway with her thumb out. She cinched her thin coat a little tighter around her neck and shrugged her shoulders to settle her guitar that hung from her back. She picked up her worn suitcase and started walking. She might as well move as just stand and wait, she thought. The cold air nipped at her like a pack of dogs. She shivered. The walking helped keep her warm, but she was still cold.

It was her damn temper, she thought. She should have planned it better. She should have calmed down and taken her time. She could have dressed warmer. She could have packed more of her things. It was, she told herself, her boyfriend's damn fault. He had known just how to push her buttons to fire her up. He knew she wanted to go to Nashville and become a singer. Sure, sure there weren't many black female country artists, but so what. The door was opening now. There were lots of crossover artists now doing country. Some of them, like Darius Rucker or Cowboy Troy, were even black. She was young, she was pretty, she had talent, she could write songs. If Mickey Guyton could break in, then so could she. It was the perfect time to try to break into the business. It was her dream, damn it.

But no. He couldn't leave it alone. Always making fun of her. Always taunting her. The bastard knew what it meant to her, but he wouldn't let up. He kept telling her she was worthless. She should just settle for the life she had. Loser.

She had lost it and punched him in his big fat face. To his credit, he hadn't hit her back. He had stood there for like a decade before telling her to get the hell out of his house. She had grabbed her stuff and stormed off, flipping him off as she walked away. Outlaw country. Fuck you.

Her rage had kept her warm at first, that and her plans to hitch to Nashville. She played the story over in her mind. It would be a great back story once she made it big. She would show him. She would show them all. Might even get to meet that white guy, Eric Church. He was so damn hot. He sang with so much soul. She wondered briefly if he liked colored girls. The cold wind reminded her that she was still along way from Nashville. And she was all alone.

She started singing the lyrics to "Better Than You Left Me", the Mickey Guyton hit. The words distracted her from her situation and bolstered her spirits. She could do it. She could make it to Nashville and become a star.

Four hours, a ride from a Baptist minister that spent the entire ride trying to save her soul, two stoner kids that wanted a three way which they didn't get, and a lot of empty highway miles and Mary had just started to have serious doubts about her plans when the police car pulled over.

The car sat silent watching her. The door opened and an old, tall white man got out. He put his cowboy style hat on. He looked hard, but his smile was soft.

"Are you okay, ma'am?"

"Yes, sir, officer. I am just trying to catch a ride."

"We got a report of a young woman out here hitchhiking. What's your name, girl?"

"Mary. But there ain't no law against hitchhiking."

"No, ma'am, there is not. But the road can be a dangerous place for anyone. Especially a pretty young woman."

"I can take care of myself."

"I believe you. Where are you headed, if you don't mind me asking?"

"Nashville. I'm a singer."

"Is that so? You must be pretty good to be heading up to Nashville."

"I am."

"It's mighty cold out tonight, especially if all you got is a little jean jacket on."

Mary smiled, slightly embarrassed. "It is a little cool."

"I can run you up the road a piece if you would like. I might even know of a place you could stay the night."

Mary gave him a dubious look.

The sheriff laughed. "No ma'am. It isn't anything like that. It's a lodge. They do me favors from time to time. They might make you play that guitar and sing some songs, but a warm bed and hot food wouldn't be too bad a way to start your trip."

"I think I will just keep thumbing rides."

The sheriff nodded his head. "Very well. You be careful."

He walked back to the car and got inside. When he slammed the door, Mary immediately began to doubt her decision. The car's blinker came on as the car started to pull away. It was getting really cold. She quick jogged to the car and tapped on the side window. The car stopped and the window slid down.

"I thought some more about it. I think I would like that ride."

"Good. I would feel better knowing you were safe. You'll have to ride in the back. Regulations."

Mary nodded and opened the door. She put her belongings in first and crawled in after them. The sheriff got out and closed the door behind her. He got back into the driver's seat. He turned and spoke to Mary through the thick mesh screen that separated the front seat from the back.

"My name is Jim Long. I'm the high sheriff in Blackwater."

"Pleased to meet you."

"Is there anyone you need me to call and let know that you are safe?"

Mary shook her head. "There's nobody that cares."

High Sheriff Long nodded like he had heard it all before. He had. He eased the police car out onto the highway and disappeared into the gathering night. Hitchhiking was dangerous business.

Jake's private cell buzzed in his pocket. He saw that it was Jenny and answered.

"What's up?"

"I was wondering what you are doing tonight."

"That depends on if you would like to get together."

"I would. Why don't you come over after you close up and we can have dinner?"

"I tell you what, I will bring some Chinese food. I know how much you like it."

"That would be great."

"I'll see you about eight."

Jake hung up. He really liked Jenny. There was something very strong and very vulnerable about her that drew him to her. Perhaps he saw a little of himself in her.

Frank Kane pulled into the Kwik Stop in Blackwater. He went inside and prepaid for five dollars' worth of gas. He told the boy behind the counter that he was looking for work. Frank told the boy a friend of his had gotten a good job at some place called the Lodge. He asked who ran the work crews up there. The boy had no idea. Frank thanked him, pumped some gas and drove to the next convenience store. He repeated the story. At the third one the older woman behind the cash register stared at him for a few beats before answering as if she were deciding whether or not she should.

Finally, she said. "Alton Crisp runs the crews up there."

"My friend said he made some good money working there."

"Must not have been working for Alton then, he's an asshole. And you can tell him Emily said so."

Frank had smiled his nearly human self-deprecating smile that he had practiced.

"I don't believe I will if I'm trying to get a job. Any idea where I can find him?"

"One of the bars in town, I would expect. He's an old-school alcoholic. Got worse after his wife left him. Runs through workers pretty fast, though. Works them hard and don't pay that well, so I hear. Still, he might have something for you. If you are strong and desperate."

"I am. I am close to flat busted."

"Well, there's that."

Frank had filled the truck the rest of the way and began a tour of the working men's bars in Blackwater. There couldn't be that many, could there?

12

The driveway to the Lodge was wide enough for four lanes of traffic, two in each direction. In the center was a heated, white guard booth manned by a Norse Man in a blue security outfit. He was carrying an automatic rifle. He peered out the side window as Sheriff Long eased up to the checkpoint. The sheriff lowered his window.

"I need to see Finris about a new guest," he motioned his head toward the back seat.

The security guard smiled and nodded.

"I'll phone ahead and tell them to expect you, Sheriff," the guard said and raised the red and white striped arm of the barricade.

"What sort of place is this?" Mary asked. "It looks military."

"No. It's nothing like that. It is a private club. It is very exclusive. They have to have security for their guests."

"I hope they like me."

"I'm sure they will. How could they not?"

The two-mile-long paved road made gentle turns as it moved toward the Lodge. The sheriff bypassed the small side roads and drove to the main building. The Lodge was fifteen thousand feet of wood, stone and tin roofs. There was a sense of solidness about it. Like it would be there forever.

High Sheriff Long parked out front and went around to open the back door of the police cruiser. He offered Mary his hand to help her out of the back of the car. He reached inside after her and retrieved her gear. A group of people appeared on the wide porch. Finris was out front. He was smiling.

"What do you have there, Jim?"

"This is Mary. She was hitchhiking her way toward Nashville. She wants to become a singer. I told her you would let her stay her for a little while if she played for you."

Mary made a small nod of greeting. "If it's okay."

Finris beamed. Heather hurried down the steps and took her hand.

"I'm Heather. We are so glad to have you."

"I won't be a bit of trouble."

"I know that, dear. Don't you worry about a thing. I'll have one of the boys get your things."

"Thank you."

Heather kept hold of her hand. "Now come with me and I'll show you to your room."

She led the girl away. Finris was laughing. The sheriff started to laugh, too, as he got back into his car. For some inexplicable reason it made Mary uncomfortable. She didn't see what was so damn funny. White folks were so weird.

The pretty blonde woman led her inside the Lodge. There was a reception desk like in a hotel. To her left, the wall was dominated by a huge stone fireplace with a blazing fire. A cache of logs was stacked nearby, ready to feed the fire should it wane. Above the fireplace was a huge wooden shield painted in blue and white. Crossed below it were a pair of strange shaped axes covered in runes. It looked medieval to Mary. There were carvings in the log walls, images of Viking long boats and huge warriors. There were depictions of someone with huge horns sitting on a throne. There were broken hammers and long spears. Runes and elder glyphs decorated the foyer. There were paintings as well, all of the same motif. Mary sniffed. Must be some man thing, she thought. Get back to your white boy Viking roots. Live and let live, she rationalized, as long as they fed her and gave her a bed, she would consider it a fair trade.

"Let me get you something to drink and have one of the men take your belongings to a bedroom. Are you hungry, honey?"

"I wouldn't mind a little something if it wouldn't be any trouble."

"Come with me to the kitchen. Let me see what I can find for you."

"Thank you. You are very kind."

Heather just smiled.

Jenny opened the door to Jake's knock. He was carrying an over-stuffed white bag filled with Chinese food. The spicy aroma filled the air around him.

"Hi," she said, and leaned in to kiss him on the cheek. Jake almost dropped the food. "You got so much. I'm going to get fat."

"I doubt that. Where do you want me to put this?"

"Follow me into the kitchen."

Jake did, scanning his surroundings as he went.

"You live here with Frank?"

"Don't say it like that," she said at the implications in his tone. "Frank lives here. I live here and so does my best friend, Caron."

"The one from the coffee shop?"

"You remember that? We only came in together that one time."

Jake smiled. "I try to be observant. I have a good memory. Frank taught me the importance of seeing everything."

"And do you see everything?"

"No. But I don't miss much."

She gave his arm a little squeeze. "Well, you saw me and that's what counts."

"Yes, I did."

"Let me get some plates."

"No. You don't need them. Didn't anyone ever teach you? You can unfold the boxes to make their own plates."

"Bullshit."

"Language, young lady. Here let me show you."

Jake spread the cartons out and deftly unfolded them and refolded them into paper plates.

"Wow. That is so cool. I can't wait to show Caron and DC. And no, I will not tell them you showed me. I plan to take full credit for discovering it."

"Of course. I'll get the silverware. You get us something to drink."

Jenny took two glasses out of the cabinet and poured them full of sweet iced tea. They took the food to the table and set it out.

"Thanks for getting dinner."

"Thank you for calling me."

"I know there is some kind of dating rule that I'm suppose to wait two days before calling or something, but I wanted to see you."

Jake chewed his food and then said, "I wanted to see you too."

"Can I ask you something?"

"Sure. Serious or flirty?"

"Serious."

"Have you been with a lot of other girls?"

Jake went silent.

"Be honest."

He seemed to be thinking how to answer. "Yes."

"You are supposed to say some or a few or something vague that implies you are not a man whore."

"I thought you wanted the truth."

"I did, but I wanted the truth to be a few."

"I meant to say a few. It was a joke."

Jenny laughed. "You aren't very good at this."

"Why do you want to know?"

"I have never been with anyone. Not really. And I am not sure I'm ready for that. In fact, I know I'm not."

"I don't understand. I haven't tried to get you into bed. Why tell me this?"

"Caron is staying at DC's house. Frank is gone. . ."

"So?"

"I want you to stay with me tonight."

"Like on the sofa as a bodyguard or something?"

"No, knucklehead. In my bed, but I don't want us to have sex. Not yet."

"What if you change your mind later and ask me to?"

"You still have to tell me no. Promise."

Jake smiled. He reached over and took her hand.

"I promise. And you say I'm weird."

13

Frank skipped dinner. Denial was a good way to forge your will power and he wanted to seem genuinely hungry. Alton wasn't at the first bar he tried, but they knew him well enough. The bartender directed Frank to another drinking establishment cleverly named The Tavern.

The Tavern sported a gravel parking lot outside a converted Pizza Hut. The inside was dark wood and dim lighting. It smelled of old beer and decades of stale cigarettes. There were three pool tables with worn green felt carpets on top. Booths lined the walls. The fake red leather upholstery was torn and duct tape repaired. They were probably left over from the Pizza Hut. The rest of the space was filled with tired wooden tables circled with battered wooden chairs. An old Lenoxx jukebox stood sentry against one of the walls. The bright blue light accents and the chrome stylings looked well cared for. But the black buttons looked like they had been beaten more than an MMA fighter.

Frank approached the long faux oak bar and signaled the bartender.

"Excuse me, friend. I'm looking for Alton Crisp. Has he come in yet?"

The bartender pointed to a corner booth occupied by a lone man.

"His lordship is in residence."

"Thanks. Give me a couple of shots of Gentleman Jack."

The bartender filled two shot glasses and Frank paid with a rumpled twenty. He took his change and the drinks to where Alton sat gloomily staring at his flat beer. Alton was in his mid-fifties. He had a face like a turtle. He was broad and thick with a belly that looked like a pumpkin was hiding under his stretched flannel shirt. He clutched his beer like he was trying to squeeze some hidden truth out of it. He raised his big head slowly at Frank's approach. He didn't speak. He just stared with tiny wet turtle eyes.

"May I have a minute of your time, Mr. Crisp?"

Alton licked his lips as he watched the shots of dark liquor in Frank's hands.

"One of those for me?"

"Absolutely."

"Then have a seat. You earned a minute."

Frank sat down and passed one of the shots over to Alton. Frank started to slip his old Carhartt jacket off. Alton glared at him.

"I said you could have a minute, not move in."

"I'm looking for work and I heard you were the man to see."

"Who told you that?" he asked.

"Emily at the convenience store. She said you ran a work crew and might be hiring."

"She don't know shit."

"She said to tell you that you're an asshole too."

Alton laughed. "I always liked that bitch. I use to long dick her before I met my wife. She still hasn't gotten over me. They never forget their best lays."

Frank laughed. It had to be one of the most insane statements he had ever heard. Alton threw his shot back. He smacked his lips and smiled a broad friendly smile.

"What's your name?"

"Jack," Frank said. "Jack Daniels."

Alton looked at the now empty shot glass and smiled. "That the name it says on your driver's license?"

"Not right now but I can get one with it on there if you want."

Alton smiled. "You're a smart ass. I like that. But I ain't got no spots open right now."

Frank smiled. He pushed the second shot toward Alton. "You sure you can't use me? I really need the work. I am about busted."

Frank saw movement off to his side. A tall man with a thick black beard entered the bar. He swept his head around looking for someone. His eyes locked on Alton. He stomped over. He was carrying a paycheck in his hand. He reached the table and glared at Alton. He tossed the check onto the table in front of Alton. Alton looked at the check and then downed the second shot of Jack.

"What the fuck is this, Alton?"

Alton picked up the check and studied it. He laid it back down on the table. "It looks like your paycheck."

"The fuck it does. It's light. It's always light, you cheap bastard."

"You do the work you get the pay. You slack off half the day, it don't seem right to give you full pay now does it?"

"I work hard as anyone on the crew."

"That ain't much of an endorsement. They are all lazy shitkickers like you."

"What about my overtime?"

"Ain't no overtime, Jim. It is what it is. Take it or leave it."

The man snatched up the check and stuffed it into his pocket.

"Get to your feet, Alton so I can knock you off 'em."

There was a flash of fear across Alton's face. Frank saw it. He understood. Alton was a bully, but he was also a coward. He knew this guy would kick his ass. Frank got to his feet. The man stepped back. He might have thought Frank was getting out of the way of trouble. That wasn't Frank Kane's way. He moved toward trouble.

He shoved the man back with one stiff hand. The man looked surprised. His face was turning red with rage.

"Stay out of this, mister. I got no truck with you, but I would just as soon beat your ass too. This is between him and me."

Frank stepped up until his face was inches away from the man.

"Raise a hand. Take a step. Blink real fast and I will rip your asshole out through your mouth."

His certainty was as powerful as the words themselves. The color drained from the man's face.

"This ain't right."

"I will give you one minute to get lost or I will consider it my duty to punch out all your teeth. Do you understand, boy? You are on the clock starting now."

The man looked from Frank to Alton and back again. He backed away slowly.

"This ain't over, Alton. You hear me? I catch you without your watch dog, we'll see who falls."

Alton shot him the bird as he hurried from the bar. Frank took his seat again.

"Well, there you go."

"What?"

"Now you got a spot open on your crew."

"Got too much crew as it is anyway."

"This solves lots of problems for you. I will out work those other sons of bitches and I'll do it for ten percent less than you pay them."

Alton thought about the offer and countered with, "Twenty-five percent."

"I got to eat."

"You said you were about busted. Something is better than nothing."

"Fifteen and you direct me to some place I can camp out."

"Camp? Like a fucking Boy Scout?"

"Sleep in my truck. It isn't too bad. Saves on money."

"I tell you what. You can park in my garage. Camp there. It's got its own sink and shitter. Damn sight better than being outdoors. But it's twenty percent."

"Alright, it's a deal."

Frank waved at the bartender who sent over the waitress. She was all the good things a waitress should be in a bar. She was young and pretty with big breasts and a big smile. She wore a tee shirt that was only two sizes too small and a pair of black jeans that looked like they had been painted on.

"What will you boys have?"

"Two more beers," Frank said.

"I got a question for you, Sallee. I was wondering how you got those damn jeans on."

Sallee didn't miss a beat. "That's the difference between you and your big friend here. You are wondering what I had to do to get them on and he's wondering what he has to do to get them off."

She turned her large eyes onto Frank and turned the wattage all the way up on her smile.

"Damn," Frank said.

"Leave him alone, Sallee. He's busted."

"What's your name?" Sallee asked.

"He's my cousin, Jack. He's here looking for a job. He can't afford someone as fine as you. Now me on the other hand, I got a right smart of money."

"You don't have enough, Alton. I can tell you. But you pay Jack real well, you hear me. Then he can come back here later and we can have this conversation again."

Frank grinned like any fool would. They watched her shimmy across the floor to turn in their orders. Frank turned back to Alton who was trying not to drip drool on the table.

"What's the business with me being your cousin?"

When Alton spoke it was with a serious tone. "Let me see your hands."

Frank extended his hands. Alton felt them and turned them over and looked at them.

"You ever hung fence? Cause that's what we will be doing. Sunup to sundown."

"I done fence work before. Anything exotic like barb wire or razor wire?"

"No, straight up chain-link fencing." Alton stared hard into Frank's face with his swollen, rheumy eyes. "You a Jew?"

"No."

"You part nigger?'

"No. I got some Scottish blood in me."

"You a cop?"

"Do I look like a cop?"

"Doesn't mean you aren't one. Are you?"

"No. I hate cops."

Sallee brought their beers and Frank paid her. She kept the change and stuffed it into her back pocket, which was a miracle of modern physics in and of itself.

"Where's the change?" Frank asked.

"I kept it on account."

"On account of what?"

"On account of I wanted it. And when I want something I get it. Do you feel what I am telling you?"

"Damn," Frank said for the second time.

Sallee walked away and twittered her fingers goodbye to them. Alton looked around the bar to be sure no one was paying them any attention. He took out a small baggy of white powder. He passed it to Frank.

"If you're not a cop, do a little bump to prove it."

Frank took his pocketknife out of his pocket and opened the blade. He dipped it into the white powder enough to remove a small pyramid. He placed it under one nostril and snorted it up. It was meth. Frank felt the adrenaline rush of the drug. He smiled at Alton who was watching him closely. He dipped the knife in and did another hit.

"Hey, you might not be a pig, but you're a hog."

"Just wanted to make sure you believed me, Alton. Now what's with all this third degree?"

Alton tucked the packet of meth into his shirt pocket. He shook out a cigarette and lit it with a red Bic lighter. Frank noticed the color. The red was a nice omen for Frank. Alton took a puff and blew the smoke into the air. He tapped the ash into the black plastic ashtray on the table. Bars didn't permit smoking in North Carolina. Either Ohio was different, or The Tavern didn't care about non-smoking regulations. Lots of small towns made their own laws.

"We do most of our work at the Lodge. The people who own it are serious about security. They got rules on who I can hire. They don't like cops. Or blacks. Or Jews. I got to vouch for everybody I bring up there to work. That or the local high sheriff runs them through the system to see who they are."

Frank ran a big hand over his shaved head. "Shit. Maybe this isn't the job for me after all, Alton. I had to get out of Tennessee because of a little misunderstanding I was having down there. The law might be involved by now."

"Don't worry about it."

"I do worry about it. I can't have the cops snooping around about me. They might lock me up."

Alton took a drag on his cigarette. He tapped the side of his own head with a stubby finger.

"That's why I told Sallee you were my cousin. The little whore had the biggest mouth in town. In more ways than one." He paused for a moment with some dirty image of what he would pay anything to do to that mouth. He shook the image off. "This is a small town. In a few days, everyone will know my cousin Jack is in town."

"Smart," Frank said. "They allow smoking in here?"

"No. Just me. I'm connected. I got friends up at the Lodge. People are afraid of me. They let me do what I want."

"The last guy, Jim, didn't seem too scared of you. I would watch my back if I were you."

"Fuck him. He won't do shit with you around. He about wet himself when

51

you ran him off. Probably at the Walmart up in Zaneville buying a pink dress right now. Might want to switch teams like that Bruce Jenner guy did."

Frank took a pair of cigars out of his pocket. He cut off the ends and passed one to Alton.

"Try one of these."

Alton didn't hesitate. He lit the cigar and puffed away like it was a giant cigarette. Frank lit his and took slow long draws on it. Alton mimicked his actions. Their smoke clouds billowed up into the ceiling and back down onto them again. Alton laughed.

"I'm glad you showed up tonight, Jack. You are alright."

"Thanks. You're alright too."

"Doesn't mean I won't work your ass off and under pay you."

"Of course. It is just business."

"That's right. It is just business."

Jeff Maurer lay in the bed beside his wife Cathy. He was pretending to sleep as he stared at the ceiling. He felt his wife move gently beside him. He did not move, hoping his inaction would help her fall back asleep. It didn't. She slid closer to him. She took his hand in the darkness and placed it on her swollen belly. He held it there and felt his child stir inside her.

"The baby is restless tonight," she said.

"It has a real kick. Going to be a handful when it gets born."

"Just like its daddy."

Maurer rolled over and kissed his wife on her head.

"I am lucky to have you. We both are."

"That's what I was going to say."

"Get some sleep. You need your rest."

"You too. Don't worry so. Whatever is bothering you will work itself out. It always does."

Maurer closed his eyes and prayed she was right. He didn't think he could stand it if anything happened to his wife or child.

14

Frank followed Alton the four miles to his house. His plan was working better than he could have hoped. He didn't need Ariadne to guide him through some twisted labyrinth. Everything happened for a reason, Sybil had told him. She said it because she saw a divine hand in what happened. Call it providence, or God, or Fate, she felt like there were circumstances that put you in place for certain opportunities and you had to seize them.

Alton's house was a run-down traditional brick ranch house. The white trim was starting to peel. The yard was mowed but weeds were starting to take over the flower garden out front. Alton parked in front of the garage and opened it with a remote control. He got out and walked toward the garage while motioning Frank to pull inside. Frank parked his truck and got out. Alton handed him the remote.

"Here is your key," he said with a drunkard's appreciation for his own humor.

Frank pocketed the remote.

"Thanks. This will be perfect for me until I can get on my feet again."

"Yeah, it's a damn sight better than camping in Ohio in the damn ass end of winter."

"Not much better."

"Come on. It's not that bad if you got the right gear and winter is done anyway. It's getting warmer."

"If you say so."

Alton made a sound in his throat that sounded like a hippo burping.

"Whatever. Can is through that door in the back. There's plenty of TP and I think there's still a half a bar of soap in there by the sink."

"Thanks," Frank said. He opened the cooler in his truck and got out two cold Buds. He handed one to Alton. "A night cap."

They popped their tops and tapped cans together in a salute. Alton drank half of his in the first gulp. Frank took a smaller sip. He pointed with the can at an old four-wheeler with part of the engine broken down. "Does she run?"

"Naw, the engine's locked up. I've been meaning to work on it, but shit happens," he said, and shrugged. "You know how it is."

"I do indeed. I'm pretty good with motors. Mind if I work on it a little at night? See if I can get it to run."

"Suit yourself. Not like you got anything else to do."

"Not until I make some money."

"I pay once every two weeks. No exceptions."

"Not a problem. I appreciate you letting me crash here. You sure your wife isn't going to get pissed?"

"Delores? Fuck that bitch. She left me last year. Run off with some Mexican fella."

"Sorry."

"Don't be. Good riddance, I say. She was a sorry wife. I'm glad she's gone."

Frank nodded like he could understand. He didn't. He couldn't. Without another word, he started unloading his supplies from the back of his truck. He tossed the camping stuff on the concrete floor of the garage. He left his food stuffs and cooking supplies in the truck. Frank turned the stopcock on the inflatable mattress and let it start to fill itself with air. He pulled the sleeping bag out of its stuff sack and shook it out on the floor. He lifted the mattress and hurried its filling along by blowing into the tube. He sealed it, put the sleeping bag on top and grabbed his pillow. Alton watched him but offered no advice or help.

"That should do it. We working tomorrow?"

"Hell, no. I like to sleep in on Sundays. If you're looking for a church, there's a bunch in town. It's a regular little Bible belt around here."

"I think I will just run some errands. Get in some supplies. Chill."

"Check in with me tomorrow night, I'll go over the routine with you. But you have hung fence before, right?"

"I already told you once. Yes, I can hang fence."

Alton lifted up his old baseball-style cap and scratched his head. He snugged the hat back on and fished a cigarette out of his jacket pocket. He lit it up and left the garage bound for his own bedroom trailing a cloud of smoke, puffing like an old-timey steam engine.

Frank watched him go. He closed the garage door. He got out his shaving kit and toothbrush. His teeth felt like they were wearing wool sweaters. He brushed and flossed. He kicked off his shoes and pants and crawled into the sleeping bag. He fluffed up his pillow and tried to get comfortable. It wasn't bad, but it wasn't all that good either. He ran over a list of items he would need to purchase to improve his little room. And of course, he would need to go to the library.

15

Jake was awake by four. Jenny was spooned next to him on the bed. They had both felt it was wiser for Jake to sleep with his clothes on. She had put on some flannel pajamas. They had not gotten under the covers. Jenny had gotten a blanket and covered them with it. Jake thought it was simultaneously incredibly innocent and incredibly insane.

He slipped out of bed and started lacing on his shoes. He reached under the bed and retrieved his gun from where he had hidden it when Jenny went to change for bed. The pistol was the new Kimber Solo, a micro-compact in a miniaturized 1911 frame. It carried seven 9mm hollow points. The gun was all blacked out except for the Tritium three-dot sight. Secured in its ankle holster, it was nearly invisible. Jake wore the gun on the inside of his left leg. That made it easy to reach and kept it from bumping into things if it was worn on the outside of his right leg like so many people did. He quietly adjusted the Velcro straps into place.

Jenny stirred behind him.

"Are you leaving? It's still dark."

"I run a coffee shop. I have to be there early to open up."

"You need a manager so you can sleep in more."

Jake turned around to face her in the darkness.

"That's a good idea. I might have to promote someone."

"Ta-dah. Can you come over for dinner? Caron will be coming home, and I want you to get to know her and DC. I'll cook."

"It's a deal. You pick the time. We close early on Sundays."

"Five. You can help me cook."

"See you at five," Jake said.

Jenny lay in the dark for a few seconds.

"Thanks for staying last night. It was nice."

Jenny listened for a response, but there was nothing. Jake was already gone. She knew she must still have been half asleep or she would have heard him slip out. He wasn't a damn ghost. He made noise like everybody else. She slipped the blanket up around her neck and switched to his pillow so she could smell his cologne. She fell back asleep dreaming they were having sex.

Jeff and Cathy Maurer liked to go to the early service at church. Jeff claimed he liked the older hymns they sang at the early service. The truth was that this way when Sunday school was over they would still have most of the day free. He looked at his wife seated beside him. She was beautiful. He was a lucky man and he knew it. Cathy turned toward him and adjusted her glasses. She motioned for him to pay attention to the sermon. His eyes drifted toward her swollen stomach and their unborn child. He said a silent prayer for their safety and health and turned his attention to the minister.

The minister was preaching about the road to Hell being paved with good intentions. Jeff felt the sting of the words. It was like the minister could see into his heart. He had brought the envelope of money with him to church. He had planned to just put it into the collection plate as an anonymous donation. His curiosity had gotten the better of him. He had looked inside. It held one thousand dollars. Ten folded crisp one hundred-dollar bills.

He had put the money back into the envelope, still planning on giving it to the church to soothe his aching conscience. But a thousand dollars was a lot of money. Cathy would be out of work for a while after the baby was born. They really needed her paycheck to get by. And what if there were complications with the birth? It wasn't like insurance covered everything anyway. And then there would be the new expenses of looking after the baby. He needed the money. He really needed it.

Maybe he reasoned, the money wasn't temptation, but the answer to his silent prayers. Maybe God had heard his pleas and sent the money to him through this odd chain of events. It wasn't like it was illegal. The high sheriff himself had given it to him.

The minister had stopped, and the choir had started to sing. The collection plates were passed out. The collection plate moved down his aisle. He put in his check for ten dollars and passed it to his left. He was supposed to have the money. He was going to keep it. What harm could it do anyway? He buried his concerns as deeply as he could and started to sing.

Masnick had been left alone, secured to the chair. The absence of other stimuli seemed to make his hearing more acute. He heard the sound of dogs kenneled somewhere nearby, the groan of the furnace as it vainly pumped its warm air, the loud clomp of heavy boots as they went about their business. He had called out to the guard or guards, but no one had ever answered.

He was exhausted. He was sore from being strapped into the same position. He had pissed and shit himself. He was hungry. He was thirsty. But mostly he was cold. The cold seemed to have reached down into his bones. He couldn't stop shivering. He imagined that he was turning to ice.

He heard the light footsteps of his torturer coming down the hallway, followed by the heavy tread of a guard. The cell door buzzed, the light clicked on and he could smell her beside him. Her perfume was delicate and airy. It reminded him of what lilacs should smell like. It smelled purple. She gently removed his hood.

56

His eyes burned from the sudden light. Tears ran down his cheeks from the irritation. She placed a soothing hand on his cheek. She turned back on the guard.

"What is the meaning of this?"

"What?"

"You left him here all night? You didn't even let him go to the bathroom?"

"Orders, Miss Heather. Finris said not to touch him."

She made an angry sigh. "Listen to me. Bring a bucket of warm water and soap. Clean this filth off of him. He is not some animal."

The guard hesitated, then his shoulders sank and he left.

"I apologize for this treatment. It is unnecessary."

There was commotion down the hall. The guard reappeared with a hose trailing behind him.

"This is all I could find."

Heather nodded. The blast of cold water took Masnick's breath away. It felt like ice daggers were tearing his paper-thin flesh. The guard turned up the pressure to wash out around Masnick's genitalia and buttocks. It felt like punches to his groin. Masnick tried not to scream. The cold water pounded his flesh and then it stopped. The fetid water circled swirled around the floor and found its way down the drain in the center.

Masnick's teeth started chattering so hard he feared they would shatter. The guard was leering. A twisted smile danced on his fat weasel lips. He started rolling up the hose as he backed out of the room.

"Bring some towels," Heather called. "And a blanket."

The guard said nothing and disappeared. Heather brushed his stubbled chin. "Hold on. He will be right back."

The guard returned with the towels. He roughly scrubbed Masnick's skin dry. Masnick could neither help nor hinder him. He tried to remain stoic. After the guard was done, he brought in a wool blanket. He handed it to Heather, who wrapped it around the trembling Spartan.

"There, that will be better. From now on I want him taken to the bathroom when he needs to go. Do you understand?"

"Finris said. . ."

"I will talk to Finris. You will treat this man with some respect. He was a Spartan peer. Bring me some water for him."

The guard disappeared and she leaned in close, tucking the blanket around him. Her warmth penetrated the blanket through his skin into his very soul. She held him like a mother holds a baby. Masnick knew it was all part of the plan, part of the breaking process. Have him identify her as his friend and protector. He hated his weakness. When the guard returned she again gave him water from a bottle. It tasted bitter.

"Would you like something to eat?"

Masnick was starving but shook his head "no." He would fight her.

Heather looked at him like a mother who has found dirty fingerprints on her kitchen wall for the third time.

"Do you know what the rule of threes is, Prometheus?"

Masnick smiled. "It would take three Spartans less than three seconds to put three bullets into your skull."

Heather laughed. "No, although that is very clever. The rule of three is that a person can go without food for three weeks. Without water for three days. And without air for three minutes."

"I like mine better."

"I am sure you do. But that isn't going to happen. Fight me if your ego demands it. Resist as long as you are able. I will treat you with a level of respect you deserve, but I will break you."

Masnick tried to spit at her but his mouth was too dry.

Heather clapped her hands. "We are going to have so much fun together."

Mary awoke in a small bedroom. She didn't remember going to bed. In fact, she didn't remember anything after that blonde lady gave her a glass of wine. She must have drugged it, she thought. Mary took stock of her situation. She still had her clothes on. She undid the waist of her jeans and touched herself. She still had her panties on.

Her pocketbook was sitting in a chair. She searched it. Someone had gone through it. Her cell phone and money were gone. She looked around. Her guitar was resting in the corner. Had she played it last night? It was all vague. Had to have been drugged, she reasoned. Her suitcase was gone.

She thought maybe she was safer on the road. She tried the door. It was locked from the other side. She went to the windows and pulled back the heavy curtains. The windows had long iron bars mounted into the frames. Her eyes swept the room looking for a way out or a weapon. She saw the camera mounted in the ceiling. They were watching her. The lock on the door clicked.

Mary stepped back toward the center of the room as the door swung inward. The giant, Finris, led the way. Two other men followed him and a girl. The men looked like typical white trash dressed in camo hunting clothes and boots. The girl was different. She was very pretty and oddly wearing lingerie.

"Put the food on the table by the bed," Finris said.

The girl meekly followed his commands. Her head was down. Mary grabbed a vase from a table by the window.

"I don't know what your game is but you ain't laying a finger on me."

Finris smiled. "You know exactly what our game is. You are my property now. I own you. I will train you to please men and you will do that to please me."

"I ain't no whore."

"When I am done, you will be. You will beg me to stay and serve. The lucky ones get to stay. The others we sell or rent depending on circumstances. Life on the circuit is hard on a young woman. The toll is high."

Mary's rage erupted. She swung the vase at Finris who brushed it aside. He caught her by the wrists and lifted her off the ground. Mary kicked at his groin but could not reach him.

"You can't make me."

"Make you? I will not make you. You will ask for the honor to serve. You will beg to serve."

She kicked again and he dropped her to the floor. She sprang to her feet and lunged at him. He struck her with a backhand that sent her across the room. Her head was spinning. A thin tear of blood trickled from her nose. She found she couldn't get to her feet.

"Bind her to the bed."

The two men pulled her over to the four-poster bed. They secured her in a standing position spread eagle to the bed. Her head was starting to clear.

"Remove her clothing."

The men took out thin knives and cut away at her clothing until she was nearly nude. Her clothes puddled around her ankles. One of the men placed a ball gag into her mouth and secured it behind her head.

"Sjambok."

One of the men left the room and returned with a three-foot leather whip. Finris gripped the handle and felt its power.

"You are fortunate. This is a sjambok from South Africa. It is one of the two items most associated with apartheid. The other, of course, is the word Kaffir. In America stupid people assume Kaffir is equivalent to the word nigger."

Mary struggled against the ropes. No one called her that word.

"Of course, it is not. Do you know what the word Kaffir means? Do you? It means infidel. A nonbeliever. It is an Arab word. They sold the black slaves and saw them as less than human since they did not follow that idiot Allah. It is funny how words change their meanings over time."

Mary tried to shout something, but the gag muffled her words.

"The sjambok is special. Historically is made from hippopotamus hide like this one. Voortrekkers used it to drive their cattle. It is also an effective teaching tool. Your kind has known the whip all over the world. You will remember the sjambok's sweet kiss for the rest of your life."

Mary felt panic and tried to pull free from her bonds. A fine patina of sweat covered her back. But the men had done this before. Their knots held fast. The first strike from the sjambok split the skin of her back and the pain erupted through her. Finris paused to let the pain fibers calm, then struck again. Mary slumped against the bed poles. He lashed her twice more and she fell unconscious.

"Go bring the doctor to treat the wounds. We can't have her getting an infection."

"You cut her pretty good," one of the men said.

Finris passed him the sjambok. "Some men prefer these scars. It shows that the woman has been broken. She will always be his slave."

"Well, these ones are going to leave a mark," the other one said.

Finris smiled. He liked breaking the new girls. He liked the feeling of complete control. Maybe one day he would have Frank Kane in his hands. He would relish breaking him. How many strokes of the sjambok could the great Frank Kane withstand before he was crying like a woman.

16

Frank Kane slept late again. It had been a long time since he had stayed up half the night drinking and doing drugs. His system wasn't used to it. He climbed out of the sleeping bag and stretched his sore muscles. He was getting old. There was a time when he wouldn't hesitate to sleep rough, without a tent or sleeping bag. On long rides, he would just stretch out on the ground near his bike and drop off to sleep like a baby. He would get up, drink a warm beer, and be ready to ride again. Those days were past. He liked a comfortable bed and soft sheets. Hell, at least he had been smart enough to bring a decent pillow. Some heat would be nice too.

In the cold garage, he went through a short series of exercises: pushups, sit-ups, and jumping jacks, until the cold no longer seemed to matter. He got out his camp stove and fixed himself a cup of coffee. It wasn't bad, he thought, for camp coffee. He dressed in the same clothes he had worn the day before and added the Marine sweatshirt to the mix. People liked veterans. Even some liberals preached support for our troops.

He took the truck into town. He went to the first McDonald's he saw and went inside for breakfast. He got a copy of the local paper and read it to see if there were any news items that might affect his plans. There weren't, it was just small-town news. He took his time with the breakfast and the paper. It was warm in the McDonald's. He stalled as long as he could for things to get open on a Sunday. He brushed his teeth in the bathroom because it was a lot better than the bathroom off the garage.

He cruised around town, getting a feel for the layout. There weren't many main roads but there were dozens of little dirt tracks that angled off the road into the surrounding woods. Hunters, he figured, or guys out drinking or trying to get lucky. He went to the local building supply store. It was a huge box store. He bought a couple of space heaters for the garage. He talked to one of the "specialists" in the DIY section about fence building. The man took his time and walked Frank through the process. It sounded straight forward enough.

He went to one of the strip malls. It was anchored by a Food Lion grocery store. He found a Mail Boxes Plus store. They seemed a fixture at every shopping center he had ever seen. It had just opened. Frank went inside.

There was a woman with a face like an old horse behind the counter. When she smiled it made Frank want to hand her an apple or find a saddle. She was so ugly he actually felt sorry for her.

"Can I help you, honey?"

"I need to get a Post Office Box, please." Frank loved the word 'please.' If you added it to the end of a request it seemed to empower the request with more intimacy. You were asking a favor of a friend.

"Well, sure thing. How long will you be needing it?"

"I don't know exactly. How short is the shortest rental?"

"Three months."

"Then that should do it. I'm trying to find work, but if I don't, I will be moving along."

She slid him the paperwork to fill out.

"And I will need to see some ID and a local address."

Frank tried to look embarrassed. "That's kind of a problem. I don't have a local address. I am living out of my truck right now. It's been hard adjusting back into the world."

She reached over and patted him on the arm. "Where were you stationed?"

"The Stan. I did three tours. Got to where I couldn't take losing any more friends."

"My nephew is in the Marines over there. Did you see a lot of action?"

Frank shook his head like he was trying to shake away demons. "I don't want to talk about it."

"I understand. You got a driver's license on you?"

"After I got out, I got into some trouble. Did some hard drinking. The cops took my license. Do I have to have it?"

"No. No. I will just fill something in. Don't you worry about it for a minute, honey."

Frank took his money from his pocket and paid her cash for the box and took his key and a business card. He thanked her and watched her slip the money into her pocket. He doubted there would be any paperwork either. Making a little leeway when the opportunity arrived. It was the American way everywhere he went. Frank could have used the fake ID he had, but he didn't want any possible strings leading back to him.

He looked back once more as he left the door. Either she was waving goodbye or swatting flies, he couldn't be sure. God, she was hard to look at. Next stop was the library. He hadn't been in a library in decades, but he reasoned it was a good place to find a computer that no one would be monitoring.

The library was a relatively small, neat, red brick building. It was a boring rectangle that they had tried to spruce up with a pair of faux Greek columns outside. The white columns were yellow with age and scarred with graffiti. But Frank took their presence as a good omen. At least it was something Greek. The librarian told him where the computer room was and the rules for using the computers. She also told him that all links to pornographic internet searches were blocked. Frank tried to look shocked.

The computer lab was empty except for Frank and two pimple-faced teenagers doing research. Frank booted the computer up and went to the internet. He went to YouTube and searched for videos on how to install chain link fencing. He watched them all. He also searched barb wire and razor wire fences. He was getting ready to shut the computer down when he had a thought. On a whim, he searched the words Spartan Rider.

Frank was rewarded with what he took to be the best omen possible. When he clicked in the words a picture appeared. It depicted a Spartan riding a large horse through a troop of birds, possibly peacocks. A winged figure followed the Spartan rider that was supposed to be Nike carrying victory laurels.

Frank sat back and studied the picture. A Spartan riding to victory. Wow. That had to be the all-time best omen. Frank read the description of the painter. His real name was unknown. He was referred to as the Rider Painter. He was a Laconian potter and vase painter who was active between 560 and 530 BC. Although considered a master in his own right, he is considered only the fifth best vase painter in Sparta. Frank noted the vase with the painting was in the British Museum. Maybe one day he would have a chance to see it in person. A man could always dream.

17

Jenny and Caron cleaned up the kitchen and then got ready for bed. They shared the same bedroom upstairs.

"Jake is really nice," Caron said.

"I think so."

"Yeah, I could tell. I was afraid you would start drooling on the floor. You got it bad, girl!"

"I do not. Well, maybe a little."

"Have you done him yet?"

"Caron. What kind of question is that?"

"One friends ask. You know all about DC and me."

"That's only because you like to brag about it."

"True. I do like being able to tell you about it. But have you guys done it yet or not?"

"Not."

"What are you waiting for? You hold out too long and he will be in the wind."

"Jake's not like that. And anyway, I want it to be special when we do it the first time."

"He's a stud. Trust me, it will be special enough."

"I'm not sure I'm really ready."

"Shit. You got to go for it. You can't spend all your time Jilling off."

"Jilling off? What's that mean?"

"You know. Fapping. Slapping the man in the boat. Masturbating. Guys Jack Off. Girls Jill off."

"You are so gross."

Caron stuck her tongue out at Jenny. "Yeah, but you love me anyway."

Jenny beamed. "Yes, I do. I'm afraid that if we do it, it will change things between us."

"It will. It will make it better."

"What if I'm not any good."

Caron laughed. "Trust me. Once he has you naked he won't remember if you were good or not. It will be all about him. Just moan a lot so he feels good about his performance. Men are very insecure when it comes to sex. And compliment him on the size of his unit. Guys want to all think their thing is huge. Do that and he will be hooked."

Jenny giggled and turned off the light on the stand between their beds. In the darkness she said, "Caron, you're a perv."

"Yeah and DC likes me that way. Goodnight, Jenny. Don't worry about Jake. It will be fine."

"Goodnight."

Masnick was exhausted but he couldn't sleep. He realized Heather must have put some kind of amphetamine into his water. It kept him alert and agitated. He fought down his fears. He was still alive. As long as he was alive there was a chance he would survive. That was Frank Kane's old maxim. Survive the day.

He smelled her scent before he heard her quiet steps. She was alone. She opened his cell and came inside. The light was turned on, but she didn't remove his hood. He could tell she was watching him. She pulled the blanket up tighter around his chin.

"By tomorrow, or the next day you won't need to be restrained any longer. You will be able to stretch out. To find what comfort you can."

Masnick didn't respond.

She pulled the blanket away from his right arm. He felt the prick of a needle. He jerked involuntarily, but the straps held him immobile. There was a slight burn at the injection site.

Heather recovered his arm. She gave it a comforting pat.

"It will take the serum about nine hours to start to take effect. I am very proud of it. It is a concoction of my own design. The bacterium of the black-legged tick, or deer tick as it is commonly called, mixed with the neurotoxins from the venom of the black widow spider. The two complement each other perfectly. It is a marvelous concoction. I will see you in the morning. Goodnight."

She kissed the top of his head through the cloth.

Masnick realized there was something seriously wrong with her. But as a mad genius himself, he understood how those two sisters complemented each other, too.

Alton knocked on the side door of the garage.

"You decent?"

"Come on in. I'm not decent, but I got my clothes on."

Frank went to his cooler and popped it open. He tossed Alton a beer and kept one for himself.

"We hit the site at eight. We'll get coffee on the way and a biscuit if you want one."

"Sounds good."

"Pack a lunch."

Frank nodded and took a sip of beer. "I saw that asshole you fired cruise by today in his truck."

Alton looked nervous.

"Is he going to be a problem? I can take care of it if you want me to."

Alton smiled. "No. He's all mouth. He wouldn't dare do anything. I got friends in the cops and the Norse Men. He knows that."

"I'd keep my eyes open just to be safe."

"Will do." Alton saluted him with the beer. "Thanks for the beer. See you in the morning."

Frank watched him go. He hadn't seen anybody cruising by in a truck. But it was good to make Alton think it was in his best interest to keep Frank around. Frank poured the rest of his beer into the sink in the bathroom. It was all part of the image.

18

Frank crawled out of his sleeping bag into the chilly garage. The space heaters he had bought worked, but only so well. He took a whore's bath in the sink and shaved away the morning stubble. He got dressed in his Carhartt work clothes. He layered up from thermal underwear. He added some gloves and the neon orange watch cap. He stuffed his work gloves into an outside pocket of the coat and put his tool belt over by the sleeping bag.

He packed a couple of sandwiches for lunch and then added three bottles of water. It was easy to get dehydrated when you worked in the cold because you didn't realize you were sweating.

By the time Alton came banging on the garage door he was already ready. Alton looked him over.

"Good to go?"

"Let's do it. You want me to follow you in my truck?"

"No. You ride with me. I got you some things you got to wear up at the Lodge. They require it. Wear it all the time on site. No exceptions. You forget, you could get shot."

Alton handed him a double extra-large lime-green nylon vest to wear over the outside of his jacket. It briefly reminded Frank of slipping on his old Spartan cut. The vest had Crisp Construction printed on the back in black block letters. Alton tossed him a lime-green watch cap with the same lettering except this time abbreviated to "CC".

"And this too. That way they know you are with me. Won't be no trouble."

Frank replaced his orange watch cap with the shocking green one. He wasn't sure which one was the more hideous.

"Thanks."

Alton nodded his bloated head. Frank scooped up his stuff and followed him to the truck. It was a big Toyota Tundra.

"Don't give me any shit about it being made by slants. The damn thing was built in Texas."

"Wasn't going to. It's a great looking truck. Wish I had one."

Alton mumbled something. They hit the local McDonald's for coffee, no biscuits, and headed to the Lodge. A second truck was waiting outside. It was towing a trailer stacked with fencing gear. The three occupants nodded to Alton as he cruised past. Alton ignored them. He pulled his big truck up to the guard shack.

"Morning."

"Morning, Alton. New guy?"

"Yeah. This is my cousin, Jack."

Frank gave a nod to the guard.

"I heard your cousin was in town. Make sure he knows the rules."

When Alton made no reply, the guard slipped back inside and raised the crossing bar. The small two-truck convoy eased through.

As they pulled away, Alton mumbled a reply. "Dick. I've known him since high school. Thinks he is a big deal now that he hangs with the Norse Men. I could have been a full member, but I got married. Fuck it."

Across the road was a huge sign that said: VALHALLA. Beneath it was written: Large Predator Rehabilitation Park. Alton drove the truck down the long winding road until he reached a second guard shack. The guard waved them through. Another sign proclaimed: The Lodge.

The Lodge was easily visible. It was huge, easily fifteen thousand square feet. It looked to be made of roughly hewn lumber. The front area was cleared down to a few old trees. Out buildings dotted the immediate vicinity. There was a large barn. A signpost directed viewers toward the park to the right and maintenance to the left.

As if on cue a lion roared in the early morning light. Frank turned and stared at Alton.

"What?"

"You got to be kidding me."

"What?"

"That was a lion."

"Yeah. It was."

"A real lion?"

"They got a lot of them. Tigers, bears, wolves, all kind of big predators.'

"You are shitting me."

"Don't get your panties in a wad. We aren't building cages today. We are working the other end of the food chain."

Finris unlocked the door to the bedroom and walked into the room closely followed by Heather. Mary lay spread eagle on her stomach, dressed only in her panties. Finris looked her over without comment. Her blood had stained the upper half of her panties as it had flowed down her back. Heather checked the wounds on her back.

"The salve is working. The swelling is down and the wounds are already healing."

"Any signs of infection?"

Heather leaned in closer. "No. It is still early, but she should be fine. If you like scars."

"Customers do."

68

Mary struggled to raise her head. "Please," she begged.

Finris and Heather both smiled. He glanced over his shoulder and two Norse Men entered the room. They stood awaiting his command.

"Please, no more," Mary begged.

"Take her down to the cells."

The two men untied her restraints and lifted her to her feet. She swung her head toward Finris. Her eyes were puffy with tears.

"Please. Let me go. I won't tell. I promise."

Finris motioned the men.

"You don't have to do this. I didn't do nothing."

Heather grabbed the blanket off the bed and the pillow. She followed the men from the room. Finris locked the door behind them. Mary was taken downstairs through a labyrinth of hallways to the basement. She saw Masnick strapped into his chair in his cell. He was still wearing the hood. The sterile horror of his condition sent spasms of fear through her. These people were monsters.

"Please," Mary continued to beg. "Let me go."

They placed her in a cell without a chair but a crude bed. Her rubbery legs wouldn't hold her and she fell to the cold floor. Heather hurried into the room and covered her with the blanket. She dropped the pillow onto the floor and backed out of the room.

"I will be back with hot food and something to drink," she promised.

Finris knelt beside the girl.

"You are mine now. You are my property to do with as I wish. We have claimed you as a spoil of war. There is no escape except death."

"Please," she whimpered.

Finris brushed her hair from her face. "There is no need to beg. It will not serve you. You will do as I say or suffer for it. The longer you resist the more pain you will have to endure."

"I'll be good. I promise. Don't whip me again."

Finris smiled.

"You are a liar. Everyone is at first. But after a few more sessions, you will learn to speak the truth. If you are very good, we will keep you here at the Lodge. You will have your own room. You will have a warm, safe place with food and comfort. If not, then we will move you into the circuit. It is a harsh life and will take its toll. Either way you will serve me."

Finris rose and closed the cell door. The lock set in place. Finris followed Heather to Masnick's cell. Masnick was writhing in the chair.

Finris pulled the hood from his head. Masnick's eyes were bleary and wild with pain. His restrained body tried to contort to the pain that racked it. Finris released the restraints and Masnick fell to the floor. His body writhed in agony as the toxins assaulted it.

Finris signaled one of the men, who used a power drill to remove the screw securing the chair. The chair was removed. All pieces that had held it into place were collected and accounted for. There was nothing in the cell except Masnick and his soiled blanket. Heather knelt beside him.

"I know it is very painful, Prometheus. The spider toxins make it feel as if your bones are being twisted apart, the tick bacteria spread it into your entire body, adding the pain to your muscles and soft tissues. Yet there is no visible mark on you."

Masnick shook as waves of pain washed over him. He could not speak.

"I told you this way was better," Heather declared.

Finris shrugged. "More effective, but not near as much fun for me."

Heather giggled and stood on her tiptoes to kiss him lightly on the lips. "You are a sadist."

Finris shrugged again. "When will we have answers?"

"When he is ready to give them. Isn't that right, Prometheus? Can you feel the fire burning your bones? They say it feels like a liquid flame coursing through your veins. I hope you, of all people, appreciate the irony."

Heather giggled again. A Norse Man approached Finris.

"Just got a call from the driver. The truck is being held up in quarantine."

"Problems?"

"No. He thinks it is just routine stuff. He said the escort is already in place."

"Excellent."

Finris wrapped an arm around Heather's waist and he pulled her close.

"Come to my room tonight."

"Of course," Heather said, and kissed him firmly on the lips.

They left Masnick alone with his agony. Masnick fought the pain in silence as long as he could. When the first scream escaped him, Masnick found he couldn't stop screaming.

They followed a side road to their work area and parked. Frank popped the door open and stepped out. The other three workers came walking up. They looked him over. Their eyes held equal parts suspicion and resentment.

"Gather round, you bunch of pussies. This is my cousin, Jack."

"Where's James?" someone asked.

"I fired his ass. Jack is taking James' place. This is Chuck, Tony and Warren."

They all shook hands and mumbled greetings.

"Well, get to it," Alton ordered. "I ain't paying you to stand around with your thumbs in your asses."

Frank looked around. A path had been hacked and lopped and pruned through the dense woods. A thin white line of twine snaked its way along the route. At regular intervals was a large X made by red spray paint. It reminded Frank of the Spartan red he used to wear. Maybe it was a good omen. Of course, it could represent blood. Maybe his blood. No, he liked his first impression better.

Alton pointed down the line.

"That's our fence line for today. We're putting up deer fence. It's nine feet tall so the bastards can't jump it."

Frank nodded. "Got it. Why they want deer fence?"

"Feeding the big cats and wolves and bears is expensive. They breed their own cattle, and hogs, and chickens and wild-raised deer to help cover the cost."

"Sounds smart."

"You should see it. My buddy let me watch when they turned a bunch of deer out into the tiger enclosure. That big bastard almost tore one of their heads off in one swipe."

"They put them in live?"

"Yeah. These animals are all from zoos and private collections. You know, pets that got too big. Finris says they have forgotten what made them predators, so he likes to live feed. He makes them hunt for their food. Granted, he removes any horns, but he says it needs to be as close to living free as it can be."

"Wow."

"It's a big operation. People and overseas zoos and shit call everyday trying to dump their animals. The park keeps growing."

"They do tours?"

"No. It's a private park. You want me to, I can ask them to give you a tour."

"No. I think I will stay as far away from that stuff as I can. Hey, where do you store your hog rings and braces?"

Alton laughed and slapped him on the shoulder. "Well, damn, maybe you are a fence man after all. Don't you worry about the gentle stuff. Your big damn hands wouldn't be able to slip a nut on a carriage bolt anyway. You get to dig the post holes. Nice and deep, like I like them."

"Fair enough. You got an auger?"

"Nope. Just a regular post hole digger."

"No gas auger? It would make it faster and easier."

"The damn things cost money. And I got lots of time. You're a big boy. It should be easy for you."

"Do you at least have a digger stick or spud bar?"

"In the back of my truck. Leave your tool belt. You won't be needing it today."

"Got it."

"Now I'm going to see if you can work as hard as you claim."

Despite the morning chill. Frank removed his jacket, replaced the lime green vest and got the post hole digger. He felt the rough wood. It was going to be a long day. It was going to be a very long day.

It was five o'clock. Deputy Maurer was sitting off to the side of the road waiting for speeders or drunks or a call from dispatch. He saw the big red Crisp Construction truck coming down the road. He knew Alton to be a hardcore alcoholic who had gotten worse since his wife had run off the year before. He also knew Alton saved his drinking for after five and on weekends. He would be sober now. He would be drunk in an hour.

The truck bounced down the road past him. He noticed there was a passenger in the front seat. He had heard that Alton's cousin was in town. The man appeared large. The man had turned his head as they passed Maurer's cruiser. Lots of innocent people didn't like to make eye contact with the police. But this had been too smooth. The head had only turned enough to hide the man's features. It set off small alarm bells in Maurer. There was something off about the guy.

As the truck sped on down the road the feeling quickly passed. Who was he kidding, he thought. The guy probably was a thug. Probably was a criminal. Probably was another Norse Man asshole. He cranked the cruiser and rolled the other way. It wasn't his business anymore. The high sheriff had made that clear. He had a baby on the way. He needed to keep his job.

Jake parked and was locking the car door when his cell phone went off.

"It's me," Jenny said.

"Hey. I had a good time last night. Your friends are cool."

"Thanks. They liked you too. You doing anything tonight? I thought maybe we could hang out."

"I can't tonight. I have something I have to do. What about tomorrow? I'll bring barbecue. You can invite DC to join us."

"That sounds great. I'll let you go."

"Good night."

Jake put the cell phone back in his pocket. He looked at the outside of the strip club. It was called Sheila's. As if a real person named Sheila ran it and not some bunch of hoods or a faceless corporation. The name implied this was a personal experience. Maybe locally owned and operated. The purple neon sign of the strip club advertised that they had the prettiest girls in town. Inside was the smell of stale beer, stripper sweat, and lust. Jake paid the cover charge and went looking for security.

He found a fat guy with no neck nodding at the bar with SECURITY stenciled in white on a black tee shirt. He tapped the guy with a finger.

"Excuse me. Can you point me to who is in charge of security?"

The fat man opened one fat-swaddled eye, looked him over and pointed to a large thick man cruising back and forth near the stage like a great white shark.

"His name's Bo."

Jake headed that way. The strip cub was nearly empty. A reasonably attractive girl was gyrating unenthusiastically around a tall chrome pole for the delight of the three or four patrons who leered at her. Other dancers, spotting a new mark, hurried to offer lap dances, special services in the champagne room, or drugs. Jake brushed them off. When he reached the head of security, he extended his hand.

"Are you Bo?"

"Yeah. Is there a problem?"

"No. I just need a favor." Jake took two one hundred dollar bills out of his pocket. "I'm looking for a couple of friends of mine. Big beefy Russians. Loud. Crew cuts, nice suits. They would be making it rain for the dancers."

Bo took the money and tucked it into his pocket.

"Haven't seen them. I'll ask the other guys."

Jake handed him a slip of paper with a phone number on it. It was for a burner phone he had just bought.

"You do that. If they come in, you give me a call. I'll give you another three bills. One of your boys calls me instead, you still get a bill, they get the other two."

Bo nodded. Jake appreciated there were no bullshit questions. "What are looking for them for? Why should I help you out? Are you a cop?" None of that mattered. It was about money and information. If you had the information, then you could sell it. It had to be enough money to be worth the effort, but not so much as to make them greedy and try to run a double cross. Steak and strippers had defined Yuri in New Jersey, so he had been right to assume he would pursue the same two vices here.

At the third strip club, The Oasis Lounge, Jake made the connection he needed. The Oasis was a very upscale Gentleman's club that tried to disguise that in essence, it was the same as the other clubs. Guys paid money to watch women dance and take their clothes off. They bought overpriced drinks and fantasized about what they would do if a particular dancer was their girlfriend or mistress. Oddly, not if she were their sister or daughter.

The chief of security said they had been here. He shook Jake's hand and took the two hundred. He told Jake he would call him direct if one of his guys saw them again. Jake knew it was so he could collect a bigger cut of the payoff. Good for him. Entrepreneurs were what made America work.

He drove home and planned his next move. He should call Carpenter and see if he had any useful intel. Jake yawned. Tomorrow. He would call tomorrow. Carpenter would have a million questions. Some he would ask. Others he would try to surmise for himself.

DC was sitting on his sofa smoking pot from a Star Wars-themed bong when his cell phone rang.

"Frank."

"DC. How are things?"

"Good. We met Jenny's new man. He seems pretty cool."

"He is. You can trust him."

"Good to know. You need me for something? It's quiet here."

"You got a piece of paper?"

"Hold on." DC scrambled around for a pen and piece of paper. "Got it."

"Take this down." Frank gave him the address of the Lodge. "I want all the intel you can get on it. Do that google Earth stuff. I want pictures. As many as you can get. The whole thing is like four miles wide so get me views of the area and then narrow it down as much as you can."

"You want all the buildings individually too?"

"Whatever you think. More is always better. I got to go in there and get somebody out. I need to know the best way in and the best way out."

"Got it. Where do you want it sent?"

Frank gave him the PO Box for the Mail Boxes Plus and his fake name. "Overnight it. I need it as soon as I can get it."

"Will do. I'll send it first thing in the morning. You should have it by Wednesday."

"Thanks. I appreciate it. I knew I could count on you."

When Frank hung up, DC sat on the sofa for a few moments, enjoying the feeling Frank's words caused. Frank Kane had said he could count on DC. Frank Kane. Damn straight. He went to his computer and logged on.

19

The golden early morning light poured into the sunroom, giving it an unearthly glow. Green plants encircled the room. Provided with constant year-round temperature and care, they had grown thick and luxuriant. A ceiling fan rested quietly like a patient sentinel.

Cyrus sat on the small sofa, drinking fresh-squeezed orange juice. The *Wall Street Journal* lay unread on the sofa beside him. Spanish Johnny paced in front of him.

"I don't like this, Cyrus."

"I realize that. But it is my plan. It maximizes our rewards and limits our exposure."

"We can't trust the Norse Men."

"No, we cannot. Working with us provides them with certain opportunities and vice versa. If they can break Masnick. . ."

"And discover some secret way he has of contacting Frank." Spanish Johnny finished for him. "Do you really think he knows how to contact Frank?"

"I have no idea."

"Then why bother?"

Cyrus held up a well-manicured hand to stop Spanish Johnny's complaints. "Offering them this task forges a bond. If they do not break Masnick, they will assume they have failed in this arrangement. They will owe us on some level. If they succeed, if there really is a way to contact Frank, then we eliminate that threat once and for all."

"And the Norse Men know not to try to do it themselves? They would only fuck it up."

"Exactly. I have a team of specialists on twenty-four-hour standby. If they are able to locate Frank, I will send you in with them to eliminate him. My jet is fueled and ready."

"And what about Helen?"

As if on cue, a strikingly beautiful woman strode into the sunroom. Her blonde hair was tied back, and she wore the beginnings of an angry smile on her perfect lips.

"What about me?"

Cyrus smiled and rose to his feet. "Darling."

She went to him and he kissed her lightly on her perfect pink lips.

"I thought you said we were going for a ride this morning."

"And we are. I decided to let you sleep a little longer. You looked so peaceful."

"That was sweet. I'm ready now."

"It is still cold outside. Make sure you are dressed warmly enough."

"Sometimes you treat me like a child."

"No, more like the goddess you are."

"Good morning, Helen," Spanish Johnny said.

Helen looked at the two men. She shook her head. "Always scheming. Always working an angle. Always wanting something."

"It is what we do."

She took Cyrus' hand and backed out of the room, pulling him after her.

"But not today. Today we are going to take our bikes on a long ride. Today we are free of any other worries or plots or business."

"You do have a security going with you?" Spanish Johnny asked.

Cyrus smiled. "Sometimes you treat me like a child," he mocked over his shoulder. "I am a god. Of course I have security. I am not a fool."

Cyrus and Helen disappeared and a few minutes later he heard the roar of their big Harleys as they came to life. He listened as they rode away. Spanish Johnny stood considering his own schemes and plans. The cook appeared wiping her hands on her apron.

"Can I get you some breakfast, Mr. John?"

Spanish Johnny smiled his wolfish smile. "I will have whatever he was having."

Masnick awoke in his cell. He didn't know when the pain had stopped or if he had just blacked out. His body ached and throbbed. His joints felt like they had been twisted apart on some torturer's rack. He guessed in a way they had. He tried to rise up, but his muscles were too weak. He could smell the woman. She still smelled like lilacs.

He opened his eyes. She was leaning over him. She was smiling a benevolent smile.

"You are awake, Prometheus. Good."

Masnick blinked in response.

"I know it is difficult to talk right now. It is an ordeal and the body needs time to recoup. It must gather its reserves. Like a computer trying to reboot."

Masnick had a fantasy of springing to his feet and bashing her pretty head in against the cold floor. It was only a fantasy. He noticed the boots of the guards behind her.

He heard a girl calling for help down the hallway. This triggered some distant dogs to begin to bark in response. Heather didn't seem to notice, or maybe she just didn't care.

"Bitch," Masnick hissed.

"Yes. I am your bitch now. When I am finished, you will crawl to me like the pathetic dog you are and lick my boots. You will debase yourself for my amusement. You will tell me what I wish to know gladly."

76

Masnick only had enough strength left to summon a tepid glare. Heather knelt closer to him. She pulled the blanket up over his bare shoulders.

"I will leave you food and water. Rest while you can. There is no way to tell when the pain will return or for how long."

One of the guards lazily placed a pair of dirty dog bowels near his head. One was half full of water, the other of some cold canned dog food. They left and he could hear Heather's tinkling laugh. He promised the gods everything he could think of if they would just let him kill her before he died.

Heather moved down the hallway to another cell. A pretty teenage girl sat quietly in the middle of the floor. Her blanket was wrapped tightly around her shoulders. When Heather appeared, she rose to her feet. She swept her shoulder length blonde hair back from her dirty face. The cell door opened and Heather entered.

"How are you this morning, Shirley?"

"Fine, thank you."

"Are you thirsty? Would you like some water?"

"Yes, please."

Heather took a bottle of water from one of the guards and passed it to the girl. Shirley took the bottle and started to open it. She paused and turned her gaze onto Heather again.

"May I?"

"Of course, dear."

Shirley twisted the cap off and drank greedily. She acted as if she was afraid they would take it from her before she finished. When the bottle was empty, she handed it back to Heather.

"Thank you."

Heather smiled. "Remove your blanket for me."

Shirley did. She was only wearing a pair of plain once white panties.

"Turn around and let me see how you are healing."

Shirley did. Heather ran her fingers along the nearly healed scars on her back.

"Excellent. You are doing so well."

"Thank you."

"Do they still hurt?"

"No, ma'am."

"You have made great strides, Shirley. Would you like to come back up stairs to one of the other rooms and join your sisters?"

"Yes, please."

Heather ran her long fingers along her cheek. "You are a very beautiful girl. Are you ready to start work for us?"

"Yes, ma'am. Whatever you want me to do."

"Good." She turned toward the guard. "Have Shena take her upstairs and let her take a nice warm bath. Feed her and find her something suitable to wear. Would you like that?"

"Yes," the girl said, as her voice broke with emotion.

"And no more trouble from you?"

"No, ma'am. I'll be good. You'll see."

"I hope so. But first, we need to give you a new name. The old Shirley is gone. Do you have a name in mind, or would you rather I chose one for you?"

The girl hesitated a moment as she thought. "What about Lexxus? With an extra x."

Heather smiled warmly. "That is a wonderful choice. Look after Lexxus for me. And bring someone in to do her hair. It is a mess."

Lexxus took Heather's hand in hers. She kissed the back of it.

"Thank you. You won't be sorry. I will do good. I promise."

Heather gave Lexxus a pat on her small round bottom as she was led away by one of the guards. Heather moved down to the next cell where Mary was kept. Heather did not open the cell. Mary was on her feet. Her blanket was wrapped tightly around her shoulders. There was a fierce fire blazing in her dark eyes.

"How are you today, Mary?"

"Fuck you, you crazy bitch."

"Now, now, such language."

"What do you expect? You lock me in a cage. You beat me like I was some animal."

"We are all animals, Mary. You are no different from any of the other girls we have trained here."

"You are a psycho."

"Are you thirsty? Would you like some water?" Heather asked taking a bottle of water from the remaining guard.

"Fuck you."

"Remove your blanket and let me see how you are healing."

"Kiss my black ass."

Heather unscrewed the cap and took a drink of water from the bottle.

"Are you sure you don't want any water?"

Mary turned her back on Heather. Heather took another sip and passed the bottle back to the guard.

"I will check on you later to see if you have changed your mind."

Heather walked away, leaving the hallway in silence. When she was gone, the lights went out.

Mary sat in the darkness planning escape. Masnick sat in the darkness planning revenge. The dogs started to howl.

20

Frank Kane sat on the back of Alton's pickup truck, eating the second of his two sandwiches. The other workers sat off in a small group talking among themselves. They still resented Frank, but he could tell he had also earned their respect. He had been the first to start work each day and the last to stop. He had dug post holes without complaint. His huge shoulders sang with the pain of overuse. His forearms bulged from the repetitive work. Even his lower back rebelled against the task. He didn't complain. Somehow the work made him feel more alive.

Alton was still being an asshole. He skulked about looking for something to focus his anger on. He raged over any imperfection. He had developed the habit of throwing rocks at the workers to motivate them. So far, he hadn't tried that with Frank. That was a good thing, Frank thought.

Alton started yelling that lunch break was over. Frank put the uneaten part of his sandwich in the bag and got to his feet. He headed to the fence line without complaint. He was starting to work on a plan and the drudgery of his task gave his mind ample time to explore other possibilities.

Deputy Maurer was seated at a back booth at a local café called Jan's Deli. He was sipping a sweet tea and looking over some flyers that had come in overnight. It was the usual stuff. Missing farm equipment or FTAs or BOLOs. He flipped through them trying to commit them to memory.

High Sheriff Long slid into the booth on his right side. Deputy Chris Durham, also known as Buck, slipped in on his left. Buck was six feet tall and weighed about one hundred seventy-five. He was athletic and quick. He wore a 70s porno mustache. It was big and bristled like a brush.

"How you doing today, Jeff?" Sheriff Long asked.

"I'm doing okay. Is everything alright?"

"Yeah, we just wanted to check in on you."

"Everything good with the wife?" Sheriff Long asked.

"Yes, sir."

The waitress arrived with Maurer's lunch, a club sandwich and fries. She looked at the newcomers.

"Get you fellows something to eat?"

"Coffee," Sheriff Long said.

"Bring me a menu," Buck said leaning back.

Sheriff Long shook his head.

"Just bring him some coffee. We aren't staying long."

The waitress hurried away.

Maurer stared at his food, unsure whether he should eat or not.

"Go ahead. Don't let us ruin your lunch."

Maurer picked up half of the sandwich and took a bite. He waited for someone else to speak.

Sheriff Long leaned in close and spoke in a low voice.

"I know this is hard on you, son. I do. It's how a small-town police force works."

Maurer nodded because he didn't know what to say.

Sheriff Long slid an envelope over to him. It bulged more than the first envelope he had given him.

"This week's bonus. Two grand," Sheriff Long said and waited for a response. When none came, he continued. "I have to have two people I trust to keep things running smooth. Can I count on you?"

Maurer picked up the envelope and slipped it into the breast pocket of his police jacket.

"Yes, sir."

High Sheriff Long patted him on the shoulder. "Good man."

"There are other perks to working with us on this."

"Like what?"

Buck laughed. "You know there are three kinds of sex you have when your wife's pregnant. The first trimester you do it missionary style. The second trimester you do it doggy style. The third trimester you do it coyote style."

Maurer looked confused. "What's coyote style?"

"That's where you lay beside the hole at night and howl."

Buck started laughing at his crude joke. Maurer managed a thin smile. He went back to eating his sandwich. Buck took one of his fries and popped it into his mouth.

"What Buck is saying in his juvenile way is that sometimes a man gets lonely when his wife is pregnant. He might desire a little female company."

"Something to take the edge off."

"I'm married. I am not going to cheat on Cathy."

"Not cheat. Not exactly. Just a little something on the side that doesn't have to mean anything," said the sheriff.

"The Norse Men got girls up at the Lodge. You get the urge, you go up and they will hook you up. Discreet," leered Buck.

"And these girls are eager to please. If you can think it up, they will do it."

"That's the damn truth," Buck agreed. "Finris says that little girl, Shirley, is on deck for tonight. He is holding her out for us."

"She would be perfect for you, Maurer. She's young and clean and pretty as a peach."

"I don't know. I'll think about it."

"Buck and I are going up there after work today. Come with us."

"I don't think I can. I appreciate the thought, but I just can't."

"Suit yourself, son. We aren't going to twist your arm. If it don't feel right, I wouldn't want you to go."

They sat in silence as the waitress brought the coffee. The sheriff passed her a twenty-dollar bill.

"This is on me. Keep the change."

The waitress smiled and left. Maurer kept eating. Buck seemed to be becoming agitated. Eventually he leaned into Maurer's face.

"Don't go all pussy on us, Maurer. This is a good deal if you don't fuck it up."

"Ease up, Buck. Maurer said he was on board."

"Well, he gets all pussy on us, he can have a sudden heart attack just like Ben did."

"There's no need for that, Buck."

Buck leaned back with a smile. "I'm just saying. Anybody can have a heart attack. Especially pussy cops."

Sheriff Long pointed at Buck. "Go wait outside."

Buck got up, took a long drink of coffee and left.

"I'm sorry about that, son. Buck is a cretin sometimes."

"Sometimes?"

"Okay. All the time. But he is a good cop. You have any problems with this you give me a call. We'll work through it."

Sheriff Long took a sip of coffee and grimaced.

"Look after that pretty wife of yours, son. You got a baby on the way. It's going to change your life in ways you can't even imagine."

He patted Maurer on the shoulder, like a father consoling a son who has failed to make the football team. Sheriff Long left the diner.

Maurer put his sandwich down. His heart was racing. He struggled to keep his face emotionless. He looked at his hands and saw they were trembling. The money was a weekly bonus. Maurer hadn't gotten As in math, but that was over fifty thousand dollars a year. That was lifechanging. That was problem solving. That was stress-relieving. That was more than cutting some drunk a favor money. What in God's name had he gotten himself into, he wondered.

21

Frank wasn't sure that his bones and muscles could ache anymore than they did. But it was a good pain, like he had been doing something important. He would like to have taken a long soak in his hot tub, or even a hot shower, but he wasn't going to ask. Instead he began a series of long slow stretches. The knotted muscles protested, but Frank cajoled and intimidated and massaged them into the moves. He took his time. There was no need to rush. What else did he have to do except eat another sandwich and go to bed. With each repetition the muscles surrendered a little to his will. Finally, exhausted, he felt limber again.

The ATV caught Frank's eye. It might be useful, he thought. He searched the little garage until he found a bundle of old newspapers. He spread them out near the ATV and got his tool belt. Alton said it didn't run anymore. Four-wheelers were tough little nuts. They were meant for tough conditions. Their motors were designed for the stress of off roading.

Frank spread his tools out like a surgeon might. He unhooked the spark plug to prevent an unexpected shock. He started to loosen the screws holding the engine in place. While his fingers were busy another part of his mind ran different scenarios to rescue Masnick. A lot would depend on what DC sent him. He would take his time and try to get it right.

Jake knocked on the door just after five. DC opened it with a huge smile on his face.

"Dude. Good to see you."

"You too. Where do you want me to put the food?"

"Jenny said to take it to the kitchen. The girls are in there. We can divide it up and chow down. I got a great indie movie for us to watch on DVD, Penance Lane. It is supposed to be scary with lots of twists and surprises. And you know girls love to get scared."

"So we can be there to look after them."

DC smiled. "You got that right."

DC followed Jake into the kitchen. Jenny ran over and gave Jake a little chaste peck on the lips. Caron smiled knowingly. Jake put the containers on the counter. He had brought a gallon of sweet tea, chopped barbecue, slaw, hush puppies and even banana pudding for dessert. Jenny started getting out glasses and plates when the doorbell rang.

"Don't stop," DC said, grabbing a hush puppy and popping it into his mouth. "I'm starved. I'll see who's at the door."

Twelve seconds later he called back to them.

"You guys better come out here."

The girls hurried from the room. Jake took his pistol from his ankle holster and slipped it into his pocket. He always expected trouble and sometimes an extra second made a lifetime of difference. When he reached the front door, the girls were standing behind DC, who faced three people. One was an older man of about fifty in a burgundy shirt. He was overweight the way athletes got when they stopped playing sports. The other two were teenagers. One was huge. He had to be pushing three hundred pounds. The other was lean like a wolf, with a handsome face that knew it. The man spoke first.

"I'm Coach Bumgardner. May I come in?"

"No," Jenny snapped.

"I would prefer we talk inside."

"You got something to say, say it where you are," DC added.

The coach nodded. "I understand. Like I said, I am Coach Bumgardner. I'm the football coach at Elon. I believe you know the two young men with me, Zach and Morgan."

"What do you want?" Jenny said.

"As you are aware, these young men had a substance abuse problem with alcohol and drugs. It led them down a dark path that culminated with them trying to break into your home."

"They tried to rape us," Caron nearly shrieked.

"I am aware of that allegation."

"It's not an allegation. It's a fact."

The coach continued without responding to Jenny's claim.

"That night was a turning point for these young men. They were arrested and as a result lost their football scholarships to UNC at Chapel Hill. At Elon, we believe in second chances. We believe in redemption. Since they were both first-time offenders, the courts eventually dismissed the charges, predicated on their completion of a court-approved substance abuse course. At that time, Elon offered them scholarships to play football with certain provisions. They entered and completed a twenty-eight-day substance abuse program."

"Get on with it, man," DC said.

"Part of that course requires that you personally apologize to the people you have hurt during your addictive phase. I knew what happened here and felt it was appropriate for me to accompany them to put everyone at ease. Boys, do you have something you want to tell these people?"

The big guy, Morgan, spoke first. "I am truly sorry for what happened that night. I wasn't myself. I was drunk and high. It made me do crazy things. I realize that you can't ever forgive me and I'm not asking you too. I only wanted to say to your face that I am truly sorry."

The wolfish one, Zach, spoke next. "It's like Morg said. The cocaine and booze got us all twisted. It never should have happened. I'm sorry and I promise nothing like that will ever happen again."

"Thank you, boys. That was great. Do any of you wish to say anything to them?"

Jenny just turned and walked away. Tears started to flow out of Caron's eyes. She didn't make a sound as they poured down her cheeks. DC looked at her and turned back to the door.

"Don't ever come back here. Ever. Do you understand?"

Without waiting for an answer, he slammed the door in their faces. Caron broke into sobs and collapsed into DC's arms. Jake stood watching them.

"You better go find Jenny, dude. That is some hard shit."

Jake walked up the stairs. When he was out of sight, he slipped his pistol back into the ankle holster. He knocked on Jenny's door. There was no answer, so he went inside. He had expected to see her crying like Caron. It was the normal response, he assumed. Jenny was sitting on her bed, just staring off into space.

"You alright?"

"Fuck," Jenny said.

"You want to talk about it?"

"That's some of my shit. I can't believe they just came here."

Jake was smart enough not to speak. He just waited.

"Sit down," she said and patted the bed beside her.

Jake sat.

She told him the story. How the guys had been flirting with them at work and then one night had shown up here, high on drugs and booze. The girls were alone. The guys had broken into the porch where they were in the hot tub. Morgan had torn the screen door off like some human Hulk. He had ripped Caron's bathing suit off and was going to rape her. Zach had hit Jenny and promised to do the same thing to her. DC had stumbled into the mix and gotten his hands on a baseball bat. He had threatened to bust Morgan's knee so he would be done with football forever. She had pulled a knife on Zach and held it against his throat. The situation had held until the sound of sirens had sent the football players running away.

Jake listened to her words, but he watched her face as she told it. He saw the nuances to the story. He felt her helplessness. He felt her rage.

She ended the story with, "Frank wasn't here."

"Of course not. He would have just killed them. You never told him what happened?"

"I told him there was trouble, but I handled it. That was enough for him."

"Frank is like that."

"I thought it was done."

"Why didn't you kill them?'

"What are you talking about? I didn't want to kill them. I don't think I could have if I wanted to."

"I could teach you how. You cut Zach's throat and while he is bleeding out you charge Morgan. He would take some killing because he is so big, but he would have been stunned, watching his friend dying. You would just have to know the right spots. You could have taken him out too."

"You are crazy."

"I saw it in your face. You were thinking it. You were thinking if you had killed them, they couldn't have come back. It would have worked out with the law. You would have skated even if the cops brought charges."

"That's not what I was thinking. I was thinking that hearing about this would make you hate me. It's like it makes me dirty somehow. Like it was my fault."

"It wasn't and I don't think that. I think you are a strong, amazing woman."

"Really?"

"Really."

Jenny snuggled against him and Jake put an arm around her shoulder and pulled her closer.

"There's more bad stuff in my past," she whispered.

"I don't care. I like the you that you became."

Jenny turned her face up and kissed him long and soft. She snuggled back against him.

"Would you really teach me?" she asked.

22

The eighteen-wheeler pulled up to the guard shack and was waved through. It meandered up the long road to the second guard shack and was directed to the right to shipping and receiving. The driver geared down and backed up to the loading dock. Finris was waiting, in his personal uniform of heavy pants and a vest without a shirt.

The driver put the truck in park and climbed down from the cab. He climbed the steps to meet Finris. Finris gave him a big bear hug and then shook him playfully.

"Everything cool, brother?"

"Just like always. They couldn't have cared less about checking it out when they saw our cargo."

"That's the plan. You expect dogs to go nuts around big cats anyway."

"I doubt they have dogs to waste on this shit anyway."

Finris smiled. "Niche marketing. When the Feds zig, we zag. When they start cracking down on heroin, we just go another direction."

A forklift chugged up behind him.

"Take the predators to quarantine. The veterinarian is waiting for them there."

Finris stepped out of the way and the forklift eased into the back of the truck. It lowered the forks and slipped them under the first cage and backed out. Finris looked over the manifest and made a check mark on it.

The first cage held an old tiger. It lay on a soiled bed of old straw. Its skin hung in loose folds over protruding ribs. The tiger didn't even raise its huge head upon the motion. The long tongue lolled out of the side of its mouth of broken teeth.

A second forklift pulled up to the back of the big truck. It removed another cage. The next cage also held a tiger. This one was younger but in equally bad health. The once thick chest strained to draw in enough air. Finris checked it off the list. He was smiling.

A third cage was eventually removed. The thick metal bars of the cage held a female tiger. Her belly was swollen slightly. Finris signaled for the forklift driver to stop. He moved closer to the tigress. She was as listless as the other two had been.

"Tell the Doc she might be pregnant."

The driver nodded and backed away. After a well-practiced turn he was off to quarantine. Finris followed the truck driver into the back of the truck. There was a final cage. This one was smaller and held a different cargo. It was a female leopard.

The leopard snarled at their approach. It charged the bars and took an ineffectual swipe at them through the bars. The truck driver jumped back. Finris did not flinch.

"A leopard?"

"I know. It wasn't on the original manifest. I guess the zoo thought they would unload it with the others. Make it our problem. They were closing anyway."

"Interesting."

The leopard snarled a warning. It crouched in the far corner of the cage.

"Got no need for a leopard. No money in it. Skin might bring something after you get it ready."

"She is so full of rage."

"Easier to just put her down, if you ask me."

"No, I think not. I like her. Have her quarantined with the others. We will build her an enclosure and see if she deserves to survive."

"Whatever you say. The foreign orders are always a pain in the ass. We should just stick to domestic acquisitions. It's easier."

Finris patted the driver on his back.

"Easier is not always better, my friend."

"Why bother? You get calls everyday about cats that have outgrown their owners, or private collections wanting to lessen their expenses, and even zoos with too many cats."

"I like to expand my options."

Finris did not bother to explain that the foreign acquisitions had nothing to do with acquiring more large predators. They were just the conduits to what he was importing from overseas. Finris took an envelope out of the back pocket of his pants and handed it to the driver.

"You are a reliable friend. That is a commodity I value in these times."

"Thank you."

"Are you heading back out today?"

The driver licked his lips and shuffled his feet.

"If you don't mind, I was hoping to spend the night up at the Lodge. I would sure like to take advantage of some of your...ahh...hospitality."

"Of course. You don't need to even ask. You are a Norse Man, the Lodge is always available to you. It is your Valhalla, your reward."

The man grinned. "I appreciate it. One night should do it. I don't want my wife to start asking questions."

Finris laughed. He went to see the veterinarian. As he walked, he scanned the loading bay. He had worked in trucking himself when he was younger. The facility would do any business proud. It was clean and orderly, with four big bays. The cargo was stacked in neat high rows that reached nearly to the ceiling.

He entered the double doors of the quarantine area. The pretty Asian receptionist nodded a greeting as he passed. Finris moved through the inner doors.

The quarantine clinic was large with an empty, sterile feel. The industrial grade tile showed the oil-black skid marks of the forklifts. Finris followed them to where they had left their charges. The veterinarian was there, so was Heather.

The old veterinarian had the female tiger on a gurney. She was sedated and hooked up to an IV. The veterinarian was sliding an ultrasound across her belly. He waved Finris over.

"You have a good eye. She is pregnant."

"How many cubs?"

"Two. They are very small, but still viable."

"Excellent. Can they go to term if we treat the mother?"

"I doubt it. She is in bad shape. If you want the cubs alive, I recommend an immediate C-section to remove them."

"Do it. But use a small incision. I don't want to damage the value of her skin."

"It would be easier if the mother's survival was not an issue."

"She is too valuable. There is still a list of potential hunters waiting. Make sure she survives as well."

"I will do my best."

"I know you will, Doc. What about the other ones?"

"They are in a similar state, but weaker from neglect. With proper care, they will recover. Once they are healthy enough, I will start the steroid therapy."

"Excellent. Make sure you sign the death certificates for the cats, that they did not survive their transportation beyond a few days."

"Will do."

Heather moved to his side.

"What do you want with a leopard? Are you going to hunt her, too?"

"Not right now. I like her. She is so beautiful and deadly. See how she is watching us now?"

As if on cue, the leopard snarled a deep throaty rumble.

"She reminds you of yourself, then."

Finris placed a hand on her chin and turned her face upward.

"No. She reminds me of you."

Heather beamed at the compliment. She rose on tiptoes and kissed him on the cheek. Finris returned her smile.

"You can be so sweet sometimes."

"Sometimes," he joked. "Is the shipment intact?"

Heather glanced to the cages. The other tigers had been sedated and Norse Men were moving them to smaller cages for transport to the quarantine. In quarantine the tigers would be monitored closely as they were nursed back to health.

A second group of Norse Men were carefully deconstructing the tiger cages. The tops of the cages were removed first. The men used special saws to section the bars at their tops. Sparks rained on the hard flooring as the diamond saws did their delicate work. When all the bars were sectioned at the top, the men turned their attention to the bottom of the bars.

As the bars came free, they were stacked on a wooden pallet resting on a hand lift. The thick bars were hollow inside and surprisingly thin. When all the bars had been removed and stacked, a man took the pallet from the room.

"Come on," Heather said.

Finris followed Heather, who followed the man with the pallet. He led them down a long corridor to another building. A Norse Man stood guard outside with an AK-47. He straightened up as Finris approached. Finris rewarded him with a nod. They went inside to an antechamber. The man passed the bars to an oriental man who carefully removed their secret cargo.

The plastic containers inside were filled with densely packed white powder. It was not heroin or cocaine or some exotic drug from Europe. The powder was anabolic steroids. It was of a purity available only in Europe. Until now. Gym rats, athletes, forty-year-olds, cops, and anyone who wanted a boost to their physique gobbled the stuff up as fast as the Norse Men could produce it.

Steroids were a wonder drug. They could transform a body seemingly overnight. They could boost libido. They could boost testosterone. They enhanced performance in sports. They made a man feel like a man. Of course, they had drawbacks. Even if you stacked its use and rotated your time on and then off the drug, it still caused acne, and baldness, and testicular shrinkage and more facial hair and even enlarged breasts in men. It could also lead to anemia, rapid cancer growth, and liver disease and heart disease. Obviously, that was a small price to pay for looking and feeling younger.

As a drug of abuse, it was low on law enforcement's radar but equally as profitable as the other drugs people abused. To enhance their product, Finris also had a small amount of methamphetamine added to the steroids. It helped ensure such feelings of euphoria that users would tolerate no substitute. The Norse Men cooked their own meth in a lab far away from the main compound, in a carefully controlled environment to limit potential explosions.

The steroids were taken into the lab where a cadre of Asians remixed and repackaged the potent mix into clear capsules.

"It was a good load," observed Heather.

Finris nodded.

"And your men know that the product can not be distributed anywhere near here?"

"Of course. You worry too much. They are aware of my rules."

"It has taken a long time and a substantial financial investment to get us to this point. I don't want to see any problems now."

Finris leaned down and kissed the top of her head.

"You and your brother are the lynchpins of this operation. You are protected from any blowback."

"That's not what I meant."

"I know what you meant. Just concentrate on breaking Masnick. An accord with the remnants of the Spartans would be a great help to our expanding our operations."

"I hate them."

"It doesn't mean we can't work with them."

"I don't trust them."

"Neither do I. Neither does Loki. Why would we? They are a necessary evil. They have contacts that would be valuable."

"The Spartans are finished. They can't do anything for us. It's all lies."

"Perhaps. But that is not your concern or your decision. Loki wants to pursue this alliance and so we shall."

"Loki. He is in prison. He does not run the Norse Men any longer. You do."

Finris smiled. He felt the same way, but he did not say so. Secrets were better kept to yourself.

"He is the head of the Norse Men. As long as he lives, he will remain so whether he is in prison or free."

"As long as he lives," Heather smiled.

Finris thought she was very much like the leopard after all.

23

Masnick lay in his cell. He was too ill to rise. He could hear the dogs barking nearby. They were always barking. The cells must be near the kennels, he reasoned. He could hear the girl, Mary, screaming that they couldn't keep them caged like animals. If he hadn't been so weak, he would have smiled. Of course they could. They were doing it.

He pitied her. She was so young. She was naive. She was wasting her time and strength fighting them. She should become docile, agreeable to their demands. She should become compliant when asked and passionate in servicing her customers. Only in that way could she hope to escape. Her anger only brought their close surveillance. Her anger only brought their beatings. In the end, she would submit or die.

Masnick's position was different. It was hopeless. He could not give them Frank Kane because he did not know where to find him. He had to prolong the torture long enough to make them believe him when he lied to them. It would only buy him so much more time. But it was more time. Perhaps in that lull he could orchestrate his own escape. He knew no one was coming to rescue him. No one was that stupid.

Jake called Carpenter.

"Jake, how are things in G'boro?"

"Fine. I need some intel if you can find it."

"That's what I am here for. By the way, did you hear the latest on me?"

"No. I stay off the under web."

"Too bad. They think I am Asian. And a woman. They are calling me the black widow. How rich is that?"

"Funny stuff."

"Jake," Carpenter sighed, "At least feign interest."

"Sorry."

"I like to enjoy the little things. The ironic moments in life give it spice."

"I know. I should have sounded more excited."

Carpenter sighed dramatically again.

"Forever, The Jake. What do you need?"

"I spotted some Russians in town. I worked a job for them in New Jersey last summer. One of them was Yuri. Can you see what they are doing here?"

"Of course. I remember Yuri. Are you keeping an eye on Frank for me?"

"Of course."

"I'll call when I find out anything."

Frank Kane was a little depressed. He had gone to Mail Boxes Plus hoping to find the material that DC was overnighting to him. But it wasn't there. He had left quickly before the horse-faced woman could ask him to take her riding. He had briefly considered doing some recon before the material arrived but discarded the idea. It would be pointless and dangerous. He took a deep breath and calmed his impatience. Tomorrow.

He had stopped by the local AutoZone for some things he needed to work on the ATV, then returned to the garage. Alton was nowhere in sight. All the lights in the house were off. There was a slim chance that Alton was snitching him to the Norse Men, but there was no reason for him to be suspicious. Frank put one of his guns in his pants pocket. Just in case.

The ATV engine had seemed sound. He removed the foam filter. It was filthy. He put on thick rubber kitchen gloves. He wiped away all the debris from the filter that had built up on it. He dunked it in the cleaning solution he had bought. He squeezed out the excess and rinsed it in the bathroom sink. He set it aside to dry.

He had a dinner of peanut butter sandwiches and a bottle of water. It was as boring and bland as it sounded. He checked the filter and decided it was dry enough. He sprayed fresh oil on the filter element and squeezed it to spread it. He reinstalled it.

Frank had also picked up some degreaser for the chain. He repeated the process three times until the chain looked clean and dry. He followed it by lubing the chain where it meshed with the cogs. Most people liked to lube the outside, but that didn't help the efficiency of the chain. He checked the clutch. It seemed fine. The brake pads seemed good too.

Frank got a cigar and took the bucket outside. He dumped the bucket over and planted himself on it. He lit the cigar and took a deep pull. He was planning on using the ATV to help get Masnick out. He couldn't take a chance on it not working when he needed it. There was a lot that Frank didn't know about the Lodge yet. But there was a lot he did know. He concentrated on that. Finris was smart. Frank knew that for certain. That meant Finris would be predictable. He would do the smart thing, not some crazy shit Frank couldn't predict. He knew there was security at the Lodge. That was a problem. He also knew, just like the Spartans had been in Asheville, the security would be lax. They would have the police in their pocket, so security was just a backup. The guards would have gotten bored by now without incursions. Flasks would be hidden in jackets. Joints tucked away in shirt pockets. Minds on other things. They would not be expecting him yet. They wouldn't be afraid.

He took another puff of the cigar. Damn, it was a good smoke. He noticed a single light on in Alton's house. Wherever he had been, he was home now. The wind sent a chill through the night. Frank pulled his coat a little tighter. It wasn't going to be long now. He would have to make a move soon. He couldn't count on Masnick holding out forever. When they broke him, they would find out he had no information and kill him.

24

Heather woke to find Finris out of their bed. He was exercising in the middle of the floor. He was nude. She watched the play of his muscles as he moved. She marveled at the flexible strength. The long thick muscles coiled and stretched as he moved through his exercises. He was the most perfect specimen of a man she had ever seen.

Finris sensed her gaze and turned to the bed. He was unashamed.

"Did you sleep well?"

"Yes. Once I was allowed to sleep."

"That was not all my doing."

Heather smiled, flashing her white teeth.

"Have you heard yet how your little Shirley did on her first night?"

"Her name is Lexxus now. She did very well. The cops were pretty rough on her, but she didn't complain."

"And the cops?"

"They were very satisfied with her performance. Of course, men are easily satisfied." Heather's smile turned into a small laugh.

"Most men," Finris added. "Their desires are small, so it takes little to placate them."

His phone rang and he retrieved it from the nightstand. He listened for a handful of seconds.

"Excellent," he said, and disconnected.

"Good news?"

"Very. Walt has located two more rhino mounts in Texas that the widows want to get rid of. He bought each for five thousand dollars, promising to add the mounts to his collection. We can move the horns for two hundred and fifty thousand a piece."

"My brother will be pleased."

"I am sure he will be. Walt is driving them up as soon as the auction ends."

"My brother will have buyers ready as always."

"I would expect no less."

Heather came up to him and lightly dragged her fingers down his back. Her claws were not as sharp as a leopard's.

"Do you fight today?"

"Yes."

"Are you worried?"

"About what? About losing? About getting hurt?"

"All of those."

Finris leaned down and gave her a chaste kiss.

"No, I am not worried. About anything."

"Are you worried about this Frank Kane I hear you talking about?"

Finris smiled. She was clever. She listened.

"No. I look forward to that challenge. He is a man much like me. We are both warriors."

"Who is he? I hear some of the men whisper his name as if they are afraid to speak it aloud."

"They are cowards. They fear ghosts and legends."

"But who is he?"

"He was the enforcer for the Spartans a long time ago. He was a very dangerous man."

"As dangerous as you are?"

"Exactly as dangerous as I am. I met him once. He gives off an aura of immense power."

"So do you."

Finris smiled.

"I heard them say he couldn't be killed," Heather said.

"Don't listen to them. They are children. All men can be killed. Now go get dressed. We have a lot to do today before the fight. I want to check on the new cats' progress."

Alton worked them hard until lunch. When they took their break, one of the other workers offered Frank an apple he had brought but said he didn't want. It was as sweet as a welcome home hug, but among guys it was probably as close as they would ever get. They asked him to eat with them and he did. He was part of the crew now.

Alton sat alone in the cab of his truck eating his lunch. The workers laughed and told stories. Frank just listened. He was not good at sharing.

He heard the approach of the other truck long before the others did. It was a Ram 1500, a very good full-size truck. But some idiot, Frank thought, had painted it in full-on camo. Nothing seemed to scream redneck like full-on camo paint job. To top it off, the owner had a confederate flag painted on the hood. There was no doubt this was a Norse Man.

The big truck skidded to a quick stop and a fat man climbed out. He was pushing his late fifties and was missing his front lateral incisor. He had a long wispy gray beard and dark droopy eyes. He was caring a red spit cup in his right hand. He looked around at the group and spat into the cup.

"Chet, what's up? Is there a problem?"

Chet shook his head from side to side. It reminded Frank of the way a bull shakes. "Good news, Alton. It is on for today."

"The fight? He got someone?"

"Yep."

"For real?"

"Big black bull from over near Tyler, West Virginia. Heard about the cash."

"Shit. Dumbass. You got to win to get paid."

"Ten thousand is a lot of motivation for a boy. Sheriff is picking him up now."

"Any chance we could watch?"

Chet slapped Alton on the shoulder. "That's why I come to fetch you. Finris said you could take a break and come down. Have a beer. Watch the show. He likes a crowd."

"It never takes very long anyway."

"No, sir. That it don't. But it's fun to watch. This your cousin?"

Frank stepped up and extended his hand. "I'm Jack."

"Chet."

"Good to meet you."

"You're a pretty big boy your own damn self. You up for making a little easy money?"

"I'm always up for making money."

"Ten thousand dollars. You good with your hands? You like to fight?"

"Leave him alone, Chet. He's a good worker. I don't need Finris beating his ass to a pulp."

"I bet he could hold his own."

"Shut the fuck up. He can't work if he's in the hospital. I need him healthy."

Chet laughed. "Blood must be thicker than mud. You're right. A man has to be crazy to go up against Finris."

"I guess I'll pass," Frank said.

Even as he said the words, he could feel his demons began to stir. He liked to think of them as locked away in a dark dungeon, behind steel and stone and walls. Shackled in heavy iron chains. But they were never far away. The dark part of Frank wanted nothing more than to go man-to-man against Finris. Frank took a deep calming breath and let his demons fall back to sleep. He wasn't here for himself. He was here to get Masnick out.

"Hop into the cab with me, Alton. You other boys climb in the back."

They all did. Frank pulled on his camo coat again, with the lime green vest over the outside and the bright green watch cap. He had not seen Finris since his time in prison. They had only been close to each other one time. All their other views had been across the yard. Frank hoped his change in appearance would be enough to fool the clever Finris.

The Norse Men had only seen Frank when he was in full biker mode, Spartan cut, blue jeans, leather. His hair had been long, now it was buzz cut short. He had worn a long thick beard, now he was clean shaven. He slipped on the thick nerd glasses to disrupt any clear view of his eyes. He doubted they would be able to recognize him even if they were looking for him, which they were not. If he was wrong, he mused, he was a dead man. He did what he could. The rest was up to the gods.

Chet worked the truck around into a turn and headed back toward the Lodge. They bounced down the dirt road in silence. It was cold in the bed of the truck. He glanced into the cab and could see Alton take a bottle of Jim Beam from Chet. They were laughing about something.

Chet parked and they all climbed out. Frank tried to slump his shoulders a little to lessen his height. He tried to move slower with a wider gait. It was not exactly a waddle, but it was close. It was the way a lot of fat guys walked. They seemed to swing their legs rather than bend them. He let his head sweep from side to side like any other visitor might. He made sure not to let it linger on anything for more than a second so there was no time for anyone to recognize him.

Chet led them to the cleared area in front of the Lodge. It had appeared flat, but it was in fact in a slight depression, the redneck version of the coliseum. The dirt had been raked and then swept clean of any debris. The perimeter was ringed with large, white painted stones. The spectators circled the outside edge of the pit.

The spectators were mostly men. It was an odd mixture. There were about a dozen Asians wearing lab coats, as if they had been forced from the warmth of their lab to view this primal sport. Frank realized they probably had been forced to come, since none of them wore a coat. There were men who worked the farm portion of the lodge. They wore bibs and looked filthy but excited, like kids going to the state fair. They lit cigarettes and joked with each other. They looked glad to have a break from a job that never ended.

There were Norse Men dressed in camo and Carhartt. The clothes were well worn but not dirty from recent hard labor. These men were all openly carrying weapons, mostly shotguns and rifles. Some carried AR-15s. One strutted carrying a MAC-10 submachine gun. Frank figured that because of the weather and the need to wear coats, most had opted for a two-handed weapon instead of a handgun. He watched some redneck trailing a large pit bull that patrolled the perimeter. The man followed the pit on a thick length of chain attached to its wide leather collar. A second man followed leading two more pits. The first was obviously the alpha.

There were a few women in nice expensive warm overcoats. They must have served some administrative position. They didn't look like prostitutes. They looked more like secretaries. Whatever the Norse Men were up to it required a lot of paperwork. They looked excited, but also a little nervous. And yes, there was a sprinkling of women watching from the Lodge that appeared to be prostitutes.

Large metal buckets filled with ice and beer had been placed at intervals around the pit. The spectators all seemed to take a cold beer as they took their spots to watch the action.

Alton's crew got a good spot right behind one of the buckets. Alton and Chet passed out beers to the men. Alton slipped a spare into his coat pocket. Watching was thirsty work. Chet had them placed on the front row. Frank drifted a little behind the others. No reason to make it too easy.

A skinny man with long Elvis sideburns entered the pit. He was carrying three chainsaws. The crowd started cheering. Alton leaned over toward Frank.

"That's Jerry. He's the pregame show."

Frank nodded and Jerry fired up the chain saws. Like some medieval juggler, Jerry started throwing the running chainsaws in the air and catching them. He went from one to two and finally to three. Frank thought of the old saying that every man had a special talent. How in hell, he wondered, did Jerry ever discover his?

When Jerry had finished his routine without cutting off a major appendage, the crowd rewarded him with clapping and obscene catcalls. Next up in the prefight was another skinny redneck dressed in camo that did a fire-breathing routine. It wasn't too bad. Frank was waiting for the clowns and elephants to arrive when the sheriff's car pulled in. The car parked off to the right of the pit. It sat motionless for a minute before High Sheriff Long and his chief deputy Buck Durham got out. They opened the rear door of the squad car.

A small bald black man climbed out. He was about sixty with a worn coat and thick canvas pants that were patched at the knees. He wore an old wool scarf. He looked scared. For the briefest moment, Frank wondered if this was the man who was going to fight Finris in the pit. Then the darkness inside the car seemed to move.

The second man who exited the car was as black as a nightmare. He was easily as tall as Finris, maybe a little taller. He was probably weighed close to three-hundred-and-twenty pounds. Yet, he didn't look fat. He was just huge. The black man didn't look afraid. He probably wasn't afraid of anything. The sheriff was talking to the two men, both of whom nodded. The sheriff pointed toward the pit.

The men walked toward the pit single file with the small man leading the way. The crowd grew silent and opened a path for them. The small man led them to the pit. The big man scanned the crowd. They watched him, intimidated by his size. Suddenly, a cheer rose up. Finris was coming.

The Norse Man strolled casually into the crowd. They parted for him. Some of the men were bold enough to pat his back or shoulder just so they could tell people later that they had. Finris looked happy. He was smiling and waving to people in the crowd.

Finris was wearing his customary outfit of thick canvas pants and a leather vest. He removed the vest, exposing his hugely muscled chest and arms. Overlaying the scars from past battles were strange Nordic runes and glyphs. They colored most of the hairless skin. The skin looked shrink-wrapped over the stretch of iron muscles. His hands were wrapped with white boxer's wrap. It wound between the fingers and across the knuckles, snaked around the wrist and was taped off at the end.

Finris made a few mock bows to the crowd. For a brief instant, his gaze swept over Frank and held. It was some primal recognition perhaps, or an instinctual response of one predator to another. Frank looked away. He could tell Finris' mind was racing, trying to sort through the thousands of faces it had seen to match this face with a name or memory. There was something. Then it was gone.

The black man seemed unimpressed with Finris, a fact that was not lost on the crowd. The ebony monster removed his own coat. He was only wearing a thin white wife-beater tee shirt underneath. His arms were long and as thick as pylons. He stretched his muscles in the cold air. He threw a few slow punches in the air. Like Finris, he was smiling.

The high sheriff had followed the men into the ring. He held his hands up signaling for quiet.

"Quiet. Quiet. Shut the fuck up! Alright. We got a challenge fight. The challenger from Tyler, West Virginia, one-time professional boxer, Neville "the Darkness" Liggins." There were shouts of approval. "In the other corner, the undefeated champion, and all time BAMF, Finris Wolf." The crowd exploded in applause. They roared and screamed and slapped each other on the back, building up the excitement.

The sheriff signaled for quiet again. The older black man was expertly wrapping Neville's hands. He had obviously worked a fighter's corner before. He secured the wraps around the wrists and sealed it with a piece of white tape.

"The challenge is simple. Finris puts up the purse of ten thousand dollars. If the Darkness can defeat him in a fight, then the money is his." The high sheriff turned back to the fighters. He explained the rules as if they had never heard them before, which Frank assumed was for the benefit of the spectators. "I want a clean fight. This is a boxing match, not a street fight. No eye gouging, biting, stomping a man when he is down. No kicks. I will let a knee or two go if it seems spontaneous. No small joint breaks. No elbow strikes. No choke holds. Fuck. You know what to do."

The high sheriff motioned the older black man out of the pit. He pointed to the two fighters, each in turn.

"Get to it."

Both men slid thick opaque mouthpieces into their mouths.

Finris extended a wrapped fist toward the Darkness. The Darkness tapped it with his own fist. Frank liked the simple act of respect between warriors. Finris moved from side to side, shaking his arms down by his side a little, then he brought them up into a good boxer's position in front of his face. Darkness just assumed the fighting position.

The Darkness stalked relentlessly across the pit. Finris danced back and left and right, keeping his distance. Finris would pepper him with stinging jabs. The Darkness came onward. He seemed unfazed.

It reminded Frank of a video he had seen of George Frazier fighting Muhammed Ali. Ali fought the same way. Stick and move. Rocky versus Apollo Creed. Frank was slightly impressed with Finris' speed and footwork. He had been trained by a pro himself, Frank thought.

The Darkness caught Finris with an overhand right that staggered him. The Darkness moved forward to close the space, but Finris was gone. Finris slipped a jab and stood the Darkness up with an upper cut. He recovered before Finris could capitalize.

It was a well-matched fight. Each man was landing hard blows, but not any significant combinations. Both men were cut and bleeding. This was not some undisciplined street brawl. No uncontrolled charges. No wild windmill punches. There was no street trash talking. No dirty tricks.

This was like watching a brutal game of chess. Each fighter tried to draw out the other fighter. They analyzed the other's tactics and tried to counter them. Darkness landed a big straight right and followed it up with a pair of lefts. The crowd groaned as their hero stumbled.

Finris was able to fight his way out of the onslaught. He caught the advance with a pair of savage uppercuts and followed with a vicious left hook. Darkness moved away. His left eye was swelling shut. Finris spit a glob of bloody phlegm onto the ground.

Frank noticed the subtle change. He saw the Darkness move a little slower on his next advance. He saw the slight smile play across Finris' lips. The black giant was tiring. His legs were going. Finris saw it too. Finris seemed freshly energized. He danced around the Darkness. He stuck him with a hard jab. The Darkness's hands were a little slow to respond. Finris hit him again. And then again.

The Darkness raised his hands higher and moved toward Finris. He knew he was tiring. He needed to end this soon. He launched a combination that might have killed a man if they had all landed. None of them did. Finris danced away. The Darkness came on. He fired a ranging jab and immediately followed with a power right. Finris countered as the right hand withdrew. Finris staggered the giant with his own big right hand. Then a left. Then a right. And another.

The blows sounded like someone hitting a paddle on the water. Boom. Boom. Boom.

The Darkness did not realize it yet, but the fight was over. He struggled on, gamely fighting through his pain and fatigue. He was bloody and bruised and beaten. He knew it. Finris knew it. Even the crowd knew it. It had been an epic battle. Maybe the best they had ever seen Finris have.

Finally, it ended. The Darkness fell to his knees. He seemed unable to rise. His chest heaved and bloody froth bubbled from his lips. It would have been easy to finish him then, but Finris let him regain his feet a final time. Finris stepped in and dropped him with a right hand. The Darkness fell to the ground. He didn't move.

The old man rushed to him. He checked his vital signs. He cradled the giant distorted head in his lap. Finris watched without emotion. Someone came out of the crowd with a white towel. He offered it to Finris, who directed him to take it to the fallen man. The man seemed disappointed but did it. The old man mopped the blood from Neville's face. The lights were still out in the Darkness.

"We need to get him to a hospital," the old man said.

The high sheriff and his chief deputy approached from the edge of the crowd. They exchanged looks. The deputy kicked the downed man in the ribs. Neville groaned and tried to roll away. The deputy kicked him again harder. The old man tried to get between the deputy and Neville. The high sheriff backhanded him across the face. The deputy kicked Neville a final brutal time. The old man rose to his knees.

"Now you can take him to a hospital," the high sheriff said.

The deputy and some Norse Men roughly hoisted the fallen man to his feet. Others in the crowd surged forward to help drag the man to the police car. They shoved him into the back seat. The old man followed. The high sheriff and his deputy climbed into the front seat and drove away.

The crowd milled around, letting their own surge of adrenaline burn away. The Asians were the first to leave. They had done their duty by watching. They were ready to get back to work in the comfort of their warm lab. The women returned to the Lodge. There were calls to make. The Norse Men surrounded their leader, peppering him with pats and congratulations.

Frank stayed back in the crowd as much as he could. He followed Chet to his truck and climbed in the back. The other workers followed him. Alton got in the front seat and dug out the bottle of Jim. They drove back to their worksite. Frank was careful not to look in Finris' direction. He had felt the connection when Finris had seen him. Frank was glad to be leaving. There was never any reason to tempt fate.

25

Jeff Maurer escorted his wife to her OB-GYN appointment. He was dressed in blue jeans and a red flannel shirt. His wife was dressed in a black pants suit made for pregnant women. He felt like she had been keeping a secret from him, but he had no idea what it was. He even thought he got odd looks from the staff and her doctor when they were led back. Maybe, he thought, he was just paranoid. He was under a lot of pressure. A lot of pressure. He had thought and prayed on it all night. Taking the money was wrong. He couldn't justify it. It was just wrong. He had decided to tell the high sheriff he was quitting. He could find some other kind of work. Somewhere else.

The nurse checked Cathy's vital signs. She checked her weight again. She rubbed gel on her stomach and waved a cold metal instrument over it. A machine on a far wall chirped and clicked as it printed out its results. She gave Cathy a knowing look. They were both smiling.

What was going on? Maurer was too tired for games.

The doctor came in. He was all smiles. They were all smiling at each other like lunatics just escaped from the asylum. It was starting to really piss him off. The doctor, a cross between Marcus Welby and a middle-aged Dr. Kildare with his white hair and gentle, wrinkled face was nodding.

"How are you today, Cathy?"

"I'm doing fine. I just feel like I am going to bust. I am so huge."

Welby-Kildare grinned. "I am sure you are. It is almost time."

"I can't wait."

"How are you doing, Jeff?"

"Great."

Welby-Kildare looked with fatherly concern. "Really? You seem to be under some stress."

"I'm a police officer. It is a stressful job."

"Getting enough rest?"

"As much as I can get. I'm dealing with it."

"And the pregnancy?"

Jeff took his wife's hand. "Not about that. That is a blessing."

"Glad to hear that. As you have probably suspected, we have been keeping a little secret from you. Isn't that right, Cathy?"

She nodded.

Irrational fear clutched him. "Is there something wrong with the baby?"

"No, nothing like that. This is a good secret. Do you want to tell him, Cathy?"

She nodded. He thought she was glowing. "I am having twins. A boy and a girl."

Cathy paused, holding her breath, watching for his response. Jeff looked around the room to see if it was some kind of joke.

The doctor smiled. "It's true. Both babies are healthy."

"I know we didn't plan on this, honey, but it's God's will."

Jeff leaned in a kissed her on her forehead. "This is incredible."

"I know it will be tough financially, but we can figure it out."

"Don't worry, Cathy. It will all work out. Twins. My God, that is the best news I have ever had."

Jeff and Cathy hugged, ringed by the doctor and his nurse. Jeff felt a sadness begin to grow inside. How could he ever break away from High Sheriff Long and his dirty money now?

After work Frank drove to the Mail Boxes Plus store again. He could tell before he opened his box that there was no package inside. He felt his anger rising. Fucking DC. The stoner had let him down, he thought. He opened the box anyway. There was a note on the store's stationary to come see the clerk. Frank took the note and approached the woman behind the desk. His anger was boiling.

She smiled. Maybe she wanted a carrot or a lump of sugar. "I got something for you, honey. It came in yesterday, but you were in and out so quick I didn't have a chance to tell you. It won't fit in your box."

The first word that came to Frank's mind was 'dumbass.' He hadn't bothered to check to see if there was anything being held for him before leaving. Stupid. His anger evaporated.

"That's why I put the note in there. I hope it's not too important."

"No. It's no big deal. Thanks for holding it for me."

She handed it to him and held it a second longer than necessary. She was giving off some kind of vibe. Frank assumed it was sexual and took the large envelope. It had to weigh three pounds. Frank smiled and went back outside and around the corner where he had parked his truck. If there was some outside surveillance camera, better not to let them see his truck or tag.

He didn't drive home. He drove to the library. He went to an empty study room. He locked the door behind him and opened the envelope. DC had done a good job. He had been very thorough. There were distant photos. They showed the surrounding area. Main roads and forests were evident. Closer in, side roads and streams and homes were all easy to discern. As the photos moved in closer the buildings became more distinct. Frank had no idea how DC had done what he had done. There were close-ups of buildings from different angles. DC had labeled some of the obvious buildings. Barn. Equipment shed. Lodge. Loading bay. Lab. Animal habitats. Small cages (quarantine?). Veterinarian clinic? Housing. Unknown. Several buildings bore the same name. Barracks probably civilian. Barracks armed men. Independent small houses.

Frank smiled. DC had spent a lot of time and skill amassing these satellite photos. He had tried to provide anything and everything Frank might want for his reconnaissance.

Some of the information was useless to Frank and he started a pile for the discards. Frank had a good memory. He studied the buildings for details that might only be visible on one photo, like security cameras. He found none. He searched for a centrally located klaxon horn that might be used to alert the compound that it was under attack. He couldn't find one. The Norse Men were confident. They had every reason to be.

The far outlying buildings were of little initial interest to Frank. These DC had marked as housing for either civilians or Norse Men or both. It didn't concern him. With that many people, there were too many unknowns. He planned to stay as far away from those buildings as possible.

There were very distant buildings and huge barns and sheds that would have no bearing on his plans. They were for the farming portion of the Lodge. He kept only the broadest shots of the areas to study possible routes for entrance and exit.

Frank wanted basically two things. The first was to figure out where Masnick would be locked up. The second was the best way to get in and out of the compound with the least amount of risk. He was glad he hadn't gotten the material yesterday. It had allowed him to look around the compound with unbiased eyes. Now he could close his eyes and see it all again. The scale of the pictures seemed more real. The distances between buildings. The sizes of buildings. The width of the roads. It all took on a new meaning to Frank.

He studied the photos for six hours. He took his discard printouts and put them in the trash can. He took out the white plastic liner bag and tied it off. He left the library and headed home. When he got back, he saw that Alton had dragged his garbage cans down to the curb for pickup. Frank put the white garbage bag inside under some of the other garbage. The lights in the house were out.

He went back into the garage. The side door was unlocked. He left the remaining information in the original envelope in the cab of the truck. He made himself two peanut butter sandwiches and washed them down with water. It was still so bland. It made him feel good. The boring food reduced it to an elemental state of nutrition, not taste. He took dominion over his taste desires. He exercised his will in a tiny way and it made him feel complete.

He took the envelope and locked it in the hidden safe in the back of the trunk. He figured there was nowhere else to leave them where Alton might not stumble on them. He couldn't allow that. That would create new problems.

Frank got out a cigar and went outside with his bucket. He lit the pale brown Connecticut wrapper. He sat on the bucket. He started working it all out again in his head. He would need to go back tomorrow night to scout it out from outside the fenced perimeter. He blew a cloud of smoke. He hoped Masnick was holding up. Couldn't really worry about that too much. It was out of his hands. Tomorrow night he would know more.

Masnick bolted upright. He realized he must have blacked out. Too bad he couldn't stay unconscious a little longer, he thought. The last series of seizures had been the worst. He had honestly thought he had felt his bones cracking during the spasms. He was sore all over. He rose to his feet and retrieved his blanket. He wrapped it around his shoulders.

While he was out, they had brought him water and food in the dog bowls. He was sure it gave Heather a sense of sick pleasure to think that somehow making him behave like a dog was a big deal. It wasn't to Masnick. He was a survivor. He would do whatever was necessary to survive. He scooped a handful of the mashed food up. He sniffed it. He knew Heather liked to hide his drugs in the food, mixing pleasure and pain. He ate away. If it was in the food or water and he didn't consume it, then they would inject him like before. It made no real difference in the end. Eat when you could. Sleep when you could. Reload when you could. The Spartans were soldiers. They knew the drill.

He lifted the bowl of water and drank. He was weak and needed to restore as much of his strength as he could. After his meal, whichever one it was, he leaned back against the wall. He closed his eyes and waited for the seizures to return. As he waited, he planned the things he would do to Heather when he escaped. For the first time in a long while Masnick smiled. She would burn, he promised himself. She would burn very slowly. Her beautiful blonde hair would shrink and crinkle under the heat. Her pale skin would blister and peel in bloody sheets. He would enjoy that. That would be his goal. That was what he would live for.

26

Frank had become so accustomed to the work routine at the Lodge that he was visibly shocked when the guard directed them to turn right instead of left as usual. Both trucks. He tensed when the guard said, "They are waiting for you by the barn. Talk to Andy."

Alton drove along the road toward the area near the Lodge. This could be bad, Frank immediately realized. Very bad. Someone in the crowd must have recognized him or thought they did. That might be why they wanted them at the barn.

Frank immediately started running scenarios in his mind. If the Norse Men were waiting, they would be armed. If they recognized him, they would surround the truck, close off any avenue for escape. Hell, if they were sure it was Frank, they would just hose down the truck with full-metal rounds and bury them all afterward. Why take chances? He doubted Alton was that important to them.

If they were unsure, they would want to see him again up close. Probably want to ask him some questions. Even the Norse Men didn't want to kill a civilian unless they had to or there was some profit in it for them. They would let him exit the truck, trying to separate him from any escape vehicle. That would be stupid. They would close in around him with guns aimed. That would be stupid too, but the Norse Men did not look well-schooled in the arts of war. Moving in close would offer Frank the possibility of seizing a weapon. Shock would slow the others' reactions. Frank could probably kill them all or at least enough to regain control of Alton's truck and escape. Then it would be all fast driving and shooting until he got away or got killed. If he got away, he would come back and rescue Masnick as he planned. If he didn't, well, everyone dies sooner or later.

There were three of them. A Norse Man carrying a shotgun motioned them toward the barn. The other two approached the truck. One of them waved them forward. Their weapons were down. Frank rehearsed his moves in his head. He would take the nearest man's weapon. Two quick taps on the others, then put down the now unarmed Norse Man. Five seconds, tops.

He could take out Alton and his men with another burst. Couple more seconds gone. It would sow chaos and confusion. It would slow down his pursuit. It was the smart thing, but maybe not the right thing. Frank was trying to do the right things when he could. No need to hurt the workers or Alton. They were decent enough guys.

Jump into Alton's truck. Blast through the flimsy guard set up at the entrance. Ten minutes one way to Alton's house for his own truck and the Benelli. Just park up in the yard beside the garage. Gun up and go. Another ten seconds off the clock. Maybe torch the garage to cover his DNA.

The Norse Men would be slowed. They would have to assess the situation. Question Alton. Arm and mobilize. Call it in to the bent sheriff's office. They would have to coordinate pursuit. It all took time. They would have to be quick to catch him.

Alton slipped the truck into park and turned the engine off. The key was left in the ignition. Alton approached the two men. The third one was loitering off to the side. The second truck with the other workers pulled in behind them. They kept the engine running, stealing a little more warmth before work.

"You Andy?"

"Yeah."

Frank slipped from the truck. Andy had an AR-15 called a Puma. Frank knew the weapon well. Fast as hell and deadly. Two more steps and it was his. Andy glanced his way and then back to Alton. Bad move. One step.

"What's the problem?"

Frank tensed his body. Any tell from the Norse Men and he would rip Andy's Puma from him and start the ball.

"Freak wind blew in last night. It took a chunk of the roof off the Barn." Andy pointed to a small stack of boards. "Probably rotted." The man noted Frank's approach and nodded a greeting.

Frank nodded back. His muscles went slack. He slumped a little to disguise his size.

"Think you can handle it for us today? We got more spare boards in back."

Alton took off his hat and rubbed his head. "Yeah. Shouldn't be a problem. These boards look pretty good. Might just have been a bad nail job. I might need to cut some spares once we check it out. Shingles look okay."

"Thanks. Finris saw the boards this morning and wanted it done first thing and you know how he gets."

Alton chuckled.

"I do indeed. You fellas go on back to the work site. I don't pay you to sit on your butts. Me and Frank got this." Then, off to the side to Frank, he said, "You okay with heights, right?"

"No problem."

"Good. You assholes get set up where we laid off yesterday. Lay the line and start bush hogging until we get up there."

"Do you want us to start the fence line?"

"Did I tell you to start the fuckin' fence line? If I wanted you to put up fence I would have said put up the damn fence. Just lay the line and clear the brush. Lay the line. Clear the brush."

Frank went inside the barn. He looked around. There were stacks of hay and animal feed along both walls. There were no stalls for animals. The barn was strictly for feed storage. There was a second level accessible by a pair of ladders on each side. Frank could see the hole in the barn roof. It didn't look too bad, but you didn't want water to ruin your feed.

Frank and Alton carried the fallen boards to the side of the barn. They seemed pretty solid. The Norse Men had brought out a half-empty box of tarpaper shingles. One of the Norse Men helped Frank and Alton wrestle a tall ladder up to the outside of the barn's roof. Alton gave Frank a rope that he looped over his shoulder crosswise.

"You got this?"

"Yeah."

"You do know how to do basic carpentry, right?"

"I said I got this, Alton. Chill out."

Frank strapped his tool belt on around his waist. He took a thick slab of shingles and tossed them over the other shoulder. He jostled them around until he got balanced and started up the ladder. He climbed the ladder with the other guys holding it steady. He reached the roofline and stepped onto the roof.

"Drop the rope and I'll hook it to the boards."

"Hold on. Let me take a look at the job first."

Frank chuckled to himself. He had no idea what he was doing. He had learned how to set fence by watching videos, but there was no way to do that now. He walked over to the hole to examine it. He figured that was what a real carpenter would do. It looked like something had just pulled off four boards. Frank knew it could be a test set up by Alton or Finris. He doubted it was. He had felt the wind last night. It was gusting.

He looked around from the advantage of the barn roof. It was a magnificent view. The Lodge was nestled neatly among the trees. It was a good ten degrees hotter on the roof without trees to block the sun. He kept his coat on anyway. Once you committed to a disguise you stayed with it.

Frank dropped the rope and Alton tied it on to the boards. Frank hauled them up and dropped them near the hole. It looked straightforward enough. Reposition the boards. Nail them all into place and then recover the bald spots with new shingles. If he acted confident he should be able to brass his way through. Who was going to bother to come up that rickety-ass ladder to check his work anyway? The repair only had to last for a couple of weeks. By then Frank would be long gone. For once he was living up to his old Spartan nickname. Frank the Hammer was now really the hammer.

He carried the pieces of wood to the hole and started fitting them back into their original place. It was like doing a puzzle with only four pieces. This was going to be easy. That was when it went bad.

Frank heard a crow caw from the trees near the Lodge. He turned to see it and saw Finris leaving the Lodge and marching directly toward the barn. Frank immediately decided that being on the roof and seeing Finris was a good omen. He had a few seconds to compose himself. He had distance from direct contact with Finris.

Finris walked down to where Alton and his Norse Men were standing.

"Good morning, Alton. Did you get to see the fight?"

"Yes, sir. It was incredible. Best fight I ever seen."

"Thank you. I try to put on a good show. He was tough."

"Nigger never had a chance. You were just carrying him for the crowd. I could see that straight up."

Finris laughed and touched his swollen bruised face. "I'm glad one of us wasn't worried. I appreciate you fixing my little problem up there."

"Glad to help. Do anything for you boys. You know that."

"I do and I appreciate it. Is that your cousin up there?" Finris asked, looking up at a kneeling Frank.

"That's Jack."

"Hey, Jack," Finris shouted. "Did you like the fight?"

Frank kept his head down as if he hadn't heard. He continued hammering.

"Hey, Jack."

Frank ignored him. Finris put two thick fingers in his mouth and blew a long shrill whistle. There was no way Frank didn't hear that. He looked around and then down to where Alton and Finris stood.

"Did you like the fight?"

Frank hoped from the distorted angle and his disguise that Finris couldn't tell it was him. He didn't shout a response. He signaled two thumbs up and smiled his well-practiced smile. The great Frank Kane did not smile, people had joked. He was a sour, grim bastard. The new Frank's smile was wide and bright. His new crowns glowed a brilliant white. That sealed any suspicion Finris may have carried. He returned Frank's thumbs up signal. Frank went back to work.

"Your cousin is a talkative fellow," Finris mocked.

"I think you scare him."

Finris slapped Alton on the shoulder so hard and fast that Alton almost fell over. "I scare everyone."

Alton forced a nervous laugh. "I don't want to keep you. We won't be long. I know you got important things to do."

"I do. I need to see a man about a leopard."

Finris strode off, leaving a perplexed Alton in his wake. Frank breathed a sigh of relief. The crow continued to caw in the tree near the Lodge. It might have been laughing at him.

27

Finris reached the quarantine area. The veterinarian was sitting at a large institutional-style metal desk. There were stacks of papers all over it. When he saw Finris he jumped to his feet.

"Good morning, sir."

"Good morning to you as well, doctor. How are the new arrivals doing?"

"Better than expected. The two male tigers are resting comfortably. They have been rehydrated and are starting to eat. Once their lab results are back to normal, I will start adding in the steroids to bulk them up."

"And the cubs?"

"I have them under twenty-four-hour care. They are small, but healthy. I do not foresee any problems with them. Although, anything is possible."

"I understand. And the mother?"

"She is not doing so well. I have instructed the cubs to be kept close to her."

"Why?"

"Maternal instinct among animals is a very powerful force. I hope the sound and smell of her cubs will encourage her to survive."

"Interesting. I am counting on you, doctor."

"I am doing my best."

"I know. If she doesn't make it, you know what to do."

Finris nodded toward a poster on the wall of a full-size male tiger. It was a diagram for traditional Chinese medicine. Thin black lines led to various body parts and the malady each was used to treat, from snake bite to love potions and many others, all at a profit to the Norse Men. The tiger's paws would fetch a thousand dollars each, but an entire pelt could bring in fifty thousand dollars or more.

The cubs could fetch fifteen thousand each normally, but since these were from Europe and reportedly wild born, he might be able to get twenty-five each. Not bad for a cat. All in all, the tigers would fetch upwards of a hundred thousand dollars on the black market. By far tigers were the most profitable big predator. Finris smiled. He had devised a secondary profit tier for the tigers. He arranged canned hunts.

Some men, some very rich men, wanted the experience of taking a fully-grown tiger. The experience, they hoped, would impart some of that lethality to themselves. It made them more alpha than their peers. It provided them with a status symbol the others did not or in most cases could not purchase. The only drawback to hunting tigers, besides the fact that it was illegal in most places, was the time it would take.

That was where Finris had stepped in. For a reasonable fee of one hundred and thirty thousand dollars he could expedite the experience, including a full taxidermy mount or rug, which normally would cost upwards of another ten thousand dollars. He could reduce your hunt to a weekend event. Fly in and enjoy the pleasures of the Lodge. After a full breakfast, suit up and take your tiger the next day in a primitive, natural, yet controlled setting. Then another night to tell stories to the mesmerized whores at the Lodge, then back to Austin, or Chicago, or New York or LA. Your trophy would follow a few weeks later.

There was already a backlog of hunters waiting for the chance to add to their collection or start one or seeking a psychological edge in business. Finris did extensive background checks on potential hunters. Finris was not afraid of a sting operation by the feds. Canned hunts were not illegal in Ohio. What he looked for were relationships that he would be able to exploit at some time in the future. Powerful men knew other powerful men. It was the way the world worked.

A private hunt was scheduled for Saturday. A freshman senator from Texas was flying in early to their small private airstrip. As a married man, and deacon in his church, he had politely declined staying overnight at the Lodge. Finris had told him he understood completely. But Finris understood the nature of temptation. It was one thing to avoid temptation. It was another thing entirely to resist it. Finris was confident there would be some mechanical problem with his plane that would prevent him from leaving on Saturday. A night at the Lodge would also introduce him to Nils, Heather's brother. Nothing forged friendships like whores and too much alcohol and testosterone.

Finris went to the loading area where the leopard was being kept. The cat watched him with suspicious yellow eyes. It sat quietly near the back of the cage watching his approach. Finris knelt outside the cage. The leopard lunged and struck the cage. It retreated and reattacked the cage trying to reach Finris. Finris did not flinch. He removed a cigarette from his vest and lit it while he studied the cat. He liked the leopard. He liked her a lot. She was a survivor. He finished the cigarette and dropped the filter to the floor. He would check tomorrow to be sure it had been swept up by janitorial.

Finris continued out of the quarantine zone to another building. A dozen Asian men were hunched over various beakers and tubes. They looked up at his approach and froze like rabbits confronted by a wolf. Finris walked through their small lab to the holding pens in the rear. Twenty-five North American black bears turned baleful eyes at him from their "crush" cages.

Bear bile had been used for thousands of years in Asia and the illegal demand for it was growing. Public outcry in China had shut down government-operated shops. Although there were many legal pharmaceutical alternatives to the UDC found in bear bile, people wanted the real thing and were willing to pay for it privately while complaining about the method of acquiring it publicly. The bears in these holding pens were lightly sedated and fed through tubes. Their intravenous diet was high in fat to stimulate the liver and gall bladder to provide excess bile.

Twice a day the Asian men would extract forty milliliters of bile. The bile was then dried into a powder that could be mixed with other all-natural ingredients into a capsule. Each capsule required about .5 grams of powder. A kilo of bear bile was worth fifty thousand dollars. Bear bile was an Asian cure all for almost every ailment, a super drug on the traditional Asian market. The demand was insatiable. Business was good.

Exotic animal trafficking was an old business. It was as profitable as the drug business, but without the risks of long jail sentences or felony convictions. The police were much more interested in serious crimes. Animal trafficking was a low priority. High profits, low risks and then mixing in some designer steroids, it was a good business plan. Finris stopped his inspection.

There was something about Alton's cousin that pricked at his memory. He couldn't put his finger on it. It was there. Just a tiny fragment. He had time before Nils arrived. He would go back and have a little talk with him, see if it sparked anything new. It was probably nothing, but it couldn't hurt. Finris trusted his instincts. He turned back toward the storage barn.

The drone of a small plane drew Finris' attention to the sky. Heather's brother was here. Maybe later. Back to work. Finris went to gather some men and meet Nils at the landing strip. Nils was the critical piece of the puzzle and he had to be treated as such.

Frank climbed down from the roof. He helped Alton store the ladder. He tossed the coil of rope into the back of the pickup. He got in the cab and they headed back toward the fence line.

"Did you see that?" Alton asked.

"What?"

"Finris. He was talking to me like friends. Just chatting away."

"Nice."

"It was incredible. Just a couple of swinging dicks having a chat."

"Yeah, while I did all the work."

"Fuck you. I pay you to do the work. I'm the boss. You're the labor force. But Finris, man. That was special. He even knew my name."

"It was pretty cool. He is a scary dude."

"I wasn't even nervous."

Alton's eyes seemed to glaze a little as he replayed the interaction. They drove the rest of the way in silence. It wasn't until they had gotten out of the truck that Frank felt safe.

Nils climbed out of the plane. He was dressed in a blue suit with a restrained red chalk striped tie. The tie was loose, and the top button of his starched white shirt was unbuttoned. The caramel-colored over coat reached to his ankles. He looked like what he was, a rich, powerful executive. He carried a worn leather shoulder bag like Europeans favored.

As the CEO of one of the fastest growing international pharmaceutical companies in the world, Nils was always in a hurry. Always, except here at the Lodge. At the Lodge he could remove his mask and relax. He could be safe from the world. At the Lodge he could indulge himself. He could be the monster he kept hidden from the world's view.

Finris' vehicle was a deep gold-colored Cadillac Escalade. Finris preferred trucks, but appearances must be maintained.

"Nils, my friend."

Finris extended his hand. Nils took it and shook it hard.

"Brother. It is good to be back. I have missed this place."

"And your sister. And me," Finris mocked.

"Of course. That goes without saying."

Finris laughed. "Come, let my men get your bags. We have business, then you can relax."

"Business first, always."

"Always."

"I was informed that you received the new shipment?"

"No problems. We have secured the product and are remixing. The new packaging should be complete and on the road to our supply network by week's end."

"Good. And the natural medicaments?"

"Medicaments. I love that word. Yes, we have the natural medicaments ready to ship. And more is being processed all the time."

"Good."

"Rest easy. The business model is still sound. But I have a special treat for you, Nils. I have a new girl I have saved for you."

Nils perked up at the news. "Really?"

"She is a fiery black girl."

"Young?"

"Are there any other kind? She is young, but not a child. Late teens."

"She is new?"

"I haven't even finished breaking her yet."

"Can I? Can I break her?"

"That is why I stopped after her first taste of the sjambok. I wanted her to fear its kiss, and not to be hardened to it. And I know how you like to discipline the girls."

"You spoil me. Thank you."

113

"As you deserve. The Norse Men would not have made these giant strides without your guidance."

"Fortuitous for us both. My company grows, my influence grows, we all grow richer."

Finris spread his arms. "As men like us deserve."

"Indeed."

Finris' telephone chimed. He checked the caller id. He held up a finger toward Nils.

"Forgive me. I need to take this. Hello. Good news, I hope."

Finris listened without response. At the end of the call he thanked the caller and disconnected.

"I just heard from one of our buyers. He has found another huge stash of ivory at the same auction he was working. All of it grandfathered in. All of it hereditary pass-downs. He has purchased it all at a pittance. It will be here in a few days."

Nils clapped him on the shoulder. "Wonderful. My Chinese buyers cannot get enough ivory. All eyes are on Africa. No one is looking for ivory coming out of the United States. Especially going to Germany."

"Traditional medicine has been a godsend. The elder gods shine on us."

Nils ticked off on his fingers as he spoke. "Market for a rare product. Acquisition of said product. Secure access to appropriate markets."

"The same model we use with the steroids. We create the market and we control the market. Buyers didn't even know they liked the meth kicker until they tried it. Now they won't use anything else. Users call it Werewolf because it changes a man into a beast."

"I find it ironic that even individuals from your law enforcement are using it."

"They are such hypocrites. They see no harm in taking an illegal drug, but they will arrest someone else for taking a different illegal drug."

"They are pigs."

"Everyone is a pig. They eat, and eat, and eat. Their appetites are insatiable."

"Good. The rich feed on the poor. The strong feed on the weak. And it is still the wolf that eats the pig."

28

After work Alton drove Frank back to his house.

"You up for a drink?" Frank asked.

"Every day. Pay day ain't until next Friday. You got some money left?"

"You going to keep me on?"

"Hell, yeah. I like you."

"You work me like you hate me."

"Fuck you. That's business. I'm talking about off the job. You're alright."

"I got a little stashed away I could get at, if you are not planning on firing me any time soon."

"Your job's safe."

"Good. Can't be too careful. I sure would like to get my drink on."

"Sounds good. Get cleaned up and we will roll."

Ten minutes later, after a quick cold-water wash in the sink and a change of clothes, Frank was in the truck. They hit the local McDonald's drive-through. Alton treated to Big Macs and large orders of fries and Pepsis. They ate on the way to The Tavern and finished their dinner in the parking lot. A couple of napkins later they went inside. There was already a small group of serious drinkers. Frank wondered if some of them slept on the floor or something.

They got a couple of beers and went to Alton's booth. There was a black plastic ashtray on it. It was a subtle acknowledgement to Alton's prestige. Frank noticed there were a couple of other smokers who had decided to follow Alton's lead and light up in the bar. No one seemed to notice or care.

Alton drank the first beer in one long gulp. He sighed, burped and ordered a second one. Alton got into talking. He was obviously lonely since his wife had left. Couple that with his personality, that was uninviting at best, and he had no one to talk to that cared to listen. Frank encouraged him with questions while deflecting talk about himself. Alton didn't seem to mind. He talked about high school. He talked about football. He talked about work. He talked about the Norse Men. He talked about fist fights he had seen and been involved with. He talked about women he had chased and women he would like to chase.

It was a good mix of truth and lies. Frank thought his embellishments were fairly reasonable. The more Alton drank the more the memories of what had been became memories of what should have been.

Frank's coat was wadded up between himself and the wall. He deftly pulled a pint of Jack Daniels from the coat's side pocket. Alton's stopped mid-story. His eyes were wet and shiny.

"Damn, son. I like your style. Too bad you didn't bring a couple of cups with you."

Frank reached back into the pocket and removed two Solo cups. He put one in front of Alton and the other in front of himself. He poured Alton's cup half full. He poured only about a shot in his. He knew Alton wouldn't notice. Frank mimed taking a big gulp just in case. Alton took a drink and smiled. He reached out and patted Frank on his arm.

"You are a good planner, Jack. Hell, I wish you were my damn cousin."

"I appreciate that," Frank said and meant it.

The air in the bar seemed to change. Without looking Frank knew that Sallee had come to work. Men sat up a little straighter in their booths. A few hopeful souls brushed thick fingers through their hair. A pretty woman was a powerful force of nature.

Frank could smell her sweet perfume as she approached. It reminded him of warm cotton candy. She set down two beers in front of them. The drops of moisture condensed and ran down the sides.

"We didn't order another round yet," Alton said.

"It's on the house."

"Thanks," Frank said.

Sallee spun around and sat in Frank's lap. She draped a long thin arm over his shoulder. She turned toward Alton.

"Alton, when you going to pay this big boy some money?"

"Payday is every two weeks. You know that. He don't get his check until next Friday."

"You are killing me. I'm not used to being put on the shelf. I may be cheap but I ain't free. Need to wine and dine me a little first."

"You bring that sugar shaker over here, girl. I got money."

"Now, you know better than that. I just got one question for you, Jack."

"What's that?"

"Boxers or briefs?"

Frank paused. "Commando."

"Oh, my God. I might straight up faint." She took a piece of paper out of her pocket and tucked it into Frank's front shirt pocket. "That's my number. You call me as soon as you get enough money to take me out proper. If Alton makes me wait much longer call me anyway and I'll loan you the damn money for the date."

Frank was smiling. He liked the brazen nature of her flirting. It reminded him of his days with the Spartans. A chance glance toward the rest of the bar changed that. James, the worker who was fired, was sitting in a corner booth watching them. He had a sour look on his face. A single beer rested between his big hands. Frank got to his feet in one move, spilling Sallee off his lap.

"Hey."

Frank ignored her. He went straight to where James was sitting.

"Get up."

James looked around.

"I ain't doing nothing. I got as much right to be here as anyone."

"On your feet. You're leaving."

James got to his feet. He took a final drink of beer and sat the bottle back down on the table. Frank had expected him to bring the bottle. A long neck was a good weapon. He took hold of James' jacket and guided him toward the exit like he was the bar's bouncer. Alton and Sallee stood open-mouthed as he marched James outside.

Frank let James go outside first. He held the door open. James stepped out back first. Frank knew a lot about James by his willingness to go first. James wasn't a thug or a criminal. Thugs always made you go first. It gave them an advantage. Thugs would strike you from behind as you passed. They would shove you down and beat you by taking advantage of any weakness you offered.

Frank watched James process the situation. He assumed wrongly that Frank was going to fight him. He would want to get in the first punch. Frank watched it begin. The muscles in James' back tensed as they started to contract. James took a big step forward with his left leg, creating some space between them. He spun with what he felt was surprising speed. Frank saw the windmill punch begin its slow-motion orbit. James was going to use the momentum of the spin to add force and surprise to the punch. He was unbalanced, essentially standing on one leg as he swung his big right fist at Frank.

Frank had time to consider how best to deal with the sucker punch. Most novice fighters threw a big looping right as their first punch. Frank could block the punch. He could slip it. He could step in and absorb it on his shoulder, depleting its force. He could lean back out of its range. Frank ducked it instead. It put him in perfect position to launch a short savage upper cut to James' solar plexus. The solar plexus was the area between the stomach and ribs. The punch forced the air out of James' lungs.

It would have been easy to follow the upper cut with a quick series of punches that would leave James unconscious. But that might bring the cops, and Frank had no desire to hurt James. As James tottered Frank just pushed him over. James sat down with an audible oof. Frank sat down beside him.

He patted James on the shoulder. "Relax. You just got the wind knocked out of you. You're going to be fine."

James nodded, but couldn't speak.

"Try to take deep breaths."

James nodded, but didn't speak.

"Listen. I don't want to have to hurt you. But I will. You can't be coming here anymore. You can't cruise past his house. You can't harass him. It was just business."

"It wasn't right."

"No, it probably wasn't. What can I tell you? Alton is an asshole."

"He owes me a hundred bucks."

"You keep pressing it and it will end bad. He'll put the sheriff on you or his friends in the Norse Men. You will end up under the dirt somewhere. Is that worth a hundred bucks?"

James stared. He almost spoke and then just lowered his head and shook it.

"I guess it ain't."

"Go home. Get another job. Make more money. It's just not worth it."

Both men got to their feet at the same time. James did an odd thing. He shook Frank's hand and went to his truck. Frank watched him go. Straights were odd people. Frank went back inside. He returned to the booth.

"You alright?"

"Fine. Sorry about that. Just had to take care of something."

"I appreciate it. If you hadn't, I would have had to take care of it myself."

"Understood."

"Take a seat. Your free brew is getting warm."

Frank sat down and took a sip. Alton patted his big arm again. Frank took out a pair of cigars out of his pocket. He passed one to Alton. They lit them and started smoking. Sallee returned. For a moment Frank thought she might be going to tell him not to smoke. She didn't.

"Call me next week. We don't have to go out. You can come over to my house. I'll cook you some dinner. I will make you something hot and tasty."

She leaned down and kissed Frank on his mouth. It was a hard kiss of restrained desire.

"I can't wait to get you naked," she whispered loud enough for Alton to hear.

Frank laughed. Alton toasted him with his red Solo cup.

A dozen beers and the bottle of Jack behind them, Alton and Frank headed home. It was nearly midnight. Alton was too drunk to even try to drive. Frank parked the big truck by the road and helped guide Alton into his house. Alton fished his keys out of his pocket but was too drunk to use them. He dropped them on the ground.

"Fuck. Leave them. I'll sleep right here on the porch."

Frank got the keys and after sorting them for a few seconds found the right one to unlock the front door. He guided Alton inside.

The house stunk. There was an underlying musty smell to it. It was unkempt. There were stacks of old dirty dishes piled in the kitchen, the food residue crusted as hard as diamonds. Empty containers of food were piled on the counters. Garbage spilled out of the overfull trash cans. Alton lived like a pig. No wonder his wife ran off with another guy, Frank thought.

The final proof of his alcoholism was everywhere. Empty beer cans and liquor bottles seemed to cover every available surface. Frank felt a twinge of pity for Alton. He was pretty far gone. It was a wonder he could work at all. Wife's leaving must have hit him pretty hard, Frank thought. Never would have guessed the guy would have a broken heart. Didn't seem like the type.

Alton pointed toward the back of the house. Frank half carried him to the back of the house. There was a large bedroom. It had been decorated by a woman. The small delicate touches were on the walls and the nightstands. Frank helped Alton out of his heavy coat and sat him on the bed.

"You're a good man, Jack. That you are. A good fucking man."

Alton smacked his lips like he was thinking about getting another drink.

"You going to be okay, boss?"

Alton waved him away with one hand.

"Never better. I'm fine as wine."

Alton leaned forward to untie his boots and nearly tipped over. Frank caught him before he pitched off the bed. He leaned him upright. Alton started laughing. He kicked until he kicked his boots off. He fell backward onto the unmade bed. Frank watched him to make sure he hadn't died of a heart attack. Alton rewarded him with a snore that sounded like a hippopotamus mating with a walrus. Frank rolled him onto his side, just in case he got sick and threw up.

Frank looked around the bedroom. He figured since he was there he might as well. The wife's clothes still filled the bedroom closet. There were shoes in every shape Frank could imagine. Her jewelry was still spread out in front of her mirror. Women who ran away with other men tended to take their clothes and jewelry with them. Frank had his suspicions.

He wandered through Alton's house, intruding as much as any guest could. When he searched the hall closet his suspicions were confirmed. Most of the stuff was pretty routine, even the old double barrel shotgun. But two items stood out. There was a well-worn woman's coat hanging on a thick metal hanger. Frank knew that people had multiple coats. Its presence didn't necessarily mean anything. He searched the pockets. There was a set of keys in the right front pocket. There were mini versions of loyalty cards attached for easy swiping by merchants. It didn't look good for Alton.

On a peg on the back of the door were half a dozen women's pocketbooks. Frank still had on his winter gloves. He searched the fattest one. He found Alton's wife's wallet with her driver's license inside. Shit, he thought.

Frank knew it all, well maybe not the details, but the story. Alton had killed his wife. They probably had another argument that got out of hand. Words led to blows and either on purpose or by accident, she died. Alton was no rocket scientist, but he wasn't a complete idiot. He knew he was in deep shit.

119

Alton would have gotten rid of the body. Buried it where he thought it would never be found. It could be anywhere. Stupid son of a bitch, Frank thought. Now he had to explain her disappearance. He made up the story about her running off with some Mexican. He probably didn't even know any Mexicans. Damn foreigners, taking our jobs and now our women. They had consoled the old drunk. It was tough. The sheriff had cut him some slack because of his connection to the Norse Men. There hadn't been any investigation, that was evident or he would be in jail. It all just disappeared. It was as if it never happened. Except Alton knew the truth. Now Frank did. He wasn't sure if it would impact his decisions or not.

Frank left everything as he had found it. He checked on Alton one last time. He was sound asleep. It smelled like he had pissed himself. Frank turned off the lights and closed the front door behind him. Let Alton sleep. It was just past midnight. Frank still had things to do.

Frank went to the garage. He put on his camo jacket and the black watch cap. He put the NVG in his pocket, along with the small handgun. He left his cell and wallet locked in the truck. No reason for ID. If they caught him, he was a dead man.

Frank slipped the four-wheeler into neutral. He opened the garage door and pushed it out of the garage. He pressed the ignition and it roared to life. He had thought about taking the four-wheeler in the back of his truck and unloading it closer to the Lodge. But doing so added different risks to his mission. Lot of folks had four-wheelers in the town. The sound should be so familiar that it was unheard. He followed the map in his head. He would go off-road on one of the many rutted tracks. If he had to run, it was better to be nimble off-road. He could go where no truck could.

The trip was nerve-wracking but uneventful. He saw no other cars. He took the route he had planned and drove off to a secluded spot near the Lodge. The rest of the way he would go on foot. No reason to be stupid.

29

Masnick was in between spasms of body-wrenching pain. He had shit himself again. He wondered if Heather's concoction would kill him. He had never known a pain to match it and he had known pain. It was hard to imagine that there was an antidote for the drug. But what did he know? He was a pyromaniac bombmaker. Once they realized he had nothing to tell them they would kill him. Or give him back to Cyrus and Cyrus would kill him. He wished he had something. He would give Frank Kane up if it bought him a few more minutes of life.

He lay there and listened to them come for the girl. There were three men. He heard them call her Mary. It seemed she was still wanting to fight. Too bad. It was going to go hard for her, but a tiny piece of the Spartan inside him was proud of her. He saw her walk pass. She was very pretty and very proud. Too bad. Too damn bad.

They took Mary to one of the bedrooms. Two girls waited for her there. One was named Lexxus and one was named Candy. They acted like this was all normal. They gave her a soft thick robe to wear and fresh silk panties. They showed her where a table had been set for her with food and drink. It was a thick heavy soup and some soft fresh baked bread. Mary wanted to refuse but she was starving.

She ate and tried to engage the girls in conversation about escape. Candy told her not to talk about that. Lexxus whispered that they were being watched and recorded. They told her about the cops in the Norse Men's pocket. They sat and chatted about life at the Lodge. Lexxus talked about her own new bedroom and how great it was compared to the cells. Candy told her not to fight. It wouldn't do any good. Lexxus asked her if she wanted to try the hot shower. Mary refused. Candy persisted. Mary was adamant. That's when the three men came in. The girls quickly got out of the way.

Mary struggled, but the men were too strong. Two of them held her while the third injected her with something. The strength went out of her. She blacked out. When she awoke, she realized someone had showered her while she was unconscious. She also learned she was in hell.

Mary was in the same bedroom where they had whipped her the first time. She was tied standing with her legs spread as before. She was nude except for her new silk panties. Consciousness came to her slowly. She was not alone.

"She is splendid, Finris," Nils said.

"I knew you would appreciate her."

"Are you sure she is secure?" Heather asked.

"Of course."

The three people approached her from her sides. One of them ran a hand over her bottom and up to the wounds on her back. She whimpered. The giant, Finris, leaned in from her left.

"She will learn to obey me."

"Fuck you," Mary snarled.

Finris laughed. "She has spirit."

Heather's face replaced Finris'.

"You will learn to like it here at the Lodge. When he is done, it will be your whole world, Mary. You will dream about coming here and working. It will be the goal that sustains you on the circuit. You will suffer anything just for the chance to come back here and serve."

"Never, you sick bitch. Never."

She felt the hand on her again. It must be the third person. It was a very delicate touch. She could not see his face. But he was close enough behind her that she could smell his cologne. It was a gentle, sweet aroma.

"I will leave you to it," Finris said.

"We will talk in the morning," Heather added.

Mary heard the door close. This might be her only chance to escape.

"Mister. I don't know you, but you got to see this is wrong. You got to help me."

"Nils. My name is Nils."

"Nils. I'm Mary. You got to help me get out of here. These people are crazy."

"Really?"

"Yeah. You don't know the half of it. Untie me and we can figure out a plan."

"How did you get here?"

"They kidnapped me. The sheriff brought me. They drugged me. They tortured me. You saw the wounds on my back."

"I don't know. I don't want to get involved. Maybe I should leave. Someone will find you. Someone is probably looking for you right now."

"No. No one is coming to help me. It has to be you. It has to be now. Help me, please."

"I like it when you say 'please.'"

"I'm begging you, Nils. You have to help me."

"I will help you, Mary. I will help you learn to obey."

She didn't have time to respond before the sjambok struck. The stiff leather hide cut her as cleanly as a knife. She screamed. Nils struck her again. And again. And again. And again. The electric shock of the blows rippled through her entire body. The pain was something from a nightmare. She screamed and screamed and screamed again. She must have blacked out.

When she awoke, she was still tied to the bed frame. She had slumped down slightly but her bonds on her wrists still held her in place. She was gasping for air. She could feel the blood flowing down her back, soaking her panties. Thick rivulets poured down her legs. Others pooled between her legs and dripped out onto the floor. The pain was so intense that she could not speak or even scream.

She consoled herself. She had survived. That was something. Not much, but something. The worst had to be over now. Someone would come and take her down and tend to her wounds.

They didn't want her dead she knew. They wanted her broken. Broken so she could be whored out to other sick men. She promised herself that she would survive to see them get theirs. She tried to think of lyrics to a country song to take her mind off the pain. Something by Rissi Palmer. She was beautiful and black and that girl could sing. She liked her songs, especially "Country Girl". She started to mentally scroll through the lyrics. In her head she sang the song, "It's a pride you feel that makes you walk the walk."

She heard movement in the room. Footsteps approached. She could smell his cologne again. Nils was still there. Why? Hadn't the sadist gotten what he wanted?

Nils didn't speak. He ran his delicate fingers over her ruined back. He pressed on the tears in her flesh and she writhed in pain. The blood that had been congealing flowed anew.

"Leave me alone. Haven't you done enough?"

Nils leaned in close to her ear. "Not yet. Not by a long shot."

She felt him cut her panties away. They fell on the floor. Mary thought she hurt too bad to scream, but when he started raping her from behind she realized she had screams in reserve. Nils raped her until she blacked out again. When she came to, he raped her again.

30

Jake sat quietly in his living room watching television. It was some old movie with Cary Grant. It was pretty good. He especially liked the part where they chased him with the airplane. That was sick. He continued killing time, waiting for the call. It was Friday night, where would Russian thugs go except a strip club? Unless, he reasoned, they had business. He hoped things weren't that far along yet.

His burner phone rang. He answered. The bouncer said the Russians were at the Gold Club. Jake thanked him and said he would bring his money right over. The bouncer agreed there was no better time than the present.

Paying now did two important things. One, it allowed the bouncer to get his money without having second thoughts. If you delayed too long, he might decide to sell you to the Russians in a double-cross. The second was it told him where the Russians were right at the moment.

Jake went downstairs. He had a car, and a used motorcycle he had bought with cash. It was one of the new Harley-Davidsons, the Street 750. It was the first new design by Harley in a long time. They had priced them at a cost that would allow new riders to enjoy the thrill of riding without the huge investment.

The bike was completely blacked out. It looked fast as hell just sitting there. Jake put on his full cover helmet and slipped the key in. He turned the switch and pressed the ignition switch and started the sleek bike. He sat there, enjoying the feel of the big bike for a few seconds, and then took off for the Gold Club.

It was still early for a Friday night and the traffic was light. He parked the bike around the back. He left the helmet strapped to the back. It took a bold man to steal a bike under the nose of the outside security guys. Back here there were no security cameras that he could see. He pulled on a knit cap and pulled the hood up on his sweatshirt. Always disguise yourself, Frank had taught him.

Jake went to the entrance. They charged him ten bucks. He went inside to find his informer. The head bouncer met him three steps in.

"You got my dough?"

"As agreed," Jake said and passed the cash to the man.

The bouncer had the good graces not to count it in front of him. If it was light, he knew Jake would have to pass him on the way out.

"Where are they?"

"They got a private table near the stage. Paid for bottle service and the whole nine yards."

"Thanks."

Jake went in slowly. No one looked his way. All eyes were on the dancers. He spotted the Russians. Yuri was getting a lap dance from a skinny brunette. The other Russian was laughing. He watched them for a few seconds. He went back to the bouncer who had called them.

"Those your boys?"

"Maybe. You happen to see which car they drove?"

"Come with me. I'll check."

He followed the bouncer back to the entrance. They went outside. He nodded to the outside security guy.

"Joe, you see which ride belonged to the big Russians?"

"The assholes?"

"Yeah."

"High-end rental."

Joe pointed to the same car they had driven the night before.

"Thanks," Jake said.

"Hey, bro," the bouncer said. "You got a little something for Joe?"

Jake peeled off two twenties and handed them to the doorman.

"Thanks."

Jake walked over to the car. He knew they were watching him to see what he was going to do. When he was on the side farthest from them, he knelt to tie his shoe. As he bent over, he attached a tracking device by a magnet to the underside of the car. It was so fast and smooth that he knew they never suspected.

Jake went back to the bouncer. "Thanks again. Someone hit my dog. The neighbors said it was a couple of Russian looking dudes, but there's no damage on their car. So maybe they were wrong. Or it's not these guys."

"Sorry, bro. Is the dog alright?"

"He'll be fine. Messed my kid up though. Neighbors said the Russians slowed down and got out of their car then jumped back in and took off. Didn't even check on him."

"Scumbags," Joe said.

"My son had the dog since it was a puppy."

"Fuckers."

"Keep your eyes open if you see any more Russians or guys that look like they might be. I promised myself I would find the bastards and sue their asses off."

"Good luck, bro."

Jake went to his bike and left. The story was simple but good. Who didn't like dogs? The part about suing them told the men he was a straight citizen. A real-world pussy. No one to worry about. End of story. He drove home and put his bike up. The hard part was going to be starting soon. Nothing to do now but wait.

Frank put on the NVG. He had hiked to an area away from the main roads. He cut the fence, folded it back and slipped inside. He folded the fence back into its original shape. He doubted they had outside patrols, but there was no reason to make it too easy for them.

He moved closer to the Lodge. He found a secluded spot and got comfortable. He studied the buildings and the routines. The dogs didn't patrol at night. That was stupid. There were only a few guards stationed at specified posts, as he had expected. Some of them slept. Some of them drank. They looked cold and bored. He changed his position twice to see as much as he could. It was nearly four when he decided to leave. He would be back.

Frank backtracked the way he had come. He rode back to Alton's house. It was still dark inside the house. He parked the four-wheeler inside the garage and changed out of the camo jacket. He unhooked the spark plug as an added precaution against Alton trying to crank it.

He got ready for bed and tried to catch a power nap before Alton got him up for work. At least there was no trouble to worry about at home, he consoled himself.

At three o'clock the strip club must have shut down. He watched the tracker finally start to move on his computer. When it finally stopped, he went back outside to his bike. He geared up like before and followed the coordinates.

The Russians liked to stay up late. He followed the GPS coordinates on his handheld device to a waffle house on Gate City Boulevard. They must have gotten hungry. He parked across the street and waited for their late-night breakfast to end.

Twenty minutes later they were on the road again. He waited twenty more and followed. The car was parked in the driveway of a modest house in Oak Hill Estates. There were lights on inside. Jake rolled by and parked down the street. He gave them another thirty minutes. The car didn't move. They must be home for the night. Jake could have gone in and killed them but that wouldn't solve the problem. Jake went home himself. He had to be at work at five to open the Black Broth. He was going to be a tired puppy tomorrow. Hell, he realized, it was already tomorrow.

Mary came to again when she felt someone releasing her bonds. She was too weak to move. She lay on the plastic-covered floor. Had it always had plastic on it? She couldn't remember. The bed had a sheet of plastic over it as well. The men left her on the floor and started balling up the plastic sheeting. She noticed the red splatter and dried pools of dark blood on it.

She could barely move her head. She looked across the room. Nils was sitting in a leather chair smoking a cigarette. He was completely nude. He was covered with blood. Her blood. The room stank of fresh blood. The stench was overwhelming. The smell almost overpowered her. She gagged and fought down the urge to vomit.

Nils didn't seem to care that the other men knew what he had done. Or even that he was naked. Or that he was soaked in blood. He seemed oblivious. He stared toward a distant wall and thought whatever psychopaths think, she thought. Then he turned his self-satisfied gaze on her. She seemed to shrink under its glare. Then he winked at her.

Something snapped. Some primal rage surged to the surface in Mary. She literally sprang to her feet. She charged at him. She saw the knife he had used to cut away her panties on a small table to his side. She swept it up. She would carve that smile off his face. She sliced at the smile but he raised his arm to block it. The cut sliced open his arm from wrist to elbow.

Nils fell backward in the chair screaming. Then strong hands were on her. She kicked and fought. She would kill them all. Then something heavy punched her and she went out again.

31

Alton had scheduled them to work half of the day on Saturday to catch up. No one wanted to work on Saturday, but everyone wanted to keep their job. No one asked about time and a half for overtime. With Alton there was never overtime. Frank expected Alton would be in a foul mood. Hungover. Tired. Full of bitterness.

He wasn't. He was almost happy. He greeted Frank with a rough slap on the shoulder.

"Damn, last night was fun."

Frank climbed into the cab of the truck. "Yeah, I got a good buzz."

"Nice not to drink alone. Forgot how good it feels to just shoot the shit."

"I hear you, boss."

"And that Sallee. Sweet Lord, that girl is so hot for you I thought she might stick to your leg."

"No explaining taste, I guess."

Alton laughed. He grabbed his crotch like he was fighting getting an erection. "I thought she was going to do you in the bar last night."

"That would have been something. She is something to look at."

"Look at? She is primo trim, Jack. You got to hit that. For all of us that won't get to."

"Soon as I get paid, I will find out if she's all talk or not."

"She ain't all talk from what I hear. But listen, you hit that, you got to tell me about it."

"Sure, boss."

"No, I mean details. Lots of dirty details. I want to know what color her nipples are. And are they big or small? I want to know everything."

"You got it."

Alton swung the big truck into McDonald's for their morning coffee. Frank fished around in his pocket for cash to pay for his.

"Two large coffees," Alton said to the drive-through speaker. He looked over at Frank and smiled. "Yeah, give me a couple of sausage biscuits and a couple of those egg and cheese ones too."

"Will that be all?" this disembodied voice asked.

"Yeah."

"That comes to eight dollars and twenty-three cents."

Alton looked over at Frank. "My treat."

If Frank hadn't been wearing his seat belt he might have fallen out of the truck. Nothing was ever Alton's treat. He fought hard not to let his mouth hang open.

"Thanks, boss."

"Off the job, you can call me AC. My friends do. Because I'm so cool."

They both laughed as they pulled up to get their order.

Masnick lay in his cell exhausted. One of the guards brought him food and water. He was so weak now after the attacks, they didn't even bother to send two guards. The guard stared at him with a smile.

"You look like shit, Spartan."

"Feel like it too."

"What you need is some Werewolf. That shit would fix you up. You would bounce back bigger and better than ever. Put some pep in your step."

"Get me some."

"Shit costs money. That's the moneymaker, baby. We don't give it away."

"Get me out of here and I will give you all the money you want."

The man laughed. "Money wouldn't be no good to me dead. And trust me Finris would kill me if I helped you. You just do what they tell you and they will make it quick."

The guard had left. Masnick lay in the darkness. He had listened when they brought the little black girl back early that morning. There was some excitement. He saw her blood-caked body carried past his cell back to her own. He heard one of the guards say she had cut someone with a knife. Someone named Nils. He sounded like a big deal. Maybe he was Finris' boss. Masnick tucked the information away.

The guards stayed in the girl's cell for longer than usual. It sounded like they each took their time raping her. She still had a little fight in her. But not much. After they were through, they taunted her. It sounded like one of them was pissing on her. She was right. Animals.

After they were gone he lay there and listened. When she began to cry, Masnick called out to her.

"Girl. Girl. What's your name?"

The sobbing stopped. He could hear shuffling. Then a quiet voice answered.

"Mary. My name is Mary."

"I'm Keith. Are you going to make it?"

"I don't know. They hurt me real bad. They might have killed me."

"Me too."

"This is a mad house. They want to sell me like some kind of animal. I ain't no whore."

"Doesn't matter to them. They want to try to turn you into one."

"Have to kill me first. What they got you down here for?"

"I'm in law enforcement. I've been investigating what goes on here. They caught me. Is there anything you can tell me that can help us escape?"

There was a long pause. "I don't think so. It's some kind of lodge. Got a big fence around it and there are guards on the roads. It looks like an armed camp of some kind. They got wild animals in cages. I seen 'em when the sheriff brought me in."

"The sheriff?"

"He's in on it too. Picked me up hitching and brought me here. Said I would be safe. Lying cracker piece of shit. No offense."

"None taken. So, they have local law enforcement in their pocket?"

"Not all of them. I heard one of the girls say the sheriff and one of his deputies, some cat called Buck are up here all the time. Lexxus, she was one of the girls. She told me they got a new deputy, Maurer or Mouser or something like that they want to get up here. He might not be bent yet."

"Wouldn't count on it. Lots of cops are quick to get dirty."

"You got someone who will be out looking for you?"

"I still got members of my team searching. But I don't even know where I am."

"Blackwater, Ohio."

"That's good to know. Rest up. Get your strength back."

"Have you got a plan to get us out of here?"

"I'm working on it, Mary."

Silence settled in again. Masnick had no plan. He had no team. He could barely walk. But Carpenter had told him that knowledge was power. Maybe he would live long enough to use it. He doubted Mary had much time left. It wouldn't take them long to realize sometimes it is better to bury your losses and move on.

Heather was busy checking Nils' arm. She had cleaned the wound and stitched it closed. She had dressed the wound and covered it with a white wrap. Finris sat quietly at his desk watching the brother and sister.

"Fucking little bitch," Heather said.

"She cut me good."

"She will pay for this, I promise. Finris, what do you plan to do about this?"

The giant sighed. "She could still be a good earner. Just got to finish breaking her in."

"I want her dead," Heather hissed. "She cut my brother. She has to be dealt with."

"Still, she does have a certain monetary value."

"Are you kidding me? After what she did to Nils? She is a liability."

Nils shook his sister away. "I'll buy her from you. Name the price."

Finris rose and walked to where Nils was sitting. He eyed him appraisingly. "You should have been more careful with the blade."

"I know. I got careless afterward. I thought she was too weak to be a threat."

Finris smiled. "But you had fun, right?"

Nils stared at him with a look of shock that transformed into a leer. "It was incredible."

"Good. I would hate to think you had no pleasure in this."

"What are you talking about? What are you going to do with her now?" Heather asked.

"I have plans for little miss Mary. It is something I have wanted to try for a very long time."

"What are you going to do?"

"Tonight. I'll show you tonight. It will be fitting punishment for her crime."

Heather spun to see if the answer was satisfactory to her brother. He didn't seem upset so she calmed down. "All right. Tonight."

"Now if you will both excuse me. I have some work I must do. And you need to check on our other guest."

Heather and Nils left together. Finris returned to his desk. He got out his cell phone. A smile inched across his square jaw. He knew exactly what he would do. He had indeed wanted to do it to someone for a long time. His smile grew. It would be an interesting test.

Masnick was regaining a little strength. The image of Heather burning seemed to restore him. He tried to imagine the sounds of her screams. He heard their approach and feigned sleep. The lock clicked and the light came on. Heather had two guards with her. She was careful.

"How is Prometheus today?"

"Dying."

"Yes, you are, I am afraid. There is really very little I can do at this point to save you. The toxins will build and dissipate. Ebb and flow."

"Sounds encouraging."

"Where is Frank Kane?"

"I don't know."

"Are the Spartans rebuilding?"

"I told you no. What more do you want?"

"The truth. For once. Tell me how to contact Frank Kane."

"I don't know how."

"Then I can't help you."

Masnick sighed. He could not tell them what he did not know. At least not yet.

"Don't be so glum. I have brought you a gift. Hold him."

The guards pinned Masnick to the floor. Heather took out a syringe. She tapped the cartridge to shake any air bubbles free. She squirted a little of the liquid into the air. She knelt beside Masnick and inserted it into his hip. She had a delicate touch with a needle, he noticed.

131

The guards released him and stepped back.

"You really think more will make a difference?"

"Of this? Yes. I have given you an antibiotic, tetracycline. It will diminish the effects of the toxins."

"Like an antidote?"

"No. It will just alleviate your symptoms."

"Why would you do that?"

"My dear sweet Prometheus. You have endured so much pain. It is time to remember what it feels like not to hurt. I will come back tomorrow and we will talk again. Bring him a clean blanket. A nice thick one."

Deputy Maurer was driving along where the highway met Norton Street. There was a white panel van parked by the side of the road. It had a flat tire. The engine was running. Maurer pulled over to help. Protect and serve.

The driver got out of the front along with a second man. They looked like good old boys.

"Is there a problem, officer?" the driver asked.

"Just thought you might need some help. I saw the flat."

"No, we got it covered. Got a tow truck on the way."

"I could help you change it if you like. Save you some money."

"No need. The spare's flat too. I been meaning to get it fixed, just never got around to it."

"I know how that is."

The men were a little too agreeable, Maurer thought. Something seemed wrong. The second man kept his right hand in his pocket. Didn't like the look of that. Two hands or none.

"Mind if I take a look in the back?"

"I would rather you didn't," the driver said.

A woman's voice cried out from inside. "Help us."

The two men exchanged looks. More voices joined the first one. Hands beating on the inside of the van.

"Help us."

"I think I am going to need you to open the van for me," Maurer said.

"Can't do that," the driver said. "Finris' orders."

"You guys Norse Men?"

"Pure bred," the driver said. "Do what you got to do, but don't open the back of the van."

The woman's voice called out again, and a second and third voice echoed her cry for help.

"Who's that? What you got back there?"

132

"You open the back, I'm going to have to kill you," the second man said. His gun was out by his waist. Looked like a Glock.

"No need for that kind of talk is there, Deputy Maurer? You know what's what. Sheriff said you were part of the team."

"Is that what he said?"

"Yes, sir. The high sheriff his own damn self."

The tow truck pulled in and two more Norse Men hopped out.

"We got a problem," the tow driver asked.

"No problem. Deputy Maurer was just leaving. Isn't that right?"

Maurer hesitated. He nodded to the men and went back to his car. He heard one of the women call out again. The passenger of the van slapped the side of the van and told her to shut up. Maurer pulled away. Serve and protect. He realized he had sold his soul.

Frank had planned to go to the liquor store and buy some more Jack for Alton, but he decided to take a nap instead. He still had a pint stashed. Just a short nap, he promised himself. Twenty or thirty minutes of sleep to recharge. The power nap turned into three long hours that only ended when Alton started banging on the garage door.

Frank got up when Alton barged on in. There was no working lock on the side door.

"What the fuck you doing in here, Jack?"

"I was sleeping."

"Not as young as you used to be."

"Feel old as hell right now."

"Good. You want to hit another place with me tonight?"

"Can't, AC, money is almost gone. I better lay low tonight. We'll tear it up next Friday when I get paid."

"Your loss."

"I hear you, AC."

"Well, I'm going over to Clancey's. Time for a little change of scenery."

Alton likely figured James wouldn't look for him there, Frank thought. Not a bad plan.

"Sounds good. I think I'll crash for a little longer. Who knows, I might show at Clancey's."

"Later, tater."

Alton waddled out of the garage. Frank listened to the big truck engine crank followed by silence. Frank got out his cell and called DC.

"Frank."

"I got another job if you are up to it."

"Sure thing. What do you need?"

"This is a little more complicated. I need you to pull up the blueprints on the main building at the address I gave you. Probably need to check county records."

"They may have built it all themselves."

"But they had to have inspections for electrical and plumbing even if they did most of the work themselves. Bureaucrats have to have their paperwork. Can you handle that?"

"Easy. They always have the cheapest security. They figure who wants what they have, anyway. I will get it printed and mail it to you. Probably won't get it until Monday. Will that be okay?"

"It will be fine. I appreciate it."

"I got your back."

"Thanks."

Frank hung up and decided to call Jenny. There was nothing to report, but it would make her feel good knowing he was alright. She answered on the second ring.

"You okay?"

"Fine. How about you?"

"Everything is fine here. Jake and DC are keeping an eye on everything while you're gone."

"That's good. No trouble?"

Jenny started to fill him in on the football players, but decided against it. He had enough worries.

"No. Just working, studying and hanging out. You know my boring life. You taking care of business where you are?"

"Working on it. Shouldn't be too much longer."

"We miss you."

"I miss you too. Tell Jake hello for me."

"I will. Stay safe."

Frank hung up and then wished he had at least said something first. Maybe a 'you too,' or 'be careful'. He was used to giving orders. He was not used to being polite. He mentally added it to his list of things he had to work on.

Frank sank back onto the sleeping bag. He had to wait for Alton to stumble home. And who knew when that would be. He decided that if Alton wasn't back by midnight, he would just take the truck as close as he could. He could hike in. He only had to have the ATV to get Masnick out fast. There was no telling what kind of shape he would be in. They would be torturing him, that was a given. If the breakout went bad, Frank didn't want to have to fight and carry Masnick at the same time. That would be a dead end for both of them. Once he went in, he would get Masnick out or they would both fall at the Lodge.

32

Jake was watching an action comedy, *Lock, Stock and Two Smoking Barrels*, with Jenny. It was a British movie directed by Guy Ritchie. It was very clever and very funny and the directing was as superb as it was odd. He really liked it. It kept his exhaustion at bay.

Jenny was very quiet. She didn't laugh at the funny parts or cower at the violent parts or even smile at the sweet parts. She was thinking about something she wanted to say to Jake. Jake was smart enough to wait. There was no need to push. People always told you what they wanted to tell you if you let them. It took a while. The movie was down to the last fifteen minutes or so. Jenny cleared her throat.

"Jake, there is something I need to tell you."

He turned the TV off. "What's on your mind?"

"Something that happened to me in Atlanta. I need to tell you about it."

"If you want to. If you don't, you don't have to."

"I want to, and I don't want to at the same time. But if we are going to be honest with each other, I think I have to."

"Alright."

"Just let me tell it all the way through before you ask any questions or say anything. If I stop, I am afraid I won't be able to finish it. Okay?"

"Sure."

Jenny told him about Atlanta. She started with how she was lured there by a boy named Vincent that she thought was her friend. How he had lied to her, drugged her and eventually sold her to an Arab sheikh from Kuwait. That was also where she met Caron and DC. She told him how her grandparents had asked Frank to find her and he did. He rescued her and brought her here. When she finished, she stared at him with her big brown eyes, trying to judge his reaction.

"That's the past."

"But does it change how you feel about me?"

"Why would it?"

"Because I did stupid things and bad things."

"We all do. You made it out the other side. That's all that matters. You just have to get past it."

Jenny slipped in closer. She put her arms around his waist. She put her head on his shoulder.

"You don't think less of me?"

"No."

"Sometimes I have nightmares about it. Sometimes I wonder what happened to all those evil people."

Jake spoke without humor. "They're all dead."

Jenny leaned back searching his face for a hint that he was being sarcastic or flippant or something worse. "How can you say that?"

Jake smiled at her and shrugged.

"Frank was our enforcer. It's not a position like being Sergeant-at-arms for a MC and keeping order among brothers at church. That was a special designation. I promise you, Frank buried them all for what they did. That's what he did. He would have made sure they answered for their crimes. Spartan honor would have demanded it."

"You're wrong. I Google searched it the year after it happened. The Kuwaiti Ambassador died in a car wreck."

Jake just stared at her.

"You don't think Frank had anything to do with that do you? Pretty convenient timing."

"I don't know. I never thought about it."

"I just know if you search for this Vincent dude, you won't find him. He is in the dirt somewhere too."

"Frank would do that for me?"

"Of course. You're family. Feel better or worse?"

"In some ways, yeah. I do feel better."

"Good. Do you want some more Coke?"

Jenny turned up to him. "No. I want you to kiss me like you mean it."

Jake was a reasonable man. He complied.

Finris went to see the leopard. He was drawn to it but was unsure why. Perhaps, he thought it was because she was a warrior and like him confined by the modern world. Or, it could just be that he liked that she was a fighter like him. Maybe because she was so deadly.

He sat outside her cage. She seemed to be asleep. Finris knew she was not. He sat down outside the bars and leaned back against the wall. He heard a noise and turned his head to look back the way he had come. The leopard sprang. Her long claws flashed through the bars trying to reach him. He was beyond her feline grasp. With a snarl she leapt back to the far side of the cage. She crouched there watching him with her dark eyes. Finris lit a cigarette.

Footsteps came down the hallway. A Norse Man was carrying a live chicken. It clucked its distress. The man didn't speak to Finris. He passed the squawking bird to the giant's hands and then backed out. He was obviously unnerved by Finris and the feral leopard.

Finris waited until he was gone. He stood still holding the chicken.

"I brought you something."

The leopard snarled. It was used to food being placed in a pan for it. But it knew prey when it saw it. The old instincts were not that dormant.

There was a latched feeding slot on the cage. The chicken began to squirm in his hands, trying to break free. Finris did not notice. The leopard's eyes darted from the chicken to Finris. The eyes locked on his. Finris unlatched the slot.

"You are a predator. You must earn your dinner from now on."

He pushed the terrified chicken through the slot. It fell to the concrete floor inside and the leopard launched itself from across the cage. The chicken died instantly in a hail of claws and fangs.

The leopard raised its blood-splattered maw toward Finris. Finris latched the opening.

"You're welcome."

Finris checked in front of the cage. His cigarette butt was gone. He smiled. He finished the cigarette he had and placed the butt under the cage. He smiled while the wet sounds of the leopard feeding filled the room.

Masnick was amazed how good it felt not to feel bad. It was phenomenal. The antibiotics had worked like a miracle cure. He was exhausted but the pain was gone. He lay in his cell under his blanket. Even its rough fabric felt exquisite on his skin. He wrapped it tighter against the chill of the cell. He savored the moments of bliss. He knew Heather would be back. He knew the antibiotic would wear off without another dose and the pain would come screaming back.

He tried to use his time to focus on escape. He had learned a lot, but most of it was useless. At least now. He would have to watch for his opportunity. Like all doomed men, he knew it could come. It would be brief, but he had to be ready to seize it when it came. He heard the sound of footsteps and feigned sleep.

Several people were coming. Heavy treads. Men. Work boots and maybe a pair of dress shoes. Softer, but still heavy. But also, the faintest hint of lilac and the click of high heels.

"She has a chip in place?" Finris asked.

"Of course. We do it first thing on arrival."

The steps stopped outside his cell. He held his breath waiting. They moved on to the girl's cell. He heard the click of her lock and then her lights come on.

"You have been naughty, Mary" Finris said.

The girl, roused from her sleep or pain or unconsciousness, moaned.

"Bitch, he is talking to you," Heather snarled.

"Quiet, Heather. Can't you see she is in pain?"

"Fuck you," Mary hissed.

"Nils is very upset with you, as is his sister. You injured him with your attack."

"Good." She turned her head to stare at Nils. "You are a sick fuck. I wish I had cut your pathetic little dick off. I wished I had killed you."

Nils started to respond, but Finris held up a hand to silence him.

"But you did not kill him. One thing is clear to me now. There is no place for you here at the Lodge."

Mary struggled to her feet. She was weaving like she might pass out. "So, go ahead and kill me then. I won't be a whore for you."

"I will not kill you," Finris said. "I am impressed with your spunk. You will have a chance to survive and escape this place."

"Bullshit," Mary said, but there was a flicker of hope in her voice.

"It's true."

"What do I have to do?"

"I will show you. Bring her. Be sure to secure her hands. She still has a lot of fight in her. Let her keep the blanket. It's cold tonight."

Masnick lay quietly wondering what they had in store for Mary. There was no way they would let her go. They couldn't. The Spartans would have just shot her. There was something in Finris' voice that he couldn't describe. It was like a secret clue to a complicated puzzle that only Finris knew. It didn't really matter. They would never let her go. She was dead. She just didn't know it yet. He hoped it was a good death. She had earned that much.

33

Jenny finally broke from their kisses. Her lips were still on fire. She stood up and took his hand. She led him upstairs to her bedroom. She sat him on the bed. She stepped back still staring intently at him.

"Will you stay tonight?"

"Of course, if you want me to."

"Get into bed while I change.'

Jake removed his shoes and lay back on the bed.

"Not tonight. You can take off your clothes if you like."

Jake was confused with what had overcome Jenny. "Are you sure?"

"Yes. I don't want you wearing your clothes tonight."

Jake pulled his shirt off.

"You don't have the same tattoos as Frank," Jenny said. She turned his arm over, there was no lambda scar on his forearm. "Or the Spartan scar."

"Frank decided it was unwise to mark me. He thought I would be more effective like this."

Jenny traced her hand over his firm chest. Jenny sighed.

"I will be right back."

As soon as she was gone, Jake removed his ankle holster and slipped his pistol under the bed. He took off his pants and hung them over a chair so his stuff wouldn't fall out onto the floor. He looked at his boxers. He was glad he had worn something dignified and not his Scooby-Doo ones. On or off? He decided to leave them on. They would be easy to remove. He crawled under the covers to wait. Damn, the bed felt good. The pillow was so cool and the covers so warm. He closed his eyes just for a second. He would rest them until she came back.

A few minutes later, the bathroom door opened, and Jenny walked out. She was nervous. This was a big step. She wanted everything to be perfect. She had shaved everything that needed shaving and lotioned all the parts that needed lotion. She had borrowed some super sexy lingerie from Caron. It was hot without being trashy. Luckily, Caron had a lot of lingerie.

She stood in the doorway letting the bathroom light silhouette her. She paused long enough for him to get a good look. She moved to her side of the bed and lit a large candle. It smelled like watermelons. She pulled the covers back. She slipped into the bed and snuggled against him. He lay quietly. Jenny snuggled closer. She could feel the warmth of his skin. It sent tingles through her. Tonight, she would become a woman for real. She was ready.

That was when she heard a faint snore come from Jake. Was he asleep? He had to be playing a joke. She waited for him to make the first move. Nothing.

Weren't men supposed to initiate sex? She did look hot, right? Maybe she should make the first move so he would know what she wanted. Jenny rose up and kissed his cheek. The skin was rough, with a day's growth of stubble. Nothing. She kissed him again. Jake sort of smacked his lips and blew out a puff of air. He was asleep.

Her first instinct was anger. How could he? Who did he think he was? She was embarrassed. Wasn't she good enough for him? Her surprise and outrage started to change into something else. It quickly morphed into a glow that seemed somehow more special. For all her intricate plans and fears, this was life. He was dead tired. She snuggled up against him. The first time was supposed to happen. It would when the time was right.

Frank waited until midnight, but Alton still wasn't back. He took his truck and drove toward the Lodge. He cruised past the guard shack. He drove until he spotted a closed gas station. He pulled into the back lot and parked among a handful of other vehicles waiting to be repaired.

He looked around to be sure there were no cameras or other watchers and left the truck. He locked it and headed back toward the Lodge. He had seen all he needed to see inside the fence. Tonight he would scout the perimeter. He might find a better way in and other options in case he had to get out quick.

Frank doubted they patrolled the perimeter. It would require too much manpower. They trusted in their reputation and the fence. Regular patrols would require coordinating a schedule. He just didn't see the Norse Men going to that much trouble. They had never been assailed in their stronghold. What did they truly have to fear? That was one of the Spartans' weaknesses when the attack had come on their compound in Asheville. They had felt too safe.

He followed a bush road part of the way until it ran out. He continued to work his way through the heavy overgrowth. It was like moving through a jungle. Briars and limbs snatched at you every step of the way. He moved slowly. There was no reason to be careless and he had all night. He used his NVG to navigate the best path. But even its green light seemed to overlook obstacles that sprang up trying to trip Frank. Branches slapped at him, but his heavy clothes protected him. The thick forest was quiet.

Along the western boundary of the Lodge was where the wild animals were caged. He smelled the predators long before he heard them. The air reeked of the stench of urine and feces and long-dead food. The pens were huge, each one at least several acres. Some were a dozen acres. They appeared empty. Frank knew they were not. Sometimes he caught only a fleeting glimpse of a figure moving away. They could smell him too. In the corner of one enclosure a tiger crouched watching him with cold eyes. It made no sound. An old grizzly bear huffed as he passed. Farther along a pack of wolves howled their calls to the night. The largest enclosure held no movement, but he smelled cat. Lions, he thought. A pride would need more space than a solitary animal. He continued clockwise toward the north.

There were more enclosures here. More predators slept or prowled or dreamed of a life without bars. Frank smiled at the imagery. Sort of like he did, he thought. It sounded so sweet. A life without bars. His passage was greeted with the odd growl or movement, but there seemed to be less wildlife here.

Frank knew from DC's pictures that there was a road about three miles on northward. It wasn't a bad option. Numerous dirt tracks connected to it before it hit the interstate. The area was freckled with small farms and houses. It was a possibility. He headed east.

The eastern corner of the Lodge contained the farming area. There were fields and housing used for raising hogs and chickens. Cattle stood in groups like they were not alive. Only their steamy breath proved the lie false. A shallow swamp stretched along the eastern boundary. The water was black and smelled of chemicals. Some natural. Some man-made. He moved carefully now.

The black water hid a mushy muck that clung to his boots. He could barely drag his feet out. There could be no escape through the bog. Of course, that was something to consider. If the Norse Men knew it was impassable it might give him an uncontested route of escape. He tested a few more steps. The swamp was suicide. If they searched that way last, he would still be slogging through the murk when they shot him down. Still, it might serve to send a false trail. If he had time. They would assume he had blundered out the wrong way and circle around to cut him off. The trouble was Frank wasn't sure how clever the Norse Men were. Finris would pursue as well as send men to circle. That's what Frank would do.

Frank paused. Too bad, he thought, there wasn't a way to get rid of Finris first. That would be a major step toward success. Maybe DC could help. Frank was pretty sure Finris lived at the Lodge. Why wouldn't he? If he had a weakness, Frank didn't know what it was. If only there was a way to lure him away from the Lodge and just take him out, but how? And how could he find out? Fuck it. There wasn't enough time. He had to make his move soon or he might have to carry Masnick out in a body bag.

Jeff Maurer knelt in the front of the church. His hands were steepled in front of him. His eyes were closed. His head was bowed. He prayed as hard as he could for guidance. He knew he was headed down the rabbit hole and every day made it that much harder to get back out.

He had been praying for nearly an hour when he heard a side door open. A feeble light shown from the hallway.

"Is someone there?"

Maurer recognized the voice of the local preacher, Reverend Roberts. Maurer had seen him leading prayers at the football games.

"Reverend Roberts, it's me, Deputy Maurer."

"Deputy, what are you doing here? You gave me quite a start."

"I apologize, sir. I just felt the need to talk to God and this seemed like the best place."

"How did you get in?"

"The front door was unlocked."

Roberts shook his head. "Small town life. I keep forgetting to lock it up at night."

"Yes, sir. You should. When I checked the door and found it unlocked, well, it felt like an omen."

"God works in mysterious ways, son."

"I believe that, sir."

"Is something troubling you? Maybe I could help. I am a good listener."

For a split-second Maurer thought about confiding to the minister but decided against it. It was his burden.

"No, sir, Reverend Roberts. Just felt the need. I guess I should have stopped and thought about it a little more before barging in."

"Don't worry about that, son. But God is everywhere. You don't have to be in church to talk with him."

"I know that, sir. I just was passing on the way home and felt the need."

"Well, you are welcome here anytime."

"Thank you, sir."

"I am going to go on back to bed."

"You live at the church?"

"The job doesn't pay much, but the parsonage hooks up to the back. I like to be available when people need me."

"That is great."

"Are you sure there is nothing I can help you with?"

"No, sir. Thank you."

"Well, son, you just lock up on your way out. Just turn the button in the knob and pull it shut. I'm going back to bed."

"Thank you. I won't be much longer I promise."

"Take all the time you need. God will show you the way. Good night."

"Good night, Reverend Roberts."

Reverend Roberts turned off the hall light behind him and went back to his set of rooms at the back of the church. He locked the doors behind him as he went. He thought about what he had just seen. It was very unsettling. The young deputy seemed to be at a moral crossroads. It was very disturbing indeed. He wasn't sure exactly what he should do.

He went to his bedroom and closed the door. He took off his robe and hung it on the back of the bedroom door. He sat down and kicked off his bedroom slippers. He shivered a little. It was cold in the little bedroom. He sighed and picked up his cell phone. He dialed a number. He listened to it ring. Finally, it was answered.

"Yeah."

"High Sheriff Long, I hate to bother you, but I believe you may have a problem with your new deputy."

34

The group consisted of Finris, Heather, Nils, two Norse Men and Mary. Finris led the way. He took the group out through the kennels. Six cages flanked the walls. Each cage held an extremely large pit bull. The zoo animals were not the only ones to get a taste of anabolic steroids. The alpha dog set the tone. When he started to bark, the others joined in. Earl, the chief handler, beat on the alpha's cage with a pipe to quieten it. It didn't do any good. The dogs snarled and snapped, aroused by the smell of the girl.

The group followed Finris outside by the side door. It was after two a.m. Finris felt the less actual witnesses the better. There were two SUVs parked nearby. Finris, Heather and Nils took one. Earl, Mary and the other Norse Man took the second.

The two vehicles went single file and parked. Mary was brought forward. She could barely walk in a straight line. Earl gave her a shove and Finris mentally made a note to discipline him for that later. Finris led the girl to the fence before her. There was a metal gate that was secured with a metal latch and bolt. Above the door was a placard. It read simply: LIONS.

Mary's eyes darted around her. She was still unsure what she should do.

"Mary," Finris said.

She turned to look at him.

"What?"

"Do you believe in a higher being?"

"The fuck you talking about?"

"Do you go to church? Or did you as a little girl?"

"Sure."

"Do you remember the story about Daniel in the lions' den?"

"Sort of."

"It is from the book of Daniel, chapter six if I remember correctly. The king is tricked into condemning his friend Daniel to the lions' den. The next morning the king hurries to see if Daniel is dead or if his god has spared him."

"I remember. Daniel is alive. God sent an angel to close the lions' mouths."

"Exactly. God found Daniel innocent and saved him."

"That's what you are going to do? Throw me to the fucking lions?"

"No. You are going to enter the cage on your own. It is a big enclosure. Twenty acres. The lion pride is somewhere inside. There are six females and a beautiful black-maned male lion from Botswana."

"Bullshit. I'm not going in there."

"Then I will let Nils have you to play with. I can promise it will be drawn out and painful. But if you enter the cage there is a chance you can escape."

"What chance? It is just a matter of time before they kill me too."

"No. At the other end of the cage is another door exactly like this one. There is no lock on it either. At nearly the end of the cage on the eastern side is a feeding pen we use to introduce food to the lions. It too has no lock. The double doors only open inward. There is a holding area behind it but again the double doors that open off it are unlocked. Slip out either way and you are almost free."

"Almost?"

"You have to get to help."

"And your cracker men aren't just going to shoot my black ass?"

"I have given a no fire order for the next ninety minutes. You must be off the property by then."

"What's to stop me if I get out?"

"The night. Mother night is cold and dark. You have no friends, no money, no clothes and you still have to get to help. Hypothermia is as lethal as the lions."

"That's my choice, face the lions or this limp-dicked perverted Nazi motherfucker?"

Nils tensed. Finris smiled. She did have fire.

"Choose."

"You're lying. There's no other way out."

"I am not."

"So, you will beat me, and whore me and kill me, but you don't lie. That's bullshit."

"No. I lie all the time. In fact, I am very good at lying. Just not this time. Choose."

Mary looked from the cage and then back at Nils. She spat on the ground.

"I'll take the lions."

Finris took a knife and slit the zip cuffs off her wrists. Mary wrapped the blanket a little tighter around her shoulders. Finris shook his head and took it from her with a sharp tug.

"Just you as the gods made you. Everything else stays here."

Mary was shaking from the cold. She glared at the big Viking. She slid back the bolt and used both hands to raise the latch. She entered the lions' den. Finris closed the door behind her. He noticed Heather flash a smile at Earl, but he dismissed it. Let them have their secrets.

"Do you really think she has any chance to get out?" Nils asked.

"There is always a chance, no matter how slim."

"We should have just killed her."

"She is a fighter. Let the gods decide her fate. She earned the chance."

"You would risk everything on the whims of your gods?"

"Of course. They determine our fate."

"If she escapes the lions and the compound, what then?"

"Let us see first of all if she does escape, before we burden ourselves with fears that may never come to pass."

Nils shook his head and kicked at the ground like a pouting child. "It's crazy, Finris, to risk so much."

"It is not a small thing. To a warrior honor is everything."

Mary tried to walk out of their view with her head held high like she wasn't afraid. She was. She was terrified. She quaked in the core of her being. She wanted to scream out at her unseen terror. But she did not. As long as there was a chance, she thought. To have chosen Nils was a sure torturous death.

There were woods on either side as far as she could tell. She moved as quietly as she could. Seconds crept into minutes. She would walk and listen and then repeat. She had no idea what she would do if she heard something. Just freeze. The thought made her smile for the first time. She was already freezing.

Her steps took her across the middle of the pen. The grass was tall and unkempt. It rose in a sea three feet tall all around her. A thousand hungry lion eyes watched her every move. She could feel them on her bare skin.

Something stabbed her foot and she stifled a scream. She pulled the briar free. She wanted to scream or cry or give up. She was too tough. She had to go forward if she had any hope to live. And oh, what she would do to them if she survived, she thought.

Near the center of the grass was a man-made pool. Mary could see the lion signs all around, mounds of cat poop and bones, but not her bones, not yet. She moved around the pool's edge and back into the deep grass.

She tried to think of the lyrics to a Miranda Lambert song to take her mind off her situation. In her mind she started singing about 'taking a ride in her little red wagon.' The grass gave way to scrub and then trees. Suddenly she realized she was almost to the other side.

She found the fence, but no door. It had to be here. She was so close. She moved along the fence toward the east. She let her hand trail along the cold metal wire of her cage. In the dim moonlight she could see something that looked like a door. It might just be her desperation tinged imagination she knew. No, it was real. Her fingers told her so. She felt the hinges. She quickly moved to the side with the latch. She was going to make it.

Mary heard movement behind her. There was still time. She found the latch and pulled on it, but it wouldn't give. More movement behind her. The lions were coming. They had heard her or smelled her fear and blood.

She felt around something was keeping the latch from sliding. She reached her hand to the other side and felt for the obstruction. Her heart collapsed. It was a padlock. In desperation, she pulled on the metal loop hoping it would snap open. It didn't.

Mary fell to her knees. The lions found her there. No angel appeared to rescue her. The lions held no mercy.

They stood outside the fence. Finris was watching a portable handheld tracking device.

"How far has she gotten?" Nils asked.

"Almost made it to the other side."

"Fuck. If that bitch escapes, we are screwed."

Finris did not answer. He watched the screen.

Heather drifted closer to Earl. She leaned close and whispered so no one else could hear.

"Did you lock the exit as I asked?"

"Yes, ma'am."

"Good. I knew this is what he had in mind. He has mentioned it many times before. After we leave, come back tonight and remove it. Finris can never know."

"No, ma'am."

"I will not forget this, Earl. You will be rewarded."

"Yes, ma'am."

Heather moved back to Nils and Finris and the other Norse Man.

"She must be almost out."

Finris nodded. Suddenly, the tracker chip started to move erratically. Then it went out. Finris stared at the small screen. He closed the cover and slipped it back into the large pocket on his vest.

"She didn't make it."

"Good," Nils said.

Finris looked from him to his sister. "As long as she had a chance."

"Of course, darling," Heather agreed. "She had her chance, but the gods found her wanting."

"Do you want me to take a detail and retrieve the remains tomorrow?" Earl asked.

"No, leave them. There won't be much left. The pride was hungry. Nature will take care of the rest."

"Yes, sir. Whatever you say."

"Let's get back to the Lodge. It's cold out."

Finris led them back to the cars and they drove back to the Lodge.

35

Frank Kane paused. He heard the lions feeding. It was a stomach-tightening experience. They growled and snapped at each other as they fed. He moved on back the way he had come. He started his trek down the east side. He had found a good spot to leave the ATV. It was secluded but close enough to the road.

Finris lay in bed, sweaty from her passion. She had seemed even more passionate tonight than normal. Sometimes killing did that to a woman. Sometimes it fired something primal at their core. Ignited new sexual flames. Sometimes it did the opposite. It made them cold. They withdrew, realizing the emptiness of life. Understanding how fragile life could be. They would sit with their arms wrapped around their knees trying to hold onto a world that had just changed. Killing no longer touched Finris. He had done too much of it.

Heather lay across his chest. She kissed his nipple.

"What are you thinking about?"

"The senator comes in tomorrow to shoot a tiger. I am just going over my mental check list to make sure everything is ready for him."

"You've done this kind of hunt a hundred times, I'm sure everything will go smoothly."

"The senator could be a powerful ally."

"It will go fine."

"I will make a note of your confidence."

"Is there something else bothering you?"

"The black girl. Mary. She did have a chance, didn't she? You didn't do something to rig it, did you?"

"No, of course not. What could I have done?"

"Locked the cage on the other side."

"That's mean. I didn't lock the cage. Go check it yourself."

Finris stared at the top of her head. He brushed a strand of hair back from her high cheek bone.

"If you made me break my word to that girl, I would be very cross with you. My word is sacred."

"I didn't. I swear."

"Alright. Is your brother satisfied with her punishment?"

"Very."

"Did he choose company for himself tonight?"

"Lexxus. He likes the new ones."

"Good. After the senator leaves tomorrow, I will let him help me break in the new girls that arrived."

"He will like that."

"I know. We need to keep your brother happy. How are things with Masnick?"

"He will break very soon. I am almost there."

"Let me know the moment he does."

"Of course, darling." She kissed his nipple again and nipped at it. "Do you want to play some more?"

"No. I am tired. Tomorrow will be a long day. Go to sleep."

Heather didn't protest. Part of her insatiable appetite was real. Part was not. She had to keep Finris happy, too. She snuggled down beside him and fell asleep.

36

Masnick awoke screaming. He couldn't stop. When the pain had returned, it seemed even more intense than before. He contorted on the cold floor. His muscles spasmed and seemed to rigidly lock into place. Bones burned and twisted, squeezing the last spark of dignity out of him. The pain hurled him around as if it were an invisible monster. Finally, the episode passed.

Masnick stared up at the cell door. Earl stood watching him without emotion. He watched a small smile edge up the corner of his mouth.

"Having fun?"

Masnick tried to speak but could not.

"Might have to gag you. All this noise is scaring the dogs, not to mention the new girls," Earl chuckled.

Masnick rose to all fours. He tried to stand, but his legs wouldn't let him. He raised his head and glared at Earl.

"Tell her I will tell her what she wants."

Earl made a clucking sound with his tongue and teeth. He shook his head. As he turned away Masnick could barely hear his parting words.

"Pussy."

Masnick slumped to the floor. He had to stall for more time. If he didn't give them something, he was a dead man. He had held out as long as he could. He began composing his answers to her questions. He felt the pain slither around inside him. He tried to hold it at bay while he concentrated on his answer.

Masnick had no idea how to find Frank Kane. But she couldn't know that. She had to believe what he told her. He would make her believe. And then she would burn.

Jake woke up to an empty bed. Jenny was gone. For a moment he panicked. He didn't know where he was. Then he realized what had happened. How Jenny had chosen last night for their first time together. And he had fallen asleep. Moron. She would be pissed. And she should be. It was a big, big step for her and he had fucked it up. Her absence from the bed told Jake all he needed to know.

He lay listening for sounds of life in the house. It was silent. He rolled to the side of the bed. He strapped on his ankle holster and got dressed. He tried to figure out his next move. Flowers? Candy? A stuffed animal? What would that say, that she was a child? If he could write poetry he could write her a sonnet. He couldn't write poetry. Maybe a card, he thought. There were lots of cute cards that said you were sorry for all kinds of things. Maybe there was one that said sorry I didn't make love to you last night. Shit.

Jake looked around her room. He could still smell her perfume. It made him smile. He would think of something to make it right. He made the bed and neatened the pillows. He left her bedroom and closed the door behind him. He moved down the stairs. At the bottom, he listened. Nothing. He opened the front door and almost ran into Jenny. She was carrying a box of Krispy Kreme donuts and two of their specialty coffees.

"You're up," she said.

"Yeah. I thought you were gone."

"I was. I went to get coffee and donuts."

"Krispy Kreme?"

"Don't start. They have a drive-through window and your place is always slammed."

"I wasn't complaining."

"Yes, you were. I saw it in your eyes. You were shocked."

Jenny squeezed passed him and carried the donuts and coffees to the kitchen table. She sat the coffees at separate seats. She opened hers and blew on it. The steam wafted up and she inhaled it. She plopped down into the chair and took a sip. Jake sat in the other chair and took a drink of his coffee. He loved coffee.

Jenny opened the box and took out a pink glazed donut and pushed the box toward Jake. He didn't want one, but he took one anyway. Jenny took a small bite of hers and smiled.

"I wasn't shocked about the coffee and donuts."

"Yes, you were."

"I was shocked to see you."

"Why?"

"I thought you had left."

"I had. To get donuts. I live here, dude."

"I meant after last night. I thought you were gone."

Jenny sat the donut down and wiped her mouth with a napkin. "Last night was awesome."

"I don't understand."

"I told you my dark secret and you didn't bolt. That is amazing."

"But I fell asleep. I mean when we went upstairs. I was just so tired..."

Jenny touched his hand.

"At first it pissed me off, but then I realized you weren't just seeing me so you could do me. That is pretty incredible. You are a very special man."

"No, I'm not. You are giving me character that I don't deserve. I was just exhausted. I still want to sleep with you."

"I know. How could you not? I mean you are a guy. But I was stupid to try to plan it out. It will happen when it happens, or it won't."

"If we keep seeing each other it is inevitable."

"I know." She leaned out of her chair and gave him a slightly sugar-coated kiss.

Frank rose early. He backed the truck out of the garage and closed it behind him. The lights in the house were still out. Alton's truck was parked by the curb. At least he had made it home, Frank thought. Frank drove north toward Zaneville. It was time to get the rest of the pieces of his plan in place.

He stopped at a convenience store and bought a copy of the *Zaneville Times* and refilled the gas tank on the truck. He took the paper to a McDonald's outside of town. He ordered a couple of biscuits and a large coffee. He took a table in the back away from everyone else and studied the paper. He knew what he was looking for.

Under the real estate section, he found a list of homes for rent by owner. He had very specific needs. He wrote the names and address of the most likely candidates down on a piece of paper. After he finished his breakfast, he got a to go cup of coffee and left. He tossed the newspaper in the garbage can near the door. He didn't want to forget and have Alton stumble on it in his truck. It might lead to questions that he would prefer to ignore.

The first two houses were busts. One was too close to its neighbors. The second was too close to what appeared to be the owner's own home. The third had possibilities. He called the number on the sign in the yard. The owner agreed to meet him right away.

Frank sipped his coffee and waited. Twenty minutes later the man arrived in a late model Honda Civic. It had mismatched tires on the driver's side and a dent on the bumper that hadn't been repaired. Both were good signs.

The man jumped out and hitched his pants up. He was tall and thin with that wiry strength farmers often had. Frank met him halfway between their vehicles. The man's teeth were bad. His breath was worse.

"I'm Bud Davis."

"James Franklin," Frank lied.

"You interested in renting?"

"Might be. Trying to find work in Zaneville."

"You from around here?"

"No. Out near Cincy. Heard good things about Zaneville."

"It's a nice town. You got family?"

"Yeah. If I find a place the wife and my son are coming down to join me."

"Well, this is a nice house."

Frank nodded. "How many bedrooms?"

"Three, and one-and-a-half baths. She needs a little work, but she's cozy. Already furnished. Be perfect for you and your family."

Frank looked around outside of the house. "I tend to work nights. Is it quiet out here?"

"Like living on another planet. No neighbors for miles. What kind of work did you say you do?"

"I didn't say."

Bud let the answer float for a minute before moving on. "Got a garage and a storage building out back. Water and power are on. Come on inside and have a look."

Frank followed the man inside. The furnishings were an eclectic mix of old and cheap. Frank didn't care. The beds didn't have sheets. There was a shower curtain in the full bath, but no towels. The kitchen was filled with cheap appliances and cheaper cookware. Frank noticed the man was uneasy about the house. Frank mumbled responses as they toured. Finally, it was over and they went outside.

"What do you think?"

"What are you asking?"

Frank had read the ad. He knew the answer.

"$650 a month. Pay on the first."

"Damage deposit?"

"One month's rent."

Frank shook his head. "A little rich for my blood. The house needs a lot of work. Thanks anyway."

Frank extended his hand. Bud didn't take it.

"The rent is negotiable. What were you thinking?"

"I don't know. More around $500. And no damage deposit."

Bud tried to look like he was considering it. He wasn't. Frank knew he wanted the money. More than that, Frank knew he needed the money. Five hundred dollars in the hand was better than a million dollars' worth of maybes. The overgrown yard proved there wasn't that much interest in a rundown house in the middle of nowhere. Frank played along.

"You seem like a good guy. Okay, I'll take it."

"Month to month."

"Sure," Bud said.

They shook hands. Frank pulled five hundred dollars out of his jacket pocket and counted it out for Bud. Bud's hands were almost trembling with anticipation. Bud folded the money and stuck it in his pants pocket. He handed Frank the key.

"I like my privacy. See you on the first."

"Yes, sir." Bud walked to his old car and started to get in. He thought of something and turned back with a final warning to Frank.

"Don't be cooking meth in there."

Frank smiled. Meth head, he thought to himself. Tweaker. Who else thought of such things? "Never crossed my mind."

The answer was good enough for Bud. He drove off. Frank put the key in his pocket and got back into his truck. The plan was starting to come together. He would have to move next week on the Lodge. He started the engine. An omen would be nice, he thought. He waited. Nothing happened. Well, maybe one would before he went in.

37

Heather swabbed off Masnick's elbow with a cotton ball dipped in alcohol. He sank back to the floor. He sounded like a dog panting. Heather lightly brushed his hair back from his forehead. She felt it for fever. She placed delicate fingers on his wrist to monitor his pulse. Masnick trembled under her touch.

"Was that really the antibiotic?"

Heather smiled. "Of course. It will take a little while to work, but it works faster since you already have some in your system."

"Okay. Can I have some water?"

"Of course. Earl, bring me a bottle."

Earl trotted off down the hall. Finris leaned against the doorway watching him. No one spoke. Earl returned and gave the bottle of water to Heather. She unscrewed the cap and approached Masnick. He raised a hand for the bottle, but she stepped past him and poured it into his water dish. She was smiling. Masnick crawled over to the water dish and drank from it like a human dog. Finris snorted.

"Now, Prometheus. You have something you wished to tell me?"

"Yes. Whatever you want to know."

Heather squatted near him. She was amused. "Are the Spartans rebuilding?"

Masnick shook his head.

"No. I would have heard. The Spartans are done."

Heather made no reply, but he saw she was still smiling. She was enjoying herself.

"How do I find Frank Kane?"

"You can't."

"I told you he was just stalling. Let me have him," Finris said.

Heather rose to her feet. She looked saddened.

"Wait. I don't know where he is, but I know how to contact him."

She knelt again. The trace of a smile danced at the corners of her mouth. "That's better. How do I contact him?"

Masnick still gasped for breath, the pain had exhausted him. "We had a private code in case either of us was in real trouble."

"Go on."

"It was simple. You put an ad in the personals in the *New York Times* Sunday paper."

"What is in the ad?"

"In the personals. Put it exactly as I tell you. Man seeking Greek. Alcman and this zip code."

"Then what?"

"Frank will reply with the same message except the name Lycurgus instead of Alcman. That is to prove it is really Frank. Then reply Alcman and the phone number or address."

"That's it?"

"That's it."

"You're are telling me Frank fucking Kane reads the *New York Times*?" Finris asked.

"Only on Sunday. He likes the travel section or something. You can find them in every city. It's an easy drop."

"I don't believe you."

"It's true."

"Today is Sunday. So, you are saying we have to wait to put the ad in and then another week to see if you are telling the truth. Then a couple more weeks. If you are in trouble that's a long time to wait."

"If I have to call in Frank it is a big deal. It is only for emergencies. Really big problems that I can't solve. I can solve most problems myself. It isn't for rapid response. I am not without resources."

Heather looked dubious. Masnick was losing her. He could feel it.

"Are you telling me the truth, Prometheus? I just don't know."

"Yes. It is the truth. We realized it was flawed because of the time. There just wasn't a better way. We modified the code for just that reason right before the Spartans fell."

"Why not just call him on his fucking phone?"

"Frank only used burner phones. The number was always changing. Maybe Cyrus had it every time he changed. I don't know. He got paranoid. Towards the end, Frank was off the grid most of the time."

"Off the fucking grid?"

"You know. After Cyrus took Helen from him, he just changed."

Finris stood up straighter. "You mean to tell me that Cyrus took Frank's woman?"

"Took her for himself. Made her a God. We all called her Aphrodite."

"Cyrus must have had a death wish."

Heather made a show of clearing her voice.

"And what was the new way?"

"We talked about doing it on Craig's List. Under men seeking men. But I don't know if Frank still remembers. It was right before the fall. Try that too."

"Why wouldn't he remember?"

"Frank was never much with technology. He's sort of an idiot with computers."

Finris laughed. Heather smiled.

"We will try both ways. I hope you are telling me the truth, Prometheus."

"I am. I swear it."

"For your sake, I hope you are. We will see what happens, but if we don't hear anything, I am afraid Finris will take you away from me."

"It's the truth."

Heather rose up on her high heels. "If you are playing us, I promise you will know only pain. I will never let you die."

Finris looked at him. "He's lying. He doesn't know anything. This is just a waste of our time."

Heather patted him on one of his massive arms. "Be patient. We have lots of time."

They left Masnick in the cell. The senator would be arriving soon.

Jake was bussing tables at the Black Broth. The employees loved that he shared the work with them. There was nothing he asked them to do that he didn't do. He was gathering up a newspaper when he saw the headline, "Tenth heroin-related death in Greensboro."

Jake sat down and spread the paper. The article detailed the emergence of a new brand of heroin in the city. It was stronger than any heroin ever seen before. Some perverted genius had started cutting it with fentanyl, a potent pain reliever that could repress respiration. The combination was lethal. It multiplied the high. Drug users weren't used to the stronger concoction, so they took too much and died. Most people would hear about it and avoid it. Junkies' minds worked differently. They flooded into the area trying to find it. This new lethal heroin was given the street name Green Apache because of the slightly green color the fentanyl added to it.

The rise in this type of heroin seemed to coincide with the Russians' arrival. It wasn't easy to get your hands on large amounts of fentanyl. It was a carefully controlled narcotic. That might be the link Carpenter needed.

Jake tossed the trash in the garbage can and finished cleaning the tables. He nodded to the remaining baristas and walked to his office. He closed the door and called Carpenter.

"Jake, what can I do for you?"

"Any word on the Russians?"

"Not much. Problem is there are so many damn Russians thugs running around that it is hard to isolate these particular Russians. If you had a little more to give me."

"I think I do. About the time of their arrival there was a huge spike in heroin-related overdoses. It was tied to a new street drug called Green Apache which is heroin mixed with fentanyl."

"Hmm. That is excellent. It should narrow the search significantly. Anything else?"

"No."

"I will call when I have something. You get any more intel let me know."

"Will do. Thanks."

"Hey, that's what friends are for."

Jake disconnected. Friends? Is that what they were, friends? Maybe. But Carpenter would be asking for a favor soon. That's what friends are for.

38

Steve Nobel, the junior Republican senator from Texas, was due to arrive. He ran on a very conservative political platform. Steve was pro-guns, pro border wall, pro-Texas state rights, anti-abortion, anti-federal government, anti-climate change, and anti-immigration. After countless years of Republican RINOs, the people ate it up. Steve had done a stint in Iraq as a Marine and played up his military hardass image every chance he got. He thought a tiger trophy would be the ultimate in machismo. He planned to have it displayed life size in his Texas home without fanfare or media coverage. There would be less questions about its authenticity. Visitors would see the tiger mount. Steve could then decline to answer questions about it, adding to its mythic background.

The twin-engine Cessna touched down on the small airstrip. Finris was waiting in the Escalade. Steve was alone. The pilot got out and helped the senator unload his gear. It consisted of single worn brown duffel and a large pristine rifle case. The senator was dressed in brown slacks, a white shirt, heavy wool sweater and an expensive Burberry winter overcoat.

"Senator, glad you could squeeze us into your busy schedule."

"It was damn hard to do. I told my staff I needed some alone time. Told them I was going up to my cabin and not to disturb me for any reason except an Iranian nuclear launch."

"What about a Russian nuclear launch?"

"Fuck. We are ready for that. I'm not scared of those pencil necks."

"Let me get you to the Lodge where you can get a bite to eat and rest up from your trip. When you are ready, just gear up and have them give me a call."

"I need to be wheels up before dark."

"Not a problem. Did you bring the clothing I requested?"

"Sure did."

"We will get a commemorative photo of you with your kill. It has to look like it was taken on a hunt in the Sundarban area of India."

"Got it all in here," Steve said patting his old duffel. "Do you have a coat I can borrow for the hunt? I promise to take it off for the picture."

"Of course. I will have a number sent up to your room. I want you comfortable when you take your prize."

"Any history on the tiger I need to know about?"

"It is a big male Bengal tiger. It was called Thaak by the locals. He took three people before our trappers captured him and brought him here."

"Thaak. That sounds badass. Sounds like a bullet strike."

"It was a name only used by the locals, so you are free to use it. There is no official history he ever existed. The government does not like to report that tigers ever kill people. It's bad for tourism."

"Hypocrites. You put me in the right spot and I will make the shot."

"With your background, sir, I would expect nothing less. Let me stow your gear and have a word with your pilot, and then we can go."

Finris loaded the gear into the back seat and held the front passenger door for the senator.

"I was told you are a Scotch man. There's a small bottle of twenty-five-year-old Macallan in the front seat. A sip or two might help keep the chill off."

"I am indeed and that is a fine Scotch."

"I like to make sure my guests are well cared for."

Steve climbed into the front seat and immediately went for the bottle. There was a crystal glass beside it and he poured himself two fingers. Finris smiled. He loved temptation. He walked to the plane.

The pilot stood up a little straighter.

"The senator wants to be gone by dark."

"Yes, sir. I will have the plane ready."

"I would prefer you had some unexpected engine problem that forces him to stay over. Nothing too big, just an unavoidable inconvenience."

"Yes, sir."

"Good. I will send someone to bring you to the Lodge to wait at the appropriate time."

"Thank you."

Finris returned to the Escalade and escorted Steve to the warm comfort of the Lodge. Once there, Steve had a couple extra drinks of Scotch. Finris didn't know if it was because he felt celebratory or because he was scared of the hunt. It didn't matter. Finris had the hunt under such strict guidelines that there was no risk.

The senator geared up, camo pants and a tan long sleeve shirt with a hunter's gear vest over the outside. His hunting rifle was in its case. He wore an old pair of hunting boots. Finris approached him with a smile and an open hand.

"Are you ready to take your tiger?"

"Yeah. I'm a little amped up. This will be awesome."

Finris reached down and scratched some dirt up in his hand.

"For effect, Senator." He rubbed some on the vest, then smeared some on Steve's face. He paused and did it again. "We want it to look like it was a long arduous hunt."

"Good thinking."

"Follow me."

Finris led him to the Escalade and they drove to the shooting area. It was a small twenty by twenty foot fenced-in area. The Bengal tiger was secured in a cage that abutted the area. Finris and Steve and Earl entered from the other side. Earl was carrying a large bore shotgun. Steve racked a round into the breach of his hunting rifle. There was sweat on his hands. He was shaking.

"If you prefer, you can take the tiger from outside the enclosure. I just assumed you would want a more authentic experience to relive."

"No, I'm fine. This will be perfect."

The tiger was from a family that could no longer safely keep him in their small home in Florida. He was sick and weak, but Finris had pumped him with a steady supply of hormones until it had grown to nearly mythic proportions. They had acclimated the old cat to the enclosure by feeding him in it for the past week. The tiger expected more food awaited it. This morning Heather had introduced a sedative into its food so that the tiger would be more pliable.

"Take up your position," Finris ordered.

Earl shouldered the shotgun behind Steve just in case.

"Are you set?"

Steve licked his lips and nodded. Finris signaled the Norse Men who had transported the tiger. They opened the connection between its cage and the enclosure. The tiger was so sedated it could barely stand. It banged into the bars of its cage trying to stumble to its next meal.

"Wait until it's clear of the cage. You want a clean kill. Aim for the chest, not the head. We don't want to ruin your trophy."

The tiger finally made it into the enclosure. It saw only men. There was no food. It made a small growl that sounded almost like a cat's meow. It swung its gargantuan head from side to side eyeing the men with bleary red eyes.

Steve squeezed the trigger without even meaning to. The large round punched a neat hole in the tiger's chest and Thaak the faux man-eater of the Sundabar fell dead. Earl kept the shotgun to his shoulder.

Finris took the stick he had carried in and poked the big cat in one of its lifeless eyes. It didn't stir. Finris turned on Steve with a well-practiced smile.

"One shot, Senator. Impressive work. When it turned its head toward us, I thought it was going to attack. You got it just in time."

Steve rose to his feet. He seemed almost stunned.

"And the roar, I could feel it inside. Couldn't you?"

Steve nodded. The adrenaline was burning away. His mind was embellishing the stalk and kill as he stared at the tiger.

"It is huge. No wonder the locals feared it."

"You have avenged those Thaak killed. Their ancestors will rest easier."

"It was a brute. I think it was studying us to attack just like you said."

Earl lowered the shotgun.

"Boys, let's get set up for a photo."

The Norse Men quickly removed one of the walls of the enclosure. Earl went to the back of the Escalade and removed a large picture. It depicted the deep grass and sparse wood of India. Earl positioned it behind the dead tiger. Finris guided Steve to where to sit and how to position himself for the picture. Head up, big smile, gun across his knee, it was a photographer's iconic dream. Finris took the Canon digital camera and took a series of shots including a few that showed the backdrop was a fake. He showed the best one to Steve.

"How do you like it?"

"Wow. I look badass."

"You are badass, Senator. I will have a dozen copies made and sent to you. It will be very professional work."

"Thanks. When can I get my trophy?"

"We will prepare the body and mount it as you described, and have it shipped to your home."

Finris hated losing the skin and head, but the other parts were valuable too and the mounting was figured into the cost of the hunt.

Steve got back to his feet again and slapped Finris on the shoulder. Earl blanched. Finris smiled.

"I will get you back to the Lodge. Get cleaned up Senator, and I will get you back on your plane by late this afternoon."

"That was the most incredible thing I have ever done," Steve said. "A man-eater. I shot a man-eating tiger."

"It is a rare accomplishment in today's world of metrosexual men. The less you talk of it the more knowledge of it will grow. Trust me."

"I do. I can't tell you how much I appreciate it."

"It was my pleasure to work with a true hunter like yourself. You never flinched."

They started back toward the Escalade. Finris took the rifle, and after he was sure it was empty, repacked it for Steve. Finris climbed in and started the engine.

"Listen, I have a favor to ask."

"Sure. We are friends bonded in blood. Whatever I can do for you, Senator."

"I might know a couple of other guys who would like to get in on this kind of thing and take their own tigers. Do you think it could be arranged on the quiet?"

"If you vouch for them, I don't see why not. But we must be discreet."

"You can trust me."

"Very well. We'll talk about it later."

"Man, I am so jazzed up right now. What else do they have in India?"

"Not much, I am afraid, that would be fitting for a senator."

"Leopards. They have leopards, too, don't they?"

Finris held his breath in. "I think you are right."

"Could you set me up with a leopard too sometime?"

"I will see what I can do."

"Thanks, I owe you big time."

39

Frank was sitting on his camp bed in the garage when Alton knocked.

"Come on in."

"What are you doing?"

"Just chilling. Resting up for Monday."

Alton came in carrying two large pizza boxes.

"I brought dinner if you want."

Frank hopped to his feet and took one of the boxes from Alton.

"Thanks, AC. That was nice of you."

"Don't get all misty on me. I figured you might want some company."

"I do. We can sit on the tailgate."

Frank let the tailgate down and Alton took a seat. Frank fished a couple of beers from his cooler and gave one to Alton. Alton tapped cans with him and opened his.

"What kind did you get? I love pizza."

"Got a meat lover's and a triple cheese. I figure we can share."

They ate in silence, only occasionally stopping to grunt their approval. Or to get more beer. When they finished, they went outside and Frank got out the cigars. They sat on the cold pavement and smoked. Then Alton went inside. It made Frank uneasy. Alton was starting to see him as a friend. He knew that when he left it would put Alton in a tricky spot. He would have to think of something to sell it to the Norse Men.

Frank went back to the garage to catch a nap. He wanted to recon again tonight just to be certain his plan could work.

Finris was exercising in the workout room at the Lodge. The workout room was reserved for guests and Finris. He liked to workout at night. He would let his mind go blank as he reviewed the day's challenges. Lifting steel was not rocket science. Normally he liked to work out alone, but tonight Heather had asked to watch. He had decided to indulge her. Her favor was important to Loki. It was important to the Norse Men's future. She then asked him to work out nude. Which he did. Finris was something of a narcissist.

She watched him hungrily. She loved to watch the flow of his muscles.

"Will you give him the leopard to hunt?"

"I don't know."

"Why not? He wants to shoot a leopard."

"We desire what we cannot have."

"Do not patronize me. Why wouldn't you let him shoot it? "

"Because I like the leopard."

"Like it? What are you talking about? It is only a product. You said so yourself."

Finris set the weights down carefully. He smiled.

"I am a complicated man, Heather. How is the senator doing? Are you taking care of him as we discussed?"

Heather moved closer to him. She let her fingers lightly trail over his hard muscles.

"Yes. He didn't even seem to mind that the plane had a problem and he had to overnight. He was so busy retelling the story of the hunt he didn't notice anything else."

"I think the Scotch helped."

"And the girls. They were all enthralled with his lies."

"And?"

"And I slipped some MDMA into his drink. To be sure he has a good time."

"Molly does that. Inhibitions disappear. Did a girl take him to her room?"

"Yes, actually two. He really liked Amber and Shena. They both went with him."

"Shena? Does he know she's got a dick?"

"Transgender, darling. And an excellent addition to our staff. Many clients enjoy specialty services."

"Shena was an easy one to convince to change teams. I think he prefers being a woman."

"Who wouldn't? We are glorious."

She rose up on her high heels and kissed him.

"I think when he discovers her extra charms he might be shocked."

"He is so high on Ecstasy that he either won't notice or won't care. And it makes for better leverage if we need it. A wife can forgive any transgression, an affair, a mistress, even a dalliance with a prostitute, but not with a transgender. She can't forgive him because the public will not. Not ever. It will destroy his career."

"Make sure the footage appears consensual."

"It will be. Later I will have her replaced with another girl. It will all be a sexual haze when he wakes up."

"I will leave it up to your delicate touch."

"Have you ever tried out Shena?"

Finris laughed. "No. Not my thing. How about you?"

Heather smiled. "Once. Just to see what it was like."

"And?"

"I had hoped it would combine the best attributes of a man with the tenderness of a woman. I was wrong. Not my thing either. Will you see the senator off tomorrow before you leave?"

"Yes. Tomorrow is a busy day. I have to get up early on Tuesday to drive to the prison to see Loki. He likes updates every other week and some information can only be exchanged in person."

"He still thinks he leads the Norse Men instead of you."

"He does. I only do his bidding."

"You only do your own bidding, darling. Do you have time for me tonight or should I let you rest up for your trip?'

Finris pulled her into his arms and held her against his heaving chest.

"Let me get a shower and we can go to bed."

"No. Take me now like a man. Covered in sweat and dirt."

Finris didn't hesitate.

Frank returned to the cut he had made in the perimeter fence. He moved closer to the Lodge. He skirted the outer edges of their security. He watched. He waited. The NVG gave him the eyes of a snow leopard waiting in the high Himalayas. He saw everything.

He had grown accustomed to the odd howls and roars in the dark. Predators were about in their cages. He watched the Norse Men. They were still lazy and cold. Frank was ready. He just needed a sign that the time was right.

He heard an owl call in the night. It was just like the night he and Helen had faced the council. She had argued for their lives. The call of an owl in the dark turned the tables their way. Cyrus had pardoned them. Frank knew it could be an omen, but he discarded it. The owl's cry was not a good omen as far as he was concerned. He would keep searching for one.

40

Deputy Maurer was on patrol when the call from dispatch came in.

"Deputy Durham requests your assistance at Bear River Bridge."

"Roger. Did he say why?"

"Negative. Just needed your immediate assistance."

Maurer drove quickly. Bear River Bridge was a small foot bridge over a shallow stream on the southern part of town. It was an isolated area. Maurer ran different scenarios through his mind. Meth? Body? Abandoned car? Missing person? Could be anything.

When he reached the gravel access road he turned off. A couple of miles later he spotted the police cruiser parked by the bridge. No one else was evident. He parked and got out. He hitched his tactical belt up where it had ridden down on his hips. He put on his hat. He scanned the area as he approached Buck. Buck was looking down the hill into the stream.

"What you got, Buck?"

"You will never believe this. You have to see this for yourself."

Maurer hurried up beside him. He followed his gaze to the stream. He didn't see anything.

"What are you talking about? I don't see anything?'

"Look closer. You got to see it?"

"What? What am I looking for?"

"Right there. It's a rat."

That's when Buck sucker punched him. Maurer went down hard. He tried to get to his feet, but Buck hit him twice more to the side of the head. Maurer fell backward. Buck was still on him. He kicked him in the ribs and the force rolled him down into the shallow stream. Maurer came up sputtering and Buck hit him again. Maurer fell back into the stream and his head went under. Water rushed to fill his lungs. He was a dead man.

Buck grabbed him by the collar of his uniform and hauled him out of the stream and up onto the bank. Maurer coughed up water and gasped for breath. Buck knelt beside him.

"That was teaching. If I wanted you dead you would be. Do you hear me?"

Maurer could only nod.

"Word is someone is having a little crisis of conscience. What have you told anyone?"

"Nothing. I haven't told anyone anything."

"Including your preacher? Yeah, someone saw your car at the church late at night. I figured it out pretty quick."

"I didn't tell anyone anything."

"Not even that pretty little wife of yours?"

"Leave her out of this. I didn't tell her. How could I? I'm taking bribes just like the rest of you. I'm no better than you are."

"That's right. You're not. You go turning snitch it will go real bad. Without evidence, we will turn it on you and you will go down for it. Best scenario, you implicate us and then you just lose your job, reputation and do some time."

"I'm no rat."

"You remember that. You don't want to end up like Ben having a heart attack on the job."

"Are you threatening me?"

"No. I'm just letting you know the lay of the land. You fuck with me on this and the Norse Men will hear. They aren't as gentle as I am. They won't just kill you, first they'll gang rape your wife and then cut your kid out of her belly."

Maurer tried to rise, but Buck slammed him back to the ground.

"Whether you like it or not, you are in this up to your eyeballs. We had you when you took that first payoff."

Maurer suppressed his anger. "Does the high sheriff know about this little talk?"

"No. He still likes you. He actually thinks he is helping you out. This is between you and me."

Buck stepped back. Maurer slowly got to his feet. He kept his eyes on Buck in case he tried to hit him again.

"I won't say anything."

"You better not. Now you might want to go home and get changed while your wife is at work."

Maurer's face was starting to swell. His head was throbbing. A thin trickle of blood crept down his cheek. Buck backed up the hill. Maurer heard him start his car and leave. Maurer slumped back to the ground. He was doomed and he knew it.

Buck called High Sheriff Long on his cell phone.

"It's done."

"Do you think it worked?"

"Yeah. He's scared shitless."

"Do you think he's told anyone?"

"No."

"Good. Any more trouble out of him and we end him like Deputy Ben."

"Understood, Sheriff."

Frank was eating with the other workers when Alton ordered them back to work. They all stashed away their trash and took final bites of food. Frank got the heavy auger and went back to work. Alton came up to him as he worked.

"How you holding up, Jack?"

"Fine, boss man."

"Payday is only a few days away and so is Sallee's fine ass."

"I know. It keeps me at it."

"I would hope so. Money or pussy. One or the other should motivate a man."

"I hear that."

Alton patted him on the shoulder as he turned away. "Ask her if you can take pictures."

"Are you kidding?"

"Yeah. Unless she says yes, then take lots. Tomorrow will be a little easier workday. We don't start until nine."

"Why the late start?"

"Finris goes up to see his boss at the prison every other week on Tuesday. Since he ain't here we take things a little easier."

"I bet everyone loves it when the boss is gone."

"Yeah, I think they do. He stays over to take care of business. Doesn't come back until Wednesday lunch."

"Think he's got a woman down there?"

"Probably. He's got primo pussy at the Lodge, but you know the old saying when you have steak every night a hamburger starts to look pretty good."

Frank smiled. It was the omen he had been hoping for. He would go in tomorrow night while Finris was gone.

Jake's burner phone buzzed in his pocket. He took it out and motioned one of the baristas to take his place at the register.

"Jake."

"I've told you not to identify yourself when you answer a phone. Just say hello. Or don't say anything at all and wait for the other party to speak first."

"I'm getting slack in my old age. I knew it was you. Who else could it be?"

"Sounds reasonable. You can never be too cautious."

"Do you have something for me?"

"The information you provided helped immensely. The address of the house and car could be traced back to a Russian we both know. It is logical to assume they are trying to expand their heroin business in Greensboro. The addition of the fentanyl obviously implicates the Chinese since they have the easiest access to high-grade pharmaceuticals. It pointed me in the right direction. It reminds me of how the great white shark hunts. It follows a scent trail. But the interesting part is when it gets close to the source..."

"You are killing me. What did you find out?"

"Life is short, Jacob. Don't be in such a hurry. Very well. Our Russian friends have indeed allied themselves with a triad out of Hong Kong. They call themselves the Black Lotus. Greensboro is their test market. It is large enough without being overly crowded with drugs."

"I thought it was something like that."

"For fancying themselves professionals, their encrypted communications were pathetically easy to penetrate. They have a meeting scheduled to exchange payment for supplies."

"Do you know when and where?"

"Not yet, but soon. Now that I am in, it is simply a matter of monitoring their contacts. I will let you know as soon as I discover something."

"Thanks."

"I assume this is a situation that you wish to resolve alone?"

"Safer that way."

"Agreed. We never talked."

The phone went dead. Jake needed to have a plan, like Frank had always taught him.

Frank had picked the package up from the Mail Boxes Plus store after work. There was an odd note attached from DC. It was a single sheet of paper, blank except for a crude line drawing. It was a wedge with a small stick on the top. Frank studied it for a minute before it became apparent what it was. It was a piece of birthday cake with a candle on top. Frank understood DC was saying that getting the blueprints was a piece of cake. Frank doubted it was true.

Frank spread the blueprints for the Lodge out on the floor of the garage. DC had done a remarkably thorough job. The schematics detailed the construction. There were overlays of water and electric. It confirmed what he had thought.

In the basement area was a series of small rooms with drainage and power. They were too small for storage, but just right for cells. He traced the access areas to the cells. There was a main staircase that led down to it. There was also a connection to the outside through what Frank knew were the kennels. The Norse Men probably thought the dogs added security. The ancient Spartans were famous for their way with dogs. Frank had a way with dogs too.

He leaned back on his bed and worked the plan out in his head. He would have to set a diversion, but he had planned for that. That was why he had brought the mosquito coils. If he was quick and lucky it could work, he thought. Hell, it should work. He couldn't ask for a better situation with Finris gone. A man was a fool to ignore opportunity.

He played with his plan, tweaking the moves he would make. Assessing risks and dangers. He worked up his escape route and then alternatives if they failed.

He knew that once he had Masnick they would be able to figure out how he got in and out, but that wouldn't do them any good. He would be long gone and none of that would lead back to him.

It was what it was.

Now or never.

Victory or death.

41

Finris went to see the leopard, as he had every day since she was brought in. Usually he brought food. This morning he did not. It was five o'clock. No one was around. The quarantine area was dark. The lights had been set on dim to mimic moonlight. Finris approached the cage. He moved quietly but he knew she heard him and smelled him and saw him. She lay in the farthest corner of her cage and did not move as he approached. Finris sat outside the cage.

The leopard had gotten conditioned to his visits and she did not attack the bars or even growl. Her nose searched for the smell of food. There was none.

"They want me to sell you," Finris began.

The leopard waited.

"They say you are like the other predators, only a product. Is that what you are? Are you like the others? Are you broken and weak?"

The leopard watched.

"Logic says they are right. You are nothing to me. A man would pay a great deal of money to kill you. It would bind him tighter to me. It would add to my influence and protection."

The leopard listened.

"It would be a kindness in a way. There is no true life left for you. A life imprisoned in a cage waiting to die is no life. The hunter's life is gone for you. The joy of the hunt, the thrill of the kill, even the pain of failure. All is gone for you now."

The leopard rose to her feet and padded to the side of the cage closest to Finris. She stood before him, then she lay down in the corner closest to him. Finris did not move. He did not reach out to stroke her fur as a man might with a house cat. Finris was not a fool. He leaned back against the wall.

"No. I will not sell you. You are a predator. We are brothers. I will find a way to free you."

The leopard slept. Finris smiled at the leopard. He sat silent as they waited for dawn to arrive.

Jenny went by the Black Broth after class. It was the perfect time. Lunch was over and it was too early for the hipster crowd to show up yet. She looked around for Jake and didn't see him. One of the sullen waifs working there recognized her and went to find him in the back. Jake appeared as if by magic.

"Hi."

"Hi, yourself. What are you doing here?"

"I just wanted to see you for a minute."

"What's going on?"

"Nothing. I just wanted to see you. Is that okay?"

"That's great. I always like to see you. Here, let's take a seat." Jake guided her to an empty table. "Do you want a coffee?"

"Sure."

Jake waved the sullen waif over, who took their order. When she left, Jake told Jenny, "I took your advice. That's Elissa, the new manager."

"Good. You were working too hard."

"Oh, it wasn't that bad, then I got this girlfriend who takes up a lot of my time now and it got to be a problem."

"Is that what I am, your girlfriend?"

"Aren't you?"

"I don't know. You tell me."

"I mean yeah, you're my girlfriend."

Jenny smiled. "I just wanted to hear you say it."

"You are so weird sometimes."

"A girl just likes to know what a guy is thinking."

"I'm crazy about you."

Jenny took his hand. "And I'm crazy about you too."

"I'm glad we got that settled."

The sullen waif returned with their coffees and sat them in front of them. She smiled at Jake and gave Jenny the stink eye.

"What was that about?" Jenny asked.

"What?"

"That look. Is she pissed at me about something?"

"No."

"She wants to do you, is that it? She's jealous."

"No. She doesn't want 'to do' me as you say."

"Yes, she does. That's what that look was. She is after you herself."

"She's not."

"How do you know?"

"She's gay, okay. She's not into guys."

"Oh, my bad. But she gave me a look. I bet if I was gay I would want to do you. Jake the lesbian breaker."

"It's my fault. I told her I liked you and she is afraid you'll break my heart."

"Your heart? What about you breaking my heart?"

"She knows I am a nice guy, so that would never happen."

"So, she thinks I'm some little skank chasing you?"

"Not skank. She thinks you are too young for me. She thinks you are playing with me."

"What a dirty bitch."

"No, she's trying to be nice and look after me. I think it's kind of sweet."

"You're not the one she thinks is a skank."

"I guess we have to prove to her you are not playing with me."

"How do we do that?"

"Don't break my heart."

Jenny leaned over and kissed him. "Never."

"I like the sound of that. Come over for dinner Friday night. I will grill something."

Jenny kissed him again. "Sounds great."

Jake finished his coffee in one gulp. "I better get back to work."

"Me too. And Jake, tell her I'm not a skank."

"I will. I promise."

42

The Ohio State Penitentiary (OSP) is a supermax prison located in Youngstown, Ohio. It houses five hundred inmates including a few facing death row. The level of the prisoners incarcerated range from 5A down to level 1. The Security Threat Group (STG) is constantly being revised and monitored. The higher rated prisoners are segregated and let out of their cells for an hour a day. The lower a prisoner's rating, the more freedom he enjoys within the double perimeter fenced prison. Some level 1 prisoners even have special low-security housing. It was a three-and-a-half-hour drive to the prison from Blackwater via US 22 West.

In most prisons Loki, also known as Robert Riggs, the leader and founder of the Norse Men, would have been seen as a high-profile inmate. He would be classified as a level 5B with limited opportunities to interact with the other inmates in his cell block. But OSP was not most prisons. Through a subtle system of bribes and influence, Loki had been reduced to a level 2 inmate. There was considerable pressure being placed to move him to level one. The only roadblock was he had to have six years or less left on his sentence. He was at eight. But things were in motion.

When Loki had first been convicted, the Norse Men were only a small criminal group. Prison allowed Loki the time to concentrate on building his crew. He was not a visionary. He was a practical man. He borrowed heavily from the principles of the Aryan Brotherhood and the Mafia and the Spartans. He designed his new organization in typical pyramid fashion, with him at the apex followed by his two chief enforcers, who he renamed Finris and Serpent in honor of mythological Loki's own children.

Together these two ancient spawn of Loki brought about the fall of Asgard. The Serpent, which was short for Mitgard Serpent, had killed Thor during Ragnarok. The Finris wolf escaped his bonds and killed one-eyed Odin, the ruler of Asgard. Except for minor details, a shaved head, a short beard, certain tattoos and scars, the Serpent could have been Finris' twin brother. They were both giants of muscle and sinew. Finris had built his body through an obsessive addiction to exercise. The Serpent had built his through the miracle of pharmacy. He was a true believer in the power of steroids. It was his passion for the benefits of steroids that had started Loki down his current path.

Below his twin enforcers, the pyramid spread out into captains then lieutenants and then street warriors. Each reported up the chain only to their immediate superior, thus insulating those farther up the pyramid.

Loki refashioned the Norse Men from meth producers and distributors to cult status. He preached a heady mix of white supremacy and Viking power.

It drew young, powerless converts, who were eventually paroled and started their own chapters. Prison requirements helped prevent infiltration by law enforcement. Loki wanted to remain as far below the radar of government eyes as possible. He was a cautious man. He was powerful, and with power came enemies. Finris was one of the only men he trusted.

One of the regulations for inmates to maintain the lowest levels was not to engage in criminal activity. That included possession of codes and special alphabets for passing information. Loki was a simple man. He liked information passed where it could not be compromised or misinterpreted. He required Finris to make visits every other week to review Norse Men business interests. After their meeting Finris would meet with captains in Pittsburgh who had important business. Captains came from the primary states where the Norse Men were building power: Ohio, Indiana, Kentucky and Pennsylvania.

Finris had taken online courses in law while he did time. He now sported a semi- legitimate law degree from the internet. He had even done part of the work himself. The purpose was to allow for non-monitored interaction with his sole client, Loki.

Finris parked in the lot and locked the Escalade out of habit. He walked up to admissions and registered with the guard. A few minutes later he was taken to his meeting with Loki. The meeting was not recorded or videotaped. It usually lasted just under four hours.

Loki rose as Finris entered. He hugged his enforcer with true emotion.

"It is always good to see you, Finris."

"Thank you. You honor me."

"Your stewardship honors me, brother."

"I am just ensuring that what we have built continues to grow. When you are released you will find a different world waiting for you."

"Things are going well?"

"Yes. I remember when we talked about hundreds of dollars of profit, now we think in terms of hundreds of thousands. We have come a long way with your guidance, Loki."

"It was a chance starting. The Serpent showed me the path without realizing it. His connections led to a world of juicers I never suspected."

"It grows daily as does our influence."

"Because we are wise enough to diversify."

"Not we, but you. I would have been content with the steroid business."

"You misjudge yourself. You would have seen it soon enough. It is just good business."

"And you are the master of it."

"Thank you. How are things at the Lodge?"

176

"All operations are running smoothly."

"And Heather and her brother? They are still an asset?"

"I don't see how they will ever be other than that. We each provide special services for the other. Not just money but safety and acceptance of their particular needs."

Loki laughed. "You are becoming a diplomat."

Finris smiled. "As you taught me."

"And my family?"

"They are well protected, as you ordered."

"Good."

"I do have a question. This business with the Spartans, you are sure it is wise?"

"Not the Spartans. Cyrus. It opens possibilities we don't even see yet. It was a smart move on our part. There is no downside. Has Masnick told you what they wanted?"

"Perhaps. Heather has broken him but we are yet to see if his information is true or not."

"Keep at him."

"Can I ask you something?"

"Sure, anything."

"Why do you think Cyrus wants to find Kane?"

"They say he is a threat to them. They hinted he was a snitch."

"But you don't believe them do you."

"Of course not. Every word they speak is a lie. A man like Frank Kane would never snitch. He has too much honor. He would die first."

"Then why?"

"They are afraid of him. They are afraid he will hunt them."

"Why would he do that?"

"I don't know. But it is only important that they think he might."

"He is only one man."

"As are you, Finris. A man would be a fool not to fear your wrath."

Finris smiled. "I hope he comes to save his friend. I would like a chance at him myself."

"Only as a last resort. Our agreement was that we would let the old Spartans resolve their issues with him."

"Still..."

"I know. You are a warrior. You would love to test yourself against someone you thought worthy."

"I am vain after all."

"As are we all."

They continued their talk in more detail about the growing Norse Men's empire and how best to promote it. Loki was a micromanager. He wanted details. When they were done, they shook hands. Finris left first. The Serpent was outside standing watch.

"Guard him well, brother."

"With my life."

"Paradise at the Lodge awaits you on release."

"Give my regards to the captains when you meet. Tell them everything is secure here."

"I will. Stay safe."

They hugged goodbye and Finris left. He drove the hour drive down I-76 East to Pittsburgh. There was trouble waiting for him there and he was ready.

Tuesday was exactly as Alton had said. The guard at the gate was even missing when they arrived for work. After a long day of putting up fence, Frank had run off to do some errands. He promised Alton that dinner was on him tonight as a way to say thanks for all Alton had done for him. Frank had two key stops, the grocery store and the liquor store. He loaded his supplies into the cooler in the back of the truck.

Frank had seen that Alton had a grill in his backyard. What man didn't? He started it up to let the flames burn off what appeared to be several hundred years of grease and burned fat. There might have even been some mastodon meat still stuck to it. He closed the lid to let the heat build. There was an old grilling scraper hanging from the side that looked like a weapon from the dark ages. Frank used it to scrape off the now burning residue.

He turned the flame down to low. He placed two good sized ribeye steaks on the grill. Frank believed grilling a good steak was a simple three-part process. Yes, you could have your own special seasoning blend or sauce, but basically you got a good cut of meat, cooked it slow with a little olive oil on it, and let it rest before serving so it stayed moist.

He also had gotten some small red potatoes. He didn't want to ask Alton for anything, so he had bought a decent knife at the grocery store, which he used to slice the potatoes into even smaller sections. He laid a piece of aluminum foil on the grill and put the potatoes on it.

He closed the grill and took out a twelve pack of Budweiser. Now he had to wait for Alton. It didn't take long. Alton came lumbering out with a smile as big as his waistline. He offered him a beer before Alton could speak.

"Damn, Jack, I thought you were broke."

"As of today, I am officially busted."

"Do I smell steak?"

"You do, AC. I got potatoes going and at the end I'll put some asparagus spears on it."

"Fuck the vegetables. Meat and potatoes are good enough for me."

"I hear you."

"Let me get some plates and shit from the house. We can eat at the picnic table. It ain't too cold."

Alton hurried into the mess he called a home. He must have been struggling to find anything remotely clean. Frank thought about getting paper plates from his truck but decided to let Alton be engaged. Ten minutes later Alton showed up with a pair of knives and forks and, surprise of surprises, paper plates. He also was carrying a roll of paper towels, the workingman's napkin. He set his load on the picnic table with a well-satisfied smile. It was the small victories that made a man happy.

Alton finished his first beer and reached for another. He paused.

"You don't mind, do you?"

Frank was startled. Alton was being polite. Would wonders never cease? "No, help yourself, AC."

Alton did and they both sat at the table. They talked about work and women and trucks. They sipped the cold beer and waited on the food. When it came off the grill, Alton said all the right things about it. It made Frank feel kind of good.

Alton fished two crumpled twenties out of his pants and gave them to Frank.

"What's this for?"

"Dinner and booze. You are too fucking generous."

"This is on me. Keep your money."

"Nope. Won't hear of it. I pay my way. You keep it. You are a good friend. Don't make me kick your ass over forty bucks, because I will."

Frank took the money and smiled. "Thanks, AC."

Alton reminded him of a lot of the Spartans he had been friends with. He was arrogant, dismissive of women, an alcoholic, a drug user, an asshole, and a murderer, but overall, he was a pretty good guy, Frank decided. He didn't want him to get burned with what he was going to do. He would have to figure out a way to insulate him.

They finished dinner and Alton started to clean up. Frank stopped him.

"No, way, AC. I got this."

Alton nodded. "Have it your way."

Frank scooped up the plates and silver ware and took it into Alton's house. Frank tossed the plates into the garbage. The sink was full of dishes. Frank tossed Alton's silverware into the sink. He slipped his own into his coat pocket. Frank knew he was being paranoid. No one would link him to what was going to happen. There was no way to trace it back to Alton. If they did the odds of them finding his fingerprints was miniscule. But Frank lived by the axiom that you should always cover your trail when you could. Someone was always looking for you. If the Spartans or the cops started looking, they had the advantage of time to shift through everything. He had even read that the Feds were developing technology where they could put in some of the culprit's DNA found at the crime scene and the computers could construct a visual image. It was like a 3D picture of the DNA's owner. It was getting harder and harder to live the outlaw life.

When he returned, Alton was puffing away on a cigarette.

"Let me get us a couple of cigars, AC."

Frank returned with two cigars and the bottle of Jack Daniels he had bought.

"Fuck me," Alton said. "You got style."

"Do it right or don't do it at all. Isn't that what you tell us at work?"

"Yeah, but this ain't work."

"Damn straight."

Frank passed out the cigars and the red Solo cups for the liquor. The next three hours passed quickly. They got into a rhythm with their stories and drinking. All of Frank's stories were lies. Most of Alton's stories were lies. The difference was that Frank knew he was lying. They were having such a good time that Alton didn't even notice when Frank started adding the sleep aid stuff he had bought at the drug store.

Eventually, Frank had to help Alton into his house. He guided him to his bed and left him snoring away fully dressed except for his boots. Frank felt like you needed to have your shoes off or you were just passed out and not sleeping. Frank went back to the garage to get ready.

He put the gear he would need into a small daypack. He put on his camo jacket and the full-face balaclava. At two o'clock he pushed the four-wheeler out of the garage and down to the street. No one was up. No lights were on. It was a work night for those lucky enough to have jobs. He turned the ignition and cranked the engine. It was now or never.

43

Finris met with the captains of the Norse Men. Plans were made and approved. Questions were posed and resolved. Payments were allocated. When their routine business was finished Finris drove to a warehouse where a special situation, a package, waited for him. He parked outside. He wore a hooded coat pulled all the way up as he went inside.

Once he was inside, he removed it and his gloves. Men were waiting for him. They nodded to him as he passed. In the back of the warehouse Mitch Straton and three other Norse Men were waiting. A man was tied to a chair. Mitch extended his hand to Finris who shook it.

"This the rat?"

"Yeah. His name's Carter. He's a fucking snitch."

Carter was tied to a chair. His face was beaten bloody. His shirt and shoes were gone. His body was covered in cuts and bruises.

"I didn't do anything," Carter whined.

"Caught him wearing a wire."

"He confess?"

"We had to ask him nicely, but he told us everything. Snitching for the FBI."

Finris knelt in front of him. "Is that right?"

"I had to. I didn't have a choice. The cops caught me moving heroin. It was my third strike. They were going to put me away for life."

"Heroin? We aren't running heroin are we, Mitch?"

"Little side project Carter got himself into trying to make some extra."

Finris turned back toward Carter. "That wasn't very wise. Heroin draws attention. We are pushing the Werewolf and nothing else."

"I know. I know. You got to believe me. I just wanted to get a little ahead. That's all."

"What did you tell the cops?"

"Nothing. I swear. They wanted to know where I got my H. I told them, but then they wanted more. Wanted me to wear a wire so they could go fishing."

"Not a bad play for a cop. No downside. But it puts us in a precarious situation."

"I know. Just give me a chance. I'll disappear. They'll never find me."

Finris nodded and stood up. "It makes sense. Cut him loose."

Mitch cut the ropes himself. Carter struggled to his feet. He started rubbing his wrists to get the circulation back.

"Thanks. You won't regret this. You will never see me again, I promise."

"I believe you. Mitch, did you bring the tools?"

Mitch went to the corner and got a large duffel bag. He unzipped it and removed two identical axes. He passed one to Finris and stood holding the other one. Carter's eyes darted around nervously.

"What are you guys doing? I thought we had a deal?"

"We do. You wanted a chance. You wanted to disappear. Here's your chance."

"What are you talking about?"

Finris nodded to Mitch, who gave the second axe to Carter.

"The Norse Men are a Viking based group. We take our strength from our Nordic heritage. You must fight for your freedom."

"Fuck that. I'm from Pittsburgh. I ain't a damn Viking."

"You were a Norse Man. Honor that. Fight like a man or by the elder gods I will cut you down where you stand."

Carter looked around the room. He stepped back and tripped over an old-style metal garbage can. He picked up the lid like a shield. He crouched slightly.

"That's the spirit, Carter. Whenever you are ready, we will begin."

Carter gulped air. He knew there was no way out. He swung a savage overhead blow at Finris, who stepped away from the blow. Carter followed up with a back-handed swipe. Finris avoided it. Carter took deep breaths and charged again, swinging the axe toward Finris' exposed side. Finris caught the blow with his own axe and struck Carter with the shaft. Carter fell. He scrambled to his feet, but Finris did not press his advantage. He let the man get to his feet.

"Can you feel them, Carter? The elder gods are watching you. They are judging you. A Norse Man who dies in battle joins his brothers in Valhalla. There he fights and drinks and fucks his days away. All is forgiven to one who dies in battle."

Carter lunged again and slashed a combination down-and-up stroke, trying to catch Finris off guard. Finris was not deceived. He caught the second stroke and once more struck Carter with the shaft of the axe.

Carter was no warrior. He was a criminal. He was a drug addict. He was a cruel, weak, petty man. He was exhausted. A sheen of sweat covered his chest. The blood from his wounds trickled down from his body like a red rain.

Finris stepped in toward him. Carter raised his tin can lid shield, planning his counter strike. Finris' blow cut through the tin like paper and through the arm behind it. Carter screamed as his arm was cut away. He dropped his axe and clutched at his ruined arm. Finris cut his head off with the next blow.

No one spoke. The others stood stunned by what they had witnessed. Finris smiled. He tossed his axe to Mitch.

"Get his other hand. The head and the hands need to be buried someplace secure. Put the body in the river."

Mitch nodded. He stepped up to the body. He used his foot to straighten out the right arm. He cut the hand off. It took three blows. His men gathered up the head and hands and put them in a black plastic bag.

"Thanks, Finris. We got it from here. We got five gallons of Clorox out back. We'll scrub the place clean. They'll never find his head or hands."

Finris smiled. "That's what he wanted."

44

Frank drove the little four-wheeler along his preplanned route. He parked it where he wanted. He saw no one. He didn't try to cover it. He adjusted his NVG and cut his way through the first of the two perimeter fences. He waited. He moved to the second fence and cut the links and he was inside. It was the same place he had entered before, or at least close to it. He moved closer to the Lodge. His plan was more complicated than he liked, but he felt it was necessary. He needed a diversion so he could get out quickly.

Frank worked his way across the grounds. The usual guard spots were empty. They were inside somewhere warm with a cold drink and a hot woman. Frank went slow. He swept around it to be sure no one was out for a smoke or a walk or to take a sudden leak. The grounds were empty.

He made it to the barn. Once inside the door he moved to the closest corner and waited some more. Frank's rule on noise was simple. Move slowly. Move quietly. When you waited, make sure you waited longer than someone would expect you too. Everything was quiet and still. He took the box of mosquito coils out of his pack. Frank made a mound of dry hay and put the mosquito coil in a little cave he scooped out of the hay. At the end of the coil he draped a pack of matches. It would take the coil an hour to burn down to the matches. When the spark reached the matches, they would flame and start the fire. He repeated the process in three other spots. It was better to expect failure and plan for it, than to put all your bets on one coil.

When he had finished the barn, he moved to the machine shed across the connecting road. It was a metal and concrete building, but it was full of flammable liquids. He poured some gas and oil along an interior wall and moved some more cans closer to both hide it and serve as accelerants once the flame popped.

He backtracked to the other side of the yard. An hour seemed like a long time except when you were on hyper alert. He worked his way around the outside of the Lodge to where the kennel should be. It smelled like a kennel. The door was locked from the outside. He had expected it to be. He used his lock picking set to pop the lock. He stayed outside waiting. He needed the timing to be close. He went inside. The dogs were waiting. He could hear their deep throated growls. One barked.

He knew they were scenting him. They were trying to determine if he was a familiar smell. They wanted to know if he was a danger to them, or prey. Dogs were acutely aware of how people felt. Frank wasn't afraid of dogs. He gave off nothing except confidence and calm leadership.

Each dog was housed in its own cage with its name on the outside of it. They were Beta and then a number. The Norse Men didn't even name them. At each cage, he tossed in one of the uncooked steaks he had bought. They weren't rib eyes, but big chunks of flank steak. The dogs all came to the bars and took the food. Until he reached the last cage. The name said it all. Alpha. This dog did not respond to the food. It snarled and crouched. When it lunged for Frank, he did the most unexpected thing. He shot his hand inside the bars and grabbed the dog's leather collar.

Frank jerked the dog's head hard against the bars, pinning it. The big dog struggled, but Frank held it firmly against the bars. It snapped and frothed and writhed. He could feel its enormous strength. Frank held it steady against the bars. He leaned closer and blew his breath into its face. He wanted it to recognize that scent. He wanted the pack to recognize its new leader. They would be loath to track him for the Norse Men.

He held it for nearly ten minutes before it began to whimper. Frank released it. The dog backed away and then came forward to take the steak back into its cage. Frank crept forward for the connecting door.

He took out his silenced pistol. He opened the door slowly. The Kimber was in his coat pocket in case things went sideways. There was an empty hallway before him. The lights were off. He moved out. There was a row of cells on his left. He looked into each as he passed. Women slept inside under thin blankets on cots. It was like the dogs' kennel. There were five of them. Two of the cells were empty. Masnick was in the last one.

Masnick lay on the cold concrete under a thick blanket. He looked like Hell. He was very thin and strangely twisted. His eyes looked sunken into his head. Frank felt the door for a lock. He couldn't find it. Masnick sat up. He didn't look surprised.

"It's me," Frank said.

"I knew you would come," he whispered.

"How do I get this open?"

"Down the hall there must be a control panel. Each cell is electronically locked."

Frank crept silently down the hall. There was a corner. He turned. There was a small office. There was a control panel. The cells were all numbered. Each had a green light on. It was easy to see which one was Masnick's. Frank pressed the button to release the door. He heard it pop from the little office. He went back for Masnick.

Masnick was still sitting on the floor. Frank found the light switch for the cell. He switched his NVG to off and pushed it up on his head. Frank pressed the button. White glare bathed the room.

"About fucking time," Masnick said.

Frank didn't know if he was joking or not.

Masnick pulled the blanket around himself tighter. That's when things went bad.

The basement lights all came on. Frank heard footsteps coming their way. A thin man appeared around the corner. He stared at Frank. He was frozen in place. Frank shot him in the forehead with the .45. The man fell.

Masnick shoved passed him.

"Help me take his clothes."

They quickly stripped the man. As a garment came off, Masnick put it on. The shirt was a little big. The pants too short. It didn't matter. The shoes fit well.

They heard shouts from outside. The fires.

The women watched them leave, a masked giant and a scarecrow.

"Take us with you," one of the women yelled.

"We'll send help," Masnick lied. "I'm a federal agent. Tell them you saw nothing."

Frank didn't answer. There wasn't time to get everyone out. They were on their own.

They went out through the kennel. They crouched in the darkness and Frank put the NVG back on. The way back was clear. They waited. The engine block house exploded. Flames were already climbing up the walls of the barn. People were shouting. All eyes were focused away, as he had planned. Everything was going perfectly. Until it didn't.

Heather rushed outside with everyone else, drawn by the explosion and fire. Norse Men poured out of the Lodge and surrounding buildings like fire ants and headed toward the blaze. Heather followed in a daze, mesmerized by the primeval light show. She froze. The fire was unnatural. Two Norse Men hurried past, but she stopped them.

"Go check around to the kennel. Check on our prisoners."

"But what about the fire?"

"Go secure the prisoners."

"Yes, ma'am."

The two men turned and headed toward the kennel. Heather hesitated and turned back to the house. She grabbed another Norse Man who was coming outside for the show.

"Are you armed?"

"Of course."

"Good. Come with me. Draw your weapon."

The Norse Man had the good sense not to question her. He fell in behind her heels. Heather went to the main entrance to the cells and led them both down. She was turning the corner when she saw Earl's naked foot. The Norse Man raised his gun. They inched around the corner.

Earl was nude and very dead. Heather hurried to Masnick's cell, knowing what she would find. He was gone. She checked the other cells. The women were all there cowering in the back. Heather ran to the control room. She opened the drawer on the cabinet. A few seconds' work on the computer and Masnick's tracking chip sparked to life on the screen.

"Well, I'll be damned," the Norse Man said.

The image was overlaid with a map of the compound. It blinked invitingly. Heather took out a pair of mobile trackers. She gave one to the Norse Man beside her.

"Let's see where our rabbit has run to."

She keyed in the search password. The blue light blinked just ahead. Masnick was just outside the kennel.

Masnick screamed. He fell away from Frank and onto the ground. For a moment Frank thought he had been shot. He rolled and twisted in pain. Frank shoved a stick in his mouth and Masnick chewed on it to keep from screaming again. It was too late.

Two men with pistols out came running around the side of the Lodge. Frank shot them both twice in the chest. One man shouted as he went down. That wasn't good. The way back was too far. Frank turned and headed north toward the animal pens and away from the shouts. He needed distance and darkness.

Outside lights on the Lodge flared to life. Frank didn't look back. Escape depended on speed now. They were into the dark. They were safe. Masnick slumped to the ground.

"What was that?"

"They got some poison shit inside me. It feels like my bones are breaking when it hits."

"Can you make it?"

"Yes."

"Rest for a second and then we run again."

Frank heard a pistol firing, but it was nowhere near them. Probably someone shooting at shadows, he thought. He watched Masnick, trying to gauge his ability to run. He waited a few seconds more to let him rest. Suddenly a dozen flashlights appeared heading in their direction. How was that even possible, Frank wondered. He helped Masnick to his feet.

"We got to go."

Masnick nodded and they took off. Frank glanced back. The flashlights were making a beeline for them from two sides. Frank pushed them faster. He could hear shouts of 'they are over there' and 'we got them cornered'. Frank would have dismissed it except it was true. The noose was closing fast. They hit a fence and stopped. It was heavy wire with reinforced poles. They skirted down to their left, hit a gravel road and the door inside the fence.

Frank knew what it was before he turned his NVG on the sign. The lion's pen. There was no way he was going in there. It was suicide. The lights swung in their direction.

45

Heather stepped outside and saw the two bodies. The Norse Man swung his gun around looking for a target. He was terrified. Fool, she thought, they are trying to escape. They are gone. She looked at the tracker. They were headed north toward the animal pens. She turned to the man.

"Give me your gun."

"What?"

"Give me your gun."

He complied and then added stupidly, "Careful, it's loaded."

Heather burned him with her eyes. She aimed the gun in the air and fired five shots at a second between. She passed the man back his weapon. They waited. Within seconds Norse Men converged on them with their weapons out. When they recognized her they lowered their guns.

"They have taken the prisoner. They have killed your brothers." She handed the tracker to one of the men. "The prisoner has a tracking chip. It blinks blue on the screen. Track them down."

"We'll make the bastards pay," someone said.

"No. I want them alive. Finris will want them alive. Do not kill them unless there are no other options available."

There were murmurs of laughter.

"The man who kills Finris' prize will have to answer to him."

The laughter stopped.

"Spread out. The fence and the animal enclosures block them to the north. They are trapped and don't even know it yet. Hurry."

The group exchanged advice and split into two, each with its own GPS tracking device. Heather watched them go and went inside. Now was the hard part. She had to call Finris and tell him what had happened.

In ancient Greece after the Greeks had fallen and the Romans had risen to power, there was a battle over Sparta. The smaller Spartan army was encamped on a large hill completely surrounded by the Roman army. The Roman watch fires swept out like a sea of fireflies. Surrounded and outnumbered, the Spartan general did what any Spartan would have done. He led his men down into battle. His unassailable logic was that sometimes a bad decision was the best decision you had left.

Frank opened the door to the lion's cage and pushed Masnick inside.

"What are you doing, Frank?"

"No other way out. We hide out in here until they pass by, then we double back. They'll never think to look in here."

"That's because it is fucking insane."

Frank didn't answer, he just moved into the enclosure. He heard someone behind them shout. "They are heading for the lions' cage."

Frank froze. There was no way possible for them to know that. Unless.

"Prometheus. You got any deep cuts while they had you?"

"Fuck. A GPS tracker? You think they hid one on me?"

"I don't know."

"With the pain and shit I have been in and out of it a lot but they never cut on me that I remember."

Frank remembered the suture marks he has seen on Masnick's back.

"How did you hurt your back?"

"Fuck. When I first woke up my back was hurting. I figure they had just manhandled my ass."

"Turn around."

Masnick turned his back toward Frank. Frank took his knife and cut a long slit down the back of the stolen shirt. There was a fresh scar in the middle of Masnick's back. It was a place hard to reach by yourself. Frank could see the scars of two stitches that had been used to close the wound. He felt the scar. Maybe something. Maybe not.

"Find something to bite into."

Masnick picked a stick off the ground and bite into it. Frank sliced the wound open. He could feel Masnick flinch and try to pull away. He dug the tip of the blade through the wound and felt something unnatural. It was hard like plastic. He dug it out as Masnick struggled to remain still. It was small, no longer than the tip of your smallest finger and no thicker than a match book. It was a tracker. Frank put it into his coat pocket.

Masnick was breathing hard.

"What now?"

"We cross the enclosure. I know what's on the other side, we can hook back to my escape route."

"What about the fucking lions? You going to take on a pride with a pistol?"

Frank didn't offer Masnick the other pistol. He didn't trust him to use it at the right time. Frank looked around and found two long branches. He snapped off the limbs to make them straighter.

"No. We're going to use spears."

Frank knew a lot about lions. He had often been called the Spartan Lion. Lions were the only felines to hunt in groups as adults. They were hard to kill because of their size but they also had relatively small hearts and lungs. Which was good news for their prey because they couldn't run long distances. It was bad news for Frank because lions liked to hunt from ambush.

"We go through slow," Frank said. "Back to back. They like to sneak up on you. Hold your spear."

"This isn't a spear. It's a stick."

"Lions don't know that. They have been hunted for centuries by two-legged creatures with pointy sticks."

"And you think that will matter?"

"I think they are genetically wired to be wary of two legs carrying spears. We go through and dump your chip farther in. I doubt they will want to come in and check on it tonight."

"You are fucking crazy."

"Let's go. Stay close and quiet. We might get lucky."

Finris heard his phone. He came fully awake. He checked the time and then answered.

"Yes?"

"There has been a problem at the Lodge."

"What happened?"

"Someone broke Prometheus out."

Finris's mind sorted possibilities.

"Was it an assault?"

"No. They slipped in and got him out of his cell."

That was only possible if someone had knowledge of the Lodge and its workings. That meant it was an inside job. Someone would have to know how valuable an asset Masnick was to risk rescuing him. The most likely suspect was Earl.

"Where is Earl?"

"Dead. Whoever broke Masnick out killed him."

Earl being dead didn't completely rule out his complicity. A partner could have used him and then silenced him. That would have been the smart play.

"Are you tracking Masnick now?"

"Yes."

"Do you know if Masnick has cold weather gear?"

"They took Earl's clothes and Masnick's blanket."

Taking Earl's clothes meant that they hadn't realized Masnick would be nude. If they had known they would have brought him suitable clothing. It could be misdirection, but it served no purpose. Perhaps it wasn't an inside job after all. But who? The answer hit him. Frank Kane.

"Where is Masnick now?"

"We have them cornered along the north fence line near the animal cages."

"I am on my way. Update me if things change. Take them alive if possible."

Finris dressed and left within five minutes. His mind ran scenarios of what he would do with Frank Kane. It had to be him. Who else could pull this off? He drove faster.

46

Frank moved slowly. He was focused on the areas in front of him. He felt Masnick leaning against his back as they walked. He could smell his blood from the cut Frank had opened. That wasn't good. Lions had a keen sense of smell.

There was something odd in the grass in front of him.

"Hold up," Frank whispered.

He knelt and picked it up to examine it. It was small and very brown. It was part of a human foot. Masnick looked over at the object.

"That's a foot."

"Yeah."

"There was a black girl in here. Her name was Mary, she was giving them a hard time. I think she stabbed one of them. I think that's her foot."

"They fed her to the lions?"

"Looks like it. These are some sick fucks, brother."

Frank dropped the girl's foot and moved forward into the enclosure. They were both surprised when the pain hit Masnick again. He screamed and fell to the ground in a twisted ball. Frank clamped a huge hand over his mouth to silence him. He held it there as the waves of pain washed over him. Seconds later they stopped. Masnick was weak and soaked with sweat.

Frank removed his hand. "You okay?"

"Hell, no. But we got to go."

Frank helped him to his feet.

"Leave the blanket here."

Masnick didn't question, he just obeyed. Frank dropped the GPS tracker nearby. Maybe they would think the lions had taken them. He had only taken a dozen steps when he realized how true it was.

The first feline head peaked up over a tangle of brush. Through his NVG he could see her long nose draw in deep breaths. A second head popped up beside her.

Frank took a deep breath. Lions were apex predators. In their world, you either ate it or you fucked it. But they were not invincible either. They recognized their own mortality. Crocodiles killed lions. Troops of hyenas killed lions. Lions killed lions. Even their prey sometimes killed them. They were cautious hunters, especially with unusual prey like humans.

"They are watching us. They see us as one thing, not two. Watch your back."

"What do I do if they charge?"

"Hold your ground. It could be a bluff charge."

"And if it's not?"

"Die with honor."

"Asshole."

Frank figured big cats were like dogs. They were somehow attuned to emotions as well. He calmed his heart. He saw himself as the alpha predator. He was someone to fear. He was a killer. He was danger and death. Frank moved toward the lions he could see. He knew there would be more that he could not.

The lion heads dropped from sight. He moved closer. Slowly. He heard rustling in the underbrush. To his right a female moved closer. She tucked her hind legs under her. The flanks quivered. Frank turned toward her. She froze. He took a step in her direction and she sprang off to the side and disappeared into the brush. He turned back onto his path.

A lion mock charged toward Masnick. In the darkness, he could not see it. He only heard and sensed its charge. He held firm. He raised his stick like he was going to throw it. The lion turned away.

They were nearly across when the great male stepped into view. It did not hide or slink. He strode like a king. He was at the pinnacle of his form with a thick black mane. Some dumbass dentist had shot one in Zimbabwe a few years ago and the world had gone crazy. They told stories of the gentle giant. They had given it a name he couldn't remember. They opened web sites and Facebook pages and Twitter feeds in its name. They screamed for justice and revenge.

This was not the lion of Disney's imaginings. This was a killer. The lion stared at Frank, well aware that Frank could see it. It began a series of deep huffing sounds. They weren't like the roars Frank had heard in the movies. He could feel the deep bass vibrate in his bones.

The big male lowered its head slightly. Frank didn't know what that meant. He raised the stick up like he was preparing to throw it. The lion showed no interest.

"What are you doing?" Masnick whispered.

Frank didn't answer. He held the big lion's gaze. Suddenly it swung its huge head to the side and disappeared. Frank didn't move. He waited. Ten seconds. Twenty seconds. Thirty seconds. A thousand years. No attack came.

He pushed forward. They reached the other side of the enclosure. Frank knew there was a door somewhere on this side but he didn't have time to search for it. He took the wire cutters out of his bag and cut a slit in the wire. He forced it open and held it for Masnick who stumbled through it. Frank followed and then stopped to bend the wire back into place as best that he could.

Ten feet ahead was the first of the perimeter fences. Frank cut through it and repeated the process of opening the cut and disguising it. It took a few extra seconds, but it might buy them minutes or even hours. They jogged down the fence line to their left and cut through the outside fence. Frank knew just where they were. They hit the corner and turned left again.

Frank was pushing Masnick beyond the breaking point. Masnick held onto Frank's belt and stumbled behind him. He was panting and weaving, but Frank didn't slow. There were no more screams of pain. They had to get free before the Norse Men realized they had slipped the trap.

The ATV was hidden just up ahead. They were going to make it, Frank thought. He reached the four-wheeler and leaned Masnick against it. He dug the key out of his pocket. He got into the seat and cranked the engine. Masnick was raising his leg to mount behind Frank when truck lights swept over him and held.

Chet jumped out of the cab of his truck.

"Hey, what the fuck are you doing?"

Frank recognized the voice.

"Chet, it's me," Frank called. "AC's cousin, Jack."

"Jack? Is that you? What are you doing out here?"

Frank drew the pistol and pulled the trigger. The heavy slug followed a slow straight two thousand-feet-per-second line from the barrel of the silenced gun through the front of Chet's head and out the back of it.

Frank jumped off the ATV and approached the truck. It was empty. Frank turned off the lights and the engine. He didn't check Chet's body to see if he was dead. He fired two more rounds into the inert body. If he hadn't been dead, he was now. Frank went back to the ATV and remounted. Masnick grabbed onto him from behind and they took off for Alton's house.

Four dead. Not bad for a snatch and grab.

Finris's phone rang as he barreled toward Blackwater.

"Yes?"

"We may have lost them."

"What happened?"

"We followed them, herding them. They went into the lion's enclosure to escape us."

"And?"

"We think the lions took them. The tracking GPs is still inside. The men heard screams. Someone saw one of the lionesses dragging a blanket. It looked like the one Masnick had."

"Did anyone enter the cage?"

"No."

"Do you want me to send men in?"

"No. If they are dead then they are dead. If not, then they are escaping."

"They couldn't have gotten out."

"Have men check all the fence around the cage to be sure. Be thorough. Every inch."

"They didn't escape. There's no way..."

"Do as I ask, please. Contact Sheriff Long and tell him I want roadblocks on every main road, secondary road, dirt track, and deer trail out of town. If they got out, they will be running."

"Alright. I'm sorry, sir."

"No need to worry over past mistakes. It's what we do now that matters."

Frank drove the ATV into the garage and shut it off. He unscrewed the spark plug and stuck it in his pocket. There was little chance Alton would try to start it, but if he did Frank wanted to be sure it still didn't start. It might start a series of questions. Why is it working? Why did Jack fix it? Did someone hear the ATV at the Lodge? Did he have something to do with that? Where was Jack now? Who was Jack really?

Masnick was weak and barely able to sit up. He still had a stick loosely in his mouth. He must have been battling the pain on the ride. Frank eased him down onto the concrete floor of the garage. Frank had already packed all of his gear into the truck and done an obsessive scrub down of the garage's bathroom.

"Hang in there. Let me make sure we are secure here and we are gone."

Frank double checked. There was nothing else he could think of. He hated to leave Alton jammed up like this, but he didn't see any other way. Frank helped Masnick into the back seat of the truck. He slipped in behind the wheel. He turned the ignition and the battery moaned. He tried it again. It moaned. He waited ten seconds and tried again. This had to be a joke.

Frank popped the hood and went to the front of the truck. He examined the battery to make sure the cables were firmly in place. They didn't show corrosion and they seemed snug. He shook them a couple of times. He left the hood up and went back inside the truck. He turned the key. Still dead. He thought he heard the gods chuckling.

Frank sighed. It was an omen. He was supposed to stay.

"You are kidding me, right?"

"Battery is dead."

"What now?"

"In a few hours, my boss will get up. We hide you in the bathroom and I get him to jump the truck."

"Then what, you just waltz me out in front of him and we leave? He'll be on the phone in five minutes. Better to go in there, get his keys and put one in his head."

"I don't want to do that. He's not a bad guy."

"Fuck him. He's not a Spartan either. Do him and let's get out of here. Or just steal his fucking truck."

"I take his ride, they will know. He will get burned. Plus, more importantly I can't leave my truck. Given enough time they might be able to follow it back to my doorstep. I can't have that."

"Spartans first, last and always."

Frank started to argue when the pain hit Masnick again. He arched and bent in the truck's cab as the pain burned through him. Frank could see him biting into the stick to keep from screaming. It was a bad one. The seizure lasted nearly a minute and left Masnick barely conscious.

"I can't make it much longer. You got to get me some antibiotics."

"For the poison?"

"Yeah, the bitch that did this to me was injecting me with antibiotics to counteract it."

"What kind? Do you know?"

"Tetracycline. She could be lying but that was what she said."

"Listen, we stay one more day. I'll get you your meds and get the truck up to speed. It won't look suspicious if I haven't run."

"Fuck how it looks if we are gone."

Masnick was right, but it might come down hard on Alton and he didn't want that. For all of his faults, Frank liked Alton.

"Just rest up. I'll roll my truck out of the garage so he can give me a jump in the a.m. I will get unpacked enough that it looks like I am staying. I will get you squared away in the bathroom so there's no chance he sees you."

"Just shoot him in the fucking head and let's go. Spartan style. Straight ahead. Shortest path is a straight line."

"Not going to do it. The guy played his part or I wouldn't have been able to spring you."

"You are going soft, Frank. Where is the old Earth shaker? Where is Poseidon?"

"Dead and gone, brother. Dead and fucking gone."

Frank helped Masnick into the bathroom. He closed the door behind him. He put his bedding back out and opened the garage door. He slipped the truck into neutral and let it roll down the hill in front of the garage. He left enough space for Alton to be able to slide up beside it and jump the battery.

Frank stored the gear from the rescue in the lockbox and buried the jacket under more stuff in the back seat like before. He put on his work clothes. He could smell them. He was getting a little ripe. The sink bath wasn't getting the job done.

He took out his real phone and did a quick Google search for what he needed.

Getting meds for Masnick was going to be tricky, but not impossible, especially if all you needed were antibiotics. Pharmacies were bunkers. Medical doctors were always suspicious. But dentists were altogether different. He located an internet list of dental offices in the area. Most were small one-man operations. He found one with an elaborate web page. There were three doctors that offered to "welcome walk-ins". A big practice meant more chairs. More chairs meant more people could just show up with a dental emergency. He memorized the address and their directions on finding it. They opened at eight o'clock. He would be there when the doors opened. He didn't mind having to wait.

Frank searched for the symptoms for his imaginary tooth problem. They were simple and easy to fabricate.

He got some more cash out of the truck. Doctors always liked cash. He put three one hundred-dollar bills into his shirt pocket. He closed the big garage door to keep the heat in. Frank would have liked to have gotten some sleep, but he was still too jacked from the rescue. He knew it was pointless to try.

He got the lawn chair he had found and slipped out through the small side door. He propped it up against the side of the house. He took out a cigar and fired it up. He had a couple of more in his jacket pocket in case Alton slept in. He zipped his jacket up and pulled his watch cap down tight. He thought about what he would do next.

47

Finris eased the big SUV into a spot just to the side of the Lodge. He didn't go inside directly. He scanned the outbuildings. He could see some slight damage and smell the smoke and fire damage. He had known it was a diversion because it was what he would have done. No one met his gaze.

He marched up the steps into the main building. He smiled as he passed the ancient Viking axes and shield hanging on the wall. This was a hall for warriors. He could hear the nervous whispers of the girls as he walked to his office. A Norse Man stood guard outside with an AR-15. Finris nodded a greeting. He heard the man mutter "sorry" as he passed. The man followed him inside the office.

Inside Heather and her brother waited. Heather was seated at a chair in front of his desk. Nils was sprawled on the leather sofa. Heather ran to him and hugged him.

"I am so sorry."

Finris stroked her hair like a man might pet a favorite horse to calm it. "It will be alright."

"How can you say that?"

"Because I am Finris." He turned to the Norse Man. "What is your name?"

"Davis, Mr. Finris."

"Davis, get a team, at least twelve people. Have a few carry the Nitro Express but everyone else carry pots and pans. Move into the lions' enclosure as a group. Find the bodies or proof that they are dead and bring them to me. Have someone take one of the mobile tracking units. I want another team of three inspecting every foot of the fence of the lions' habitat from the outside. Be certain they did not slip out."

The man didn't object. He just nodded and left.

"Why risk any of our people? They are surely dead."

"They are not our people. They are my people. I believe this is the work of Frank Kane. I do not believe he would have gone down so easily. I must be certain."

"If it makes you feel better."

"It does. You did well, Heather. You nearly stopped their escape with your quick thinking. You were very close."

Heather smiled at the unusual praise. "Thanks."

"Any word from the roadblocks?"

"No. They are in place. If they didn't get out immediately, they are locked in. The only way out would be on foot."

"Excellent. They killed three of our people. The sheriff can get a door to door manhunt started once everyone is in place."

Finris' desk phone chirped. He walked to it and answered. He listened and hung up without comment.

"Well?" Nils asked.

"They found Chet shot in the head and chest outside the main fencing. They escaped."

"You must be kidding me. What do we do now? We could lose everything."

"Calm, yourself, Nils. That is not going to happen. We have this contained."

"How can you say that? They escaped."

"Suppose we don't find them. Who are they going to tell? Are they going to say I killed some people rescuing a criminal from some other criminals? I don't think so. If they get out, they will disappear."

"What about the Spartans?" Heather asked.

"What about them?"

"They will not appreciate that we let Prometheus escape."

"How will they know?"

"They will be wanting results. If we don't provide them, they may want him back."

"I will call Cyrus today and explain that Masnick hasn't broken yet, so we are intensifying his interrogations. Then when Masnick proves too weak to withstand our questions and dies it won't be a shock. They will look into other avenues to find Frank Kane and they will remain our allies."

"You are very clever. What if they recapture Prometheus?"

"How? He will be more cautious than ever. And they aren't even looking for him anymore."

"What if we do find them? What then?"

"So many questions. So many worries. We kill them both. Frank Kane is too dangerous to wait for the Spartans to arrive. He has always been quick to use guns and it will have to go down that way."

"If I could ask a favor? If Prometheus can be captured I would love to spend more time playing with him. I have some new toxins I want to try."

Finris kissed the top of her head. "You are such a wicked girl. I will give the order to take him alive if they can."

Heather beamed. "We will get back to business then."

Nils shook his hand and followed his sister out. Finris smiled. They seemed so confident, but underneath they were ready to panic. That was the trait that set him apart, he thought. He did not bend to the whims of the gods. He went to change clothes. He had things he needed to take care of.

The lights came on in Alton's house at six thirty. At seven thirty Alton came rumbling outside. He was making a beeline for the garage when he saw Frank.

He slowed his roll. Frank stayed seated.

"You're up early, Jack."

"Couldn't sleep. Thought I would have a smoke before work."

Alton took a pack of cigarettes from his own jacket pocket and tapped one out. He lit up and started smoking. Frank didn't say anything. Alton took two deep drags before he spoke.

"We got problems."

Frank waited. When it was apparent he wasn't going to ask, Alton continued.

"There was an incident up at the Lodge last night. Fire got started. Some people got shot. They killed Chet."

"That was the big guy who drove us to the fight. He was a friend of yours, right?"

"Yeah. Since we were kids. Biggest redneck motherfucker I ever knew."

Alton puffed on his cigarette, remembering his old friend. Frank worked on the cigar.

"Sorry to hear it."

"Yeah. They said work is suspended for the rest of the week while they get things sorted out up there. That's what I came to tell you. I know you need the dough."

"That's okay, AC. Listen, the reason I couldn't sleep is I got this killer toothache. Since we aren't working, I thought I might run in to let a dentist take a look at it."

"Man, I hate dentists. They give me the willies."

"Me too, that's why this one went bad. You mind if I take off and get it looked after?"

"No. I'll go with you if you want."

"No. I got this. But I could use a jump. Battery is dead in my truck."

"Sure thing, Jack. Let me get my keys."

"Thanks."

Frank watched Alton head back inside for his keys. Work was suspended for the rest of the week. That would work well. He would get a new battery and some antibiotics for Masnick and then as soon as possible slip out of town. No fuss. No muss.

Maurer was parked near the campgrounds beside the service road. His face was swollen and his ribs ached. Buck had kicked his ass. He had lied to Cathy. He told her he got jumped by some drunks. She was so sweet and good that she believed him. She could never imagine the world he was living in now. It was a world gone crazy.

High Sheriff Long had said some strangers had gone crazy at the Lodge and started shooting people. That didn't make any sense. How did they get up there? Why were they shooting people? How did they escape? Maurer figured in a way it didn't really matter. They had a detailed description of one of the men as thin and bearded, medium height, brown hair, sickly with dark eyes. They had his picture. Where did they get a picture of him? The other was described only as a very big man, probably six foot four inches and two hundred and thirty to two hundred and fifty pounds.

Maurer's job was to stop any car carrying more than two people that attempted to use the service road. If the occupants even remotely matched the description, he was to detain them and call for backup. The suspects were considered armed and extremely dangerous and he was authorized to use lethal force if necessary.

It was pointless duty. The service road was barely more than a dirt track. It was narrow and barely wide enough for one car. He drove up it until he found a place to turn his cruiser and park on the side facing down the road. No one would see him until they turned the corner and by then it would be too late. Only a handful of locals probably knew of it in the first place. Except for the game warden, Maurer doubted the little road was ever used except by adventurous kids looking for a slip off spot to neck or smoke pot.

The high sheriff had stationed him here to get him out of the way. They didn't think they could trust him. They didn't think they could count on him to spin an encounter the way they wanted. He knew they were probably right.

He knew he was going to have to do something to get out of this mess. He had to protect his family, but he had to get free of this or it would kill him. It was a cancer eating him up from inside. Maurer sat in the warmth of his car and tried to figure a way out.

48

Frank stopped at the first automotive store he came across. He bought a new battery and had the salesman install it for him. It took ten minutes, tops.

The next stop was the dental office. It was on Friendly Avenue and appropriately enough called the Friendly Dental Building. The parking lot was pretty full. Frank parked and went inside.

A pretty girl at the desk greeted him with a warm smile. When he explained that he was there because of a tooth that was bothering him, she gave him a stack of new patient forms to fill out. Frank diligently filled each one out with lies about his name, where he was from, and where he lived. He gave her back her novella of forms and took a seat.

The magazines were current, so he picked up a Sports Illustrated and read about sports teams he knew nothing about and cared even less about. On the plus side, it was very warm in the dental office. He got a little sleepy and had to fight it back.

Fifteen minutes later, another pretty girl in a blue smock came and led Frank back to an operatory. She got him comfortable in the chair and put a matching blue napkin around his neck on a chain. She asked him about his symptoms. Frank had done his research. She took a digital x-ray of his tooth and left him alone in the room. A few minutes later the dentist came in.

Frank was surprised. The dentist was a woman. She was a petite brunette with her hair worn long. She was thin and walked with an athlete's confidence. He figured she was a runner or a competitive tennis player. She extended her hand.

"I'm Dr. Rebecca Howe."

"Nice to meet you."

"They tell me you have a toothache. Tell me about it."

"It is really weird. It comes and goes."

"What makes it hurt?"

"Sometimes when I chew on it there is a sharp pain. And lately it hurts to hot. Not all the time, but sometimes."

"Does cold hurt it?"

"No."

"Does it wake you up at night?"

"No. Sometimes when I am getting into bed I feel it a little, but it doesn't keep me up."

She sat down in a little chair on rollers and moved closer. "Let's take a look."

She laid the chair back. The pretty girl in blue had come back and took a seat in another little chair. She adjusted a light so it shone into his mouth. The dentist took a little mirror and explorer and poked and prodded around a little where Frank indicated the pain had started. After a few minutes, she slid her chair back.

"You have great teeth. Those are nice implants you have in the front."

"Thanks."

"You obviously take good care of your teeth. The x-ray didn't show any abscess or fracture, but they don't always show up either. From our tests, I would think you have a crack in your tooth. The pain is caused by the force when you chew. The tooth separates a little bit and you get that jolt."

"That's exactly what it is, a jolt. Like touching a light socket."

"I think the nerve in the tooth is dying. You have three choices of treatment. You can delay, but you run the risk of the tooth splitting and not being able to restore it. You could have it removed. But it is very important for chewing. I recommend a root canal and then a crown. That way you get to keep the tooth."

"That's what I was thinking. I don't want to lose it."

"I can fit you in this morning if you like."

This was the tricky part. Frank tried to sound sincere. "How much is a root canal?"

"I think on a back tooth they run about twelve hundred dollars."

"That's what I was afraid of. The truth is I don't have that much money right now. I might need to delay getting it treated for a couple of weeks while I get the money together."

"That's fine, just don't wait too long. I want you to keep this tooth."

"Me too. Thanks."

Dr. Howe started to get up and then stopped. "Listen, I know times are tough right now. If you want, I can go ahead and do the treatment and you can pay me when you get the money."

Frank was shocked. He hadn't thought of that. But he was quick on his feet.

"I couldn't have you do that, Doc. I pay my way. I always have. I'll just make an appointment to come back in two weeks after I get paid, if that is okay?"

"That's fine, but you baby that tooth. Try to chew on the other side until you get it fixed."

The pretty girl in blue set his chair up and unhooked his napkin.

"Oh, Doc. Could I get a prescription to hold me over until I come back?"

Frank saw her suspicions rise. It was a physical change. Her back went stiff.

"What kind of prescription do you want? Something for pain?"

"No. I can handle that. Something for the infection. Maybe some antibiotics."

Frank watched her shoulders relax. Dr. Howe smiled. She had a stunning smile.

"Sure. I will write you a script and leave it at the front desk." She picked up his patient folder and scanned it quickly. "You say you are allergic to penicillin and erythromycin both?"

"Yeah. Tetracycline usually works for me."

"It is not the ideal choice for a bad tooth."

"I would prefer it. It's worked well for me in the past."

There was that smile again. It made you feel safe.

"All right. But two weeks and not a day more. I want to see you back in here."

"Absolutely."

Frank watched her leave. The pretty girl in blue walked him to the front desk. The equally pretty girl took his paperwork and asked how he wanted to pay his bill. She was so smooth and reasonable, it would have been impossible to decline to pay. He paid cash. She gave him the written prescription and he left.

Finris was wearing his normal outfit, thick canvas pants and a vest. He was sitting outside the leopard's cage sipping a cup of coffee. The leopard had devoured the live chicken Finris had brought it and now lay curled asleep in its cage near Finris. He glanced under the cage. The old cigarette butt was still resting there. Everything had its limits.

Finris lit another cigarette and stretched his legs all the way out.

"Well, friend, it is good to see you doing so well."

The leopard lay sleeping, dreaming whatever dreams a leopard dreamt.

"I think I have things under control here. It is always important to seem in control. If they ever see doubt in you, they will begin to doubt your ability to lead them."

Finris sipped his black coffee. He felt his phone buzz in his vest pocket but ignored it.

"I should know in a few days if my plans will work out or not. If things come apart here, it will get very bloody."

He took another sip.

"But that is alright too. Warriors weren't meant to live forever. We were destined to die in battle surrounded by enemies."

The leopard stirred and turned its head toward Finris.

"You will not be forgotten, I promise. I will set you free to live or die as fate determines. Your kind used to hunt these remote woods and valleys. You could survive. Maybe you will find others of your kind hidden from our view. Maybe you will die alone. But you will have that chance, my friend."

The leopard looked at Finris. Perhaps it was the timbre of his words, or the sense of raw power in Finris. It was hard to know. The leopard fell back asleep feeling safe.

"Well, I have goofed off long enough. I must get back to work. Rest well."

49

Frank was feeling pretty good when he got back to the garage. He had the battery and the medicine and a plan to shield Alton from retribution. That all went to hell as soon as he pulled into the garage. Masnick was sitting on his bed.

Frank parked and closed the garage door.

"He's at the house waiting for you."

"What are you talking about?"

"Big fat guy. He came by to see if you were back. I was having a seizure. He saw me. He knows.

Frank sighed. This could be very bad. He took a deep breath. He opened the pharmacy bag.

"Here are the antibiotics."

Masnick snatched them from his hand. His hands were trembling. He opened the bottle and swallowed a pill dry. He managed a weak smile before lying back onto Frank's bed.

"Thanks, brother."

Frank went back to the truck and took out the small Kimber and put it in his pocket.

"I guess I better go talk to him. Anybody else show up?"

"No. I think he wanted to talk to you first."

Frank nodded.

"Just do him and let's go. I will put the stuff back in the truck and rewipe everything."

"Be thorough and fast."

Masnick got slowly to his feet and started breaking the bed down. He turned to look at Frank. He made a gun with his hand and pointed it at his own head.

"This won't take long."

Frank trudged up to the house. He knocked.

"It's open."

Frank went inside. His hand was on the pistol in his pocket.

He worked his way into what was supposed to be the living room. Cans and boxes had been hastily swept aside. Alton sat on the sofa. He was holding his shotgun. Frank thought about just shooting him before the talking started, but he didn't. That Frank Kanc was long gone.

Alton stood up. The shotgun was at port arms across his chest with the barrel pointing away from Frank. Frank stood in front of him but didn't speak.

"I saw your friend. He's the one they are looking for?"

Frank nodded.

"It was you up at the Lodge shooting up the place?"

"Yeah."

"You the one killed Chet?"

"Yeah."

Alton nodded and stared at the ground. He shook his head.

"This is fucked up, Jack. I thought we were sort of friends and stuff."

"We are."

"You put me in a fix. They figure out it was you; they will come after me."

"You could always run."

"Too damn old. Got nowhere to run to. I ought to call them and give you up."

"That's the smart play."

"Don't see any other way out."

Frank smiled and punched him just below the right eye. Alton went down hard. He dropped the shotgun. He struggled to his feet.

"What the fuck was that?"

"It's me saving your ass."

"What are you talking about, Jack?"

"Shut up and listen. I've been trying to figure a way to cover your ass."

"So you punch me? Some plan."

"Part of it. Hear me out. You got a cousin?"

"Sure."

"Any that you are close to?"

"Yeah, one up in Pittsburgh, Lizzie's boy."

"You call him up and tell him you need a big favor. Tell him if anyone ever asks, he tells them this story. He says he met some good old boy. Big redneck shit kicker in a bar one night. They were having a drink and this guy asks if he knows anybody hiring. He says if he's down this way to look you up. That's it. That's the whole story. Doesn't know the guy. Never saw him before or since. Seemed like a good guy."

"I don't get it."

"That eye is going to swell and go black. Tomorrow night anybody asks you say we got into a beef over money. Tell them I sucker punched you, so you fired me. When they ask if it was your cousin that hit you, you tell them not your fucking cousin, your cousin's friend, Jack."

"I still don't get it."

"Listen, everybody you introduced me to is a retard or a slut. They will think they misheard you. That explains why I'm gone. Somebody comes asking, you tell them I was some friend of your cousin's. Hard-working fat guy who said my name was Jack Daniels. They may check with your cousin. If he backs it up that should do it."

"It's pretty thin."

206

"It's the best we got. You stick to that story and you'll skate. You get wobbly and they will bury you. You call James, tell him his spot is open if he wants it. Argue with him over money. Bitch that you aren't going to be cheated. Word will spread."

"What about you and your friend in there?"

"Either way, we are leaving. You can play along or go for the shotgun or call your buddies. But if you rat me out, they will kill you for being a fool. It's your call."

"You not going to try and stop me?"

"From calling? Hell no. I don't think you are that stupid. You go for the shotgun and try to keep me here, I will kill you."

Alton nodded. "It sounds like a plan."

"Best we got."

Alton smiled. "I sure would have like to have gotten the details of you and Sallee from the Tavern."

"Me too. She was hot as fire."

Alton stuck out his beefy hand. "Good luck, Jack."

"Thanks."

As he turned to leave he heard Alton behind him. Frank turned. Alton had taken two steps toward him.

"One more thing. They told me they got road blocks up on all the roads heading out of town. You got to take a back road if you want to get free."

"Any suggestions?"

"Near the campgrounds there is a service road that cuts off the back. It runs around through the deep woods until you hit up with I-70 North. That's your best bet. I used to spotlight deer out there. Nobody hardly knows about it. You know how to get to the campground from here?"

"Yeah. Thanks. I'll look for the road. You stick to the story. No matter what, you stick to it. Things get rough. They start pushing you around. You stick to it. They start pounding on you. You stick to it. Tell your cousin the same thing."

"Roger."

Frank went back to the garage. Masnick had tossed everything into the back of the truck bed. He was stretched out on the back seat under the camouflage jacket Frank had worn. The Benelli shotgun was beside him.

"Did you do the fat man?"

"No. He told me a back way out of town. They have roadblocks on all the other roads."

"Sounds like an ambush to me."

"Then you better keep that shotgun ready."

Frank cranked the engine. It started on the first try. He backed out of the driveway. He hoped Alton followed his advice. He hoped Alton wasn't setting him up. That would be real bad.

50

Frank worked his way through the local traffic and took the turn for the campground near the park. The road was deserted. The service road was supposed to be up ahead. He could just make out the overgrown tire ruts. It looked like someone else had been up it recently. Frank took the gun from his pocket and put it in his lap.

You never knew what a man was capable of until he did it. It would only take one tearful phone call to the Norse Men. If they were quick or the route was a dead end, it would be red. There was nothing you could do about that now. Worrying only slowed you down. Frank turned his truck up the rutted dirt track.

He glanced over his shoulder. Masnick was asleep or passed out or pretending. He drove slow with his window down. He didn't see or hear anything until he rounded a turn in the deep woods. There was a police car parked off to the side of the road. Its engine was off. A police officer leaned against the hood.

The man was young and in good shape. His face was beat up. He was in a pose that represented boredom more than hostility. He looked surprised to see Frank. That was a good sign. Frank's hand slipped to his gun. He would hate to have to shoot him. But he would.

Maurer was lost deep in thought when the old truck suddenly appeared around the corner. He hadn't seen anyone all morning and hadn't expected to. It was a lone driver. It wasn't the car he was supposed to be looking for. A bored man would have let it pass. Maurer was a policeman. There was something off for the truck to be here at all. He moved to his feet. He raised his right hand in a halting signal. The truck braked to a stop.

Maurer walked toward the truck. He had no idea that Frank was seconds away from ending his life.

Cyrus was sitting on the porch smoking a Turkish cigarette. A cup of fine Jamaican Blue Mountain coffee steeped on the little table in front of him. He was gazing out the window in the trees around the compound. He was thinking.

Spanish Johnny was on the other side of the room, pacing.

"I don't get it, Cyrus. You said he called to say everything was okay."

"That is what concerns me."

"But you talk to him frequently."

"Yes. But I call Finris. He does not call me. I ask myself why?"

"And?"

"I am not sure."

Spanish Johnny ran a hand through his thick dark hair as if he could massage meaning into his brain. "All he said is nothing has happened. No results. No Frank Kane. No information."

Cyrus smiled. "Yes. He called to tell me everything was fine so therefore it must not be. Why call except to reassure me? Why bother? Finris knows I want results. He knows I don't care how he gets them. So why call?"

Spanish Johnny smiled. "You think Masnick is dead and they are scrambling to cover it up."

"Something like that, but why? Masnick is only a piece in our play. Letting the Norse Men have him bound them to us. It increased the resources that would be looking for Frank. It might open new business opportunities for us."

"He was always bait to lure Frank in anyway."

"Nothing more. He was expendable. I was never convinced he knew how to contact Frank in the first place."

"So why let him be tortured by those animals?"

Cyrus shrugged and took a drag on his cigarette. He lifted the coffee, blew on it, and took a sip. He sat it back down.

"I could have been wrong. I might have not used enough leverage in questioning him because he had been a Spartan."

"I could have asked the hard questions myself."

Cyrus tapped the ash off his cigarette.

"No. He was a Spartan. He deserved better than a slow death at our hands. This seemed cleaner."

Spanish Johnny laughed.

"What you did was better?"

"Of course. Helios' long boring stories taught me one rule."

"And?"

"Never let yourself get caught in your own trap. If Frank Kane comes, it is better we seek him out than lead him to our home here."

"Let him come."

Cyrus took another puff. "Brave words, brother. But there is something special about him. I knew it when I first met him when he was a boy. He is like a force of nature, so pure in his being. He is death. It is his special talent. He is a dangerous adversary and we should always remember that."

"I would love another chance at him."

"I am sure you would. He proved himself difficult to kill the last time you met."

"I remember."

Cyrus took another sip.

"I meant no disrespect, Johnny. You are every bit his equal. If the circumstances ever presented themselves, I am sure you would best him."

Spanish Johnny mumbled something under his breath.

"Can I get some breakfast?"

"Sure." Cyrus pressed a button on a remote that slept on the table.

A female Latina voice answered. "Yes, sir."

"John would like some breakfast."

"Of course."

"What would you like?"

"Eggs, over medium, coffee, bacon extra crispy, toast."

"Did you get that?"

"Yes, sir. I will have it sent right up."

"Thank you."

Cyrus puffed his cigarette.

"Is that any good?"

Cyrus studied the Turkish cigarette. "Not really to my liking. I just felt like trying something new. You are welcome to the pack if you like."

Johnny looked for a moment and then shook his head. "No. You can keep them. All I want is breakfast."

"Just be patient. It is coming."

Cyrus looked out across the bleak woods and worked his schemes and counter schemes.

51

Maurer knew he was in trouble when he reached the truck. Tiny alarm bells started firing in his mind. The driver raised a pistol and pointed it at the center of his chest. Maurer froze. His gun was holstered a thousand miles away on his right hip. He was alone. He thought about his wife and unborn children. He felt a wave of sadness for the life he would not have. For the life he had given up with his weakness and greed. For a wife he would never kiss again. For children he would never love and hold and see grow. All his dreams of advancement and achievement were dust motes in the universe.

He had had a good life. He had followed the plan. He had found his soulmate and married her. He had known the joy of waiting for his children to be born. He had had great friends and great parents. He had known success in sports. He had lived his life the way he had felt was best. He had served God. Well, except for this last part with the sheriff. Maybe this was God's way of stopping him before he went too far. Maybe God was giving him a way out without disgrace and humiliation.

Maurer felt a sudden sense of calm. He felt himself relax. This was his future and he had created it for himself. He was ready. This was God's will. He would do whatever his God told him to do. He handed his life over to God.

Frank Kane was close to the young policeman. He could read the name tag, Maurer. He saw the changes sweep over Maurer. He saw the man's surprise turn to tension and then complete relaxation. Frank lowered the pistol in his left hand. It was not so low that he could not bring it to bear in a split second, but it was off target. His message was clear. I can take your life if I want to.

"Can I help you, officer?" Frank asked.

Maurer looked into his deep blue eyes for a sign of his impending doom. They were blank wells. Maurer was not afraid. He took a step closer and looked into the cab of the truck. A man lay sprawled in the back seat. His face was etched with the scars of intense pain. These were the two men he was supposed to find. These were the two men he was supposed to shoot on sight.

A thought crept forward in his mind. Why? Why was he supposed to apprehend them? Who wanted them dead? He immediately knew the answers. This was a test from God.

"No, sir. No problem at all. You looking for the highway connection?"

"Yes, sir."

Maurer looked over his shoulder and up the road behind him.

"You are heading the right way. Just follow this track. It dead ends at the highway."

"Thank you, officer."

"Not many vehicles use this route. Road gets worse farther in, so take it slow. There could be limbs down blocking it. Have a blessed day."

"Thank you, officer. You too."

Maurer smiled. He was having a blessed day. God was showing him the way. He stepped back from the truck.

Frank eased the truck forward. He crept past Maurer and watched him in the rear-view mirror. If Maurer went for his gun he would kill him. If he hurried to his cruiser to call it in, he would kill him. Maurer didn't. He stood in the middle of the road and watched them pass. He waved a hand at them.

Frank watched him. Maurer seemed oblivious to any danger. He went back to his cruiser and leaned against the hood, just like Frank had seen him when he rounded the corner. Frank knew it was an omen. The elder gods were clearing the way for him. He drove slowly down the road until he knew he was safe.

Maurer had said the road was rough ahead and to take it slow. Frank was no fool. He picked up speed and bumped and banged and lurched down the road. When he found I-70 North he accelerated onto it and raced toward Zaneville. He glanced in the back seat at Masnick. He was still breathing evenly, cradling the shotgun. He looked like he would make it after all. Frank breathed deeply. It was finally over.

Jake's private cell phone buzzed. He stopped working and went to the back. He answered the phone. It was Jenny.

"Hey."

"Hey, yourself. What's up?"

"I know we were going to go out Friday, but we have career day on Thursday and Friday."

"What's career day?"

"Where you get to skip school to visit colleges you might want to attend."

"But you already decided. You've been accepted at UNCG."

"I know. But I still get the days. So, why don't we go out tomorrow?"

"Are you asking me out on a date?"

"Yes. But you still have to cook for me."

"So many rules. Okay. I'll pick you up tomorrow before lunch."

"Sounds good."

"I'm not being too forward, am I?"

"Not at all."

"Good."

"One more thing, make sure you dress warmly."

"Why?"

"I'll tell you tomorrow. Comfortable but warm."

"Okay."

"I better get back to work. You better get back to class."

"Bye."

Jake disconnected. He had a special date in mind.

52

Frank pulled up into the driveway of the little rental house in Zaneville. He parked around back. Masnick was still out so he unloaded the truck. When he was finished, he woke Masnick up.

Masnick was weak and drenched in sweat, but he seemed stronger too. He helped him into the little house and to one of the old beds. Masnick insisted that he keep control of the shotgun and Frank didn't object. Frank put it beside him on the bed. Frank got Masnick to tell him his clothing sizes before he let Masnick fall back asleep.

Frank went into the kitchen and got a glass of water. He drank it and then a second and third glass. He turned up the heat. He was tired of being cold all the time. The little space heaters had done their best, but garages were not insulated. He felt cold in his bones. Finally, he took a leak.

He stumbled a little as he was walking. The adrenaline was all burned off now and the lack of sleep was catching up to him. Frank went to the other bedroom. He unlaced his work boots and stretched out fully clothed. He planned to rest his eyes for a few minutes and then get back out buying supplies.

Frank woke five hours later. He was a little embarrassed. He put his shoes on and checked on Masnick. He was still asleep, but the lines on his face were relaxed now. Frank left by the front door and locked it behind him.

Frank went out to buy some appropriate clothing for Masnick. He also got food and drink and a bottle of Masnick's favorite liquor. When he returned Masnick was sitting on the front porch. The shotgun was resting by his feet. Masnick helped him unload the truck.

They sat out food and both ate without comment. Frank was a big eater, but Masnick ate like a starving man. Frank guessed his body was trying to refuel to repair itself. Frank tossed the paper plates in the garbage can and went out back to smoke a cigar. Tomorrow he would call Carpenter and tell him the job was done. He would give Masnick some road cash and see him off to wherever the old kook wanted to go. Then he would drive home.

The thought warmed him. He missed Greensboro. He missed Jenny and Caron and DC and the guys at work. He was looking forward to catching up with The Jake too. He had a fleeting urge to head north and check in on Dorian. It wasn't that far. She had helped him with his business in Fort Worth and he hoped she had gotten her little hair styling business started like she had planned. He could imagine the surprise on her face when he walked into her shop. He imagined how she had looked naked in his arms. His little brain between his legs stirred. Frank smiled. No, it was better to leave her alone. Give her a chance to make it. He could only bring trouble to her. Still she had looked mighty fine without her clothes on and she was passionate.

The back door opened with a screech and Masnick came out, spoiling Frank's daydream. He was wearing some of his new clothes. The improved fit almost made Masnick look normal. Almost. He still looked gaunt like his parchment-thin skin might rip if he moved too quickly. He sat beside Frank.

"Want a cigar?"

"No. That shit will kill you."

"Funny, coming from the god of fire."

"Fire is different. It is religion and beauty and life. A cigar is just burning leaves and breathing in the damn smoke."

Frank took a deep pull and blew the smoke away from Masnick. The wind caught it and blew it all over Masnick. If he noticed he didn't care. Frank smiled. Not his best smile but close enough to be genuine.

"You got me out, brother. You saved my ass. No one else could have done it."

"You would have done the same for me."

"No. I wouldn't have and you know it. I might have tried. But I couldn't have pulled it off."

"You could have done it."

"How did you know they had me in the first place?"

"Helios, Carpenter, called me said he had word the Norse Men had you and were going to use you to draw me out. He wanted me to get you out."

"That was nice of him. So, he knew about this Lodge of theirs?"

"No. I figured that part out. I figured you would resist as long as you could and then feed them lies, biding your time, looking for a way out. I wish I could have come sooner, but it wouldn't have worked out."

"That's just what I did. I gave them a fake code for contacting you to stall for more time. Hey, by the way we should have something like that in place."

Frank nodded and went back to his cigar.

"It was Spanish Johnny that nabbed me. He and Cyrus turned me over to the Norse Men."

"That's what Carpenter said. Said I had a duty to try to get you out."

"They were like my own brothers."

"People change, Masnick."

"That's the bad part. People don't change. They are who the fuck they are. Sometimes you get to see inside to the real person. Trouble was I never saw it."

"You were never a good judge of character anyway. You were a criminal."

Masnick chuckled. "True words, brother. I had my own demons. The roar of explosions and the warmth of cleansing fire."

"We all have demons. But we can change. We can control them. We can be better than who we were."

"There aren't any men better than you." He patted Frank on the back. "Thanks again, brother."

Frank nodded. Masnick stared off into the darkness. He paused.

"You know we have to go back, don't you?"

Frank looked up at him but didn't speak.

"We have to for what they did to me. It's Spartan honor."

Frank started to answer, when Masnick raised his hand to silence him.

"You sit out here with your smoke and think on it. You know I'm right. They put something in me that is killing me. They tortured me. They have to pay for that. They have to be the example so others will fear us again. Honor depends on this. Frank Kane would go."

"What about Cyrus and Spanish Johnny?"

"I don't think I will be around long enough to handle that business. That's up to you if you want. But these Norse Men need to pay Charon for what they've done to me. Think about it. Push it around in that big head of yours and when you realize I am right we can figure out how we do it. Either way I'm going back. I don't have much time left. My body is shutting down. I would enjoy taking some of them with me."

Masnick went back into the warmth of the little house. Frank felt its inviting warmth sweep over him as subtly as the tease of a woman's perfume. He puffed his cigar and considered Masnick's words. Spartan honor. He had a new life now. He had a new family that mattered. He had new friends. He was out. He was hidden and safe and invisible. Spartan honor. The ash grew longer on his cigar. He wouldn't die for Masnick. He wasn't worth going back in on a suicide mission. Spartan honor. Maybe it could be done. Maybe Masnick was right. We couldn't change who we were in our core. He stubbed out the nub of the cigar against the porch beam. He ground it out in the shape of a lambda. Frank felt the first stirrings of his own demons. Spartan honor.

He went inside. Masnick was watching some home renovation show on HGTV. He looked up at Frank. His face was blank. He nodded.

"Three conditions. First, it has to be survivable. Second, we bring in help. Third, you follow my plan. I am lead on this. What I say goes."

"Agreed."

"Let's get down to it. I'm going to need coffee."

The two warriors sat up most of the night. They started with Masnick telling everything he knew about the Lodge. He told it in minute detail. Every word carefully cataloged for just such a possibility. There was no telling what was important and what wasn't until it was all out. Then Frank told all that he knew about the Lodge and getting Masnick out.

Frank brought out the blueprints and the diagrams that he had of the

Lodge. They started running scenarios. There were a lot of pieces to consider. There were logistical concerns. There were police considerations. There were problems with the number of Norse Men and their fire power. There were issues with the presence of civilians on the property. There was the potential for outside intervention from other law enforcement agencies or the Norse Men who lived off the premises. None of it mattered. Not really. Frank knew they would make their plans and then they would go. They were Spartans. This was what they did.

Frank's demons did not rattle their chains or roar. He felt them quietly slip out of their fetters. Cells opened. Gates were raised. They moved calmly into position. They lined up patiently and waited for the last barrier to free them. They were polite and disciplined, waiting for the battle horn to sound. They were calm. They were eager. This was war. This was their time of harvest. This would be a reckoning. This would be a reaping.

53

Carpenter was smoking a menthol cigarette when his phone buzzed. It was five a.m. in Fresno, where he was currently staying. He checked the caller ID. Frank Kane.

"Poseidon. Good to hear from you. I am still working on finding this Valhalla, but I have it narrowed down to Ohio or Kentucky."

"I got Masnick out."

Carpenter tried to disguise his shock. He paused, collecting himself. The timbre of his voice betrayed him. "You amaze me. How did you find him?"

"I have my own talents."

"Yes, you do. How is he doing?"

"About like you would expect. But we have a slight problem."

"Ahh. So that is why you called. How can I help you?"

"We are going back in."

"What on earth for?"

"For what they did to Masnick. It requires an answer."

Carpenter understood only the concept not the sentiment. "What do you need?"

Frank got out his list and read off the items he needed. It was a very detailed list.

"And I need all the background you can find on a Deputy Maurer down in Blackwater."

"Why?"

"Not sure. He might be useful."

Carpenter mumbled his agreement. "Give me three or four hours to round everything up. I will UPS it to your location. You should have it by Friday."

"Do you need the address?"

"No. Leave your phone on. I can track the chip I put in it." Carpenter paused to gloat at his cleverness.

"I figured. That's why I keep the battery and sim card out unless I needed you."

Carpenter smiled. Frank was still sharp. "Indulge me, Frank, and leave it in for now. I might need to update you on the situation if it changes."

"I might need you to track down some phone numbers for me."

"Spartans?"

"Yeah. Guys I can trust."

"Give me the names and I will text you the phone numbers."

"Thanks, Carpenter. And I'm glad you sent me to get Masnick. It wasn't right what they were doing to him to get to me."

Former FBI Special Agent Richard Redding, recently retired, was enjoying a nice glass of fresh-squeezed orange juice on his sun porch when he heard his front doorbell chime. Then a second time. Then a third. He took a final sip and placed it on the glass-topped table beside the crossword puzzle he had been working on. He hated crossword puzzles. He sucked at them. He tucked his pistol into the back of his pants just in case. In Redding's long career he had put away a lot of dangerous people.

Redding moved with an easy stride to the door and opened it without checking to see who was on the other side. A delivery man in a brown UPS uniform was carrying a brown box. He was standing in front of a brown UPS truck. The man was about twenty. He was lean like a cat burglar. Blue tattoos winked out of the top of his short sleeved brown shirt. Redding let his right hand drift back to his gun. UPS would try the door once and if they got no answer, always leave your package on the doorstep.

"What you got there?"

"A package for a Richard Redding." The man said reading the label. "Are you Mr. Redding?"

"That's me. Man, it's already hot out. Would you like to come in and get a cool drink? I have ice water."

The man smiled. "Yes, sir. That would be great. It's always hot in Florida."

"Good. Come on in. You can set the package down on the table by the door. I'll get you that water."

The UPS man turned and set the package on the table. Before he could turn back around Redding had the gun up to the base of his neck. He slammed the UPS man against the wall and held him there. Redding knew that UPS men are not allowed to enter peoples' homes, too much liability.

"Who the fuck are you?"

"I'm UPS."

"And I am former FBI. I can blow your fucking head off and no one will ever ask why. Now who the fuck are you?"

"Just a guy trying to make a living."

"You ride around in your brown uniform in your brown truck and nobody ever notices, is that it?"

"Pretty much. We contract out to deliver stuff. We get a call, pick up stuff and deliver it where we are told."

"What kind of stuff?"

"I don't know. We never open the packages."

"Make a guess."

"Guns. Maybe drugs. Shit, whatever."

Redding released the man and stepped back three long steps. The man didn't move. Redding kept the pistol pointed at him. "Step away from the wall. Do not turn around."

The man did.

"Open the package."

The man looked scared. He knelt by the box.

"What's in it, dude?"

"Let's find out."

The fake UPS man took out a folding knife and cut the tape on the top. He opened it slowly. He rose to his feet. He showed the contents to Redding.

"It's just some papers and bullshit."

"Put it on the table. Now get out."

"Thanks, bro."

The UPS man scampered out the front door to his truck and drove away. Redding approached the box. He recognized the documents. They were proof of his taking money from a criminal. The criminal's name was Keith Masnick, aka Prometheus, one of the Spartan elite, part of their inner council, a Spartan peer, a Spartan god. He was a brilliant mad explosives genius. Through a series of events, he had become Redding's CI, providing intel of questionable importance about the Spartans and their enemies. During this relationship, Redding's sister had contracted cancer. The treatments were long and arduous and incredibly expensive. Masnick had provided the necessary funds to procure new experimental treatments. Ultimately, the treatments had failed and his sister died.

Redding locked the front door and took the package out to his sun porch. All the documents proving his criminal activities were here. There were transcripts of phone calls, bank records, and medical reports from physicians. It was a nice tidy package. One that would send Redding to prison for a long, long time. When he had read through it all he took it outside to his chiminea and burned it piece by piece. He waited for the call he knew would come.

It came after lunch.

"Special Agent Redding, how are you this afternoon?"

"I got your package."

"All the originals. No duplicates anywhere. Your secret is safe with me."

"Why?"

"What do you mean?"

"Why send it?"

"So suspicious. I have a favor to ask and I didn't want overt coercion involved in your answer."

"I'm listening."

"We were friends once."

"We were never friends. You don't have any friends, Masnick. You were my CI that's all."

"Yet when you were in need I helped you, did I not?"

"Yes."

"And when I disappeared I left you as a star for the FBI."

"You used me."

"Of course. You know me so well. I am capable of almost anything. I did kill my own brother. But I know you too. After a few months of sitting in the sun and failing at golf, you miss the hunt. You are bored. It is a waste of your special skills."

"I don't deny it. Retirement isn't for me."

"I have a deal to make you, but it must be in person and it must be now. I need you to come alone to a meeting in Ohio."

"Why should I? It sounds like a set up."

"I am sure it does. But if I wanted you dead there would have been an explosive device in the package, not records. I will make it worth your while."

"What are you offering?"

"If you accept my proposal, when it is complete, I will turn myself over to law enforcement for prosecution."

"Uh huh. Why would you do that?"

"I am dying. I have been poisoned with an incurable poison. I don't have long to live. And I will sweeten the deal. I will give you something else you have always wanted."

"What's that?"

"You can meet Frank Kane. How's that?"

Redding's heart raced a little at the mythical name. He took a slow breath. "Are the Spartans rebuilding? Is Frank Kane settling old scores like they feared?"

"Come to Ohio and ask him yourself."

Redding paused to try and hide his excitement. He wanted Masnick to think he was considering the deal even though he had already made his decision.

"Where and when?"

"Today. There is a three o'clock flight to Zaneville, Ohio. Get a room at the Best Western hotel nearest the airport. If you are alone, I will contact you. I promise you won't be disappointed."

"I guess I have to pay for my own flight and room?"

"Really? You are so frugal. I can reimburse you in cash for any expenses you incur, but it is important that each step of the trail is traceable to you."

"Three o'clock. See you in Zaneville, wherever that is."

54

Finris walked through the research building. Beneath the strong smell of industrial cleaners, it still stank of urine and pain and fear. Along the back wall the black bears were secured in their tiny "crush" cages that prohibited any movement. Finris looked at them. In the trade, they were called "battery bears." This was the existence they could expect for the rest of their lives.

Finris did not feel any sympathy for the bears. They were not the leopard. To him they were no more than sheep being shorn. Livestock that were raised to be slaughtered. Those that died had their other parts harvested for other traditional medicines. Business in the natural remedies world was booming. Finris loved the Chinese appetite for their traditional medicines. The Chinese were a subhuman species.

Heather met him in the collecting room.

"Our friend the senator has referred several of his important friends to come hunt with us as he promised."

"Excellent."

"He is insistent that he wants to hunt a leopard. Money is not a consideration."

"He has trophy fever. We always covet the things we cannot have."

"Let him have the leopard, Finris. She means nothing to you and it will bind him tighter to our enterprises here."

Finris smiled. "I will consider your request."

"Don't consider it. Just do it. It is good business."

"Life is not all about business. I have plans for the leopard."

"What kind of plans?"

"I will tell you when I want you to know."

"What does that mean?"

"It means what it means. When I want to share my plans with you I will."

Heather made a huffing noise of anger. It was slightly catlike. It made Finris smile.

Finris took her small face in his huge hands. It was a gentle move. He leaned down and gave her a light kiss.

"Later, perhaps. Any word on the search for Prometheus and Kane?"

"Nothing yet. The roadblocks are still in place, but so far nothing. I don't like it."

He kissed her again. "Don't worry. He'll turn up."

"How can you be so calm?"

"Life is chaos. It does not serve anyone to race through it in a panic. I will deal with real problems, not potential ones."

"And if they come?"

"I will deal with them."

Finris could feel her start to relax. The tension went out of her shoulders. She moved in a little closer.

"I know. You always do. It is just that we are all exposed here. If something was to go wrong. . ."

Finris gave her another light peck. "Things always go wrong. It is the nature of the world. But we can handle anything. Let me handle it."

Frank dialed the number that Carpenter had gotten for him. It was answered warily on the third ring.

"Yeah."

The all too familiar voice made him smile.

"Blanco?" Frank asked.

There was a moment of silence.

"Frank? Is that you buddy. Been a long time."

"I've been off the grid."

"I heard you were dead."

"Me too."

"I knew they couldn't kill Frank Kane. What do you need?"

"You, brother. I have business that requires additional manpower."

"And you need someone to watch your six?"

"Yes. Some members of this enterprise are unknown to me, as are their motives. It would help me to have people I can trust with me. I will pay you ten grand for a night's work."

"Fuck the money, Frank. It's not about money between us. Is it going to be bloody?"

"I believe so. Very."

"How are the odds?"

"We are Spartans. Does it matter?"

"No. I'm in."

"Is Reaper with you?"

"Yeah. How did you know? Never mind. I know you have your ways. You need him, too?"

"Of course. I need solid hitters on this one. I need boatmen."

"Good. He would have been pissed if you didn't include him. Tell me when and where and what we need to bring."

Frank did. There was still a lot to do before they went back in.

Richard Redding checked into his room. It was a decent enough room with a bed, a desk, a couple of nightstands and a TV. He sat down on the bed. It was comfortable. He didn't know what he should do. He assumed Masnick would call him. He glanced at the phone. He turned on the television. He liked FOX news. The minutes crept by as he waited for the phone to ring. After an hour of waiting, Redding was starting to get angry. He got up off the bed and went into the bathroom to take a leak.

There was an envelope on the toilet lid. He picked it up and opened it. The message was only an address. Redding took care of business and went out to his rental car. He punched in the address in his cell phone and followed the route to a small diner in a questionable part of town.

The diner was called Alice's. It was busy, but not too busy. He found a booth in the back and sat down. He scanned the customers for any sign of Masnick or potential threats. There were a lot of rough-looking men alone or in small groups. No one stood out.

The waitress brought him a menu and he ordered a coffee, black. When she came back, he ordered a cheeseburger with chips. He had just finished eating when Masnick came in. Masnick walked straight to his booth and sat opposite him.

"It's about time, Masnick."

"It is good to see you, too."

"What is all the cloak and dagger about?"

"In due time. How was your flight? Is your room nice?"

Masnick pushed his empty plate away from himself. "Do we really have to do this song and dance? I've come a long way, as you requested. I came alone."

"I know. I have been watching you."

"And."

Masnick leaned in a little closer. "First, I must have your word."

"About what?"

"If what I am about to tell you does not get you to help me, then you will walk away. You won't report it to other agencies. You won't try to arrest me. You won't do anything. You will just walk away. Go home and do the crosswords and waste your days trying to improve your short game."

Redding thought about it. He was officially retired. He didn't owe anybody anything. "Okay. You have my word."

Masnick nodded as if he hadn't been sure he would get it. Then he told him about the Lodge, and the Norse Men and a drug called Werewolf, and exotic animals and the sex trade. It was not a neat story. There were holes in the picture he painted of the Norse Men's operation. When he finished, he leaned back.

Redding took out his phone and punched in a code that allowed him access to an FBI search engine. He searched for information on the drug, Werewolf. He searched for missing girls in Ohio. He researched number of deaths and disappearances in Blackwater. He researched the Norse Men. He searched for data on illegal uses for exotic animals on the assumption that the Norse Men would be using them for some illegal means.

Masnick ordered coffee while he watched Redding work. Redding worked methodically. He didn't make notes. Thirty minutes in and Masnick ordered a second cup of coffee and a piece of apple pie with extra ice cream. When Redding looked up to study him Masnick just smiled.

"You are meeting with a CI off the books. He would order something. Got to leave a paper trail too."

Redding went back to work. He nodded his head as he read. At the end of an hour he shut his phone off.

"The FBI will log your searches into their data base I presume."

"Yeah."

"Good."

Redding put his phone in his pocket.

"Well?"

"Alright. I will do what I can, provided it is nothing illegal."

"Your part isn't. You got a tip that I was down here at the Lodge. I assume there is a sizeable reward out for my capture."

"There is."

"Even though you are retired you came to investigate. I was a perp that was hard to let go of. I was a cold case that haunted you."

"How does that help you?"

"I need a reason to involve you. You can spin the story as we need it spun. If I don't make it out, it will all be up to you."

"And if you do?"

"I turn myself over for arrest."

"What about Frank Kane?"

Masnick motioned with his right hand. Frank Kane got up from the counter where he had been eating and walked over. He slid into the booth beside Redding. Masnick felt his heart race.

"You're Frank Kane?"

"As ever was. There is no paper out on me."

"No. There isn't."

"Prometheus said you had questions for me."

Redding cleared his throat. He had always dreamed of talking to the Spartans' enforcer, but in his dream, it had been in a police interrogation room with Frank in restraints.

"Are the Spartans rebuilding?"

"No. Not that I am aware of."

"Are you settling old scores with your enemies?"

"No."

"Did you have anything to do with the deaths of the motorcycle gang in Atlanta?"

"I think I will skip that one. Next."

"Why are you involved in this if you are clean?"

"Spartan honor."

"That's it. Spartan honor? That seems a poor reason."

"It is enough. After this is resolved I will disappear again. I don't want you looking for me or ratting me out."

"Agreed."

Masnick interrupted. "We are going to shut them down. People will die."

Redding sighed. Masnick had just admitted to planning a murder. "I don't know if I can let you do that."

"You don't have a choice. It is going to get done with or without your help. Afterwards the Bureau will be all over the scene. We need you to tell the tale in a way that protects Frank."

Redding stared at his hands. This was a big step.

"You will be a star again. You can get any job you want. Sure beats the alternative."

"What's that?"

Frank turned toward him. "This was Prometheus' idea to bring you in. If you are out, there are consequences."

"Such as?"

"I kill you."

Redding knew it was not an idle threat. In for a penny in for a pound. "What do you want me to do?"

"First, go for a ride with us. We need to see a policeman who can help too."

Redding signaled the waitress who brought his bill. He paid it with his credit card. He left a decent tip. He smiled at Masnick.

"Paper trail."

Frank Kane followed them out.

55

Jeff Maurer was sitting in his living room watching television with his wife when the doorbell rang. He started to get up, but his wife beat him to it. He slumped back into his recliner. She came back with a puzzled look on her face.

"What's wrong?"

"There is an FBI agent that would like to speak with you."

Maurer got to his feet. He was found out. He knew it was over. But he reminded himself that it was God's will. He had placed this problem into the Lord's hands, and he would take what God gave him. Maybe going to prison was the only way. He walked to the door.

Redding showed him his badge.

"Are you Deputy Jeff Maurer?"

"Yes, sir."

"I am former Special Agent Richard Redding. Can I speak with you a moment?"

"Sure, come inside."

"I would rather speak in private if you don't mind. Would you mind following me to my car?"

Maurer called inside. "I will be right back, Cath."

He followed Redding to his rental car. There were two men inside. He couldn't make out their faces. He got into the front passenger's seat and turned toward the two men. They were the men from the truck.

Redding climbed into the front.

"Stay calm. These men are deep-cover operatives. They work with me."

Maurer nodded.

"You will never mention having seen them to anyone. Is that clear?"

"Yes, sir."

"I have a dossier on your time as an officer with the Blackwater police force. We believe it a compromised department."

"It is."

"These men attest to your aiding their escape from a place called the Lodge."

Maurer nodded.

"I do not know what kind of hold they have over you, but that is not why we are here. I think you are a good officer who has gotten caught up in something he can't find a way out of."

"Yes, sir. I don't know what to do."

"That's neither here nor there. I will do all I can to shield you from any prosecution and repair some of the wrongs you have committed."

"Thank you, sir. I will do whatever you ask."

"For now, do nothing. Do not report this meeting to your superiors."

"I can't. High Sheriff Long and Deputy Durham are complicit in the crimes up at the Lodge."

"I am aware of that. If you follow my orders at the conclusion of this operation they will be arrested and charged. The Lodge will be shut down. My investigations reveal that it is involved with illegal drug manufacturing and human trafficking."

Maurer nodded. "I think it is true. At least the trafficking part. I don't know about any drugs."

"Doesn't matter. You will report solely to me on this matter. I will contact you soon and explain what you need to do. You need to follow my orders on this."

"Yes, sir, I will."

"I was never here. These men were never here. From this point on all our contact will be logged."

"Yes, sir."

"This visit is a courtesy. I have reviewed your record and I believe that your involvement is minimal. I believe you deserve a second chance."

"Thank you, sir."

"Now go back inside to your wife and enjoy what's left of tonight. I know this is a lot to digest."

"Yes, sir, it is. I have been praying about it."

"Well, your prayers just got answered. The Lodge is a disease that is spreading all through Ohio. We have a chance to stop it."

"Yes, sir."

"What time do you go to work tomorrow?"

"I have to be at the station at eight for roll call. The high sheriff likes to meet with everyone before we go on duty."

"I will see you there."

"Yes, sir."

Maurer got out of the car and went inside. God was truly listening to his prayers.

Jake had the television on a local news station. The handsome talking head was blathering on to his equally attractive female co-host about the rise in drug related overdoses in Greensboro.

"Gretchen, there have been four more deaths related to overdoses of this new lethal form of heroin that has surfaced in Greensboro."

"It is horrible."

"Yes, it is. Authorities are warning locals to avoid this new mix of heroin and fentanyl that goes by the street name, the Green Apache."

"It is a terrifying mixture that can cause complete respiratory depression and death. Stay away from this terrible, terrible drug."

"Authorities have informed me that despite warnings about Green Apache, usage is actually increasing. Drug addicts are flocking to Greensboro to find this dangerously potent and potentially toxic drug. Police officers are now carrying Narcan, a special drug, to use on overdose victims to try to save their lives."

"Are other cities in the Triad experiencing the same thing that we are here in Greensboro?"

"Not yet. But authorities are afraid with its growing popularity that it will spread."

"That is just terrible."

"If you have any information on this drug please contact the police tip line. There is a reward offered and all calls will be kept strictly confidential."

"Call if you have any information."

"Now let's switch to a look at our local weather. . ."

Jake clicked the television off. He picked up his phone and called Carpenter.

"Jake."

"Any news?"

"I have been searching. There's not much new. Russians, Chinese, new heroin."

"It's called Green Apache on the street. That's how they are marketing it."

"That's good. Might link to something. But you already told me this."

"Sorry. I forgot. I need to take care of this before they get established here."

"I am fully aware of that, Jake. I will contact you when I have something."

"Thanks."

"You're welcome."

Jake hung the phone up. He went to his computer and booted up the tracking app. The Russians were out at the same strip club. He watched for a while and tried to figure out his next move. He felt frustrated.

Greensboro was his home now. He had a straight business that was doing very well. Frank Kane was here. Jenny was here. He wanted to stay. He would do whatever he needed to do protect it.

56

Redding parked in one of the visitor's parking spaces outside the Blackwater Police Station. He went inside and introduced himself to the secretary at the front desk. The morning briefing was just ending, and the officers were walking out to their patrol cars. Redding asked to meet with High Sheriff Long. The secretary pointed to the sheriff, who was talking to Maurer.

Redding thanked her and approached the two men. They stopped their conversation and turned to face him.

"Excuse me, I am former Special Agent Richard Redding."

"Former?" High Sheriff Long asked.

"Yes, sir. Retired."

"I am the high sheriff. Name's James Long. This is Deputy Maurer."

"Pleased to meet you," Redding said, and shook everyone's hands.

"How can I help you?"

"It is about a fugitive, a former CI of mine, named Keith Masnick. Can we speak in private?"

The name shook the sheriff, but he showed no sign. "Sure, come on back to my office. Can I have Sue get you a cup of coffee or something?"

"No thank you, Sheriff. I just need a couple of minutes of your time."

Redding nodded a farewell to Maurer and followed the high sheriff to his office. Once inside he took a seat across from the sheriff's heavy oak desk. The sheriff sat behind the desk.

"How can I help you?"

"I have a tip that a notorious felon, a Mr. Masnick, has been sighted in the area."

"Who is this fellow?"

"He was a former elite member of the Spartans Motorcycle Club. He is a sociopath with a penchant for bombs."

"Correct me, but in what capacity are you searching for him in? You did say you were retired."

"I did and I am. It was my final case and he slipped away after murdering a United States senator and a number of other people, including my partner."

"And you can't let it go?"

"No. The Bureau is aware of my ongoing interest in the apprehension of this felon, but this is all entirely unofficial."

"You said you had a tip that he was in the area. Can I have the name of your source?"

"I am sorry. It is confidential." Redding took a mug shot of Masnick out of a manila envelope he carried. "This is what he looks like."

The high sheriff made a show of studying the picture. He shook his head. "This is a small town. I will put the word out. Can I keep this photo?"

"Of course. I have lots."

"I don't mind telling you I think you are on a wild goose chase, Mr. Redding. Why would a big-time criminal like this be in our one-horse town?"

"I have no idea, Sheriff. This is a courtesy call. I just wanted to let you know I would be poking around."

"If you turn something up, don't hesitate to contact me directly." He handed Redding a business card. "Anything that I can do to help, don't hesitate to call me."

"I will, Sheriff."

"Well, we all want the same thing here."

"I appreciate your cooperation."

"Glad to help. You staying in Blackwater?"

"No. Up in Zaneville at the Best Western." He took a card out of his pocket and passed it to the sheriff. "If you turn up anything, give me a call."

The high sheriff looked at the card and slipped it into his shirt pocket.

Redding rose to his feet and extended his hand. They shook and Redding turned and left. The high sheriff watched him stop and speak to the secretary at the front desk. He passed her a business card. He watched him pass his card out to Maurer and the other officers as he left.

High Sheriff Long picked up his cell phone and called Buck.

"What's up, Boss?"

"Might have a problem. We got a former FBI guy poking around."

"What's he looking for?'

"Masnick. He got a tip he was in the area."

"Shit."

"He's staying at the Best Western in Zaneville. Go check him out. I don't want it to be able to be traced to me if this thing goes sideways."

"Got it, boss."

High Sheriff Long hung up and called Finris. He explained what had happened.

Finris seemed unconcerned.

"There is no reason to believe his search will lead him here. He can't come up to the Lodge without an invitation or evidence of a crime."

"Except with a court issued warrant."

"That won't happen. The local judges are locked down. They would never approve it."

"I think you are right."

"If he becomes a problem, I assume you will take care of it."

"That won't be a problem. Just wanted to keep you updated."

"I appreciate the call, Sheriff."

The sheriff hung up. He had an uneasy feeling that Redding was going to be a problem. He just felt it in his gut. Buck would keep an eye on him. Redding would get bored and leave. If Redding got close to something, he had options. He could try to scare him off. He could slip him a little of the old Bill Cosby and film his fun time at the Lodge. Blackmail was always easy. He could plant evidence and arrest him. Or if things got too bad, he could let Buck make him disappear. Buck wouldn't have a problem with that. The high sheriff hated to do that because Redding was a fed. Normally that would bring a rain of shit down on you. But on the other hand, he was retired. How hard would they look? He would do whatever it took to protect what he had built here.

Jenny was waiting for Jake. She was trying to look like she wasn't. But she was. She had showered and dressed and then redressed and then a final change of clothes. She was starting to think her first outfit might have been the best choice. It was hip and comfortable. But it wasn't very warm. And the second was warm but dull. This one was a classic. It was black jeans, three-buckle Madden Girl calf-high boots, and a deep black sweater sprinkled with gray. She had her coat and favorite vintage scarf and a funky little wool knit cap laid casually on a chair near the door.

Every time she heard a car she sat up a little, hoping it was Jake. It wasn't. She checked her watch. Okay, to be fair, he wasn't due for another fifteen minutes. But he should be early, she reasoned, if he was really looking forward to seeing her. She went to the bathroom and checked her makeup. It looked good. Maybe she should run change one more time? Where was he?

The doorbell chimed. Jenny's heart raced. She hurried to the door. She finger combed her hair and opened the door. Jake was on the doorstep. He was smiling. She felt her heart melt.

"You look fantastic."

"Thanks. You said comfortable, so I just threw on the first thing I came across."

"Perfect choice. Are you ready to go?"

"Yeah. Let me get my coat."

Jake let her come outside and lock the door behind her. She scanned the curb for his car. It wasn't there. A sleek Harley 750 Street crouched at the curb. She spun around.

"Is that bike yours?"

"Yeah. I thought it might be fun to ride."

Jenny slapped his shoulder. "Oh, my God. It is gorgeous."

"Have you ever been on a bike before?"

232

"No. I mean close. Jet skis and four-wheelers, but not a real bike."

"Then this will be a treat."

She followed him to the motorcycle. She walked around it, admiring its simple beauty.

"This is a sweet little ride. Smooth, fast, and nimble. It is the first new design by Harley-Davidson in a long time. And best of all, I could afford the price. Perfect for what I have planned."

He handed her a full helmet.

"This will mess up my hair."

"Put it on. Better your hair than your pretty face. A friend of mine used to say dress for the slide not for the ride."

Jenny slipped it on. Jake put on a second helmet.

"But we aren't going to crash, right?"

"I promise."

He straddled the bike and pressed the starter button. The bike roared to life.

"Get on."

Jenny climbed behind him. She could feel the almost sexual rumble of the bike between her legs. She placed her hands lightly on his back.

"Where are we going?"

"To lunch at the Bohemian. It's a hip little bistro. You'll love it."

Jenny smiled, but she didn't think he could see it through her tinted facemask. He pulled her hands a little farther around his waist.

"Hold on tight and trust me."

Jenny gripped his waist and pressed lightly against his back. Jake moved the bike into first and gently pulled away from the curb. A few quick flicks of the gears, a twist of the accelerator and they were flying.

Jenny thought the feeling was phenomenal. It was free and fast and dangerous and the roar between her legs was stirring dirty ideas. Very dirty ideas. Now she understood why people loved riding motorcycles.

57

The three huge packages arrived via UPS. They were stamped golf clubs. Frank signed for them and lugged them inside. He took them and placed them on the bed in his room. The gear from Carpenter was all packed inside the empty heavy golf bags. He took his knife and slit the tape on one of the packages and dumped the contents out on the bed. There were seven sets of identical tactical body armor with the protective plates already in place. Frank had his own body armor, the Dragon Skin. There were eight tactical vests with ammo pouches that could be reconfigured to the wearer's specifications. There were eight Glock 40 caliber semiautomatic pistols, each with three magazines. They were droppable weapons that could not be traced back to Carpenter or his contacts. There were eight boxes of ammo for the handguns.

But the most important items were the jackets. There was one for each man. The navy-blue nylon windbreaker jackets were stamped with large yellow letters on the back, DEA. There was a smaller configuration over the left breast that could be covered be a flap. There were also badges and fake DEA credentials for each man.

There were eight IFAKs, individual first aid kits. These miniature medic kits could be secured with a Velcro strap to your leg or placed in one of the tactical vest pockets. These kits were meant to be worn on your front so you could self treat your wounds. In this scenario, it was almost certainly going to be single or multiple guns shot wounds. The IFAKs had been modified for that purpose.

Frank unzipped one of the kits. The first compartment contained a CAT tourniquet and vacuum rolled packs of gauze. The inside pocket contained two packs of Israeli dressing. The Israeli dressing could be placed in a GSW and would mold itself to fit. There were also two packs of QuikClot Combat dressing. The last section of the kit contained three syringes, each loaded with an ampule of morphine. Good to go. He zipped the kit back up and went to Masnick's room with the other two golf bags.

Frank knocked on the door to Masnick's room. He was lying on the bed.

"The gear."

Masnick sat up. "Great. Is it all there?"

"Yes. Same basic things in each box: vest, backup gun, jacket, med kit. Are your guys bringing their primary weapons?"

"Yeah, they got their own guns. My main guy, Keating, is bringing the special weapons and cash and some other supplies I need. The other three have the coordinates to this place and will follow after they acquire extra vehicles."

"You mean steal."

"Of course. I need a minimum of four vehicles for your plan to work. Each man brings a ride. Makes it easier to escape at the end too."

"I know. Can't have too many escape vehicles."

"Your guys bringing heavy firepower?"

"No. I plan to acquire it onsite."

Masnick looked surprised but tried to mask it. "You sure it will be available?"

"Based on my intel it won't be a problem."

"Whatever."

"Carpenter says all the gear is droppable. Nothing can be traced back to him."

"If we lose something or someone, it can't come back on him."

"Exactly. There will be a lot of lead flying."

"Yeah. Listen, Frank, I trust Kevin, but the other three are straight up Merc thugs Keating hired. I can't vouch for them. They are here for the money, nothing else."

"Meaning?"

"Meaning. There may or may not be a bounty out on you. Keep your eyes open."

"Thanks for the warning. I got Blanco and Reaper."

"Good men. Reaper is a bit of a loose cannon, but solid enough."

A car pulled up outside, then the sound of several more.

"Sounds like the party is starting."

Masnick lifted himself off the bed. He seemed grayer than he had earlier. He paused for a moment like he was trying to get his balance. There was a glass of water on the bedside table and a stack of pills. Frank tried not to stare. Masnick took a few pills and washed them down with the water. Masnick smiled and headed toward the front door. Frank turned and followed Masnick outside. He kept his hand on the pistol under the back of his shirt.

There were four cars outside. The lead car was a dark sedan without a license plate. The other three were nondescript junkers. Each man stood beside his vehicle. Masnick smiled when he saw Kevin. Kevin Keating was average height and build with a mop of hair on his head, curious eyes and a broad boyish smile. He wore dark slacks and a white shirt with a nondescript blue tie. He looked like a federal agent. The two men embraced. Frank couldn't hear what they were saying. Kevin was nodding. At the conclusion, he straightened and approached Frank. His hand was out. Frank shook it.

"I'm Kevin Keating. I've headed his security detail for a long time. I was off-site when they took him."

"Frank."

"These private contractors are going to be referred to as simply Able, Bravo and Charlie for added security."

The contractors nodded. Each man was dressed in a dark blue suit with a red tie and white shirt. They looked like cops or military operators. Masnick went to the back seat of Keating's car and removed a pair of large duffel bags. The other men followed his lead and gathered their gear. They all went inside. The three men placed their gear in the small living room. They each returned to their cars and brought in new AR-15s. They laid their weapons on top of their bags.

Masnick and Keating took their bags to Masnick's bedroom. After a minute where no one spoke, they returned. Masnick handed each man a thick stack of bills.

"Ten thousand up front. Five more at the completion."

The men all smiled at the thick stack of bills. The nudged each other. Today was a good day. They put the money in their bags.

"Sweet," Charlie said.

Masnick passed out the fake IDs and the nylon jackets. The men examined the documents and slipped them into coat pockets.

"Kevin, I got that job for you. Take Able and Bravo with you."

Kevin smiled. "Let's roll."

"What about some food?" Bravo asked.

"We can pick up supplies on the way back."

"Roger that."

"We will go over the details of the op tonight."

The men all nodded.

"Listen up. This is Frank's gig. You do what he tells you or you will end up dead. This isn't a security detail. This is no bank heist. This is some serious shit," Masnick said.

The men nodded some more.

Frank watched the contractors. No one seemed overly interested in him. They seemed a little excited with a touch of professional boredom.

Masnick handed Kevin a list. Kevin looked it over.

"These are the other things I need. You can get them on the way back too."

"Will do."

Frank didn't like going to war with men he didn't know, but there was no other way.

58

Jake paid for lunch and they remounted his bike. Jenny was feeling more comfortable on the bike.

"Where to now?"

"Wait and see. It is a surprise."

She tried to put her lower lip out, but it didn't work very well. Jake didn't seem to notice. They rode for fifteen minutes. Jenny thought she could ride all day. Finally, Jake pulled the Harley-Davidson into a parking lot outside Calibers.

Calibers was an indoor gun range. It was a nondescript one-story brick building. The only entrance was covered with a dark green awning. There were thick concrete security barriers to prevent knuckleheads from trying to breach the building through the front door.

Jake led Jenny inside. The people working there seemed to know Jake. He joked with them. He picked out a half dozen targets and four guns for them to try and a box of ammo for each. Jake took Jenny over and got them both a pair of ear protectors and safety glasses. The tall red-haired guy behind the desk gave them a lane to use. Jake laid the guns out on the counter in front of them. There was a .22 caliber pistol, a .38, a 9mm and a .45.

Jenny was nervous. She could feel her heart starting to race. She was starting to tremble a little. The recirculating fan groaned over her head as it sucked the air up from the lane. It felt like she was outside in the wind. Even with the muffling effect of the ear protectors she was overwhelmed with sound. Guns boomed and popped and banged all around her. There were different tempos to the sounds. Some stitched like a sewing machine with long continuous ribbons of noise. Other gun fire was in groups of two or three. Some in lonely single sounds like the roar of cannons. She could smell the tangy smell of gunpowder.

Jake took something leaning against the wall that looked like a squeegee on a long pole and pushed the spent brass casings off the carpet into the shooting area. He leaned it back against a wall. He taped up one of the targets, a silhouette of a man, to the hanger that would take it out into the shooting part of the range. He sent it down range about seven yards. He opened the box of .22 caliber ammo. He ejected the magazine and fed the rounds into it with his thumb. He snapped the magazine back into place. Jake waved her forward. Jenny felt her legs trembling. Her hands were wet, so she wiped them on the sides of her jeans.

"You need to know how to handle a gun. You need to know how to protect yourself."

Jenny nodded. Her mouth was too dry to talk.

Jake leaned in a little closer so he didn't have to yell as loud. "I know you are scared. I'm going to teach you how to shoot."

He handed her the gun. It was a twenty-two with a long barrel. He showed her the proper stance with one leg in front of the other, about shoulder width apart. There was a slight turn to her body. He showed her the proper two-hand grip. He showed her how to sight down the barrel and to place the center dot in the sight picture. He had her open both eyes.

"Now take a deep breath. Let most of it out. Calm yourself and squeeze the trigger."

"Will it kick?"

"It doesn't matter. If you ever have to use a gun you won't even notice the recoil. Now gently squeeze the trigger."

Jenny did and was shocked when the gun fired. It didn't have much recoil and the sound wasn't that bad. Her first round hit the target in the midsection near the outer edge of the left hip. She turned toward Jake and smiled.

"Very good. Now aim for the center of the chest and give me two shots."

Jenny licked her lips. She aimed and fired. Both rounds were off the mark, but they were close together.

"Nice grouping. Aim up and over to the right a little."

Jenny did and put the next two into the center zone. She felt a rush of excitement. She turned to Jake and he was beaming.

"Are you sure you haven't ever shot a gun before?"

"No."

"Well, you're a natural."

"It's not as scary as I thought it would be."

"No, it's fun."

"Your turn," she said extending the pistol toward him. Jake just shook his head.

"I come here all the time. Today is about you."

Jenny looked at the weapons and boxes of ammo.

"That's a lot of bullets to shoot."

Jake smiled at her. "That's just the start. Once we run through these, we'll know which gun you like best. Next time we can concentrate on that one. We will start to refine your techniques a little more."

"Oh, my God, this is so much fun! Do you think Frank will be mad?"

"Why would he be? This is how he taught me."

For a brief moment Jenny could picture Frank showing a teenage Jake how to use a gun. Not for protection but to kill other men. It sent a shiver down her spine. She buried the thought. Frank was a good man, she told herself. Jake was a good man.

"Aim for the head."

Jenny worked through the different guns. She noticed the differences in weight. And what she called the "kick and roar" of the different guns. The longer the barrel was, the more stable the gun, but it also made it heavier. It was fun trying different guns and different calibers trying to determine the right fit for her.

The .22 was scary at first but it seemed to lack power. The .38 revolver was the easiest to load and never jammed. The .45 was just too big and heavy and loud. In the end, she settled on the 9mm, the standard choice. It seemed a perfect compromise between weight and power. And she liked having more rounds if she had to shoot.

She had fired two hundred rounds, but Jake bought her another box of fifty for the 9 since she was having so much fun. Her shot placement was precise. She felt relaxed and excited at the same time. When she finished her last round, she had a moment's temptation to shoot one more box. But her trigger finger was getting sore, so she didn't.

Jake policed the brass casings and carried the rented guns back to the front desk. The guys were all smiling. They liked seeing a pretty girl who wasn't afraid of guns. She waved goodbye to them and followed Jake outside to his bike. He handed her helmet to her.

Jenny looked at the helmet. Why did Jake have a helmet for a woman? She felt a sharp pang of jealousy. Maybe this was how he played women. She stuck the helmet out toward Jake.

"How many other girls have worn this?"

Jake looked back at her without expression.

"None."

"Then why do you just happen to have one that fits a female?"

"I bought it for you to wear."

Jenny looked closer. The helmet was brand new. The DOT sticker on the back was shiny. Her heart leapt.

"Why?"

"You can't just ride bitch all the time."

"Excuse me?"

"It's just a term for riding on the back seat. It doesn't mean anything. You'll need a good helmet when you learn to ride on your own too."

"Drive my own motorcycle?"

"Sure. I'll teach you and when you are ready you can go to the DMV and get an endorsement so you can ride legal."

"Do you have one?"

"No. But you should."

She leaned over and kissed him on the cheek.

"What was that for?"

"The best day ever."

"Hey, I still have to cook dinner."

Jenny smiled. "I know. I figured I better kiss you now in case you can't cook at all."

Jake laughed. She got on behind him and wrapped her arms around his waist. The bike sped away. It really was the best day ever.

59

Kevin Keating and the two contractors drove to the Best Western Hotel where Redding was staying. They were wearing the faux DEA jackets. Able and Bravo took positions near the entrance. Keating approached the check-in desk. He looked around and smiled. The pretty ash-blonde girl behind the counter smiled back. He reached into his breast pocket and removed his fake id. It was a perfect replica of the real thing. Keating badged the girl behind the counter.

"I need the room number of one of your guests. He is an FBI agent named Richard Redding."

The girl didn't hesitate. She went immediately to work typing on her keyboard.

"Room 304."

"Thank you. I would appreciate it if you did not alert him to our presence."

"No, sir. Is he in some kind of trouble?"

"No, ma'am. We just need to speak to him about an on-going investigation."

"One of those joint task force things you hear about?"

"Something like that."

"Do you need a room key?"

"No. That won't be necessary. Thank you."

Keating nodded some secret command to Able and Bravo who followed him to the bank of elevators. The three men went up to Redding's floor. They walked single file to his room and knocked. There was no answer, so they knocked again.

"Masnick sent us."

There were muffled sounds. The deadbolt was released. A voice said.

"Come in slowly, one at a time. Hands where I can see them."

Keating led his men inside. Their hands were raised about waist high with the palms out. Redding was lying on the floor in the bathroom off to their right. He had his Glock aimed at them. Keating smiled. He liked a man that wasn't a fool.

"Face down on the bed, all three of you."

Able and Bravo complied without comment. Keating tuned slightly.

"I am going to reach into my left outside pocket. I have a cell phone there. I will place it on the floor. Press One on the speed dial to verify we are who we say we are."

"Go ahead."

Keating did and then joined the others lying face down on the bed with their hands raised. Redding got to his knees. Damn, they were stiff, he thought. He didn't much like lying on a hotel bathroom floor. God only knew what had been there. He scooped up the phone and pushed the button. Masnick answered on the first ring.

"Agent Redding."

"What do you want?"

"To verify that these men are who they say they are. I knew you would be suspicious."

"Damn right. Some stooge in an unmarked car has been tailing me all day."

"I thought so. I am sure he noticed our contact."

"I am sure he has. What do you want?"

"Just establishing the chain of events. You were approached by three DEA agents who all appear to have the proper credentials about their ongoing case."

"Which is?"

"They would not elaborate, but it involved illegal drugs, steroids and amphetamine mixture."

"Sounds good. What did they want with me?"

"To see what the FBI's interest is. To share information."

"Bullshit. They never share information. Neither do we."

"But you always promise too."

"True. Good move. It confirms my involvement."

"Would you mind letting my people up? I assume you have them at gunpoint."

"Hey, you can get up."

The three men rolled over and got to their feet.

"Just let them stay ten or fifteen minutes for the show."

"Got it. Don't forget our deal."

"I won't. I am many things, but I am honorable."

Redding laughed. "Whatever."

"Keep this cell phone so we can communicate. I will retrieve it when next we meet."

"Out."

Redding hung up the phone. He spoke to Keating, who was obviously the leader.

"Do I know you?"

"I don't believe so."

"Good. Didn't want you to carry a grudge into this thing."

"Not from me."

"What do I call you? I mean when they ask me later. What name did Masnick want you to use?"

"Special Agent Erskine."

Redding laughed out loud. Keating smiled. Able and Bravo looked confused.

"Masnick choose the name?"

"Yes, he did."

"I thought so. What a dick."

"I don't get it," Able said. "Who's Erskine."

Keating looked to Redding. "You want to tell him?"

"Go ahead."

"Inspector Lewis Erskine was the name of the character played by Efrem Zimbalist, Junior, on the television show The F.B.I., back in what, the seventies?"

"Mid-sixties. It ran for a decade and a half."

"So, it is the name of a fake FBI agent. So what?"

Able shrugged.

"Masnick didn't think you would recognize it."

"Hell, I am old. I watched the damn show. It's what made me want to get into the Bureau in the first place."

Keating laughed. "I think he just recently passed."

"May 2, 2014. He was ninety-five. The FBI presented him with an honorary special agent's badge in 2009."

"I guess Masnick didn't realize how well he was remembered by the FBI."

"Yeah, I'll just make a name up for you and your men. Easier to remember."

60

Frank heard the car easing up the gravel drive. He slipped his pistol out and held it by his leg as he went to the front door. The car, a late model gun-metal gray Honda Accord, stopped, but no one got out. Charlie came up to his side. The AR-15 was on a sling over his shoulder. The pistol grip and stock were in his hands.

"Trouble?"

"We'll see."

Charlie pulled back on the charging handle. The bolt pistoned back into place. Frank glanced at the weapon. Thirty round magazine, four-X scope, probably chambered for .556. It was a devastating weapon in the hands of someone who knew how to operate it. Charlie seemed very comfortable with the weapon.

The passenger's front door popped open. A man stepped out. He turned away from the house and appeared to be stretching. Frank could tell there was something in his hand. Might be a weapon. Charlie raised the barrel three inches. He flipped the safety off.

The man turned toward the house. He was Robert Ziglar, aka Blanco Grande, the Great White. He was so named for a long scar that ran down his face and neck and through his close-cropped beard. Blanco was about five foot ten with a thin build. The item in his hand was a can of beer. He turned the can up and killed it. He tossed the empty back inside the vehicle.

The driver's door opened and out stepped Reaper. He was smoking a cigarette, a Camel Silver, as Frank recalled. Reaper was taller at about six one, and a little thicker. He had broad shoulders and big arms. He was a blade man. He was good with a lot of weapons, but he preferred a blade. He and Spanish Johnny had always had some kind of beef between them. In retrospect, it would have worked out better for Frank if he had let Reaper cut Spanish Johnny's black heart out. As it was, Spanish turned on Frank and almost killed him and now he was messed up with this shit about Masnick. Spanish Johnny was off the rails.

Frank couldn't think of two better warriors to go into combat with than Blanco and Reaper. And the Jake too, of course. That kid was superhuman. But Blanco and Reaper would do just fine. They had all been Spartans together. They were all boatmen. They had all been members of the Kryptea, the Spartans' kill squad.

Frank placed a hand on the barrel of the AR-15 and eased it down.

"These are my boys."

Frank stepped away from Charlie and went outside.

The joy at seeing their old comrade was unfeigned. Reaper and Blanco took turns hugging Frank. Backs were slapped, biceps squeezed, shoulders shaken, heads rubbed and even fists were bumped.

"Damn, it's good to see you, Frank."

"It is good to see you both, too."

Charlie walked onto the porch, still carrying his AR.

"Do I get one of those?" Blanco asked.

"Yeah, later. This is Charlie."

Charlie nodded and they nodded back.

"You hold the fort down, Charlie. Keating will be back with your friends soon. I'm taking my boys out for something to eat."

"Masnick in there?" Blanco asked.

"Yeah. He's taking a nap. You can talk to him when we get back."

"Sounds good."

They all piled into Frank's truck. Reaper got into the back.

"Just like old times," Blanco said.

Reaper leaned forward and shook Frank's shoulders. "I can't believe you are still alive. Word was you got whacked."

"You can't kill Frank Kane," Blanco said. "Everyone knows that."

"Truth, brother. Truth."

"What have you guys been up to?"

"Same old," Reaper said.

"Did some crime, did some time."

"Well, Helios swears he wiped your histories from the data bases. No prints on file, no DNA, no photos, clean slates," Frank told them.

"For real?"

"Part of some deal he was working on for Cyrus. You know Carpenter, always working an angle."

"No shit."

"Me and Blanco have been working this cool little bank deal."

"You mean knocking over banks?"

"Well, yeah. But it is so much sweeter now."

"You are masked up, right?"

"Frank, we aren't stupid. We go in wearing full painter suits. Coveralls, hair covers, masks, buckets of paint, even a tarp. It looks so legit no one says shit at first. We hold the place up, get the cash from the tellers."

"Most punks are so stupid they only get the top drawer."

"Yeah, we get both drawers. Take is usually about fifty or sixty K."

"Tell Frank the best part."

"Right. Banks have started to use these GPS trackers now instead of dye packs. The fake stack sits on a little pedestal in the top drawer. When the teller slips it into your stack it sends out an alert and the cops can track it."

"That sounds bad."

"No, it isn't. The cops are spoiled. They let the perps get away and just follow the tracker. In a couple of hours after the adrenaline has burned off and the perp feels safe, they send the SWAT team to go pick them up. We do it a little differently. I politely ask for the money with the tracker. She is stunned I know about it but will comply. Blanco tells each of the other tellers if they slip the tracker in with his stash he will hunt them down and kill them."

"And they do it?"

"Hell, it's not their money. Who wants to get killed for bank cash?"

"Plus, it's only easy to do something like that if you don't think you will get caught."

"Tell him the best part."

"I'm telling this. After we get away, we dump the getaway at a Walmart. We put the tracking cash in the back of a truck and split."

"That way the cops follow the wrong car."

"Exactly. We've pulled it a couple of times and it has been slick as snot. The banks will start to get wise sooner or later, but it's fun."

"That's why you said this wasn't about money."

"Yeah, brother, we are pretty flush."

"Knuckleheads."

"Beats a real job."

They found a restaurant on the water with outside tables. They took the most remote one. They ate and talked and drank beer. Blanco and Reaper could do some serious drinking. Frank gave them the run down on the plan and what he had seen. He explained his concerns about the mercs and Masnick.

"So," Blanco asked, "what did you end up doing with this Alton dude?"

"You ice him?"

"No. I left him alive. He won't rat. It would be his ass too."

"But after this thing is resolved, you are going to go back and take care of him, right? No loose end to come back and hang you."

"I don't know. Probably just let him go. No reason to do him if I don't have to."

Blanco shook Frank's big shoulder. "You're getting soft. Back in the day, Poseidon..."

"Those days are gone, brother. I'm trying not to be that guy anymore. Living the straight life. Keeping my head down."

"Yet, here you are. Gearing up for war."

"It's fucked up."

Frank shrugged. "It is what it is."

"We got your back on this, Frank. You can count on us," Reaper said.

"Yeah. Whatever you need."

"I appreciate that. He handed each of them a piece of paper."

They looked at it. It was a phone number.

"What's this?"

"My private cell. I owe you both. You ever need me, call."

They both realized the importance of the number. It signified Frank's total trust in his brothers. It was a promise of unconditional help. It was the bat light on top of Gotham City. It was Superman's phone number. It was the red phone in the White House.

61

Buck called High Sheriff Long.

"Buck."

"We got a problem."

"What?"

"Some DEA boys met with the FBI guy at his hotel."

The high sheriff pondered the information. It could mean a lot of things. All of them bad.

"Where did they meet?"

"In his room. They showed up, got his room number from the front desk. Then went up."

"I wonder what they are up to. I'll make some calls see if I can turn up anything. Could be they are old friends, or their investigations have crossed."

"Think they'll tell you?"

"No. I'm nothing to them. But sometimes you can learn a lot by what they don't say."

"Got you."

"We got to keep our eyes on this. It could spell big trouble if they are looking down in Blackwater."

"Yes, sir. Just tell me what to do."

"I'm not sure. Come on back. Let's meet at Ruby's and talk."

"On my way."

Jake's house was small. It was an old nondescript two-bedroom home. She noticed that the yard was slightly unkempt. There was a scattering of leaves over it. The white paint on the house was starting to peel. The house looked old and weathered and adorable, she thought.

He parked the bike beside his car in the two-car garage. They left their helmets on pegs on a wall board in the garage and went inside. The inside of the house was neat and clean. It was lightly furnished with some secondhand pieces. Jenny could tell it was recently cleaned. She didn't know if she wanted it to be like this all the time or if she wanted it to be like this just because she was coming over. There was a modest television in front of the sofa. There were no pictures on the walls, which she thought was odd.

The kitchen was small and neat. The appliances looked new. There was an elaborate coffee machine and a tiny microwave. There was a small round dining table with four chairs tucked into a nook off the kitchen.

"This is nice," she said.

"Thanks."

"Where can I hang my coat?"

"Just toss it on the bed."

Jenny's heart was racing when she stepped into his bedroom. It seemed very daring and adult. The bedroom was sparse. There was only the bed and a nightstand with a lamp and a phone charger on it. She sat down on the bed, it was medium, not too soft and not too hard. The comforter was pale gray swirls with red designs in it. She thought it seemed tasteful. She placed her coat and gloves on the bed and went back to the kitchen.

"You can chill out and watch TV if you want while I get dinner ready."

"Okay. Can I have a drink?"

"Of course. I don't have a lot of choices. I'm not much of a drinker. I have a couple of bottles of red wine if you would like."

"That would be great."

Jenny did a little look around for the wine and spotted the two bottles on the back of the countertop. Jake opened a drawer and removed a corkscrew. He handed it to her and went back to the dinner. Jenny felt very grown up as she looked at the wine. They were both the same kind. She searched the cabinets and found two wine glasses. They were dusty so she rinsed them in the sink and then poured them each a glass of wine. She put Jake's in front of him.

"What are you making?"

"Something I think you will love. It's salmon sushi."

"Ew. Really? Raw fish?"

"It is really good."

"I don't like sushi."

"Have you ever tried it?"

"No. But in the south, we call it bait."

Jake smiled. "Sounds like something on a tee shirt."

"That's probably where I saw it. I just don't think I will like it."

"You have to be willing to try new things. That's what makes life fun."

"What if I hate it?"

"Then I'll make you a peanut butter and jelly sandwich. But you have to at least try it. It is simple to make but very good. You could even make it for Frank. He loves sushi."

Jenny didn't think she had ever seen Frank eat sushi or even mention it. It gave her a twinge of sadness that even after all this time there was a lot she didn't know about Frank. And she had never taken the time to find out.

"Okay. I'll watch as you play chef."

Jake prepared the rice, boiling and cooking and cooling until it was ready. He spread it over a baking tin he had lined with cling film. The sticky rice clung to his fingers as he spread it out. He placed the smoked salmon slices over the rice, completely covering it. Then he pressed cling film down over the salmon to mold everything together. He got a ceramic knife, dipped it into some hot water and cut the food into sixteen rectangles.

"That's it," he said proudly.

It looked ghastly. Raw and unhealthy. She managed a weak smile.

"It looks nice."

"Don't be a baby." He got out some sauce from the refrigerator. He picked one sushi roll up and bit into it. "Yum. Try it."

Jenny psychologically held her nose. She knew it had to stink. She picked up one and took a little nibble. She faked a smile.

"No. You just got rice. You have to taste it with the salmon."

She managed another weak smile. She did really like him. She took a bite. She was stunned. It was good. No, it was incredible. The mixture of flavors and textures was incredible. She couldn't believe it.

"Oh, my God. This is so good."

Jake toasted her with his glass of wine. "I'm glad you like it. Let's take it over to the table so we can have a proper dinner. I also have a small spinach salad chilling in the fridge so you can have a balanced meal. Normally I just eat the sushi."

They ate and talked and sipped the wine. It was a perfect day.

Jeff Maurer was watching television with his wife. It was some old movie with Errol Flynn playing a French man during WWII. Cathy watched him watch it. He seemed so peaceful these last few days. Something had happened. She didn't know what, but something profound. All the stress and worry were gone. When she pressed him on it, he had told her that he had given his life over to God. God would show him the path and he would follow it.

When the FBI agent had come to talk to him it had not upset him, although it had scared her terribly. He had only told her it was part of God's plan for them. She felt the babies stir and she placed a protective hand over her swollen belly to soothe them. They flipped and flopped and settled. She prayed for her unborn children. She prayed for her husband. She felt like everything was going to be alright. God had a plan.

62

Nils was stretched out on the king size bed. He was leering. He was not alone. Shena and Lexxus were with him. They were dressed in provocative lingerie. Lexxus wore six-inch stripper heels and a pale pink baby doll ensemble. Shena was wearing a black number with thigh-high leather boots. They moved expertly around his body licking and touching and stroking and teasing.

He mounted them in a variety of positions. They voiced their enthusiasm and submission to his desires. Nils was both a part of the sexual dance as he was separate from it. An undercurrent of cruelty seemed to pulse in him. He disentangled himself and leaned back against the headboard. He pointed at Shena.

"Now I want you to fuck her."

Lexxus tensed. There was a blur of pain in her eyes. She didn't move. Her mind scrambled to come to grips with the changing tableau. A harsh smile played across Nils' lips. Lexxus didn't move.

"Are you refusing?" he asked.

Before she could answer Shena moved to her. Shena brushed the blonde hair back from Lexxus' face. She kissed her cheek and then the top of her head. Lexxus was trembling.

"I don't think I can do this."

"Shh," Shena whispered. "That's what he wants. He wants you to refuse so he can punish you."

Lexxus was as stiff as wooden doll. "I can't get my head around it.'

"Shh. You can or he will hurt you. Let me help you."

Lexxus was shaking now.

"Go someplace else in your head. Go there now. I will take care of this."

Lexxus looked at her. Tears were streaming down her cheeks.

"Just think of a better place. Leave your body here for me. I will put on a good show."

Lexxus nodded. She let Shena ease her back onto the bed. She could see Nils' leering face over her shoulder. She tried to think of something else, somewhere else, someone else. Shena moved on top of her. She could feel the transsexual's excitement.

"We will have our day," she whispered again into Lexxus' ear as she pretended to nibble it. "I promise."

Frank and the boys finished their lunch and spent the rest of the afternoon buying supplies. They bought clothes from Target, more burner phones, and a can of red paint. They bought groceries and beer and then hit the liquor store for booze. They gassed the car and Reaper got a couple of packs of Camel Turkish Silvers. They drove back to the house to find everyone there.

Frank got the whole fifteen thousand for Blanco and Reaper. After the mission they wouldn't be coming back. After dinner, before the hard drinking started, Frank called them all together in the little kitchen. He laid out the maps and went over the battle plan.

"Sounds awfully simple," Charlie asked.

"It is. It is my experience that when the shooting starts most plans fall apart. KISS."

"I heard that."

"So that's it? We set it up and see how it plays out?"

"More or less. You each have your assignments. Do that and we walk away from this. If you don't, then some of you don't come back."

"What are the rules of engagement?"

"Shoot everyone," Able mocked.

"You are green-lit to take any viable targets. That means anyone with a weapon."

"What about collateral damage?"

"Use your best judgment. But if you put down a lot of innocents it will draw more intense scrutiny afterward. I want the feds focused up here, not looking for us."

"Sound good."

"This isn't our first op. We know what to do."

"Everything set on your end, Masnick?"

"Good to go. Wired and primed."

Frank nodded. "Chill out tonight. Tomorrow we do a final weapons check, and police the grounds."

"What's the point?"

"No evidence left behind. Make it tough for anyone looking."

The beer and liquor were brought out. Masnick excused himself to go to his room. He looked pale and frail. Blanco and Reaper joked with Frank about when Pan had run whores for the Spartans and the good times riding under the lambda. Around one o'clock, people drifted off to sleep where they could.

Frank went outside after the last man was asleep. He took one of his cigars. He sat on the back porch smoking and reviewing his plan. It was bold. And it could work. His phone buzzed in his pocket. He let in vibrate. A minute later it buzzed again. Frank took it out of his pocket and checked the caller id. It was Carpenter.

"Yeah."

"Frank. Did you get my care package?"

"Yes. Just like the doctor ordered. Anything else?"

"Just checking in. I got my end covered. I will be able to disrupt the cellular service like you wanted, even if Masnick's plan fails."

"Good."

"There is one other issue."

"Yeah."

"How's Masnick doing?"

"He says he is dying. He looks like it too. But I think he can rally through tomorrow. This is important to him."

"Revenge always is. That's what worries me."

"What are you talking about?"

"After Masnick gets done there, he may start looking for a new focus for his revenge. He might start looking at my part in all of this."

"Masnick is not looking at you. He knows you are helping him."

"For now. But later."

"Later he says he will be dead."

"What if he isn't?"

"Spit it out."

"Masnick can't come back from the Lodge."

"What are you talking about?"

"Make sure he doesn't get out alive. Is that clear enough for you?"

"You want me to do it?"

"If it needs to be done. Do I have your word?"

"No. I'll think about it."

"Frank..."

Frank disconnected. He smoked and thought about the ocean at night. He closed his eyes and saw the green waves rising like ghosts in the moonlight. He could hear their roars as they charged the distant shore. He missed the ocean.

63

Finris sat outside the leopard's cage. The great cat was busy licking her dinner from her paws and muzzle. She eyed the giant man without fear or rage. He drank a bottle of water as he watched her. Her head popped up at the distant sound of high heels. Finris turned toward the sound.

Heather clicked down the tiled hallway. She approached him and stood over him with her hands on her hips.

"So here you are."

"Yes."

Heather sat beside him. She took the water from his hands and took a sip. "What are you doing?"

"Just thinking."

"There is something unhealthy about this relationship you have with this leopard."

"All relationships are unhealthy on some level."

Heather sat quietly. Finris didn't speak.

"Do you love me?" she asked.

"No."

"Is that why you sleep with other women?"

"I never thought about it."

"I think I am in love with you."

Finris looked at her. "You aren't. You desire me. There is something in you that is drawn to a strong man."

"I need you."

"No, you want me. It is not the same thing."

Heather glanced at the leopard. She was watching the humans with dark curious eyes.

"We make a good team. You said so yourself."

"We make an exceptional team."

Heather stood up. She slid her dress up and removed her panties. She dropped them on the cold floor.

"I want you now."

Finris smiled. "Here, on the floor? Now?"

Heather knelt down. She unbuckled his pants and pulled them down. Finris was not wearing underwear. She stroked his cock and it immediately grew hard. She straddled him. She slowly lowered herself onto his erection. She sighed deeply as he sank into her. She started to ride him. Slowly at first and then faster as her passion grew.

The leopard withdrew to the far side of her cell. It left them a hiss as it withdrew.

Jake and Jenny finished their dinner and the bottle of wine. Jenny excused herself to go to the bathroom.

"Do you want me to open the other bottle?" he asked.

"No."

"Are you sure?"

Jenny returned from the bathroom. She was wearing only her underwear.

"I'm sure. I want you to make love to me."

This time the Jake did not fall asleep. He swept her up in his arms and kissed her. They kissed standing in the doorway of the bedroom for a long time. Then he led her into his bed.

64

Redding was sitting in a back booth. He had finished his breakfast of ham and eggs and was working on his third cup of coffee. A local newspaper was spread out on the table next to his plate. Masnick slid into the booth opposite him. Redding didn't look up. He had spotted Masnick when he had come in.

"Good morning, Agent Redding."

Redding took a final glance at the paper and folded it closed.

"Good morning yourself."

"It seems the good sheriff has pulled your tail off."

"Yeah, I haven't seen any sign of him. Still, this is risky. What are you doing here?"

Masnick took out some folded paper and passed it to Redding. Redding opened it. It was a map of the compound. He spread it out on top of the newspaper.

"Maurer needs to believe this raid is legit. He has to have a story he can tell and retell and not change details because it is the truth. His truth as he knows it. But I figure you could use a little intel. Get a lay of the land."

"Where are they keeping the girls?"

Masnick tapped the side of the Lodge near the kennel. "This is where the new girls were when they had me."

"Umm," Redding mumbled and stared at the map.

"This is the way Frank got in to get me out. It is straightforward. They should be focused elsewhere when you go in. But they may be trying to use it as a rat hole to escape so go in ready."

"Thanks, mom."

"Don't be an asshole."

Redding glared at him. Masnick looked like death. He was pale, and his skin looked as thin as paper stretched across the bones of his face. His eyes were blood red. They were as sunken into his skull-like head as far they could go.

"Sorry. How are you holding up?"

"I can make it a little longer."

"Then you turn yourself in like you promised."

"If I make it out, I will. I gave my word."

"Okay."

"There will be other women in the house. After you free these girls you can go back for them."

"Got it."

Masnick got to his feet. Redding thought he moved like an old man.

"Good luck."

"You too."

Jenny woke up with Jake's arm around her waist. It felt good. She snuggled back a little into his arms. She could feel his warm breath on her back. She thought she could feel his heart beating in his chest. She wondered if she could synch her heartbeat to match it. She even tried until she realized it was foolish.

Last night had been amazing. It was all she had hoped it would be. He was slow and gentle, but also strong. As her comfort grew so did his passion. It was a blur of kisses and touches until he was inside her. They had tried several different positions to find the one they liked best. Some had proved impractical and they had laughed together at the absurdity of the positions. She loved the sound of his laugh. She loved the way his teeth seemed to glow in the dim light.

When it was over, he held her and kissed her. They had fallen asleep in each other's arms.

Jenny was not a fool. She knew the afterglow could not continue forever, but for now it was good, and she promised to enjoy every second of it. He was an amazing man.

She felt him stir beside her. She wondered if he would want to make love again. Was her breath stale? Why didn't she bring her toothbrush? Because she wasn't a whore, that was why she reminded herself. She wondered if she stunk a little. They had worked up a sweat. And her hair must look awful. And in the morning light he would be able to see every flaw. She was starting to get a little acne outbreak on her nose, but she had hidden it with makeup. It was probably smeared all over her face now like a damn Kabuki dancer. God, she needed to take a shower and fix her hair and rub a little toothpaste on her teeth. If he saw her now the way she really, was he would vomit.

Jake kissed the back of her neck and she melted.

"Good morning."

"Good morning."

"I need to get to work. Elissa will think I died I am so late."

Jenny rolled over to face him. She kissed him lightly on his lips.

"I probably need to get going too. Will I see you tonight?"

"If you want too."

"I do."

"Let's say I pick you up at eight."

"Sounds perfect. And Jake, last night was amazing. Thank you."

"Yeah, it was pretty amazing."

He leaned in and kissed her. They held it for a few seconds.

Jenny broke it first. She rolled out of bed and scooped up her underwear. She carried it to the bathroom to dress. There was no way she was going to get dressed in front of him. When she got to the safety of the bathroom she couldn't help but stare at her reflection in the mirror. She was a woman now, she thought. She couldn't see any difference in her face. There was no sparkle, or gleam, or aura like she thought there would be. There was a light knock on the door.

"Do you want coffee?"

She smiled. Maybe she was glowing a little. He was so damn sweet.

Deputy Maurer's cell phone buzzed in his pocket as he was driving into Blackwater. It was the high sheriff.

"Yes, sir."

"Just wanted to give you a sit rep. You back on board?"

"Yes, sir."

"I can count on you?"

"One hundred percent, sir."

"Good. Buck said the Fed has been meeting with some DEA boys. I can't find out what they are up to. No one says they know anything. Keep your eyes and ears open. You hear anything suspicious; you let me or Buck know. You got that?"

"Yes, sir."

"The Fed can snoop around all he wants he won't find out anything. Blackwater is my town. People know what's what."

"Do you think he can get a warrant to search the Lodge?"

"No way. I got all the local judges on lockdown."

"What do you think he's up to?"

"Who knows? He'll snoop around for a little while and then he will go his way. We just got to sit tight and wait him out."

"Yes, sir."

"Remember. Anything strikes you as out of the ordinary, you call me direct so it can get handled."

"Yes, sir. And thank you, sir, for giving me this opportunity to redeem myself. It took me a little while to realize how big an opportunity this was."

"You're a good man, Maurer. You do what I tell you and you will do just fine."

"Yes, sir."

65

Helen was surprised when she went outside to her bike. It had been brought from the garage and parked out front next to Cyrus' bike. But instead of Cyrus, she found Spanish Johnny sitting on his own bike. It was a 2008 Harley Sportster in red and white. There was skull painted on the gas tank. He was wearing jeans and sneakers and a heavy coat. He was leering.

"What are you doing here?"

"Watching you walk toward me. Could any man want to see anything more beautiful?"

Helen laughed. "You should do stand up, you are so funny." She looked his bike over and walked up closer. "Isn't this Hades' old bike?"

"It was. He gave it to me just before the old fool blew himself up."

Helen nodded. "I didn't know you two were that close."

"We were pretty tight. I did him a solid and he gave me his ride. Said he wanted to get a bigger one."

"If you say so. But this is supposed to be my ride with Cyrus. Just the two of us. Does he know you are here?"

"I'm not afraid of Cyrus. If I truly wanted you, I could take you from him."

"You think so?"

"I know so."

"You are so arrogant."

"That's what you like about me. Plus, I'm damn near as good looking as you are."

Helen laughed. "You are a fool. And too stupid to realize it. One day that is going to get you killed."

Spanish Johnny smiled. "That or my big dick."

Cyrus came out of the house zipping up his Harley-Davidson jacket. He didn't look happy.

"Are you okay?"

"Fine. Ride on ahead, Johnny. We'll be behind you in five. We'll meet up at the rendezvous as we discussed. Be thinking about what we talked about. I am getting a strange vibe."

Johnny pulled his helmet on and rode off.

"What do you have a bad vibe about?"

"The Norse Men. Something is going on out there. I told Johnny I think he should take a little surprise trip out to check it out."

"What business do you have with the Norse Men?"

Cyrus smiled. "You know me. Always planning. They are supposed to be doing something for me, but I got a weird feeling something isn't right."

"Your feelings are usually right. It is probably prudent to send Spanish Johnny."

Cyrus touched her delicate face.

"I know you don't like him."

"I don't trust him. He's a snake."

"Perhaps."

"One day he will try to kill you and take everything that is yours."

"I'm not afraid of Spanish Johnny. I can kill him whenever I need to."

"You are too trusting with him. Are you carrying a gun?"

"Of course. Aren't you?"

"Well, yes."

"We are in a dangerous world, my love. We must do all we can to protect ourselves and the ones we love. Ultimately, we have to be able to count on only ourselves for that."

"Then why don't I see security for our ride?"

"I thought we might ride like the old days without the benefit of black SUVs shadowing us."

"And?"

"Ronnie refused. Can you believe it? He refused me. He said that it was out of the question."

"When I told him I could look after myself, he said, now get this, that he never doubted it, but he was paid to protect you too."

"Who would have thought the little Guido had real balls."

"So, what did you decide?"

"I told him he could ride sweeper in one of the vehicles just in case."

"That was very nice of you."

"It was so funny. Ronnie thinking he could protect you. He has no idea how dangerous you really are."

"You are the only one who knows me that well, baby."

Cyrus leaned in and kissed her softly. They held the kiss for a few seconds.

"Let's ride."

"Let's."

He climbed on his Harley-Davidson and they rode off.

66

Jake drove his car to the Black Broth and parked in the back. It was only eight o'clock. The place was still packed, but the peak was usually at eight as students and workers and teachers grabbed a final cup on their way to work or class. Jake slipped around to the front.

He got the glare from his new manager, Elissa.

"Good morning, boss."

"Good morning."

"Did you have fun last night on your play date? Did you go to Chuck E. Cheese?"

"Elissa, she's not a kid."

"She's jailbait. With her cute little statutory rape smile."

"She's eighteen."

"Oh wow. Are you kidding me? Eighteen, well that makes all the difference in the world. She's still a baby. I got tee shirts older than her."

"I like her."

"She's too young for you."

"Maybe I'm too old for her."

"Whatever. I hope this little fling got it out of your system."

"I am going to see her again."

Elissa actually looked stunned. "Why?"

"I told you. I like her a lot."

"You had her now you can just move on. Isn't that what guys do nowadays? Put a notch on the bedpost."

"I'm not that guy."

"You deserve someone better. A grown woman, not a little girl. Someone who has lived a little and gotten her head on right."

Jake smiled. "Give me a hug."

She stepped into his hug and held him. When they stepped apart Jake spoke first.

"I know you mean well. I know you are trying to look after me. But I really like her. You would too, if you gave her a chance."

"No shit? You really like her?"

"Yes. Now get back to work. I got to make some money if I am going to pay you to be a manager."

Elissa smiled. She hurried to deal with the customers. Jake stepped in too, bussing tables, pouring coffee, taking orders, even checking the patrons out. By nine thirty it was over. The shop was nearly empty. The madness was over. One of the part-time waitresses was leaving. She worked the dawn shift from six to nine. Jake was manning the cash register when the blonde came in.

The woman who came in was dressed in slim jeans, hiking boots, and a ragg wool sweater with an open coat over it. She wore a wide scarf around her neck. She was incredibly beautiful in the way only Nordic women could be. Her blonde hair was pulled back in a ponytail, which emphasized her perfectly shaped face. She moved like an athlete or a dancer or a cat. She had a shy smile and brilliant blue eyes.

She ordered the daily special, a pumpkin spice latte. Jake got it. Elissa had suddenly disappeared. He gave it to her and took her money. She was smiling and looking around.

"Is this your place?"

"Yes, it is. My name's Jacob."

"I am Sabina."

"It's nice to meet you, Sabina."

"You too. I love the name of this place. It reminds me a little of Croatia. Did you come up with it?"

"No, a friend gave me the idea. Have you been here before?"

"A couple of times. I know Elissa. We work out together."

"Elissa works out?"

"Hot yoga."

"Who would have guessed."

"You should come sometime. You would love it."

"I just might."

Sabina picked up a pen from the cup where they kept them for guests by the register. She gently took Jake's hand and turned it over, she wrote a phone number in his palm. She held him with her eyes.

"Or you could just call me."

Jake smiled back.

"I just might."

She turned and he watched her walk away like a fading dream. When she was gone, Elissa peeked out from the back. Jake smiled.

"Really? That was not subtle."

Elissa held her hands up. "I surrender. I was just trying to help. I'll tell her you're not interested."

"I'm sure it will break her heart."

"She's not used to rejection. It might change her world view."

"There's a first time for everything."

67

The day dragged slowly by. Redding drove around Zaneville. It was really a very nice town. He had lunch at a small restaurant. It was very good. He walked the streets. It was just the right size of a town, he thought. Later he had dinner near the hotel and took a nap. When he got up, he showered and shaved. He hung his dark suit in the bathroom and closed the door so the steam could get rid of some of the wrinkles. He took his gun and rechecked it. He spread his ID, gun, badge, and spare clips on the room desk. He tuned on FOX news and tried to watch. He missed Bill O'Reilly's show.

Jenny futzed about the house. She tried to study but couldn't. She tried to watch Netflix, but she couldn't concentrate. All she could think about was last night and Jake. When she thought about Jake her body seemed to have a little hum to it. She could still feel the pressure from his lips on hers. If she closed her eyes she could almost feel his fingers on her skin. She worried that she hadn't been a good lover for him. He knew she was inexperienced, but he might have expected more. She had enjoyed it, that had to be obvious to him. But what if once he had slept with her he didn't want her anymore? Or what if having sex changed how he acted or how he treated her. What if he thought she was a slut for asking him to do it? What if he hadn't really liked her body once he saw it? She was thin, but she could do more sit ups. She had a tiny tummy. Guys wanted a girl to have a six pack. She had read guys liked a round butt. Was her butt round enough? God, she was going crazy. Was this what life was going to be like now, she wondered.

Helen had her fingernails and toes done at the spa. She worked her own plans and machinations. Did she need to make some kind of move? Was she being too compliant by waiting? She thought about Frank Kane. She reexamined her feelings for him for the ten thousandth time. They loved each other. She never doubted that. There was something magical there. It was something rare and beautiful. She wondered why Frank had never called her. Maybe he didn't get the phone number she had left behind for him at the hotel in the Bahamas. She thought about the pretty brunette in the jail. What had happened to her? Did Frank rescue her? She wondered about Cyrus and Spanish Johnny. That was the difference between them and Frank. They would both kill for her, to protect her, to possess her, even to avenge her; but Frank Kane would die for her. She thought she would die for him too. In the end, she called Johanna and set up a tennis match. She didn't want to be alone.

After dinner Frank's team went over the plan for the millionth time. They spent some time burning all the maps and info outback in a crude fire pit that had come with the old house. Then Frank had made them police the house. They balked, but Frank insisted. Every scrap of paper and empty can was bagged up. They went room to room wiping the house down. Except for Masnick's room. He had gone to rest before the mission brief. Frank thought he looked really bad.

Blanco and Reaper said they had some final business and took off. Reaper said he needed a long ice pick or one of those skewers for shish kebabs. An ice pick for God's sake, Frank thought. Why would he need an ice pick? It had to be a joke, right? Frank didn't ask them where they were really going. He knew they wanted another escape vehicle to maximize their options. Probably going to a strip club. Keating and Charlie took two of their vehicles and put the plan into motion.

Frank was sitting out front when Keating returned a few hours later. Charlie went straight into the house with only a nodded greeting.

"Everything go alright?"

"Yeah. We parked it right beside the cell tower and then relocked the gate. We used our lock so no one can tamper with it. Can't imagine why anyone would be up there tonight, but better safe than sorry."

"Good work."

"How's Masnick?"

"Not good. He's in his room resting."

"Don't worry about him. We talked it all out. He's got his drugs and the ones I brought him. He can do this."

"I have no doubts."

Blanco and Reaper pulled up in two separate cars, as Frank had suspected they would. Keating patted Frank on the shoulder and went inside.

"You boys have a nice ride?"

"Took care of business."

"We will put a car out by the park like you told us. You can park your truck there too. We'll take one vehicle to their compound. If we can't get out in it we can hoof it down to the park and get out the back way down that old logging road."

"Sounds right. I like the way you are thinking."

"One more thing," Blanco said. "We took care of that other problem."

"What other problem?"

"That dude, Alton, bro. We couldn't have it bouncing back on you."

"What are you talking about?"

Frank got to his feet.

"He's off the field," Reaper said with a smile.

"He's gone," Blanco said.

Frank's face could not hide his shock and anger.

"Shit. You don't think sticking some guy in his house won't bring attention? I told you to let him alone. He was solid."

"Look, we talked about it. He was shaky at best. We figured you told us about him so we could take care of it for you."

"Yeah. There won't be any blowback on it, brother. We told him we were the law. We showed him our IDs. Dude broke down right away and confessed about killing his old lady and burying her under the rose bushes. We had him write it all down along with his sorrow for having done it."

"Poor old fuck thought he was going to jail or the gas chamber."

"He didn't even flinch when I stuck his shotgun under his chin."

"He knew what was coming and didn't care anymore. He must have figured he was getting what he deserved."

"It looks like a straight up suicide. His gun. His note. No other prints. Just like you taught us to do."

"Fuck. I was hoping you guys might be interested in getting out of the outlaw life. Getting a second chance and going straight."

Blanco and Reaper looked from each other back to Frank. They were genuinely shocked.

"Not us. We love it. Outlawing is all we were ever good at."

"But you can start off clean."

"And do what? A straight job? Not for us, brother."

"Outlaws are what we are."

Frank nodded. Not everyone wanted what he had found. He didn't blame them. They were who they were. He had a moment's regret for Alton. Frank had liked him. But what was done was done. He couldn't go back and change it. He followed them inside.

68

Jake was turning off the lights to leave his house when his cell buzzed. It was Carpenter.

"You got something for me on the Russians?"

"It's not much. I set a word trap..."

"What's that?"

"An alarm tripped by key words. Greensboro, Russians and Chinese meeting, a bunch of code words for fentanyl like Green Apache, China Girl, goodfella, Murder 8, Tango and Cash, a few other newer ones."

"And?"

"I got something. Too damn much, but I sifted through it all. Your Russians are set to meet tonight with their new partners."

"Do you know where and when?"

"Sorry. They were too careful. You'll have to figure that out for yourself."

"Alright. Thanks."

"Wish I could have done more."

"Not a problem. I got this."

Jake went to his computer and pulled up the tracking device. The Russians were at dinner at 1618, an upscale restaurant just outside of downtown Greensboro. Jake thought for a minute, trying to develop a quick plan. Frank had told him sometimes the direct approach was the best. He closed the computer.

Jake went to his bathroom and removed his makeup kit from the closet. He set it on the counter. He removed the spirit gum and painted the outline of a goatee. He dabbed at it with the brush until it became tacky. He took out a ball of black hair from the kit. He stretched it and rolled it around in his hands. He cut a straight edge with a pair of scissors and pressed it into place. He used the scissors to position it. He painted another tiny swipe between his eyebrows and added a little hair for a unibrow look. He thought it would look more European. He shaped the goatee and trimmed the loose hairs until it looked natural. He did the same for the brow extension. When he was satisfied, he closed up the makeup kit and put it back into the closet.

He took some hair gel and slicked his thick hair back.

He went to his bedroom. He was wearing black jeans and a gray sweater for his date. He took them off and replaced them with a dull black suit and dark blue shirt without a tie. He replaced his tennis shoes with a dark dress shoes that looked a lot more expensive then they were.

He opened the closet in his bedroom. There was a five-foot-tall gun safe inside. It was made of forged steel with a triple lock system. He opened it. He took out a Glock G22. It carried fifteen rounds in .40 caliber. He had scored the gun from an underground Russian arms dealer in New Jersey who didn't need it anymore. It was a cold piece. It couldn't be traced back to him. He picked out an inside-the-pants holster and secured the gun in the small of his back. He replaced his mouse gun on his ankle. He liked a back up gun, but it could be lost. He might use it and leave evidence that could be traced to him. If he couldn't resolve his problems with the Glock then he would run.

Now the hard part, he thought.

Jake took out his regular cell phone and called Jenny.

"Hey, baby. Are you on your way?"

"There's a problem."

"A problem?"

"Yeah. Something has come up that I have to take care of."

"Oh, no. Can I help?"

"No. It's something I have to do alone."

"Are you going to come over afterward?"

"I'll try. But it could be late."

"Okay. Come if you can. I miss you."

"I miss you too."

Jake hung up. He could sense the anxiety in her voice. He didn't have a choice. If he didn't take care of this now it might be too late. He went outside and took his motorcycle. He rode to the restaurant where the Russians were.

Jenny hung up. She flopped down on the sofa and turned the TV back on. She felt her disappointment start to turn to anger. A million doubts rose to her mind. She wondered if he was seeing another girl. She wondered if he had simply used her for sex. Maybe it had been terrible for him. What if he wanted to just reduce her to a booty call? Was this the way he really was? She felt the anger grow. Bastard, she thought. That motherfucker was not going to treat her this way.

Jake reached the restaurant and parked his bike. He found the Russians' car. They were still here. He went inside. The hostess stepped around her station to greet him. She was holding a menu. He raised a hand.

"I am meeting some friends here."

He scanned the small restaurant. He spotted the two Russians sitting at a corner table just off the bar with a clear view of anyone who entered. They saw him as he walked toward them. Yuri leaned over and said something to the other Russian.

"Yuri."

"Stephan. What are you doing here?"

"I was told you might require extra security tonight."

"By whom?"

"My employer. He didn't give me specifics beyond that I was to come and watch your backs."

"Do they think there will be treachery?"

"Always."

The two Russians spoke quickly in Russian. The second man who hadn't been introduced spoke.

"They said only two from each side at the meeting."

"I know. If there is a problem, I can explain it to them.

The second Russian looked unconvinced.

"If you don't want me to accompany you, it is fine. I get paid either way."

The second Russian started to speak but Yuri slapped him on the shoulder.

"He is a good man, Mischa. Don't be so suspicious. Have a seat."

Jake sat down.

"Vodka?"

Jake smiled. "Of course."

Frank's crew did a final check. Ultrathin liner gloves were slipped on. Balaclavas were positioned for quick access. Combat vests were cinched. Loads were checked. Magazines were secured in the Velcro-closed pockets on the front of the vests. Backup handguns were holstered. DEA nylon jackets were donned. Frank did a final sweep of the entire house except Masnick's bedroom where the rest of the money was kept. Masnick said it was spotless. He didn't doubt it. The rest of the house appeared clean. It was game time.

They stood on the front porch looking from man to man.

"One day we may be out gunned and out manned," said Blanco.

"One day we may miss our shots and our weapons jam," added Reaper.

"One day fuses may not light. Explosives may fail their objective," said Masnick.

"One day we may be betrayed and trapped and killed," Keating said.

Each man looked at Frank. The Spartan enforcer just smiled. "Hoy no es ese dia."

They all repeated the phrase, "Today is not that day." Shoulders were shaken and fists were bumped for the final time.

They loaded into their cars and left for Blackwater at staggered prearranged times. Afterward, Masnick's team would rendezvous back at the house for their final payment. Frank's boys would be gone. When the caravan was only minutes out from Blackwater, Masnick called Redding. There were things that needed to be in place before the FBI agent was on site. He would only allow Masnick so much latitude.

Jenny tried to watch television, but she was too angry. She didn't care if he had an emergency. She was going to talk to him. That was not negotiable. He owed her that much. He needed to act like a man and tell her the truth. She dialed his phone. She would have answers. She held the phone to her ear and waited. It rang on. There was no answer. If iPhones weren't so expensive, she would have thrown hers across the room.

They left Frank's truck and Reaper's exit car down by the park. They repositioned and drove to the Lodge. The cars pulled into the parking area before the guard shack at the Lodge. Reaper and Blanco burst out of their car. Their guns were out.

"Hands where I can see them," Blanco screamed.

"Don't move. Don't move," Reaper added. "DEA. DEA."

"Show me your hands."

The skinny guard in the guard shack raised his hands over his head. It wasn't the first time he had taken orders from the police. Blanco held his gun on him.

"Hands on the counter."

The man complied, leaning forward. Reaper swept into the guard shack. He swept his hands down his left arm and down his left side. He swept them up past his groin and down and up his right leg. The man was calm. He had been through this routine before. Reaper's hands eased up the man's right side. One hand drifted back and took the ice pick from Reaper's belt. Reaper paused to line up the correct angle. He punched the nine-and-a-half-inch blade through the armpit and into the right side of the heart. The man lurched up and then fell to the ground.

Reaper watched him as life left him.

"See, Blanco, I told you. It's like instant. Like turning off a light switch."

"I wouldn't have believed it if I hadn't seen it myself."

"Tip goes right into the heart."

"Dude."

Blanco helped lift the dead man and they placed him in the trunk of one of the stolen cars. The faux DEA agents spread out, waiting for the next stage of Frank's plan to begin.

Deputy Maurer got the call from the station. He took out his cell phone and called the high sheriff.

"What you got, Maurer?"

"Sorry to bother you, sir. I just got a call from that FBI fellow, Redding."

"Why did he call you?"

"He said he tried to reach you, but they told him you were off-duty, so he remembered meeting me and asked to be patched through to me."

"What is he up to?"

"I'm not sure. He said he was with a team of DEA agents and they were heading out to execute a warrant at the Lodge. He said he didn't want to proceed without local law enforcement being informed and present."

"How did they come up with a warrant?"

"I don't know, sir."

"Could have gotten a judge to sign at his home, I guess. We can't have them tromping around at the Lodge."

"Should we warn them?"

"No. There isn't enough time to hide what all's going on up there. We got to keep the law from going up there. Where are you?"

"I'm on my way to meet them. They said they would wait for me."

"You stall them. No matter what you don't let them approach the Lodge. I am en route."

"Should we alert Buck too?"

"Yeah, I'll call him and he can meet up with us there. No one goes up until I get there. Are we clear?"

"Yes, sir."

"You did good, Maurer. I'm counting on you now. There will be a big bonus in this."

"Thank you, sir. I will hold them until you get there and figure something out."

"You do that, son. No one in or out."

"Yes, sir."

70

Redding parked his rental car and got out. Frank went to meet him. They shook hands. Neither spoke. Maurer pulled in. The faux DEA agents all pulled their balaclavas into place to hide their faces. Maurer got out. He was relaxed. He acknowledged Redding. He opened the trunk on his patrol car and took out his AR-15. He stood quietly by beside his car.

Seven minutes later the high sheriff arrived and so did Buck. Buck got out carrying his AR-15 across his chest. High Sheriff Long jumped out. He was agitated. He was shaking his head from side to side. He approached Redding.

"What the hell is going on here, Agent Redding?"

"Sheriff, glad you are here. These men are from the DEA and they are preparing to execute a warrant on the Lodge and surrounding grounds."

"Why wasn't I informed?" he demanded.

"I don't know. I contacted Deputy Maurer to provide local support and assistance."

"No one is executing anything without my approval. Not in my town. Let me see the warrant."

"Yes, sir. I'll get it for you."

Keating went to retrieve the warrant from his car.

"It better be all in order or I am calling this off. Who signed the damn thing in the first place?"

No one answered.

High Sheriff Long scanned the DEA agents that were assembled. Something seemed off about them. Buck moved up to his side.

"I don't like this, Boss. They look like they are kitted up for a damn war."

"Something is off. Stay ready."

Keating stepped up with a tri-fold piece of paper. He handed it to the sheriff. The high sheriff opened it. It was a flyer from a local cable company. The high sheriff stared at it, dumbfounded. He raised his head up to see who thought this was funny. Frank Kane stepped up and punched him in the stomach. The high sheriff fell to the ground. Blanco pressed a gun behind Buck's right ear. He reached around and took the AR-15 from him.

Frank knelt beside the sheriff. He took his sidearm and stuck it in his coat pocket.

"You are fucked. You got once chance. Be a hero or a victim. It's your call."

The sheriff stared up at him. "Who the fuck are you?"

Frank pulled him to his feet and ushered him to his police car. He pushed him to the front door.

"Get inside."

He pointed the high sheriff's own gun at his head.

"Pop the trunk."

The sheriff did. Reaper went to the back and took out the AR-15 and two spare magazines of ammunition. He slammed the lid. He used the barrel to guide Buck to the front seat of the other police car. He got in behind him and pressed the barrel of the AR-15 to the back of his neck.

"Just give me a reason," Reaper whispered. "Now pop the trunk."

Buck did. "Listen, you got this all wrong. I don't know what you heard but we are in this with you guys."

Blanco took the spare magazines for the AR-15 and climbed into the front seat beside him.

"You don't know what you are getting into. I can help you."

Blanco smiled back at Reaper. Neither spoke.

Frank got into the back of the sheriff's car.

"Eyes front. Do exactly what I tell you and you might get out of this alive. You fuck with me and I promise you will not make it."

The other DEA agents got into their cars. Masnick approached Redding.

"You know the plan. When the shooting starts, you come up. Charlie will give you back up. Go through the kennel and free the girls."

Redding nodded. "Don't try to skip out on me."

Masnick's laugh deteriorated into a series of wet hacking sounds. Masnick went to a car and got into the back.

Redding walked to Deputy Maurer.

"You good to go?"

"Yes, sir."

"Keep it simple. Tell the truth. I called you. You alerted the sheriff as you were required to do. DEA agents arrived and showed the sheriff what you took to be as a legal warrant and then drove off. The sheriff and deputy went willingly."

"That's what happened."

"No one comes up. You hold them here. Fire trucks, ambulances, more cops. You got your orders."

"The high sheriff ordered me to not let anyone up."

"People may try to get out this way. It is up to you to arrest and detain any Norse Men that try to escape. They may be armed. You may have to fight."

Maurer smiled and patted his rifle. "I got an AR. I'll hold this position. No one will get past that shouldn't."

"Put the noncombatants some place safe. Do you have restraints?"

"Zip-cuffs. I'll be fine."

Maurer went into the guard shack and pressed the lever to raise the gate. The other cars disappeared up the driveway.

273

71

Dinner was finished. The plates had been cleared. The Russians laughed and joked in Russian. Occasionally Yuri tried to include Jake, but Jake didn't share their background or experiences. He positioned himself to watch the door.

Near midnight, Yuri paid the bill with cash and they went outside. The restaurant was empty behind them. The staff was glad to see them finally leave.

"Do you want to ride with us?"

"No. I'll follow. When we get there, give me five minutes to scout the location to be sure it isn't a trap."

"Da. It is an old warehouse near downtown. It is near the police station." Yuri paused. "Less chance of a double-cross with the police so close. Gunfire will attract them."

Jake nodded. He got to his bike and fell in behind their car. He parked near a dark access road. It was going to be tricky to pull off, he thought. He slipped into the dark area around the abandoned warehouse.

Buck's car led the procession followed by a DEA car, then the sheriff, and then the car with Masnick. They stopped at the second security booth. The man stepped outside to see what was going on. Keating shot him three times with a silenced pistol. They left the man where he fell.

When they reached the barn, they stopped by the side.

"Watch for snipers," Reaper said.

Blanco just smiled. He hopped out and went to the barn. He got the ladder from inside and placed against the side of the barn. He climbed it toward the roof. The caravan continued. Buck parked where he was directed, directly in front of the Lodge. Keating and Charlie pulled off to the side and drove toward the barracks. They parked their car there and got out. The sheriff parked to the side of the other police car. Masnick pulled his car to the left flank and stopped. He and Bravo got out.

Masnick pulled a large duffel bag out of the back seat. The two men crouched in position behind the car. Keating jogged to the rear of the Lodge. Charlie jogged back toward the far-right flank of the Lodge and took up a position behind a row of trees. Reaper tapped Buck on the shoulder.

"Turn on the light bar. Leave the siren off."

"Listen, this is crazy."

"Keep the siren off."

Buck flipped the light bar on. To his side, the high sheriff did likewise. Then they all waited for the lights to draw the insects. It didn't take long. A man appeared on the front porch carrying a rifle. A second man joined him.

"Light them up with your spotlight," Reaper said.

Buck did. The men on the porch shielded their eyes. Another man and a woman in a long skirt joined them.

"Hand me the mike," Reaper said.

Buck turned it on and passed it back.

"Now get out. Stand by the side of the car." Buck got out.

"Everyone in the Lodge," Reaper started in his best cop voice. "This is a joint task force of the DEA, FBI and local law enforcement. We are here on a federally-issued warrant. You are all under arrest. Please lay down your weapons and get down on the ground."

Finris came onto the porch.

"What's this all about?" he hollered. "Buck, what are you up to?"

"Get down on the ground," Reaper continued.

That's how it started.

72

Jake moved quickly through the area surrounding the warehouse. He moved into the back and crept silently through the darkness. He spotted two Asians standing in a pool of light in the center of the warehouse facing the main entrance. Behind them and to the left was a third Asian carrying an MP5 submachine gun. There was a large duffel bag at his feet. It was enough. He drifted back outside.

Jake circled the warehouse back to the Russians' car. It was empty. They were already inside. He removed the tracking device from their car and slipped it into his jacket pocket. He did not see anyone else near the old warehouse. He walked toward the entrance. He could hear voices.

"The results were satisfactory?" a tall Asian asked.

"Very impressive. Sales exceeded our estimates by nearly twenty-two percent."

"The fentanyl dramatically boosts the effectiveness."

"There was a concern over the overdose deaths, but it did nothing to lessen sales. We are satisfied."

"Now we can start doing business in earnest."

Jake walked up to the group of four men. The Russians did not even look his way. The tall Asian was alarmed.

"Who is this man? We agreed on only two representatives from each side."

"This is Stephan. He is a security specialist."

"Why is he here?"

"There is a problem." Jake said.

Yuri didn't look his way. He watched the tall Asian. The second Russian moved his hand into his jacket near his pistol. The tall Asian raised a hand for calm.

"What is this man talking about?"

"There is a third man hiding in the back with an automatic weapon."

The tall Asian visibly relaxed. "He is with me."

"You said only two," Yuri said.

The tall Asian laughed. "Like you, I am a careful man, especially with new partners. He is here to guard the fentanyl. Nothing more."

"Then have him come up," Jake said.

Yuri looked at Jake's impertinence but dismissed it.

"Do as he says. Have your man up here with us."

The tall Asian nodded and called out in Chinese to his man to come forward. The man did, carrying the duffel bag, and the MP5 on a sling. The high-powered machine gun made the second Russian nervous. Mischa slowly drew his gun and let it hang by his leg so that the tall Asian could see it. The tall Asian motioned again for calm.

"Is there anyone else?"

"No, no. He is the only one."

Yuri looked to Jake. Jake shook his head.

"Okay, if we are all here, let's do some business. The Russian knelt and unzipped the black nylon bag he was carrying. It was packed with stacks of money. The money looked old and used.

The tall Asian motioned to his second who stepped up with a small handheld device. He swept it over the bag and then stepped back.

"Do you think I am stupid enough to track you?"

"Caution is a businessman's best friend."

"Sweep that thing over your own bag then."

The tall Asian nodded and spoke to the man who repeated the procedure and stepped away.

"Satisfied?"

"Yes. Show me the drugs."

The man who had used the tracker unzipped the bag and turned it so they could see it was full of blocks of greenish-white powder.

"I hope as our relationship grows we can dispense with some of this paranoia."

"I like being paranoid," Yuri said. "It is a criminal's best friend."

The tall Asian smiled.

73

The triggers on the explosives were electronically synched. When Masnick pressed the trigger, the car near the cell phone tower exploded. The blast toppled the tower and pancaked the surrounding transformers. All cell service in Blackwater disappeared. The second car parked in front of the barracks exploded as well. The blast force crushed the front of the building. The unsupported structures crumbled. Electrical fires started immediately in the rubble. One hundred yards away on his stomach, Charlie felt the force of the blast wash over him. The heat singed his hair.

The people on the porch cowered down. Stunned by the massive explosion, no one moved. Reaper leaned out the side window of the car and emptied Buck's pistol at the group on the porch.

The Norse Men on the porch returned fire. In a blinding roar of sound and fire the porch erupted. Buck was struck a half dozen times and went down dead. Reaper dove down on the floorboard as bullets tore up the car. He threw Buck's pistol out of the window and crawled out the other side of the car. Bullets struck like rain drops against the car. Glass shattered and sprayed him.

Far to his left, Masnick and the mercenary crouched behind their car. Masnick started to dig through the large duffel bag he had laid on the ground. He was whistling a tune, unconcerned that death in the shape of little slugs of lead were flying all around him in the air. The concerns of dead men were different than those of the living. Masnick envisioned Heather on fire. He smiled. He could almost smell her burning. The merc shouldered his AR and fired at the group on the porch.

Redding looked at the remaining mercenary and then over to Maurer.

"Follow the plan. Secure the road."

"Yes, sir."

"You will be fine. Just follow your training. I will try to send hostages up to you."

"I got this."

The mercenary got behind the wheel of the car. Redding climbed in beside him. They took off up the empty road with their lights out. When they reached the firefight, they turned off to the left to position closer to the kennels. The car slid to a stop.

Redding hopped out and crouched beside the car, trying to visualize what he had only seen on paper. He could see Masnick off to his right with the mercenary, Able. They looked over toward him. Masnick waved in the direction of the kennel.

Redding nodded. The mercenary crouched beside Masnick was firing at the

Lodge. Suddenly his head exploded in a shower of gore. Redding dove to the ground. It had to be a sniper.

The mercenary in the car threw the car into reverse and disappeared in a cloud of dirt. He spun the car around and took off back the way they had come. Money doesn't buy courage, Redding thought. Fucking mercenaries.

High Sheriff Long was nobody's fool. When he saw Buck get out of the car he knew what was going to happen even if Buck was too stupid to. When the first shot was fired, he took his chance. He leapt for the opposite door of the patrol car. He scrambled over the computer set up between the seats and lunged outside through the passenger door. Bullets struck all around him as he ran for the nearby barn. A bullet burned a trench across his back, but he didn't stop. He made the barn alive.

He was unarmed, between two groups that at the moment wanted him dead. He had to find a weapon fast. He looked around and spotted some farm tools hanging from hooks along the wall. He ran to them. He started to take one of the machetes, but he wasn't sure he wanted to get that close to the big guy if he followed him. He chose a pitchfork and flattened himself against the wall near the wide doors. He gripped the pitchfork and waited to see if he was followed.

Frank ducked the first wave of gunfire. He felt the sheriff lurching in the front seat and thought he had been hit. Then the side door opened and he knew the sheriff was trying to bolt. Frank opened his own side door and ran after him.

Finris saw the sheriff run. Then a moment later a big man in a DEA jacket followed him. Something in Finris recognized the man. Whether it was his size or his speed or the way he moved, Finris did not know. It was a subliminal awareness. He knew the big man was Frank Kane. He fired three times with his forty-five. At least two of the rounds struck the man in the center of his back. The big man in the DEA jacket went down. With a .45 round it was a sure kill shot.

Frank went down as if a truck had hit him. The air rushed from his lungs and he struggled to breath. Dirt filled his mouth. He tried to assess the damage. He hurt but he wasn't seriously wounded, the Dragon Skin armor vest had worked. He thought a rib might be broken, maybe two, but that wasn't enough to stop him. He lurched to his feet and ran into the barn.

Finris saw the dead man rise. He fired twice more but the man disappeared into the barn. Bullets took down the Norse Men on either side of him. The gunfire was mingled into a solid deafening roar.

The sheriff watched Frank regain his feet and enter the barn. The big man was looking for him. He turned his head to the left. It was the opening he had hoped for. He charged from the right. The big man turned toward him, but there wasn't time for him to raise his shotgun. The sheriff crashed into him with his shoulder low like a football player crashing into the defensive line. Frank went down. The shotgun spun from his grasp.

The sheriff raised the pitchfork and stabbed at Frank's exposed chest.

Heather was in the kitchen when she heard the gunfire. She froze like a deer trying to comprehend the danger. There was more gunfire and screams.

The Latina kitchen staff started jabbering at her in that gibberish that they claimed was a language but sounded like a monkey's chatter to her. They surged around her, wringing their hands and screaming. She hated them.

"Go on," Heather shouted. "Go on. Get the fuck out."

They looked to each other and the three of them fled the kitchen toward the back of the house away from the gunfire. Heather grabbed a kitchen knife from one of the wooden holders. She had to find Finris. He would know what to do.

A rifle slug passed by Masnick's head as he pulled something from the bag. It was an odd-looking tube gun of some kind, Redding thought. It was vaguely familiar. Masnick wrapped the strap around his right arm and stood up. He sighted the weapon and fired at the sniper in the upper floor window.

Blanco didn't have a shot. Frank had told him that he wouldn't have one. The roof of the porch hid the people there and it was worthless to waste ammo trying to get a lucky shot in. He held his position and waited. Frank had said the Norse Men would send people to the roof and he had to eliminate them. He heard the boom of the hunting rifle from the far corner of the house. He tried to find the sniper, but the structure blocked his view. He sighed and waited. Frank had everything under control.

Nils lay naked on his bed. Lexxus lay beside him pretending satisfaction.

"Shena, go get a bottle of the Dom Perignon from the kitchen."

Shena got up from the chair where she had been watching their perversion of love making.

"Whatever my man wants," Shena said. "What are we celebrating?"

"My last night here. The pilot says we leave at first light. I want it to be grand."

"It will be, darling. You just tell us what you want."

Nils laughed. He stroked Lexxus' soft blonde hair.

"When you get back, I am going to take the sjambok to Lexxus' sweet back again and then you and I will fuck her at the same time."

Lexxus looked panicked, but Shena just smiled.

"Whatever you say. You are the master."

"Damn right. Now hurry along. I can feel my erection returning."

Shena stepped out into the hallway. Nils' dinner tray sat outside with the remains of his meal. He was cruelly twisted, she thought. But she knew there was nothing she could do about it except endure. He would be leaving soon.

The sound of gunfire erupted outside.

Frank rolled to his left to avoid the pitchfork. The sheriff slammed it into the ground where he had just been. He wrenched the points free to strike again. Frank lashed out with a savage kick to his knee. The blow snapped the knee like a dry branch. The sheriff screamed and fell to the ground. Before he could rise, Frank struck him across the side of the face with a back fist. The sheriff fell back into the dirt of the barn. Frank rose to his feet and picked up the pitchfork. The sheriff raised his hands to ward off the blow.

"Wait," High Sheriff Long pleaded. "We can make a deal."

Frank slammed the tines downward through his left hand and into his chest and through the back. Blood erupted from the sheriff's mouth as the prongs punctured his lungs and nicked his heart. The light started to go out of his eyes.

Frank knelt down beside and lifted the shotgun from the dirt.

"Never go against the Spartans," he whispered.

As the sheriff died, a voice sounded from the back of the barn. Followed by running feet.

"What's going on?" a man yelled as he raced forward.

Frank shot him twice with the shotgun.

Frank put the sheriff's pistol in his dead hand and pointed the gun upward. He squeezed the trigger until the slide locked open. He dropped the gun beside the body. The forensic guys would find the GSR. That would be good. He reloaded his shotgun up and went back to the fight.

Finris emptied his pistol toward the figure crouching behind the car. He turned to go inside for more ammo when Frank stepped from the barn. He got a glimpse of movement and then heard the roar of the shotgun. Boom. Boom. Boom. Boom. Boom. Men on the porch screamed as the double-aught buck found them. A pellet chanced to strike Finris in the back of his right knee, hurling him through the doorway.

Three Norse Men tried to flank them by going out the right side of the Lodge. Charlie shot them as they cleared the building. He turned as a pair of figures in white lab coats ran from one of the buildings behind him. They didn't look to be armed, but he didn't care. He shot them anyway.

Bravo barreled down the road toward the entrance. He wasn't afraid. He was greedy. All he could think about was all the money Masnick had left at the house. Money they were meant to divide if they survived. Well, not if he got there first. He saw Maurer standing in the driveway. He flashed his headlights and beeped the horn. Maurer stepped aside as he sped past. Fuck them all, Bravo thought. Every man for himself, that was his motto. He would be to Zaneville before they had figured out where he was going.

Redding recognized the sound of Masnick's weapon. It had a distinctive thump sound. It was a grenade launcher. The round was high and to the left. The blast shook the Lodge. Masnick broke the barrel and ejected the spent shell. He loaded another and fired again. This one went through the window where the sniper had been hiding. The explosion blew out a huge hole in the side of the building.

Masnick turned toward Redding.

"Hurry."

Redding got to his feet.

Masnick fired another round and this one broke into flames when it detonated. The side of the Lodge started to burn.

"Past the cells is a control room. There are electronic switches that unlock the cells. And don't worry about the dogs. If they aren't on patrol, they should be in their cages."

Dogs, Redding thought. No one had mentioned anything about dogs. He hated dogs.

He sprinted toward the kennels and the back way inside.

The three Latina women from the kitchen broke out through the back door of the Lodge. They looked left and then right and turned left to circle the building. A gunman followed close behind.

Keating shot him with a quick double tap.

A second Norse Man ran outside with his gun up. Keating shot him too and then moved his position.

A few seconds later a barrage of bullets struck where he had been hiding. They were fired from a second-floor window. Keating emptied half a clip through the window and the gunman went silent.

A woman in a business suit ran outside and Keating let her pass. He didn't shoot women.

Yuri turned to speak to the other Russian. One of the Chinese men started to bend over to pick up the satchel of cash. Jake knew it was time.

"Gun," he shouted and drew his pistol.

He shot the nearest Chinese guard in the center of the chest with two quick rounds. He swiveled the gun a few feet. The leader of the Chinese was opening his mouth to say something. Jake shot him in the center of the face, blowing out the back of his skull.

The Chinese guard swung his MP-5 up toward the group, his finger already pulling the trigger. The big Russian had drawn his weapon and was trying to bring it into play. The MP-5 caught him across the front of his body and cut toward Yuri. The big Russian only managed to get off one involuntary round and that struck only concrete.

Yuri fired at the gunman as his bullets killed him. Yuri's round caught the Chinese gunman in the throat and he collapsed holding his throat. Jake swept his eyes over the men. He picked up Yuri's gun and shot the Chinese gunman with the throat wound, twice in the chest to be sure he died.

Yuri was dead. The top of his head was gone. The big Russian was cut nearly in half, but he was still alive. Jake went to him and helped him to his feet. The Russian moaned and Jake tried to guide him to where Jake had taken his own shots from. It would make the forensics better when they tried to recreate the scene. He sat the big Russian down.

The man sat covered with blood, rasping for breath. Jake reached beside him and took his holster from his pants. He swapped his pistol out for the big Russian's. It was a nice Sig 223. He dropped his in front of where the big Russian slumped. He watched the big Russian finally die. He checked his carotid to be sure.

Jake went to the moneybag. He knew Frank would say to leave it and get out. Frank wasn't here. And Frank was rich. Jake took three bricks of cash out of the bag. He fanned the money to make sure it was real. Maybe, he reasoned, the cops would think the payment was light and that was why it went bad. The truth was Jake thought it was stupid to leave so much cash behind. He might need it. He stuffed a brick in each outside pocket of his coat and one under his shirt.

Sirens screamed outside in the night. Someone had kicked the hornets' nest. The cops would be there any minute. He jogged outside to where he had left his bike. A few seconds later, he was heading down West Market Street toward his house.

76

Shena watched the women from the kitchen run out the back door. She was going to follow when she saw two Norse Men head out the same way. She heard the sound of Keating's gun. She made a split-second decision. She went back into Nils' room. He was standing beside the bed.

"What is happening?"

"We are under attack."

"Who?"

"The cops, I think."

"What should I do?" he asked.

Suddenly he was like a lost little boy. He was scared and helpless. Shena saw her chance.

"Come on, we have to get you out of here."

"What about my sister?"

"You can't do her any good if you are dead or in jail. We get you out of here and then you can help her."

"And go where?"

"Back to Europe."

Nils nodded. "You are right."

He started to grab his pants.

"No," Shena said. "They are shooting any man who tries to exit out the back door. But they are letting the women pass."

"So?"

"If we get you out of here do you promise to take us with you?"

"Sure. Sure. Whatever you want."

"Can you fly the airplane that brought you here?"

"No. We must get the pilot."

"Alright, I'll go find the pilot. He's probably in one of the rooms up here. Lexxus, you help Nils get ready. Put on women's underwear. A bra and panty set and then one of the silky robes. Help him fit into one of the wigs. Something bold. The Dolly Parton one should work. I'll be right back. Wait here for me."

Nils started to protest.

"Do you want to live?"

Nils nodded.

"Then do as I tell you."

Nils nodded again. He was looking at the floor like a scolded child.

Shena stepped into the hallway. The building shook with an explosion. She knelt down and picked up the steak knife off the dinner tray. She went to the room where she knew the pilot was. She made it her business to know where everyone was and with whom.

The pilot was sitting on the bed in his boxers. A pretty teenager was beside him on the bed. They both looked scared.

"Candy, you got to get out of here, it's a raid."

"How? They are shooting everywhere."

"Go out through the kennels where the cells are and slip out the side."

Candy grabbed a blanket off the bed and wrapped it around her shoulders. She ran from the room.

"What about me?" the pilot asked.

"Nils has plans for you. We got another way out for us. Get dressed."

The pilot nodded and got off the bed. He pulled on his pants and sat back on the bed to put his shoes on. Shena stepped in close.

"Let me help you."

"Get the fuck away, whore. I don't need any help."

Shena stabbed him in the side of the neck. The pilot screamed and lurched away. When he pressed his hands to the deep neck wound, she stabbed him twice in the stomach. He fell forward onto the bed and rolled off onto the floor.

Shena picked up the lamp on the nightstand and smashed it against his head. She kept smashing it against his head until the base of the lamp snapped off. She was breathing hard. The pilot didn't move. She went into the bathroom and washed the blood from the knife then slipped it under the back of her nightgown.

She checked the pilot to be certain he was dead. She found a clasp knife in his belongings and slipped it into the outside pocket of her flimsy nightgown.

She turned off the light and went back to Nils' room.

Finris hobbled up the stairs toward his office. His leg was no good. He kept spare ammunition there. The building shuttered under a series of explosions. A Norse Man rushed in.

"What do you want us to do?"

"Get men on the roof. Send some to flank them."

The man ran off. Finris opened the desk and took out the box of ammunition. He reloaded the gun and got a spare magazine from another drawer. He loaded it and poured the rest of the ammo into his pockets. There was an armory in the basement, but he didn't think he could make it that far on his leg.

He hobbled over to the window and tore the curtain down. He wrapped it around the knee to try and stop the bleeding. It felt like it was on fire. He thought again about Frank Kane. He knew the legends, the bullshit they told about him. That he couldn't be killed. Finris knew he had killed him, but then he had risen again. It sent a small shudder down his spine.

Shena knocked on the door and went inside. Nils was dressed like a slut. She smiled at the once-fierce sadist.

"There are cars parked out back. We will take one to the airplane and get out of here."

"What about my pilot?"

"Candy said he had left for the plane to check on something before the shooting started. He should be waiting for us now."

"He wouldn't dare leave without me."

"I know he wouldn't. Let Lexxus and I check outside to make sure it's safe and then we will come back for you."

"Don't leave me here, please. Promise you won't leave me here."

"We won't."

"Promise? You have to promise."

"We promise. Come on, Lexxus."

She took Lexxus by the hand and led her out of the room.

"You aren't serious about helping him, are you? After what he has done to us?"

"I have a plan."

"Let's just get out of here while we can. Fuck him."

"Do you want to be rich and famous?"

"What?"

"You heard me. Do you want to make some money off the hell we've been put through?"

"Sure. How?"

"You be ready. You do what I tell you when I tell you."

"Are you sure? What about that twisted fuck?"

"Trust me. He won't ever hurt anyone again."

"I'm in."

Shena handed her the clasp knife. Lexxus stared, confused for a moment then put it into her own robe's pocket. Shena opened the door.

"Come on."

Nils came out on bare feet. He looked around. More bullets broke glass on the front of the Lodge and there was another explosion on the roof. He looked terrified. Shena took his hand.

"Keep your head down when we get outside. Hold my hand. Stay with us and we will take care of you."

"I will. Thank you. Thank you both. You won't be sorry, I swear."

They went down the back stairs and out through the back door.

"Don't shoot. Don't shoot," both women shouted as they ran. No one did. They got into Finris' Escalade. The key was in the ignition. Shena started the car.

"Keep your head down in the seat until we get to the plane. There might be more of them out there."

"Thank you. Thank you," Nils whimpered.

Keating watched the three women come running out. He let them go. He was bored. He took a phosphorous grenade out of his pack and lobbed it up onto the deck behind the second floor. It exploded and bathed what remained of the stairs in flames. He tossed another one near the doorway. It blew the back of the Lodge in and bathed it in flames. Let the rats find another way out, he thought.

A man jumped out of a second-floor window. He hit the ground and rolled to his feet. Keating shot him three times and changed his position again.

Blanco saw the two men come out of a hatch on the top of the roof. About fucking time, he thought. They moved in a crouch toward the front of the Lodge. Tactically it was a great position. Unfortunately, Blanco was waiting for them. He used half a magazine killing them.

Movement caught his eye. There was someone in a second-floor room tearing the curtain down. The man was wearing some kind of biker vest. The man disappeared before Blanco could fire. The room was quiet, offering no second chance at a shot. Suddenly the man stood back up in front of the window. Blanco emptied the rest of the magazine through the window and watched the man drop.

77

Redding reached the door near the kennel. He tried the handle. It was locked. He started to try to kick it in when it opened in front of him. A young brunette stared back wide-eyed at him.

"Who are you?" she asked.

"FBI."

She hugged him.

"I'm Candy."

"I am here to help you."

"Thank God. We're all prisoners here."

Redding shook her loose.

"Where are the others?"

"Back this way. Come on, I'll show you."

He followed her into the kennel. The dogs were barking and whining and snapping at the bars of their cages. They moved through the kennel. Redding moved the girl behind him. He opened the door and stepped into the long cold hallway. He could hear girls screaming for help nearby. He moved slowly.

There were five of them. It was exactly as Masnick had said. They were huddled nearly nude in bare cells. They were wrapped in thin blankets.

"Help us. You got to help us," They pleaded.

"I will," he promised. "Let me get these cells open."

"Hurry. For God's sake hurry. They might come back."

Redding moved carefully toward the end of the hallway toward the control room. He heard running boots coming his way. He knelt into a shooter's position and waited. A Norse Man turned the corner in front of him. He was carrying a shotgun.

"FBI. Drop your weapon."

The man must have been an idiot. He tried to swing the shotgun toward Redding. Redding shot him in the center of his chest. He went down and after a few seconds didn't move. Redding held his position. He heard another pair of boots running toward him.

"FBI," he shouted.

The footsteps stopped, paused and ran the other way.

Smart man, Redding thought. He moved to the control room and released the cells. He went back to the women.

"Follow me," he said.

They did. When they got to the outside door, he checked to make sure it was clear. He turned to the women and pointed toward the entrance road to the Lodge.

"You go that way. There is a police officer waiting there. His name is Maurer. He will protect you."

"No. Don't leave us."

"I have to. There may be other women in there who need my help. Now go on. Stay away from the barn and just run as hard as you can."

One of the girls kissed him on the cheek.

"Thank you."

Then they were gone. Redding went back into the building. He had forgotten all about Masnick.

Heather called out for Finris. There was no answer. The building shook with a series of explosions. She crouched down. There was more gunfire. There were more explosions. She noticed her hands were shaking uncontrollably. She had to find Finris. He could orchestrate the defense. He would turn the tide. She called for her brother, Nils, but again no one answered. Either he was hiding or he had fled without her. Coward, she thought.

A Norse Man started shooting at Masnick from a second-floor window. The shots were wild, but one round blew out the window on the car Masnick was hiding behind. The shards of glass ripped his face open in a dozen tiny wounds. The man kept firing. Finally, a lucky round punched through Masnick's shoulder. Masnick staggered backward. He loaded his last grenade and fired it at the window where the shooter crouched. It missed badly to the right. Masnick tossed the grenade launcher aside. The Norseman started firing again. Masnick picked up the dead mercenary's AR-15 from the ground. He checked the charging rod. He turned toward the Lodge and emptied the magazine at the window. He ejected the clip, slapped in a second magazine and did it all again. The window went quiet.

Masnick sat back onto the ground. Blood poured freely from the bullet wound. A little lower and it would have hit the vest. A little higher and it would have missed all together.

He pulled the large duffel toward him. He found the first aid kit inside and opened it. He pulled out the stuff to stop bleeding, tore it open and used it. It hurt like hell. He popped the cover off one of the morphine syringes and stabbed it into his thigh. He waited for the pain to ease. It did. He took out a second one and stabbed himself in the leg again. He laughed and slipped the other syringe into his jacket pocket. He dug around in the bag and found a bottle of water. He gulped it down and followed it with a handful of pills. Masnick laughed again. It wasn't like he was going to make it anyway, he thought. He struggled to his feet and calmly walked toward Frank's position.

Reaper was out of ammo. He tossed the AR-15 onto the ground. He took out his pistol. Slowly he moved farther back down the side of the patrol car and leaned against the rear tire. He took out his cigarettes and lit one. He savored the acrid smoke as occasional bullets continued to ping off the car.

He saw the headlights of the truck coming toward them from the right. He took a final drag and stubbed the cigarette out in the dirt. He tucked the butt into his jacket pocket. The truck was driving wildly, its headlights strobing through the trees and brush. He knew Frank saw them too. He aimed his pistol. When the truck was within ten yards he started shooting. He concentrated his fire at the driver's side of the windshield. The truck veered hard to the left and struck a tree.

A man in the back of the truck was thrown out. The passenger pushed his door open and jumped out. Reaper had already slapped in a second clip. He could only see the man's legs clearly, so he shot them first. When the Norse Man fell to the ground, he shot him in the head.

The man from the truck bed staggered to his feet. He picked his AK-47 from the dirt just as a blast from Frank's shotgun touched him. He was hurled back against the truck before sliding down to the ground in a red puddle.

78

Heather ran from room to room searching for Finris. She found him in the study. He was sitting in the floor wrapping one of the curtains around his knee. The leg was covered in blood. She felt faint. He saw her and smiled.

She felt suddenly safer. He was a Viking God. He would save them. She stepped toward him. Finris lifted himself off the floor. She opened her mouth to speak when the window beside him exploded.

Finris was spun around and slammed to the ground by the bullets.

Heather screamed. She crawled toward him. He was still alive. She grabbed his vest and helped drag him away from the window. He had been hit four times. There was a wound through his left bicep, a second through the left shoulder, but the third and fourth were in the center of his back. They were the man killers.

Finris moaned. She could hear his teeth grinding against the pain.

"Help me," he said.

"I will. We must get you to a hospital."

"No. Norse Men do not run from battle. Help me get downstairs and back into the fight."

"If I don't get you to the hospital you will die."

Finris smiled at her. His teeth were wet with blood.

"We all die. This is my time."

Heather picked up her knife. She helped lift him to his feet. His left side was useless, and he hobbled like an old man. She could feel his blood oozing across her and she shivered.

"I won't leave you," Heather whispered. "I promise."

Blanco could see no more targets from the roof of the barn. He climbed down. He only had a couple more rounds in the AR-15. He fired them at an unbroken window. He tossed the gun to the ground and took out his pistol.

Reaper was crouched by a truck with an AK-47. A second one lay on the ground at his feet.

"Hey, buddy," Reaper called, holding up one of the AK-47s. "Look what I got you."

Blanco crab walked to him and took one of the guns.

"Sweet."

"I figured we could always use some extra fire power."

Blanco patted him on the shoulder.

"Nice work. You okay?"

"Not a scratch. You?"

"Same."

They saw Masnick walking up. He wasn't trying to hide. If anyone in the house had been looking, it would have been an easy shot. No one was looking. Masnick squatted with them.

"You're hit," Blanco said.

"Not bad. I feel great. You guys alright?"

They all nodded. Frank came over.

"You ready?" Frank asked.

Masnick got to his feet. "I need to find the bitch that did me."

"We will," Frank said.

Masnick stuck out his hand to Blanco.

"No need for you boys to stick around anymore. They're done."

"No way," Reaper said. "We stay to the end."

Frank put an arm around Reaper's shoulder and turned him away. Blanco followed.

"You did good, but you're done here."

"You need us in there, Frank."

"Maybe. Probably. But you got to go."

"Give me one good reason."

"Prometheus doesn't want you to see him die. He was a God. He still has pride."

Blanco and Reaper exchanged looks.

"I get it," Blanco said.

"Thanks. You got your wire cutters?"

Blanco patted his fanny pack and Reaper checked his. They nodded.

"Cut a hole in the fence and circle back to the park. Don't go back down the driveway. You can't trust cops."

"I hear you."

"It was good working with you again, big man."

"You got our digits if you need us."

Frank shook their hands.

"And you have mine if you need me. Anytime. Anywhere."

"Spartans forever."

The two Spartan hitters jogged out of sight toward the fence. Frank smiled. They were good men. No, they were the best of men. He was glad to know they would escape unharmed and uncaptured. He turned to see Masnick strolling casually toward the entrance of the Lodge. Frank spotted Keating coming their way. He saw him signal the mercenary to come in from the side. It would all be over soon.

Maurer saw the women coming down the driveway. Looked for weapons. They didn't have any or clothes either. He waved them over. He placed them in one of the cars and turned the heat up.

A man came jogging down the drive carrying a rifle. Maurer swung his AR-15 to his shoulder.

"Drop the weapon. Drop the weapon," he shouted.

The man looked at his rifle like he was surprised it was there. He dropped it.

"On the ground. Hands above your head."

The man complied. Maurer rushed up and zip cuffed him. He put the man in the back of his police car just as another man appeared running down the drive.

Maurer disarmed, controlled and cuffed him as well and he went into the back of the car. It was looking like it was going to be a busy night.

The mercenary called Bravo had reached Zaneville and driven back to the little house. It was dark and quiet and empty. He drove up close to the front door and slammed on the brakes. The car skidded to a stop. He got out. He left the engine running. He wouldn't be long.

He had to hurry. They could be after him. He ran up the front steps and started to open the door. He hesitated. It could be booby trapped. That cat Masnick was supposed to love bombs. He went to the window on the porch and used his pistol to break out the glass. He unlocked the window and slid it up. He climbed inside the house.

Nothing stirred except dust motes. He moved to the front door. It looked clean from this side, but you could never tell. He started to turn on the lights but thought better of it. Might be another booby trap.

He took out his flashlight and swept the room. It looked clean. He went toward Masnick's bedroom. The door was half open. He scanned the room for a trip wire or electric eye. Nothing. He eased the door open. Again, it was clear. The black duffel bag sat in the center of the bed. It was now or never. He crossed the room. There would be time to count the cash later.

He grabbed the bag and turned to leave the room. There was a barely audible click from something under the bag. He turned as the bomb went off.

The explosion leveled the house, the car and the surrounding yard. Karma was a bitch.

Charlie pulled open the side door of the Lodge. He took one step inside when a man appeared. The man raised his hands and started to speak. The mercenary shot him anyway. A second man appeared behind the first. Charlie shot him too. Fuck 'em if they couldn't take a joke, he thought. He stepped over the man's body. He only had one more goal and it would be over.

The mercenary knew there was a bounty on the head of Frank Kane. He never thought it would be possible for him to be in position to claim it. But now, the dark gods had smiled upon him. A bullet. A picture. Then the rewards he deserved.

Keating met Frank and Masnick on the front porch. There were bodies everywhere. He nodded to Frank. "We clear the first floor. If the little bitch isn't there, we'll head upstairs."

"Don't forget Charlie is coming from the right side. Don't shoot him by mistake."

"Good to go."

Keating went in first and cut left. He disappeared down a long hallway.

Masnick looked up and saw Heather leading Finris down the stairs toward them. The giant was covered in blood and as pale as a ghost. He was walking dead, just like Masnick.

When Heather saw Masnick she screamed. It was as if her nightmares had all come true and stood before her. She let go of Finris and bolted down the stairs toward the basement rooms. Finris fell down the stairs. His big pistol skidded across the room. He lay unmoving at the bottom of the stairs.

"Run, little bunny," Masnick called. "The God of fire has come for you. Walk with me for your salvation."

Heather turned the corner and headed down the stairs. She had to find another way out. There must be a way out. There was always a way out.

"It is time for our walk, little bunny. You must walk into the fire with me. We must complete the circle of fire."

Frank approached Finris. He stared down at the giant warrior. He kicked the big pistol farther away. He lifted Finris and carried him to a long leather sofa against the wall. He set him there and stood back watching him. His pale blue eyes swept the inside of the Lodge. It was all stone and rough timber and exposed beams. There were huge fireplaces and a decidedly Viking motif in the carvings and paintings. Frank liked it. He liked it because it spoke to the warrior in him and because he saw it for the icon it was meant to be. Just like the Statue of Liberty was meant to inspire immigrants, and the World Trade Tower inspire businessmen, and the big Hollywood sign meant to inspire actors and dreamers, and just like the Spartan compound in Asheville, the Norse Men's Lodge was meant to inspire. It was a promise of what you could achieve. Loki was smart.

Finris opened his eyes.

"Frank Kane," he rasped and forced a wolfish grin.

"Finris Wolf."

Finris spit blood. "I am sorry for this. I wish we could have met man to man."

Frank moved closer and knelt. The shotgun was across his knees. It was easy to reach.

"It would have ended the same way."

Finris laughed and it turned into a ragged cough that seemed to have no end. Blood bubbled from his lips.

"You are an asshole," he said.

"So I have been told."

"I guess we will never know who the better man was, Frank."

"I am."

Finris looked down at his ruined body. He wiped up some of the blood and stared at it. He looked back at Frank.

"I am dying. There is little place in this civilized world for men like us. Warriors."

"True. Death is the way of the warrior. We knew that going in."

"True. But this," he shrugged. "I had hoped to go down fighting like the ancient ones. Now..."

Frank understood.

"Will you do me a favor before you leave?"

"If I can."

"In the white building is a laboratory. In the back, there are animals kept in cages. One of the cages holds a leopard. A female. Before you leave free her."

"That is not going to happen."

"Yes. Take one of the forklifts. Take her in her cage through the fence and just open the cage. Give her a chance. Please."

"Why?"

"She is out of time and place just as we are."

"They will find her and kill her."

"Perhaps. The national park is not far. If she is lucky, she can reach it. If she is careful, she can survive. Leopards were once seen in this area a long, long time ago."

"She doesn't have a chance."

"Do it anyway. For the predator in all of us. Set her free to her fate. Please. A favor for a brother warrior."

Frank nodded. "I will."

"Thank you."

Frank looked over and saw the shield and twin Viking hand axes hanging above the huge rock fireplace. They looked very old. Frank walked over. He took down one of the axes and the wooden shield. He left one axe on the mantel piece and went back to Finris who was watching him. He leaned the shield against Finris' legs and laid the axe beside his right hand. Frank then backed across the room and retrieved his shotgun.

Finris didn't move. He watched Frank.

"Well?" Frank said. "A true Viking would take up his weapons and face his enemies. Isn't that the only way for a true son to reach Valhalla?"

A blood-caked smile split Finris' face. He leaned forward and used the shield to leverage himself up. He slid it up his numb arm and wedged it against his body. He reached down with his good hand and lifted the axe. He looked at the ancient glyphs that decorated the blade. He tested its weight. He made a small swing in the air. He turned toward Frank.

"Whenever you are ready," Frank said.

Finris stood for a dozen seconds enjoying the feel of the ancient weapons, the ancient ways. Finris drew back the axe and stumbled toward Frank. Frank shot him twice with the shotgun, cutting him nearly in half.

Frank moved up to the body. He was gone. They were a lot alike, Frank knew. He was glad he sent him out this way.

The mercenary, Charlie, saw Frank from behind as he looked over the body. It was perfect. He shouldered his rifle and adjusted his aim. It had to be a head shot. The bulletproof vest might save him otherwise. It was money in the bank. He never heard the gun that killed him.

80

Redding rushed into the room. His gun was still trailing smoke. He knelt over the mercenary and checked his carotid. Dead. Redding never trusted mercenaries. Frank smiled back at him but didn't rise.

Keating came jogging in from the left. His gun was down.

"Masnick has gone after the girl. It's over."

Keating looked around the room.

"See you on the other side."

Frank nodded.

Keating slipped him a piece of paper. "My digits in case you need me."

Frank nodded again.

Without another look at Redding, Keating jogged out the front door. He climbed in the pickup truck and drove toward the entrance to the Lodge.

"What was that all about?" Redding asked, pointing at the dead mercenary.

"Bounty, I guess," Frank said.

"No, the business with Finris."

"Honor. He wanted an honorable death. He had been a warrior his whole life. He deserved it."

A man came running down the stairs in just his boxers. He had his hands up.

"Down the road to the street. Go."

Two girls came out of a third-floor room.

"Don't shoot."

"FBI. Come on down."

Black smoke started to swell up from the back of the house.

"Hurry. Down the street to the entrance, there will be an officer to look after you."

Another girl and a man in boxer shorts came out from another upstairs room. The man had a big revolver.

"Drop your weapon."

The man did, throwing the gun across the room.

"Is there anyone else up there?" Redding shouted.

"I don't know."

"Get out. Down the street to the entrance. Run."

Frank watched them all go. He didn't say a word. After they were gone, he followed them out.

"Where are you going?"

"It's over. I told you. I have things to do before I leave."

"Are you really going to free that leopard?"

"I gave my word. And I have some painting to do before I go."

"Where's Masnick?"

"Back there. He went after the girl."

Redding looked down the hallway and up the stairs. He had to choose. He could check the rooms to be sure no one was still being held there or he could go after Masnick. That had been the deal. Frank watched him. The choice would say a lot about the man. Redding ran past him and headed up the stairs.

"Go on. I've got to clear the upper rooms before the fire gets there."

Frank nodded and went outside.

81

Masnick went down the stairs. He was methodical. He searched each room carefully. He could smell the aroma of smoke and fire. It buoyed his feelings. He was home.

"We are born from ash. We burn through our time and in the end, we return to ash. It is the circle of fire. Come walk with me, my little one."

He followed the scent of her perfume. She left a trail of lilac as clear as blood on a snowy field. He opened a door and Heather lunged at him.

She stabbed him in the side twice with her knife. Masnick struck her with a backhand that sent her tumbling back against a wall. When she righted herself, he punched her hard in the face. She crumpled to the floor. He leaned over her and punched her again.

He pulled the blade out. It hadn't penetrated deeply. He tossed it aside. He pulled the last syringe of morphine out of his pocket. He held the tip cover in his mouth and removed it. He spit it out and injected himself in his right hip. He felt incredible. He knelt over Heather's body. She was struggling to rise. He hit her again. She went down.

"It is our time to walk in fire together."

Masnick removed a pair of metal handcuffs from his back pocket and clipped one to her wrist and the other to his. He tossed the AR-15 across the room and drew his pistol. He stood up and pulled her to her feet. She was swaying.

"Come, we have a walk to make together, little one. You need to be awake."

Heather tried to pull away, but he jerked her back close to him and took her hand.

"Don't fight. There is nothing you can do now."

Masnick led her from the room and back toward the stairs that led back up. Heather was crying. It made him smile. She would burn as he had promised himself. Her clothes would burn away. Her skin would blister and bubble and blacken and wither.

"Don't, please. You don't have to kill me."

"It is only fair. You killed me."

"No, I didn't. I lied. There is an antidote."

Masnick started his climb up the stairs. "No, there isn't. You're lying."

"There is. I swear. You had to think you were dying. It had to be hopeless to break you. It was all a ruse."

"Now, my little pretty one, stop lying to me. We both know I am a dead man. I can feel life slipping away. You killed me as surely as a blade or bullet."

"No. I can save you. I'm the only one. I can do it. There is an antidote."

Masnick cleared the stairs and stepped into the hall. Fire danced up the walls all around him. He turned the corner. At the far end of the hallway Redding stood, directing people to the front door. Redding turned and their eyes met.

"A bargain is a bargain, Special Agent Redding. But I don't believe I will be walking out of here alive."

Masnick turned toward the back of the Lodge, toward the flames and thick wall of black smoke.

"Help me," Heather screamed. "You have to help me. He's crazy. He's going to kill me."

Then they were gone. Redding started down the hallway to follow when a portion of the roof fell in blocking his way. He paused, then turned and ran out the front door.

Shena drove toward the small airfield. It was deserted. She parked the car.

"Keep your head down, there is someone up there," Shena lied.

She took out the steak knife. She hesitated for a second. When the full realization of what Shena had planned dawned on Lexxus, she snatched the knife from her own robe's pocket.

"Is it safe?" Nils whimpered. "Please tell me we are safe."

"Almost," Shena said.

She raised the steak knife. She lifted it as high as she could in the car and stabbed Nils in the back. Lexxus attacked him from the other side, stabbing in a mad frenzy. Nils managed to rise up, but whichever way he turned they kept stabbing him. He lashed out and hit Shena with a backhanded blow that stunned her for a second. She recovered before he could press any advantage he had. Within a minute, he was dead.

The girls looked at each other. They were drenched in blood.

"We did it," Lexxus said. "He's dead."

"Now to be rich and famous."

"You keep saying that. How?"

"We need to go over our story of our daring escape. How we overpowered him and saved ourselves. We will be all over TV. We'll get a Hollywood agent and write a book. They may make a movie about us."

Lexxus smiled. "Maybe you better punch me a couple of times to help sell it. We don't want anyone asking questions."

Redding found Frank Kane by the barn. He was painting something with red paint. Redding saw it and smiled.

"You better go, Frank. I got to call the cavalry in."

"I put the guard dogs in the barn. Make sure they get good homes. They're good dogs; they deserve that much."

Redding smiled. "I will. I promise. You got to go."

"On my way, but first, take a look at this."

He handed Redding a piece of paper. There was a phone number on it.

"I owe you," Frank said. "If you need me, call."

Redding memorized the number and handed the paper back to Frank.

"I hope I never need to."

"I trust you can keep this between the two of us. It wouldn't look good me being too friendly with a Fed."

"My lips are sealed."

82

Jake made it to his house without incident. He parked his motorcycle in the garage and slipped inside with the outside lights still off. Once he was inside, he locked the new gun in his gun safe. He cut the ties on the bundles of cash and spread it out on his bed. He shuffled through the money once more to be sure it wasn't tagged. It wasn't. He put the stacks of money in the bottom of the gun safe and closed and relocked it.

Jake went to the bathroom and removed his fake beard. He took scissors and chopped it up into small amounts and flushed it down the toilet. He scrubbed the glue and few remaining hairs off his face. He took off all of his clothes down to his underwear and shoes and put it into the bathtub. He sealed the tub and dumped a gallon of Clorox bleach on top of it. He added more cold water from the tap until the clothes were covered. He swirled the clothes around in the tub to be sure the Clorox saturated everything. He closed the bathroom door. Clorox was the best way to destroy DNA evidence. Unfortunately, it also stunk.

Jake went into his kitchen while his clothes soaked and got a bottle of water. He went to his cell phone to check it for messages. He saw that he had missed ten calls from Jenny.

Fuck.

He checked his watch. It was two o'clock. He dialed her number, but she didn't answer.

Fuck.

He put on jeans and a clean shirt and took his car to her house. He rang the doorbell. There was no answer. He beat on the door. Still nothing. He rang the bell again. He saw a light come on in the house. He heard footsteps.

Jenny cracked the door.

"What?"

"We need to talk."

"About what? I hope she was worth it."

"What are you talking about?"

"Whoever you blew me off to see. I won't be your whore."

"There wasn't anyone else tonight."

"Then why didn't you come over as you promised?"

"I had to kill some men tonight."

The truth was like a slap to her face. Jenny opened the door and pulled him inside.

"What are you talking about?"

"Some men. Drug dealers. Their stuff was killing people. They were trying to set up business here. It would have been very bad. I had to eliminate them."

"You're serious. You killed them. Why are you telling me?"

"You asked."

"Can't you make something up?"

"No. There can only be truth between us. I won't lie to you, ever."

Jenny led him into the living room, and they sat on the sofa. She didn't speak for a moment, trying to decide what to ask. Finally, she asked, "What was it like?"

Frank found his truck where he had left it. It was a long drive home, but he was ready. He thought about Dorian again. He missed her. He could drop by and say hi, he thought, again. No, he knew better than that. She had a chance to go straight. He wasn't going to ruin it for her. He thought about Helen. She had left him her number to call, but he hadn't. Why? He wasn't sure. Maybe he was afraid to find out.

There would be time to figure all that out. He took out a cigar and lit it. He never smoked in his truck, but tonight seemed like a special occasion. It was. He rolled the windows down and let in the cold dark air. He reached over and patted the rump of the big dog curled up on the front seat. The dog raised its head and licked his face.

"I got you now. You'll like your new pack. No more hassles trying to be the alpha. That's my job."

The big dog blinked its heavy eyelids and lay back down on the seat. Frank drove back to Greensboro and his home and family.

Spanish Johnny found Cyrus sitting in front of the television.

"What happened in Ohio?"

"Isn't it obvious, Johnny?"

"No. The Norse Men are taken out. Masnick is involved. He was supposed to be their prisoner. Fake Feds. It doesn't make any sense."

"Of course, it does. It is plain to see. Did you see the painted message?"

"Yeah. A red lambda and fear the Spartans painted below it and some numbers. We used to paint that shit all the time to scare people. Wait, does that mean Masnick brought in old Spartans to help?"

"Johnny, you don't see what is right before your eyes."

"What are you talking about?"

"The numbers are not meaningless. They are a message."

"For who?"

"For us. For you and me. Look closely again."

"9731426085. It's some kind of code, but I don't get it. So what? If it's a message, shouldn't we be able to understand it?"

"What is the third number?"

"3."

"That is where it starts. His messages always start with three. What are the next two letters?"

"14."

"No. 1 and 4. 314. Do you understand now?"

"No."

"314 is the mathematical symbol for Pi. The Greek letter Pi was used to represent the letter P which we used to designate Poseidon. He even wears a burn scar of it on his shoulder."

"Frank fucking Kane. He did all of that? No way."

"Yes. I told you before. Death is his gift."

"So, his message is that he did this. So we would know."

Cyrus sighed and took a drink of coffee. "No. That is his signature. The message is not Fear the Spartans. It is not plural. It is fear the Spartan. Frank Kane is warning us to leave him alone."

Eight weeks later

Former Special Agent Richard Redding knocked on the door at the top floor of the FBI building in Miami.

"Come."

Inside were two men. Each dressed anonymously in expensive dark suits with white shirts and bold purple power ties. The man seated at the desk was the Assistant Director of the FBI. His name was Franklin. He had a file in front of him. Redding did not recognize the man standing. Neither man introduced themselves. Franklin gestured toward an empty chair across from the great expanse of teak. Redding sat.

"Former Special Agent Redding, thank you for coming."

"Always glad to help, sir."

The man at the window smiled.

"I was just reviewing the ongoing investigation in Ohio."

"Yes, sir. Is that why I am here, to be debriefed again?"

Franklin looked up. "No. It is a very interesting case. The Bureau will be chasing and untangling these strands for years. You were instrumental in this."

"I was lucky."

The man at the window smiled again. Franklin looked at him and back to Redding.

"You were more than lucky. Sheriff Maurer says you were the key element in the resolution of this case. The key element. That is high praise. But let us be frank. You are a star. You have always been a star at the FBI. Although not always by following protocol, I must point out. And you had your enemies in the Bureau, but that is normal. You had an interesting career. You managed an extremely high value CI, one of the principals in the Spartan criminal organization, off the books. You were the Bureau's lead in its prosecution of the Spartans. You helped bring down a score of dirty politicians, including the senator who oversaw the NSA. Now this. Drugs, human trafficking, exotics, collusion and corruption that will lead to where we cannot even guess as yet."

Redding did not answer. There was nothing to say. He looked to the man at the window. He caught and held his gaze until Franklin continued.

"How many times in your career have you drawn your weapon?"

"Three."

Franklin thumbed through the documents. "Shouldn't that be four? You drew it twice before Ohio but did not discharge it and then twice while on this last operation."

"No, sir. Once I drew the weapon in Ohio, I did not reholster until the situation was under control."

"You killed two men."

"Yes, sir."

"Two men, two shots."

"Yes, sir."

"Very efficient. Less than ten percent of police officers ever fire their weapons, probably closer to five. And less than three percent of those ever kill anyone."

Redding shrugged. "I was taught in the Bureau to shoot to kill."

"How did that make you feel?"

Redding shrugged again. "I did what I had to do."

Franklin returned to his documents.

"No nightmares. No insomnia? No PTSD?"

"Not that I am aware of."

"You do not like retirement, I see."

"Not so awfully much. I get bored."

Franklin chuckled. "Gets bored," he repeated. "Very good."

The man at the window cleared his throat. Franklin nodded.

"You are officially retired from the FBI, but I have a proposition for you that I assure you will not be boring."

"What would that be, sir?"

"We have established a team of independent contractors to handle some of the nation's more complex problems."

"Homeland Security?"

"Not exactly."

"NSA? DNI?"

"Again, not exactly."

"You will officially be working as a special contracted investigator for the FBI. You will still carry your rank as Special Agent," the man by the window said. "But you will work without their aegis. We will provide all the support that they would at a substantially higher pay."

"Is this black ops stuff? Some off-the-books division?"

"The specifics aren't important. What is important is that we bring the full and complete support of the United States government with us."

"So, if I agree, I don't have to worry about stepping on someone else's toes?"

"Stomp on them if you like. You will be one of a very elite group of men charged with investigating and resolving certain crimes that might put this country at risk."

"Resolve? Do you mean arrest?"

"Resolve as necessary. You will have great latitude in deciding what is necessary. Your choices will not be second-guessed by the Justice Department or some bureaucrat later in Washington."

"Special Agent Redding," Franklin said, "you were born in North Carolina, isn't that right?"

"Yes, sir, on the coast near Atlantic Beach."

Franklin shared a knowing look with the man at the window.

"We have a situation that we need you to look into. Approximately two months ago a wealthy family was murdered in their home. Graffiti was painted on the walls. There was a paw print and talk of one percenters. The next month another family was murdered the same way. The local police, SBI, and FBI have been unable to resolve this case."

"I haven't seen any of this on the news."

"We have had the scenes scrubbed after gathering the evidence," said the man by the window. "There has been a news blackout."

"How does this concern national security?"

"As you may know the governor of North Carolina, Pat McCrory, is very well connected in Washington. There is talk that he may become our next president. One of the murdered families were big supporters of his. He would like this matter handled. Will you help us?"

"Of course. I am honored, but to be truthful I am not sure I can do anything that hasn't already been done."

"One man can often learn things a troop of policemen cannot. See what you can do."

"You will be operating on your own as you see fit. It is a dangerous task and I advise you to bring along appropriate backup personnel. If you would like we can provide you with the names of several vetted contractors to assist you."

"Mercs?"

"Ex-Seals, Rangers and Delta Force. The best of the best."

"If you don't mind, I would like to arrange my own."

"As you like it. But you need to leave as soon as possible. We need to stop this thing. Here is all the information we have so far."

Franklin pushed a telephone book-sized file toward Redding and then a second one. Redding picked up the files like he had already agreed.

"We have established a support system for you. Take this phone. Someone will monitor it 24/7. Let us know what you need."

Redding took the large black phone and rose from his seat. No one extended a hand toward him. He started for the door and turned back for an instant toward the man by the window.

"Excuse me, sir. May I ask you your name and operating title?"

The man at the window smiled. "No, you may not."

Redding smiled and slipped out of the office. He felt the exhilaration of the hunt all over again. He knew exactly who he was going to call to back him up. There was really no one else he could call.

On May first, a local hiker in Tennessee claimed to have seen a large leopard crossing a field just before dawn. Authorities could not verify his claims and dismissed the sighting as a hoax. A similar report of a black leopard had been made the year before in the same area and was also dismissed as a hoax.

ABOUT THE AUTHOR

John is the author of three previous Frank Kane novels, **THE LAST SPARTAN, SPARTAN NEGOTIATOR,** and **SPARTAN KRYPTEA.** He is currently working on the fifth book in the series, **SPARTAN VENGEANCE.** In addition to being an author, he is a screenwriter, producer and actor. Look for the Spartans to make their first on screen appearance in Mane Entertainments thriller, PENANCE LANE scheduled for release in the summer of 2020. The author lives in North Carolina with his wife and two dogs.

To order additional copies of:

SPARTAN
HONOR

Earlier action-packed adventures with
Frank Kane are available at
www.savpress.com and Amazon

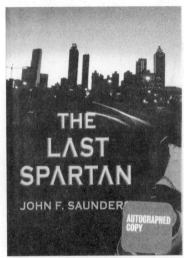

THE LAST SPARTAN

SPARTAN NEGOTIATOR

SPARTAN KRYPTEA